CRIMEUCOPIA

Let Me Tell You About...

A Murderous Ink Press Anthology

****

CRIMEUCOPIA

Let Me Tell You About…

First published by Murderous Ink Press
Crowland
LINCOLNSHIRE
England
www.murderousinkpress.co.uk

Paperback Edition ISBN: 9781909498600
eBook Edition ISBN: 9781909498617

Acknowledgements

To those writers and artists who helped make this anthology what it is, I can only say a heartfelt Thank You!

Special thanks must go out to V. S. Kemanis for helping out with the grunt work – very much appreciated.

And to Den, as always.

Contents

* Black Mack first appeared in *Malone's White Fedora* (2001)
** Package of Pain first appeared in *Mind Slices* (2012)
† An earlier version of *Two Nights with Suzie Wong* appeared in the e-zine, *Oyster River Pages*, in 2019

If Looks Could Kill
She Would Have Been An Uzi....
(An Editorial of Sorts)

...Or more likely a shotgun. I mean, Lawd knows what those two ever saw in each other in the first place, and that's a fact. Don't believe me? Well, let me tell you about the time when....

And that's how it usually starts, doesn't it.

Only this time there's 19 storytellers gathered around the front counter of the Crimeucopia *Shots to Hell* Bar & Grill. And all of them are more than willing to tell you about how it is, or was, or even will be....

Over the background sound of an old jukebox loaded with worn out 45s (vinyl rather than the likes of a Px4 Storm), at one end **Vinnie Hansen** tells everyone that she knows of **A Perfect Place to Die**, while at the other, **V.S. Kemanis** carefully explains what **A Father's Duty** really is.

David Krugler knocks on the bar top to gain our attention and tells us about a family he knows, with **A History of Violence in 24 Minutes, 10 Seconds**, before **Robert Jeschonek** opens up about someone's cousin, Abe Birnbaum, who might still be alive if it wasn't for those **Blue Laws**. Or so he believes.

Beverle Graves Myers finishes her martini – dirty, of course — and while she waits for the barman to refill her glass, she tells us about Jack, who's just a regular **Jewboy in Dallas** — a story that she assures us is as kosher as a dill pickle.

Not to be outdone, **Kirk Landers** also winds the clock back to the 1960s, as he recounts **Two Nights with Suzie Wong**. And as fast as you like, **James Lee Proctor** counters with his tale of something that certainly qualifies as both **Cruel and Unusual**.

In the silence while the jukebox flips another 7-inch as neatly as opening a Balisong butterfly knife one-handed, **Victor Kreuiter** says he'll **Just Keep Talking**. And, when he stops, **K. Arlington Andrews** talks street patois, and explains **How the Devil Stole Pastor Henry's Soul**.

Then *Michael Bracken* shifts into gear and takes us along a different track while revving up the pace by letting everyone know the fate of **Black Mack**.

Accessing a video file on his phone, *Kevin R. Tipple* picks up this after hours verbal 'show and tell' in the form of a **Package of Pain**. When he goes back to his phone again, *William Flores* shakes his head as he introduces the night time clientele to **The Brothers Jackson**.

Then, while some nod to the bar staff for refills, *Robert Sumner* explains about Edgar, and why he did what he did when confronted with a **Martyr**....

Jim Guigli adds to the subtheme of influences and motivation, by telling us that it's all just a matter of **Supply and Demand**. As he sits back, *James Roth* takes us to Tokyo's murky world, and why Kawayama Tomoyuki needs to offer up **A Prayer for My Daughter**.

Michael Zimecki nudges a damp coaster, clears his throat, and assures us that **While the Moon Comes Out of the Sea**, his tale is totally true. Honest....

Sebastian Corbascio looks up from contemplating his near empty glass, and to everyone and no one he asks: 'Did I ever tell any of you about... *noelle*? This is how I remember it....'

There's a short pause in the group conversation while the bar staff check the clock above the entrance door — way above eye level, so as not to distract the patrons with such trivial a thing as the passing of time.

It also gives *Martin Zeigler* a chance to explain why he's writing **Your Ticket to Freedom**, just before *John Bertram Fawet III* claims to lead by literary example in regard to **The Last Gunfighter**. Crimesapleanty indeed....

Which is the cue for the Editorial bar staff to call for glasses and ask the age old question:

"Don't any of you writers have homes to go to?!"

As with all of these anthologies, we hope you'll find something that you immediately like, as well as something that takes you out of your late night cocktail comfort zone — and puts you into a completely new one.

Because, in the *Happy Hour* spirit of our *Murderous Ink Press* motto:

You never know what you like until you read it.

A Perfect Place to Die
Vinnie Hansen

Buford Callahan already had the gun. The Colt .45 semi-automatic had been his father's in World War II. He wanted a silencer, too, but had discovered, to his chagrin, that such a request raised eyebrows, even in large, anonymous gun shops.

Buford glided his white Mazda sedan into the place where he and Marcia had parked in their courting days. Setting the brake, he peered out the windshield, but the lake was gone.

That fit, he thought. With his health insurance business sinking, he had been left high and dry.

Buford heaved himself out of the old car. He wasn't fat. He was in good shape for almost sixty, but he felt heavy. When he pushed through the weeds, his meaty hand brushed a slick, sticky blossom from a bush. He bent down.

"A condom," he muttered in disgust. "A used condom."

How naïve to imagine this pull-off in the sycamores had remained "their" spot. He passed a small pile of crushed Budweiser cans.

Down the dusty, gravel road he tromped for a quarter of a mile before he reached the water. The area where they used to swim was now beach and the edge of the lake a reedy marsh.

This had been a perfect place — serene and beautiful. Now the damn kids and drought had ruined it.

He trooped back to his Mazda Protege, slammed the door, and sat vacantly inside. He'd made the decision, cleaned the gun, written the note, and polished his shoes. Buford didn't want to turn back. But he couldn't kill himself parked in a trashy place. It would not do. He extracted the creamy envelope from his battered leather briefcase, ripped it open, and reread the letter.

Composing the note had been the hardest part. Marcia, his wife, had been a loyal companion for thirty-one years. How could he reassure her that it wasn't her fault? While not exactly stimulating, Marcia was a steadfast and kind partner.

In his letter, he'd done his best to forestall any conclusion his suicide was the result of their childless marriage. The first four or five years, he'd been disappointed, but as his friends' children developed into gangly and surly adolescents, Buford had gradually grown smug. He and Marcia didn't have to haul kids to and from soccer games. They didn't have to shell out money for "cool" clothes and the latest cell phones. They didn't have to endure blaring music and slamming doors, calls from the principal, or worse, the police. Buford's best friend had a son who was twenty-five that he couldn't get out of the house, and Buford's poor slob brother had a daughter who'd gotten pregnant at sixteen.

No, he and Marcia were lucky.

He tucked the letter into an insurance brochure and started the car. He couldn't do it here. He wanted a perfect place.

In his head, Marcia softly mocked, "Type A to the end."

That evening, after they ate their dinners in front of the news, Republicans and Democrats attacking each other as usual, Marcia asked, "Are you okay, Bu?"

"I'm fine," he said.

"You seem down."

He patted her hand adorned with her wedding band and clear polish with glitter, simple, but maintained. His wife took care of herself. "After work, I drove out to the lake."

"You did?" A smile flickered. "I haven't been out there since our camping trip."

She meant the ill-fated camping trip. Buford acknowledged how dense he'd been. With no children, it had been easy for them to travel, but it had taken him many adventures before he realized Marcia didn't like strange beds or foreign foods. She'd much rather go out for dinner and a movie.

"It's like a swamp now," he said.

Marcia picked up their dishes and laughed. "I thought it was a swamp back then."

The next day, after work, Buford resealed the letter in another creamy envelope. He drove toward the neighboring town in his sedan. It was a modest car with cloth seats, but he'd never been the kind of guy to want something racier. He thought about the park in the town, the grassy knolls and surrounding woods. A perfect spot.

Buford didn't consider himself depressed. He just couldn't see the point of continued existence. His birthday loomed in a week. The big 6-0. Marcia wanted to throw him a party, but Buford couldn't see any call for celebration. The business was going under. With government health care, his expertise was outmoded. And, full-service insurance companies wanted young employees with lives ahead of them.

Buford fiddled with the air as he drove the flat, straight road that led to the park. Getting old sucked. His father lived — no, *existed* — in a skilled nursing facility. His father, decorated with a Gold Star and a Purple Heart, a man who married, had two children, owned a five and ten store, a house, and the latest model Oldsmobile. A man with friends, a better than average income, and chest-thumping, robust health.

Switching on the blinkers, Buford turned into a parking lot tucked between low green hills. His father's life had come down to a single bed in a shared room, a few clothes in a closet, a wheelchair. What was the point?

At the end of the lot, Buford steered the Mazda carefully up a fire road into the trees. He passed up two pull outs that weren't deep enough. He wanted the car to face in, so he viewed the woods. The third time was the charm. With the bumper up to a tree trunk, the car fit. He faced a footpath, but he couldn't imagine anyone using it.

Quiet hush surrounded the vehicle. Buford sat for several moments, bird song breaking through the silence. He extracted the old Colt from the briefcase. His hands trembled. He took a deep breath and raised the barrel to his mouth. His father would not even know he was gone. Buford and his brother had never gotten along. *Marcia.* Marcia would be shocked. Stunned. But he didn't know if she'd actually be sad. She'd have the house, her book group and her knitting group and....

Kaaaaa-thump! Bang!

Buford threw back his head in time to see a leg in blue jeans and a huge Nike sneaker.

Wham! The shoes hit the roof of the car.

Ka-thud onto the trunk. Buford whirled. A fleeing boy sprinted across the fire road and into the trees on the other side.

Buford's heart raced. He stashed the gun below the seat.

A huffing policewoman emerged from the trees and trotted to his car.

He stared at her.

She made a motion for him to roll down his window.

Perspiration filmed Buford's forehead.

"Did you see a tall boy, blond dreadlocks, run by here?"

Buford pointed numbly. "He ran over my car."

The woman glanced at the hood of the Mazda. "Cool," she said. "I may not be able to keep up with teenaged punks, but I'm great at lifting shoe prints."

She walked to the edge of the woods and used her radio. She was a short woman, compact and solid, but she strode back to his vehicle with an air of authority. She pulled out a notepad.

"What's your name, sir?"

Buford found himself unable to speak. "Nikes," he sputtered.

"Nike is your name?" she asked.

"His shoes," Buford said.

"Good, good." She jotted down the information. "Don't be alarmed," she reassured him. "The kid is only a purse snatcher, probably not dangerous."

She went on to ask his address and what he'd seen. Grateful she didn't ask what he was doing in the park, Buford stammered his responses.

When the police officer disappeared into the trees to fetch her kit from her vehicle, Buford could have driven away. But he waited as instructed. Even as the woman sprinkled his car with black powder, he watched mutely through the glass. With pursed lips, the officer pressed strips of tape onto the hood.

Buford glanced at his Rolex. His father's watch. He'd donned it for the occasion. Marcia wouldn't be worried yet, but she'd be wondering.

Head nodding and eyes bright, the officer peeled up the strips. "Perfect," she said. "Sorry about the mess."

When Buford pulled into his driveway, Marcia was dumping the day's news into the recycle can. Buford had wanted the moment between killing the engine and opening the door to examine himself in the rearview mirror, make sure he appeared normal. He had hoped to enter the house anonymously and spirit away his briefcase to a secret spot.

Instead, Marcia descended on him.

When she reached the car, her smooth forehead drew into a frown and her sandy eyebrows arched into question marks.

Her eyes pinned him to the seat like a bug on display — homo insectus. He had considered going to a carwash, but he was already two hours late getting home. Unable to bear the thought of his cell phone ringing beside his dead body, or worse yet, as he was about to pull the trigger, he'd turned the damn thing off. And left it off. Not wanting to know if he had messages.

Marcia's neck lengthened. He must move before she became alarmed.

Gripping the briefcase and marshalling his will, Buford pushed himself up out of the car.

"I'm sure there's a story here," Marcia greeted him. From her gold hair and rosy skin to her sparkly toenails, she exuded optimism. *Perky.* His wife was a perky person.

From years of selling, Buford knew the best way to lie was to tell the truth, just not all of it.

He sighed. "After work I drove out to Dixon Park."

"What's gotten into you?" she asked, moving toward the house. "First the swamp and now the park?"

He shrugged and told her about the thief and the cop while she warmed their dinner in the microwave.

"What a bizarre event!"

Marcia had recorded the evening news for him, and when they were seated before the television, watching what seemed like a re-run, she said, "Maybe we should go on a camping trip."

Buford's forkful of casserole stopped midair. "You hate camping."

She tilted her head and oscillated one hand. "It's not my favorite thing, but I miss that time with you — the adventure. Afterwards I get to come home and fully appreciate my mattress."

Buford laid down his fork and muted the television. His heart fluttered with panic. She knew. Those blue x-ray eyes had seen through the leather of his briefcase parked beside him on the couch. Had seen the gun. Read the letter. She was proposing a camping trip to cheer him up. To change his mind.

"You don't want to sleep on the ground," he insisted.

"Maybe we could try a rustic cabin," she said. "How about Natural Life Hot Springs?"

"Too many hippies."

"Ahhh." She leaned her golden curls against his shoulder. "True. There's no place like home." She raised her head.

"Right." *So right.* Here on this couch was about as good as it got. He reached to his briefcase.

Marcia stood abruptly. "How about dessert?"

He nodded. "Okay."

"Strawberry shortcake," she trilled.

Marcia loved anything with whipped cream. She'd suck her spoon, relishing the last little bit. Happy. Content.

Right here. On the couch together. A perfect place to die.

A Father's Duty
V.S. Kemanis

My father was gunned down when I was twelve, the age my son is now.

It was 1932, many families hungry and homeless. I never knew want. We were doing well in our four-bedroom house on two green acres in Massapequa.

My father was laid out in the living room. The house teemed with people who'd pulled up in their Packards and Lincolns. The women wore black veiled hats. Broad-shouldered men wore double-breasted suits. They mingled and whispered in rays of sunlight shot through the dust, holding crystal tumblers of amber liquid. Lilies and gladioli crept up every corner and jammed the hearth, giving off the sickly sweetness of gradual rot.

The assassins had spared my father's head. On my way upstairs, I caught a glimpse of his rubbery face. I felt no sadness. Far from it. In my young mind, I thought the man meant little to me. While in his presence, I was expected to stand tall, listen attentively, call him "sir," and obey his commands without question. He was King. But now that he was dead, I would not have to do any of those things again. There was a freedom about it along with the uncertainty.

I sat on my bed to wait out the hours for all the visitors to go home. But before long, my mother came upstairs. When she entered my room, I realized I'd been expecting her. I lived for my mother's approval. While I *needed* to please my father, I *wanted* to please her. In the uncertainty of the moment, her approval of my absence from the wake would be reassuring.

My mother was strong and well put together. Beautiful. She didn't cry. Didn't appear to be grieving. To this day, I'm not sure if she hid her emotions or had nothing tumultuous inside her that needed to be masked. With my father, she'd never put on phony displays of feminine weakness. She commanded respect through firmness and reason. I don't mean to say that she disdained her need for a man. She was practical and understood the value of masculine strength, especially for a man in my father's line of business.

My mother sat down next to me and put a hand on my back. "Let me tell you a story about your father," she said. "One afternoon when you were four years old, you and I were in the house together, alone. I was pregnant with your little brother. The doorbell rang, and I took you with me to the front door. I never had cause to worry about who stood on the other side of a closed door. I opened it."

*Never had cause to worry…*because my father, or one of his men, would always be nearby, watching.

"The man on our front porch was about your father's age, well groomed, good looking, and very polite. He introduced himself, but I don't remember his name. He said, 'I'm sorry to impose, ma'am, but I was in the neighborhood and couldn't help stopping by. You see, I used to live in this house when I was a little boy!'

"He said a few other charming things and asked if he could step inside for a quick minute, just to take a trip down memory lane. He put a hand on your head, ruffled your hair, and said you reminded him of his own boyhood. His teeth sparkled and he knew how to put a person at ease. It seems I had no trouble believing him.

"With my big belly and you by my side, I walked the man through the first floor as he made lively comments about family possessions that were in the house during his childhood. His mother's cookie jar here, a gonging grandfather clock there. We strolled through the kitchen, the dining room, the den, the sunroom, and ended up in the living room where we were sitting when your father rushed in.

"I hadn't expected him home. He'd been given word, belatedly, what was going on in the house.

"When he walked into the living room, he kept his composure, but I could tell. A look passed between him and the visitor. They pretended not to know one another, and I played along. I explained why the man had come, and your father offered to take him outside for a 'memory tour' of the grounds.

"Next thing I knew, five minutes later, your father came back inside and said the man had gone.

"We spoke no more of it. In the following days, I went about my daily life caring for you and keeping house. Your father was gone every day, from dawn to dusk, taking care of his usual business.

"I had my assumptions, but nothing was said. After three or four days, I asked your father, 'Do you suppose that man will come back? The one who said he used to live here?' I tried to make a joke of it. 'You know, I never did give him a tour of the upstairs!'

"Your father's face grew dark. 'That man,' he said, 'did not come here with good intentions. He lied to you. He believed I owed him something. He was wrong. He was the one who owed *me*. You don't have to worry. I took care of it. He will not be back.'

"After that, I never raised the subject again. Your father was sensitive to his failings, no matter how small. Like everyone, he had moments of neglect or inattentiveness but always made sure to put the consequences in order again. One objective guided him. To protect us, his family. That day, it was the man he'd hired who'd been inattentive, but your father felt he'd let us down. He was quick to correct his mistake, for our safety. I always felt safe. We *were* safe. Because your father understood his duty. He provided for us. He protected us.

"A few days ago, a moment of inattentiveness cost your father his life. You might not understand this now, but you will, one day. His ultimate sacrifice was made in fulfilling his duty to you. To provide. To protect."

She paused, but I knew this wasn't the end of it. The most important message was still to come. She took my chin firmly in her hand and turned my face toward her for a direct, penetrating look. "For all that he's given us, you owe him your respect."

My mother got me to stand up next to the bed. She examined my suit, brushed off the shoulders, pushed up the knot in my tie, made sure the Brylcreem still tamed my cowlick. We walked downstairs and passed my little brother, who was tucked into a corner of the living room. I felt my mother's hand on my back, giving me a gentle push. The crowd parted and I walked through, up to the coffin.

I knelt, pressed my hands together, and bowed my head. After the expected minute, I stood up again. I would not touch or kiss that lifeless figure. The face was sunken, the color and texture of modeling clay. Quickly, I looked away, preferring to recall the fire in his eyes whenever he delivered a reprimand. My focus settled on the middle of his chest. I imagined the flesh under his suit jacket, mentally counting the number of holes. I had a new appreciation for his "sacrifice," as my mother put it, but vowed never to end up like he had.

*****

When I finish my story, we sit facing each other without talking. The usual sounds float in from the corridor. Clattering keys and chains, footfalls on linoleum, men shouting in the distance.

Not many seconds do we stay like this, just long enough for the priest to understand that I have nothing more to say. His eyes are a cloudy blue under sagging eyelids and a tented brow.

He puts a hand on my shoulder and says, "Son. Little time remains. Cleanse your conscience, confess your sins, and ask for forgiveness."

I can say nothing, thinking only of the necessity of what I've done, something the priest wouldn't understand.

He persists. "Do you wish to be accepted into the Kingdom of Heaven, to meet your Father, Lord Jesus the Savior?"

"I've met my father and have no regrets." My own father wasn't given last rites. He received grace in the performance of his duty. His life, sacrificed for his sons.

A small, troubled look passes the old man's face. I realize then why I've asked for him in my final hour. He has served a need, allowing me to voice my mother's lesson. I wanted only to hear it, out loud. Her words, and the memories that have kept me company, countless times, sitting alone in this concrete box. I'm ready now, lifted by the righteousness of purpose. My purpose. A father's duty.

I don't explain. If the priest is puzzled at my resistance, he gives no indication. He has seen many men worse than me. Despite my failure at the sacrament of confession, he anoints me and gives me communion. "May the Lord Jesus, in his love and mercy, forgive you your sins, protect you, and lead you to eternal life."

I've run out of time. The guards arrive. The priest bestows a final touch before I'm shackled and led into the corridor.

The way is long and straight. Three pairs of shoes scuff and echo. Cells on either side hold men I've come to know in these years of useless waiting. As I pass by, they murmur their goodbyes.

The blinds are closed when we step into the room. Spectators are not allowed to see the preparations. They strap me onto the hard wooden chair by my forearms and ankles. I begin to feel the excitement of the moment. Before anything is placed on my head, the blinds are opened.

Among the dozen people in the tiny theater, I seek out three. They sit in the front row, at center. If my mother hadn't succumbed to cancer, there would have been four.

My wife is poised and regal, wearing a hat and suit in the style worn by the First Lady last year in Dallas. A different color, a pale lavender. We exchange a look of deep understanding. Her eyes are wide and dry, like my son's. He sits tall in his suit and tie, almost a man. His focus drifts past my shoulder. Maybe he's thinking of the days he stood at attention in my presence, replying, "Yes, sir," to my demands. He doesn't know me. Not really. The start of all this happened when he was only eight.

Next to my son sits my "little" brother. He's physically bigger and stronger than me, fierce and menacing when needed. But today, his strength means something else. He's the protector, in my stead. An enforcer. In his final visit to me, he conveyed the understanding he'd negotiated with those people — the man's allies and family. They are satisfied with this. It is enough. An eye for an eye, me for the man I killed.

Like my father, a moment of neglect put me where I am today. I'd planned well, so I thought, until the point I was cuffed and led away. Maybe it's better this way. Clearer. If I've let my family down, if my flawed performance landed me in this chair, I go to my grave knowing I haven't failed in my ultimate duty. I've provided. My wealth is bedrock. I've protected. The confirmation resides in my brother's eyes. We lock into a hard gaze and he nods his assurance. His word is sealed in my fate.

The final minute is for my son. He submits. Our eyes meet. He will watch, will not turn away. My wife has prepared him. She has done her duty as mother, has instilled the lesson of respect. *Your father has fulfilled his duty. To provide. To protect.*

The executioner, bag in hand, steps closer.

A History of Violence
in 24 Minutes, 10 Seconds
David Krugler

On a cool April night in Chicago, Ronnie and Clem sat in the front seat of a gleaming, brand-new baby blue 1970 Ford Galaxie and watched the corner of Broadway and Clifton. A young man wearing a top hat and paint-splattered overalls wobbled by on a unicycle. Three boys, barely teens, tumbled out of Ace Hardware, spray paint cans in their hands. They shook the cans like maracas. The pinging drowned out the scratchy bowing of a violinist standing beneath the el. One of the boys shoved the musician. He stumbled but kept playing. The boys moved on. An elderly man wearing two coats trudged by. He stopped every few steps to pull out a worn notebook and leaf through it. After peering intently at a page, he looked around suspiciously, as if afraid someone was reading over his shoulder. A middle-aged woman in a house coat and slippers swerved her shopping basket past the man. The head of a stuffed muskrat jutted from the basket.

Welcome to Uptown, Ronnie thought.

Clem turned his head and watched the younger man watch the street. "You think this is somethin'? Lemme tell you, this ain't nothin'. I seen crazier."

"You sound like that hobo in the book," Ronnie said.

Clem cocked a bushy eyebrow. "A hobo? In our book?"

"No, a book book. The kind you read."

"Oh, so you read books, do you? About hobos."

"The book isn't about hobos — there's just one in it."

"So you read a book that ain't about hobos. What's your book about then, P'fessor?"

Ronnie hesitated. "The war. You know, the one you and Pop were in."

Clem stared hard. "You don't think I know which war we was in?"

"A'course I do, I'm just—"

"Lemme tell you somethin', P'fessor. Any book with a hobo in it ain't a book about the war."

Ronnie didn't say anything. He had once overheard Pop tell an associate on the phone that Clem had been one of the first Marines ashore at Tarawa. *What's Tarawa?* Ronnie had asked when Pop hung up.

Pop had stared hard, like Clem just did. *What's Tarawa?* Pop had mimicked in a falsetto voice. Ronnie hadn't asked again. The falsetto was Pop's way of telling Ronnie to shut up.

"What time is it?" Clem demanded. He wore a watch, but the question was his way of telling Ronnie they had a job to do.

"Six forty-eight," Ronnie answered.

Clem grunted.

Ronnie looked at the television and radio repair shop across the street. Al, the owner, would be flipping his sign from *Open* to *Closed* in twelve minutes. In eleven minutes, Ronnie and Clem would exit the car.

What was the name of that book with the hobo in it? Ronnie had read it last year, when it came out. The novel was about a guy named Billy Pilgrim, who was a prisoner of war in Dresden, Germany, when he wasn't time-traveling through space. How could he remember all that but not the title?

"Let's go over what you're gonna say to Al," Clem said.

"Okay."

"I'll be Al, you be you."

"Okay."

"'Good evening, gentlemen,'" Clem said. Al was unfailingly polite. Even though his hands would be trembling.

"'Hi, Al.'"

"Stop!" Clem clenched the steering wheel. "Jesus Christ, Ronnie, how many times I gotta tell you?"

"Sorry, I forgot. It's just Al's such a nice guy and when—"

"He ain't nice. He ain't even a guy. All he is to us is a debt, you understand? An *overdue* debt."

"Right, an overdue debt."

"Okay. I'm still Al. 'Good evening, gentlemen.'"

"'You're late, Al. Again.'"

"'Is it Saturday already?'"

"'A'course it's Saturday, Al. Just like it was Saturday... um... last Saturday.'"

Clem grimaced but stayed in character. "'Well, I ain't got it. I'm very sorry.'"

Ronnie had never heard Al say 'ain't' but he kept going. "'That's not good, Al. We've given you all the breaks we can.'"

"'I don't know what to tell you. You can't get blood from a turnip.'"

Ronnie gave Clem a blank look.

"Forget that. Whatever Al says, it means he don't have the vig. And you gotta be ready to do what your dad told us to do. You understand?"

"Yes."

"So say it."

"'We gotta take the keys, Al.'"

"Then what do you do?"

"I hold out my hand for the keys."

"No! You grab Al like this" — Clem's right hand shot out and seized Ronnie's collar — "and you shake him like a rag doll and then you tilt him upside down and shake the keys outa his pockets."

Ronnie nodded. He'd seen Clem rough up overdues plenty of times. He knew Pop wanted him to start doing it. *Clem's not getting any younger*, he'd told Ronnie. But why couldn't they just ask Al for the keys? He was an old man who walked with a limp.

"Jesus, Ronnie, I can't understand how a big guy like yourself ain't itchin' to crack heads."

How many times had he heard that? *A big guy like yourself* ... Ronnie stood 6'3" and weighed 210 pounds. No belly, wide shoulders, thick biceps. Fast feet, too, according to the boxing coach Pop paid to work Ronnie out.

"I hit the bag hard," Ronnie protested.

Clem shook his head sadly. "It ain't the same. Not even close."

"You really want me to shake Al up?"

"Just get the keys."

"I will."

Clem answered by lighting an Old Gold and blowing a mouthful of smoke out the window. Ronnie looked down at his massive hands. Meathooks, Coach called them. Made for jabs, uppercuts, and roundhouses. But only if Ronnie wanted to punch. *All gift and no grit, that kid.* So Coach had told Pop.

Ronnie couldn't see why they had to get rough with Al. The old-timer knew he was going to lose his business. When Clem had glided the Galaxie to the curb, Ronnie had seen Al peek out the window. This was the third Saturday he hadn't paid. When he took the loan, Pop had made him repeat aloud what the vig was and what would happen if he didn't pay.

Ronnie turned his left wrist. 6:52. Seven minutes until they left the car. He tried mentally rehearsing what he would say to Al but the exercise felt silly. He gave up.

You think this is bad? This ain't bad. So said the hobo, who had become a soldier, in the book Ronnie couldn't remember the title of. The hobo, Billy Pilgrim, and other American soldiers were packed into cattle cars in winter, on their way to a German P.O.W. camp. They had been captured in a battle during World War II. How could he remember all that but not the title?

"Look at that hippie," Clem said with disgust. Ronnie followed his gaze. A young white man loitered outside the hardware store, which was on the north side of Al's shop. He wore combat boots, jeans, and a denim jacket with a Confederate flag patch on the right shoulder. His straight brown hair fell to his shoulders and brushed his eyebrows. He was short but looked powerfully built.

"He's one of those Young Patriots," Ronnie said.

"D'hell are they?"

"They're from those people moving here from Kentucky."

"The hillbillies? They got a gang? Those crackers can't hardly tie their own shoes."

"I don't think it's a gang. It's more like, I don't know, a community group?"

Clem snorted with derision. "Yeah, that freak's just waitin' to help little old ladies across the street." He shot Ronnie a look. "How come you know so much about the hillbillies? Read another book, P'fessor?"

"No."

"If you're so smart, why don't you tell me what that *brutha* over there thinks about your hillbilly friend?"

"Brutha" was Clem's latest slur for blacks. This man was standing outside the Drift-In Lounge, which was on the south side of Al's shop. He was tall and thin, dressed in black jeans, a sleek leather jacket, and a black beret.

"Well..."

"Well what?"

"Nothing," Ronnie said, even though he had an answer. A week ago, he had seen fliers around the neighborhood. *Tired of Rats and Pigs?* Underneath this headline was a garish sketch of landlords, rich men, and police as rats and pigs. The flier urged residents to attend a meeting to "unite Uptown against the crooks, capitalists and cops who harass, oppress and abuse us." Intrigued, Ronnie went. Hadn't Pop told him he needed to keep his ear to the ground?

The meeting was in a church basement. Every folding chair was filled. Ronnie had to stand in the back. An old man with a Southern accent and scraggly gray hair addressed the crowd. Most were white but quite a few blacks were present. The old man spoke quietly but clearly. "Y'all tired'a the cops hassling us over nothin'?" The whites nodded, the blacks said uh-huh, uh-huh. The old man talked about landlords who didn't care about rats biting their kids and ceilings caving in from broken pipes. He asked if they were sick and tired of Pay Day, the outfit that took twenty percent of day laborers' wages as a commission. Pretty soon, the whites were uh-huhing and giving the blacks knowing looks and the blacks were giving knowing looks right back. Meanwhile, four young white men and four young black men stood on either side of the old man, legs apart, hands laced in front. The whites wore blue jeans and denim jackets with Confederate flag patches. The blacks wore dark pants, leather jackets, and black berets. One had on wraparound sunglasses.

The old man said, "I want y'all to meet some young bloods who're gonna clean up this neighborhood." The blacks were Panthers who had come from the West Side. The whites called themselves the Young Patriots.

"How come y'all sportin' those flags on your jackets?" an elderly black man called out, to approving murmurs. One of the Patriots tried to explain it was a symbol of their Southern heritage and no offense was intended. That didn't go over well. Then the Black Panther in sunglasses stepped up. He started talking. He said injustice didn't know color, not when money called the tune. He said the Man worked hard to divide the People. The Man wanted whites to hate blacks and blacks to hate whites. "Are we gonna do the Man's work for him?" he shouted. "No sir!" came the response, from blacks and whites. "We gonna let a little scrap of cloth divide us when we all need to come together?" Now the crowd was on its feet, roaring approval. At a feverish pace, the young man in sunglasses spoke of how the Black Panthers and the Young Patriots were uniting to—

"What are you doing here?" The hostile challenge came from the old man. Ronnie hadn't noticed him sidle up.

"I'm just listening," Ronnie answered.

The old man glared. "Dan Griel's son ain't welcome here. You get gone, understand?"

Ronnie had left quietly. Which is why he didn't want to now tell Clem how he knew who the Young Patriots were. Or how they were working with the Black Panthers. If he said he went to the meeting, Clem would berate him. *D'hell you doin', showin' your face to people like that?* And if Clem found out Ronnie had allowed the old man to roust him, he'd really lose it. *Goddamnit all, Ronnie, you represent the organization! You let the mooks push you around, the organization gets pushed around!*

Ronnie didn't want any of that to happen. He knew he should tell Clem and Pop the Panthers and Patriots were talking trash about Pay Day. Pop owned Pay Day — he'd want to know if trouble was afoot. But that, too, would mean revealing he'd attended the meeting.

"What time is it?" Clem asked.

Ronnie looked at his watch. "Six fifty-nine."

"Let's go."

They exited the car and crossed Broadway. Al had already flipped his shop sign to *Closed*. When had he done that? Ronnie hadn't noticed. He looked at Clem to see if he thought this was unusual, but Clem already had that one-thousand-yard stare that came over him when they visited overdues. The black man in the leather jacket glanced at Ronnie and Clem and then went inside the Drift-In Lounge. The Young Patriot Clem had derided as a hippie was nowhere in sight. Ronnie couldn't remember seeing him leave his spot outside the hardware store.

"Don't forget what you gotta do," Clem said as he reached for the door handle.

"I won't."

A bell jangled as they entered. Al stood behind his counter. He offered a tremulous smile. "Good evening, gentlemen."

Clem scowled.

"You're late, Al," Ronnie said. "Again."

"I know. But tonight is different."

"You got the money?"

Al hesitated. "Yes, I do."

"So let's have it," Clem said. He strode toward the counter. Ronnie followed. Tools and the guts of a radio were spread across the worn wood. Wires, tubes, clips, screws. Pliers, screwdrivers, cutters.

"I have to go get it."

"From where?"

"In the back."

"Ronnie'll go get it. Tell him where it is."

"Sure." Al looked at Ronnie. "It's in an envelope beneath the open chassis of an Admiral Celestial."

Ronnie looked at Clem.

"Jesus Christ," Clem muttered. "Go with him," he ordered Al.

Ronnie and Al went into the back. Metal shelves brimmed with the carcasses of televisions, radios, reel-to-reel and cassette recorders. Wires and cords festooned a pegboard. A thick sheath of plywood fastened to sawhorses served as a worktable, which was empty except for the base of a large radio — the Admiral Celestial, Ronnie assumed. Why would Al leave the envelope there? Had he hidden a gun under the radio?

"Al, stop," Ronnie ordered.

Al froze.

"You better let me get the envelope."

"Okay. It's right there, like I said." He pointed.

Ronnie lifted the radio base. No envelope. He looked at Al.

Who tried to look puzzled. "What the hell...?" He made a show of snapping his fingers. "Ah! I left the envelope in my car." He gestured at the back door.

Ronnie frowned. Just because he didn't like to crack heads didn't make him stupid. "Al, lying is only gonna make this worse."

Al smiled weakly. "Ronnie, really, I got the money, it's in—"

"D'hell's taking so long?" Clem demanded. The door to the front flapped noisily.

"Al says the money's in his car."

"Bullshit." Clem moved toward Al. Ronnie saw him roll his shoulders and clench his fists. The wind-up. Al saw it too. He took two steps backward, toward the rear exit. Ronnie started around the table to block his path. Al bolted. Even with his bum leg, he was out the door before Ronnie could grab him.

Clem and Ronnie raced after him. The door snicked shut behind them. Al stopped in the middle of the narrow street, where two men stood. Clem and Ronnie halted, hard — the two men had handguns trained on them. A black man in a sleek leather jacket and a long-haired white man in a denim jacket with a Confederate flag patch.

"You two! D'hell you think you're doin'?" Clem advanced.

"Stop," the black man ordered. "Take out your weapon, real slow. Set it down and kick it toward me."

Clem told him what he could do to himself, using his preferred slur for blacks.

The man lifted his gun and squeezed a shot that passed dangerously close to Clem's head.

Clem didn't flinch. He didn't obey the order. He stood still, drilling the shooter with a sharp stare. Ronnie dared a quick look around. Their situation wasn't good. Clifton, the street behind Al's shop, was a short block with a ten-mile-long reputation. Blood Alley, locals called it. Muggers preyed on the drunks who lived in dilapidated SROs. An abandoned warehouse was a shooting gallery for addicts. The streetlights were broken, the sidewalks cracked. On the opposite curb, a sewer grate had caved in beneath a rusty Ford Falcon, catching the car's front tire like a raccoon's paw in a trap. Vandals had stripped the car. From behind it, four shadows rose. Two more Panthers, two more Patriots. They spread out alongside Al's two guardians. They were armed too.

You think this is bad? This ain't bad. Ronnie couldn't stop remembering the hobo's lines from the book he couldn't remember the title of. This seemed awful bad, though.

"You really want a shootout, old-timer?" asked the Black Panther who had fired the shot.

Clem slowly reached behind his back and took out his Colt 1911. He bent and laid it down on the pavement. He straightened up. "I ain't kicking my piece — that'll scratch it. You want it, come get it."

The Panther hesitated. Ronnie held his breath. Clem didn't care about damaging the gun. Kicking would expose the Beretta in an ankle holster on his right leg.

"All right. Take five steps back."

Clem stepped back.

"Now you," the long-haired Patriot ordered Ronnie.

Ronnie took out his Smith and Wesson, set it down, and backed up.

One of the other Patriots retrieved the weapons.

"Know who you're messin' with?" Clem said.

"That's why we're here," the Panther said calmly. He lowered his weapon. "We have a message for your boss."

"Write a letter," Clem said. He pointed a finger at Al. "You still owe us, you understand?" Then he addressed Ronnie. "C'mon, we're goin'." He turned and strode toward the rear door of Al's shop.

It's locked, Clem. Ronnie remembered the sound of the lock clicking in place. But he couldn't say the words. What would Clem do — what would Pop do — if he sounded afraid? Clem pulled on the door. It clanked securely against its reinforced frame. He swore under his breath. Ronnie started to whisper "What now?" but Clem shook his head. He turned around, squared his shoulders.

"Look here," the Panther called out. He made a show of securing his weapon behind his back. He gestured at his comrades to do the same. Then he held up his hands, palms out. "Like I said, we got a message for your boss. The guns are just to get your attention. Now that we got that, we do this all peaceful, alright?"

"You got our attention? Dontcha mean you got our guns?"

He smiled. "Don't worry, you'll get them back."

Clem scanned the street. The sun had set. With the streetlights out, the cracked pavement and uneven sidewalks disappeared into a murky darkness. Not a single window in any building was lit. That troubled Ronnie. A crowd in the street, a gunshot — why weren't the residents of the SROs gawking out their windows? The Panthers and Patriots must have ordered everyone to mind their business.

"Don't think about running," the Panther told Clem.

Who snorted. "We ain't even thinkin'a thinkin'a runnin'."

The Panther pointed at Clem, then Ronnie. "Here's the message for your boss and your old man: no more loan-sharking. Tomorrow, Al and everyone else who owes will pay their debts. But no vig, understand? They've paid plenty of interest already, so they're only gonna pay the principal. And once the debts are paid, Griel folds up the operation. He's done screwing over working folks."

Ronnie watched Clem's jaw grind. His face was florid, his eyes coals. He looked like a bull about to charge. No one talked to him like this, ever. The Panther said no more, arms crossed.

Clem wasn't just being watched on the street. Atop Ace Hardware, a Young Patriot named Lyle was crouched on one knee beside the roof's parapet. The Remington Woodsmaster rifle that had belonged to his deceased father was trained on Clem. Lyle had just joined the Young Patriots. He was seventeen. The other Patriots told him he was too young for this "mission." He was tired of being told he was too young. That's what the guidance counselor had said when he quit school. That's what the Marine recruiter told him when he tried to enlist without his mom's permission. And what his mom said when he demanded her permission. Hell, wasn't their name the *Young* Patriots? If he was old enough to belong, he was old enough to do his part. He had tailed his comrades, staying out of sight, then clambered onto the roof after they took their positions.

"And if we don't quit business?" Clem asked.

"Like I said, we wanna do this peaceful. That's why you're getting this polite warning. You don't quit, well, you'll see what happens next. So just deliver the message to your boss."

"Do I look like a Western Union boy, boy?"

The Panther's face tightened. "Maybe you think we're doing this 'cause we wanna take over the loan-sharking. We're not criminals, you understand? We're here to get rid of the crooks. To get rid of you. Just ask your *boy* here — he heard us explain what we're about."

Clem looked at Ronnie. "D'hell he's talkin' about?"

"Well, I, uh...about a week ago, they had this — there were fliers all over the street, and you know how Pop keeps telling me—"

"C'mon, Griel. Tell him how you came to our community meeting."

"You been talking to them?" Clem was incredulous.

"No! I just went to see what they're about. That's all, I swear."

"Next time you wanna spy, don't send an ox," the long-haired Patriot said with a sneer.

"He heard us say we're gonna clean up this neighborhood," the Panther said. "Well, now we're cleaning up."

Clem wasn't listening. He was looking at Ronnie, who had never seen such an expression of disgust on the older man's face. Not when overdues begged for more time, or begged him to stop hitting them; not once when Ronnie had messed up before.

"I was going to tell you, Clem, I just..." Ronnie caught himself. *Never show weakness, never admit a mistake.* How many times had he heard Pop say that?

"Looks like you two got something to work out," the long-haired Patriot mocked them.

Clem released a gritted, almost inaudible exhale. That one-thousand-yard stare was back. Ronnie had seen it on Pop, too — lots of vets had it. Looking like they weren't looking at anything, yet seeing everything. Clem was calculating. Clem was deciding. *Never show weakness...*

"Put our guns right here, *brutha.*" Clem pointed at the pavement in front of him.

"Uh-uh, no way, *uncle,*" the Panther said. "Chuck here'll put 'em in your car." He ticked his head at the Patriot who had picked up their weapons. Chuck set out toward Broadway.

On the hardware store roof, Lyle shifted. His right foot was going numb. How did snipers in the action-adventure paperbacks he loved to read stay crouched this long? He kept his rifle trained on Clem. The darkness made it difficult to stay on center mass. He shifted his aim to Ronnie. The old man seemed to be the primary threat, but what if the big guy made a sudden move? Lyle had better be ready to take out either one. *Take out*, was that the phrase? It didn't sound quite right. *Fell the target*, that was better. He couldn't believe his unit had failed to secure the high ground. And to put their weapons away like they had? How could they do that? Lyle imagined the debriefing back at HQ (actually his cousin's apartment). They'd cuss him out for disobeying orders, but when he told them how he'd covered the field from the roof, they'd come around. They'd say they were dead-wrong for leaving him behind. "Man, this one's a natural," he imagined William, the leader of the Panthers, saying to cheers and claps on his shoulders.

"Al!" Clem shouted.

The old man winced.

"Gimme your keys."

Al looked at the Panther, who nodded.

Al fished in his pocket, threw the keys to Clem.

Who caught them. But the keys slipped through his fingers, clattered on the pavement. He bent to get them. Ronnie knew it was no accident. Clem had the hands of a juggler. He never dropped anything. He was going for the gun strapped to his ankle. Ronnie leaned in, using his bulk to block the sight line of the Panthers and Patriots. Would that make up for him not telling Clem about going to the meeting?

As he stood, Clem palmed his gun and handed the keys to Ronnie. His eyes told Ronnie what to do. Unlock the door, open it. Ronnie dipped his chin to let him know he understood. The lock was a Schlage. Ronnie looked at the keys, found the one stamped Schlage. He unlocked the door, pulled it open...

What was that? Peering down at the targets, Lyle caught a flash of metal as the old man bent down. He was taking something off his ankle as he picked up the keys he'd dropped. Another gun! Lyle's heart raced, his breathing became shallow. Had his comrades seen it? But the big guy had stepped in to cover his partner. Lyle adjusted his aim. *Steady, hold, squeeze.* His finger applied pressure to the trigger as he held his breath. Between the V of his rifle sight, the old man was holding the gun to his side. Any second, he would fire at Lyle's men. How many could he hit before he and the big guy ducked into the store? Two or three, at least. Or none, if Lyle kept squeezing the trigger...

Two men immediately dropped to the street — Clem and Gary, one of the Young Patriots. Like Clem, Gary was a combat veteran, two months back from Vietnam. Gary scrambled to a crouch and raced toward the gutted Ford Falcon.

"Take cover!" he shouted at his comrades. They ran, some to the car, others to the loading bay of the hardware store. Al stood alone in the middle of the street, bewildered.

"Ronnie, get down!" Clem hissed.

Ronnie's knees buckled. His abdomen was burning. And wet. The wetness seeped into his pants, his underwear. He pressed his hand against his stomach.

"Clem, I, I—"

He toppled into the doorway to Al's shop. Clem saw the wound. The round had torn through Ronnie's back and come out just above his waist line. Blood slicked Ronnie's fingers.

The Panthers and Patriots didn't see Ronnie fall. They were whispering furiously. They thought the shot was aimed at them. Was anyone hit? How had the loan sharks known to bring a third man? Had someone betrayed them? Where was the shooter? They scanned the rooftops. But Lyle had ducked beneath the parapet. He wanted to remain hidden, so the targets wouldn't know where the shot had come from. Any moment, his comrades would take out their weapons and finish neutralizing the threat. Lyle's heart pounded. He had saved his men. Alone on the roof, the greatest rush he'd ever felt brought forth gasping laughter.

Clem shoved his handgun into his belt. He nimbly vaulted over Ronnie and pulled him into the shop. The door slammed shut once Ronnie's boots cleared the threshold. Blood smeared the cement floor.

"Ronnie, look at me," Clem ordered. He cradled the young man's head.

"I'm burning, I'm burning," Ronnie whimpered. He tried to touch his wound; Clem seized his wrists.

"Keep your arms down, okay?" Clem looked again at the wound. He had seen gut-shots like this on Tarawa. The medics treated them last.

"What happened—"

"Look at me."

Ronnie met Clem's eyes.

"This ain't — it's gonna be okay. I seen worse. I gotta call for help, but I'll be right back. Don't touch the wound, hear me?"

"Don't leave."

"I'll be right back."

The burning surrendered to coldness. *I'm going into shock*, Ronnie thought. Did that mean Clem was right, that he would be okay? Shock was the body's way of protecting itself, wasn't it? He needed to stay conscious. But his eyelids fluttered. His legs and arms felt like stones. The back room of Al's shop grew dark. He thought he heard the whisk of Clem's shoes.

"Tell Pop, tell him..." The words weighed on his tongue, as heavy as the boxing gloves felt on his hands when he was in the ring. Ronnie didn't finish the sentence.

Clem wasn't there to hear Ronnie's last words. He was on Al's phone, waiting for Dan Griel, Ronnie's father, to be summoned to the line.

"Clem?" Griel said.

"We're at Al's. I need the doctor and every man. Bring the BARs. It's bad."

Clem hung up and checked his watch. A few ticks past 7:12. In two minutes or less, Griel would be there with their crew, the gambling-addicted doctor they kept on a string, and the black market Browning

Automatic Rifles from the gun safe at the office. And then the punks out there would find out who really owned Uptown. He rushed to the back to check on Ronnie.

Outside on Clifton, the Panthers and Patriots were regrouping. Using hand signals, Gary had guided them behind a dumpster shielding them from the sniper. They were arguing. Gary wanted some of them to trap Clem and Ronnie in the shop while the others found the sniper and killed him. William, the leader of the Panthers, wanted to retreat. They hadn't come to start a war with Griel. How would a shootout help the People?

Lyle didn't hear any of this. Flattened out on his back on the hardware store roof, he was looking up at the stars, cradling his father's rifle, waiting for the gunfire.

Blue Laws
Robert Jeschonek

My cousin, Abe Birnbaum, stares up at me from the floor of the department store, all trace of life gone from his dull, sunken eyes. They remind me of my own eyes, every time I look in the mirror, ever since the war.

His security guard uniform reminds me of something, too. It reminds me of a photo he sent me once, with him in his Army khakis and helmet, on a hilltop somewhere in Italy. Hard to believe he survived his time in that uniform, only to die in this one.

"It happened sometime yesterday," explains the local cop, Officer Demarco. "The store was closed Sunday, so no one found him until this morning."

"Right." I swallow hard, cursing the blue laws that keep most businesses closed on Sunday in the state of Pennsylvania. If Ziegler's Department Store had been open yesterday, Abe might not be dead on the speckled white linoleum floor with a pool of crimson blood spread out under his crushed skull.

Demarco clears his throat and checks his notepad. "Started his shift at 8am Sunday, pulling a double to cover for another guard, whose wife was having a baby." Demarco scowls and flips to the next page. "Didn't matter, I guess. Kid was stillborn anyway."

"Uh-huh." For a moment, I turn my gaze away from Abe and look around. We're on the second floor of Ziegler's, in the middle of the men's suit department. How long has it been since I was back here, in Ziegler's Department Store in Morley, PA? Twelve years, almost. Since before the war, for sure.

It's been a long stretch from 1942 to 1954, but the place looks much the same as I remember it. Circular racks of suit coats arranged around us; racks of trousers hung from the wall that spans the department. Men's casual clothes to one side, and boys' suits across the aisle. Section by section of merchandise, set up from wall to wall, cut through by a carefully planned path designed to maximize sales. And every floor the same as this from basement to attic, providing a world of shopping under one roof for the people of this small city...though those people are all elsewhere this morning, kept out until cousin Abe can be cleared.

Overlaying it all is the smell I remember so clearly from my visits to the store — the aroma of peanuts and cashews being roasted on the ground floor. It's the greatest marketing strategy of all time, if you ask me, the scent equivalent of comfort food wafting throughout the building. I guess the staff started up the roaster before Abe's body was found this morning.

I almost wish they hadn't. I was practically raised in this place; the smell conjures up memories both good and bad that distract me from the task at hand.

I'm a Pittsburgh cop, a detective. Time to act like one instead of mooning over the past. "You said Mr. Zeigler found the body?" I ask.

"The company president, yes." Demarco smirks, but at least he doesn't mention that Mr. Zeigler is my father. "He was the first one in this morning."

It figures; Dad has always been like that. "And no one that you know of disturbed the crime scene?"

"Correct." Demarco snaps the notepad shut and stuffs it in the pocket of his black trousers. Reaching up, he adjusts a brass button on his black uniform shirt, then fiddles with the badge over his heart. "Mr. Z locked the place down and called the station right away."

As I crouch beside the body, my eyes are drawn to the awful wound in Abe's head. From what I can see, his skull was caved in with some kind of object; the bone is crushed between forehead and crown, the skin gashed open, blood soaking his thin gray hair.

But what interests me most is the edge of the wound, nearest the forehead. "What the heck is that?" I slip a pencil from the vest pocket of my suit jacket and point the tip at the wound's ragged fringe. "Some kind of blue residue?"

Demarco leans down for a look. "Beats me. Paint, maybe?"

The residue is sky blue and smeared all around the wound. Inside it, too, maybe, though I can't tell through all the blood. "Go get me a Q-Tip, wouldja? I want a sample of this stuff."

"Q-Tip?" Demarco frowns like he doesn't appreciate my request. Could it be he doesn't like taking orders from a Jew?

If it is, that makes us even. I spent two years fighting Italians during the war, so he's not exactly putting me at ease. "Ground floor, Demarco. Look in toiletries or cosmetics, all right?"

Demarco hesitates. "Sure, okay." Then he shuffles off toward the elevator bank at the front of the store.

Leaving me to poke around Abe's body some more. It's then I realize his head wasn't the only thing damaged. The fingers of both hands are also smashed and smeared with blue residue. His rib cage feels broken too, and the unnatural angles of his splayed legs suggest they were also snapped.

What a mess. Not much in the way of clues, either, except for the blue residue...and one thing that seems out of place in his wallet. A business card for someone called Madame Kashmir. Her name is written in flowing, exotic script, like something out of *Arabian Nights*; her address is on the far side of town...the *dark* side of town, if you ask most people.

Leaning back, I take another look at Abe with a less clinical eye. He was never my favorite person, I admit. He was a thug and a bully as far back as I can remember, though he spared me the worst of his abuses. From time to time, he even looked out for me. He was an asshole, but he was also family.

And I will not deny him the justice he deserves.

*****

I get my sample of the blue residue with the Q-Tip from Demarco, then stow it in a paper envelope from the stationery department. Just as I step out of the elevator on the ground floor, on my way to follow up on Madame Kashmir, my dad intercepts me.

"Leonard!" He marches over briskly, his thick, black brows pulled together in a deep frown under his cloud of silver hair. "What do you have so far?"

Leave it to Dad not to beat around the bush. "Not much. I've got to check a few things and see where they lead."

Dad straightens his gray, tailor-made suit coat. "What things?"

I'm not about to share what I've got with him. He called me in, he asked for my help, but I know him too well; he won't be able to stop himself from trying to take charge. Once a boss, always a boss. "I'll let you know when I've got more solid information, Dad," I tell him.

He steps closer and thrusts out his chin in a challenging pose, locking eyes with me. But then, he just nods. "You do that, Leonard." He reaches out and pats my left shoulder. "And please be careful."

"I will." I turn out of his grip and head for the door.

"Watch your step," says Dad. "What if they're targeting the family?"

"I handled the Nazis, Dad," I say over my shoulder as I push through the door. "I think I can take care of myself at this point."

*****

I've got a Lucky Strike cigarette in my mouth the second I get outside. Been dying for a smoke for a while now, but I didn't want to light up around my poor, dead cousin.

As I pull out my Zippo lighter and flick it to life, I notice how relieved I feel now that I'm out of the store. It became like a cage to me when I was growing up; there was an expectation that I'd fill my dad's shoes someday, which was the last thing I wanted to do.

I think Dad would still love it if I went to work there, especially since my two brothers died in the war. After all, it's the family business, built from the ground up by my grandfather and his brothers after they escaped the pogrom killing sprees by the Cossacks in Poland.

But no. Being a plainclothes cop, a detective, is what I've always wanted to do. And the truth is, I never fit in here. There are things about me that have always made me feel like a stranger, things that keep me forever at arm's length. Being who I am, with my particular secret, I could never play a significant role in this company or this town, with my life permanently under the magnifying glass. I could never withstand the scrutiny.

Retail and Morley ought to be in my blood, but they aren't. My blood is blue, all right — *cop* blue — and that will never change.

Speaking of blood, I see splotches of red on the sidewalk when I step around the corner of the front of the store. Crouching, I take a closer look, wondering if I ought to get a sample.

The splotches look more like paint stains than blood...though they glisten in the morning sun in a way that makes me think they might be fresh.

I dab one with a finger, and the tip comes away bright red. Definitely recent. But why someone would splatter paint on this spot is beyond me.

Puffing on my Lucky Strike, I wipe my finger on my handkerchief and get to my feet, thinking about the next place I need to go.

*****

"Come in, dear seeker, come in." A woman's voice with a British accent calls to me as soon as I open the door of the rundown little shop.

Her accent's as strong as the smell of incense wafting out of the place, which is enough to make me cough. I can actually see puffs of it rolling through the doorway as I lean inside and have a look.

Incense, crystal ball, beaded curtains, Ouija board: at least I know what business she's in at this point. I didn't know this town had its own fortune teller, but obviously, that's what she is.

The bell on the door jingles as I step through and close it behind me. "Madame Kashmir?"

There's a flurry of gold jewelry and brightly colored scarves through one of the beaded curtains. She enters with a twirl and stands revealed before me, arms spread dramatically.

"I am the one you seek," she declares, her voice a rich baritone. "I foresaw your arrival in the tea leaves this morning, and so you are very welcome in this sanctuary." Her dark hair falls around her face as she makes a little bow.

As she straightens, I realize she must have been beautiful once. Twenty or even just ten years ago, her dark eyes and thick lips might have mesmerized me. Forty or thirty pounds ago, her figure with its ample bosom and prominent buttocks might have enticed me to offer a proposition. But those years are gone, those pounds are here to stay, and her stocky frame, abundant wrinkles, and oversized nose have no better attributes to distract from their combined unattractiveness.

"Tell me how I may help you, seeker." She presses her palms together in a prayerful gesture.

I produce her business card from my vest pocket and hold it out to her. "My cousin, Abe Birnbaum, had this. I take it he was one of your customers?"

Her dark eyes flick from the card to my face. "Alas, that is not within my power to divulge."

"Please. This is very important."

A big, sad smile spreads across her pudgy features. "If he *were* one of my customers, that knowledge would be private between he and I. Think of the Catholic confessional." She presses her hands over her heart and nods slowly, sincerely. "Our personal, spiritual interactions must remain sacrosanct for as long as we both shall inhabit this mortal plane."

"Then we're in luck," I tell her. "Because Abe's not *in* this mortal plane anymore. He's been *murdered*."

That takes the helium right out of her balloon. Her face drains of color, and she wobbles on her feet. "Murdered?"

"That's right." I nod and slip the card back into my vest pocket. "So much for the confessional seal."

Madame Kashmir staggers a few steps across the room and drops into a chair at the little table with the crystal ball. "Oh my God."

I pull back my coat, revealing the police badge clipped to my belt. "I'm more than his cousin, too. But you already foresaw that, didn't you?"

Madame Kashmir continues to deflate, slumping against the table. "I don't...I..." She lets out a heavy sigh.

"So let's start over, shall we?" I plant my hands on my hips, keeping the jacket open and the badge visible. "How did you know Abe Birnbaum?"

"He was a customer." She still has the British accent, but the over-the-top dramatic projection is gone from her voice. "A very good customer."

I nod. "And what kind of services did you provide him with, exactly? Fortune telling?"

Madame Kashmir's elaborate gold earrings tinkle when she shakes her head. "I didn't kill him, and I don't know who did."

I narrow my eyes and lean toward her. "What kind of services?" I snap out the words.

That raises a little fire in her eyes. "Nothing harmful, all right? Nothing you need to worry about."

Glaring, I step forward. "*Tell* me. What *services*?"

Kashmir flinches, then pops out of her chair. She stomps across the room and squats by a set of curtained-off shelves. I watch her every move carefully, sliding my hand close to the .22 revolver in the shoulder holster under my coat.

I tense when she parts the curtain and reaches for something on one of the shelves...but I quickly relax when I see there's no kind of weapon in her hand. As she stands up and walks toward me, she's carrying a stack of big, glossy photos, not a gun.

"Here." She hands me the stack. "This is the service I was providing."

As soon as I see the top photo in the stack, I understand. It's a shot of a voluptuous young woman, completely naked, performing a sex act on a very excited young man.

Flipping through the stack of black-and-white 8 x 10s, I see that the rest of the photos are all variations on the same theme. It's possible cousin Abe was in the market for such pictures; any red-blooded man might be susceptible to this particular photo gallery.

"Just a little blue photography, you see." Madame Kashmir's gold bracelets jangle as she flutters her hands. "Nothing harmful about it, as I said."

Tell that to the models, I think, but I don't argue the point. "And you were providing these to Abe? Selling them to him?"

"I admit *nothing*." She chops her right hand through the air. "That would be *illegal*, officer."

I flip through a few more photos, noticing the same faces keep popping up. "I wonder if these girls have boyfriends." I linger on a shot of a woman servicing two men at once. "What would happen if one of them came across some of these pictures, I wonder?"

Madame Kashmir shrugs. "It wouldn't have made any difference to Abe, I assure you. These photos were taken God knows where. Not even in the States, so I'm told."

I look at a few more shots, then drop the stack on her table by the crystal ball. Walking slowly around the room, I wonder what other shady business Madame Kashmir is into.

"Tell me more." I lift the curtain from the shelves and look at the contents — more stacks of photos and magazines, from what I can see. "Who could have wanted to hurt him?"

She shakes her head. "I've told you everything there is to tell, seeker. Your cousin came to me for a particular kind of entertainment, no more. Our relationship was of a strictly professional nature."

I let the curtain fall and walk to the opposite wall. A painting hung there catches my eye and draws me to it. "What's this?"

"It's from India," says Madame Kashmir. "A portrait of the goddess Kali."

I can't look away from the four-armed figure in the painting. Her face is twisted in a sneer, her hair a tangle of dark coils, her skin a brilliant shade of sky blue. "What is she the goddess of?"

"Many things." Madame Kashmir clears her throat. "Including death."

"You don't say." Frowning, I pull out the sample envelope I've been carrying and hold up the swab with the smear of blue from Abe's head wound. It's a perfect match for the goddess's skin color. "So where else can I find this Kali in the city of Morley?"

Madame Kashmir steps up beside me. "A library book, perhaps? This town is hardly a hotbed of Indian culture."

I put away the swab and pocket the envelope. "There's no one from India living in the area?"

"No one, no one." Kashmir narrows her eyes and taps her wrinkled chin with a fingertip...then grabs my upper left arm and squeezes. "Wait, I spoke too soon. There is one man, an occasional client."

I turn to her expectantly. "Who is he and where can I find him?"

*****

As I walk through the door of the local VFW, it seems much the same as any other post of the Veterans of Foreign Wars that I've been to. A U-shaped bar occupies most of the room, tended by a balding, middle-aged guy in a plaid shirt and khakis. Six men are scattered on stools around the bar, slouching over glasses of beer without looking up when I enter. A haze of cigarette smoke hangs over them, forming a misty layer that ripples like seafoam in the breeze from the open door. Everything seems afloat in a timeless, melancholy murk, a fog in which all movement, sound, and thought are slowed and suspended like insects in amber.

At first, I don't see the man I'm looking for, and I wonder where else I might find him. But then the men's room door swings open on the other side of the place, and he walks out big as life, impossible to miss with his dark brown skin and glossy black hair.

As he takes a spot at the bar and orders a beer, I walk over and stand beside him. "Naveen Shrivastava?"

He looks over his shoulder at me, his big white eyes bulging under tar-black brows. "Do I know you?" he asks.

"You do now." I show him the badge on my belt and watch carefully for a reaction.

Nothing but the mildest interest is visible on his face. Not exactly what I'd expected to see from the current prime suspect in Cousin Abe's murder.

He shrugs and reaches for his beer. "To what do I owe the honor of your visit?"

"Her, actually." I hold up the painting of Kali, which I borrowed from Madame Kashmir.

"What about her?" Naveen's accent has a sing-song rhythm. I've heard it before, from the occasional Indians I met in passing in Italy during the war.

"You tell me." I put the painting on the bar and slide it closer to him. "Ever seen her around town?"

"This town? No." Naveen sips his beer calmly. "Why do you ask? Has she committed some offense?"

I push the painting closer still. "Are you sure you haven't seen her recently?" Locking eyes with him, I look for the slightest flicker of nervousness.

But there is nothing. "I am sure." He smirks a little and shakes his head. "I think I would remember if I ever crossed paths with *her*."

"I suppose you would." With a shrug, I sit down on the stool beside him. "So where did you serve during the war, Naveen?"

"Italy." He sips his beer. "You've heard of Monte Cassino?"

"Hell yes." Bad memories rush back at the mention of the place. Suddenly, I feel like having a beer myself. "I was there for the end of that mess."

"Then perhaps you remember the Gurkhas," says Naveen.

I look at him with new respect. "You were a Gurkha?"

He nods slowly. "She was there, you know." He points at the painting on the bar. "So very much business for Lady Death to attend to in those days."

"This is true."

"Perhaps you yourself even encountered her," says Naveen. "Perhaps you came closer to her than you ever knew."

With that, his lips spread wide in a toothy grin that makes me wonder if Kali the death goddess might be close to me again. Close to the both of us.

Because his teeth are stained with red...the same red as the spots on the sidewalk outside Zeigler's Department Store that morning.

There's a paper sack open on the bar in front of him, and he reaches into it. His hand comes away full of red-tinted nuts. He pops a few into his mouth and chews, still grinning his crimson grin.

"Betel nuts." He holds out his hand toward me. "Want some? Guaranteed to make you feel good."

"No thanks." I get up from my stool. "I just remembered something I need to do."

*****

I follow him when he leaves, trailing on foot from a distance through the streets of downtown Morley. I never worry about losing him because he leaves a trail of red Betel nut stains on the pavement, spitting scarlet juice every few steps he takes.

Eventually, he arrives at a ramshackle bungalow in the shadow of a vacant Bund meeting house — the local branch of a German-American association that was pushed out of town during the war.

As I wait in the shadows across the street, I think about Naveen and Abe. Italy is the common factor between them, the only one I know of. Whatever led to Abe's murder could have happened there...but who knows? They could have a whole shared history here in Morley that I'm not aware of, one that led to Abe's skull being smashed in on the second floor of Zeigler's. Interrogation will tell the tale.

But first, surveillance. I want to see what Naveen does now that I've turned on the heat.

Fortunately for me, he has no curtains on the front window of the bungalow. Now if only he'd do something that gives me some kind of insight. So far as I can see, he just sits on a ratty sofa and flips through a newspaper, chewing those Betel nuts from a paper sack and spitting the juice in a bowl.

The reading and chewing goes on for a while...long enough for me to start craving a smoke. But I know better than lighting up while on a stakeout. Lots of ways a lit cigarette can attract unwanted attention.

Finally, Naveen does get up from the sofa and walk into another room, where I lose sight of him. Annoyed, I walk a little to one side, taking care to stay in the shadow of the alley where I've been lurking.

Squinting, I try to catch sight of him, but can't. The angle of the window cuts off the view beyond the doorway. For all I know, he could have gone right out the back door and disappeared into the night.

Did he make me? Cursing under my breath, I wait another moment, then start planning the least obtrusive way to get across the street.

It's then that two hands shoot out from behind me and yank a wire over my throat.

The wire tightens fast, and I react. Times like this, I'm glad I spent time in a war zone. No substitute for combat-honed reflexes.

Instead of grabbing the wire or hands, I go for the attacker's weak spot. Lashing my fists back over my head, I plow them into his face with everything I've got. Then, I haul up a foot and blast it back into his shin.

With a pained exhalation of breath, he drops back, pulling me with him. I use the momentum to take him all the way down with me on top of him.

When we hit the pavement, his grip on the wire finally loosens. I grab one of his hands with both of mine and twist it as hard as I can.

Bones snap in his wrist, and he cries out. The end of the wire in his damaged hand springs free, releasing the tension against my throat.

I press the advantage, grabbing his other hand and rolling over fast in one smooth motion. But he's still in the game. As I come up on my knees, he lurches his body in the same direction, heaving me off.

Before I can go for my gun, he plants a kick deep in my crotch. Now it's my turn to cry out.

In that moment of disoriented agony, he rolls to his feet. I finally get a look at his face: brown skin, black hair and mustache, flashing white teeth bared like an animal. Indian through and through.

I recover enough from the kick to get a hand on the butt of my revolver. In the same instant, he thrusts his one good hand into the pocket of his jacket.

It takes an extra heartbeat for him to reach the pocket, since it's on the same side as the damaged hand. That gives me the time I need to free the gun from the holster.

I swing the .22 out and pull the trigger. Bullet tags him in the shoulder, and he drops what he was pulling out of his pocket.

A statue of the four-armed, blue-skinned goddess of death Kali.

It falls to the pavement, and so does he. Groaning, he pulls a knife out of a belt scabbard, and I kick it away like it's a rabid rat running for me.

Then, keeping the gun trained on his head, I walk over and pick up the statue of Kali. It's heavy, made from some kind of metal. Holding it up in the glow of a streetlight, I realize I've found the murder weapon.

Her sky-blue skin is tainted red with the blood of my cousin.

*****

The man with the statue killed Abe. That much seems obvious from the start, given his possession of the murder weapon and the fact that he tried to kill me. But it takes time and "convincing" to get to the rest of the truth.

His name is Dinesh Shrivastava, brother of Naveen. It's a good thing we also bring in Naveen before he skips town, because apparently he's at the heart of the murder in more ways than one. Plus, most of what we learn, we get from Naveen, who is much less of a hard case than his brother.

Apparently, Dinesh is an assassin for hire, part of a cult of Kali-worshipping criminals called the Thuggees. Supposedly wiped out long ago by the British Raj, they survived in the shadows and gained a foothold in the Americas after the war.

According to Naveen, he hired Dinesh to settle a blood debt left over from his Monte Cassino days. In the chaos of the extended Allied assaults on the Italian/Nazi stronghold, Naveen lost a good friend — a *very* good friend, an *American* friend — because of Abe. Because Abe murdered him.

Thinking back, I wonder if Abe might have done the same to me if he'd known my own personal secret. If he hated faggots enough to shoot one on his own side in the heat of battle, might he have murdered me, too?

I can't say I don't believe it happened. I remember his many comments through the years before I left town — the many things he said about so-called "faggots" he knew or came in contact with...comments that I let slide. Maybe I shouldn't have let them slide.

I remember he said he "rolled" a few, too. Tuned them up for laughs and talked about it later. Never got in trouble for it, of course, because the unwritten law of the land was that it was perfectly okay. And the written law said it was illegal to be a sodomist faggot anyway, so there.

So yeah, I believe he could have done it.

And I believe he could have lied about it, just as Naveen says. He could have lied and said the faggot he killed on the battlefield was a deserter, running for the hills.

And his story might have been accepted by the powers that be, who after all had much bigger fish to fry. The burden of proof is lower in wartime, especially in the aftermath of a pyrrhic shitstorm like Monte Cassino.

Who knows? Maybe it was easier to sweep it under the rug just because Naveen's much-more-than-a-friend was a suspected faggot. And it probably didn't help that he was a white American, so the races were mixing, too.

In the end, it only matters that Naveen could not find justice until after the war. That it took a Thuggee brother to put down the man who'd taken the life of Naveen's lover.

Which is why it hurts me so much to see the two of them, especially Naveen, charged with murder and taken away. My heart goes out to him.

There but for the grace of God goes I. I believe in the depths of my soul that Naveen and Dinesh only did what was right, what I might have done in their shoes...though I dare not say it to anyone, especially in this town.

So I clench my teeth as the bus pulls away, carrying them off to prison to await trial. I clench my teeth to keep from crying for that broken-hearted man.

Jewboy in Dallas
Beverle Graves Myers

"Jack, I need money."

"Who is this?" the man in the rumpled cotton pajamas growls into the phone receiver.

"Karen. Our rent's late and I'm broke. Fucking landlord is about to toss us out."

Karen? Jack rubs sleep-bleared eyes with thumb and forefinger, sits up on the edge of the bed. The diet pill he'd swallowed when he first came to life has him a little buzzed, but he's muzzy with exhaustion at the same time. Since President Kennedy was killed he hasn't been able to sleep more than a few minutes at a time.

"You there, Jack?" The female voice with the Texas twang rises to a whine. "I need twenty-five dollars. Now. Or we'll be out on the street."

Yeah, yeah. Now he has it. Karen is Lynn — Little Lynn — one of his strippers down at The Carousel Club. He'd given her a few bucks when she showed up to dance last night and found he'd closed the club. Now she wanted more.

"Well, I had to close, didn't I? To show respect. You could show some, too, Sweetie." Jack pauses to shove his dachshund's wet nose out of his ribs. "How can you even think of anything besides President Kennedy's brains getting blown out with Jackie sitting there right beside him?"

The phone in Jack's hand feels heavy. His arm begins to sink, but he jerks the receiver back to his ear when he hears panic in Lynn's voice. "We don't even have the dough for groceries — no food in the house at all. Please, Jack. Help a girl out, will ya."

He puffs out his cheeks, exhales real slow. Yeah, he'll help. Lynn is a good kid, a steady worker always on time. She and her useless bum of a husband live way out in the sticks, but she says she can get to the Western Union office in Fort Worth. *Who the hell would live over at that hillbilly pigsty Fort Worth when they could live in a modern, lively town like Dallas?* Jack shakes his head, but he'll wire the twenty-five. He'll help.

Just like always.

Just like he pitches any punk who harasses his dancers right down the stairs. Like he coughs up a couple of bucks or a hot meal for any sad sack down on his luck. Like he takes coffee and sandwiches to his cop friends pulling the late night patrols. And way back when, just like he stood up for his sisters in their tough Chicago neighborhood where Jews and Italians constantly battled for turf. None of those Greasers ever messed with the Rubenstein girls, because Jack — Jacob then — was famous for hunting them down and beating the living crap out of them.

Once he's agreed to his errand of mercy, Jack begins to feel better. He showers, drags a razor over his jowly mug, and dresses in his usual neat fashion. Dark suit, white shirt, silk tie. He straightens his spine and studies his image in the bedroom mirror. *Hey, you wanna be somebody, one of the big shots, then dress the part.* Then he pads into the shabby living room. His roommate, George Senator, is out but at least he brought in the morning paper and tossed it on the couch before he left.

Jack gobbles up news like cops inhale doughnuts, though admittedly entertainment and sports are the sections he usually turns to first. He's always had this itch to know what's going on — and then to somehow wiggle himself right in the middle of it. That's why he drove over to Parkland Hospital when he first heard news of the shooting. With ears flapping, he mixed with the crowd, questioning strangers and hoping the doctors would come out and announce they'd managed to save Kennedy after all. When that didn't happen he drove to his club and sat in his office calling everybody he knew. The President is dead. Why?

How? Jack couldn't get over it. *John F. Kennedy, the classiest, handsomest prince of a guy to ever sit in the White House. The war hero of PT-109 who always stands up for the little guy. And now he's gone in the blink of an eye.* Jack hadn't felt this bad when his own parents died.

Still knotted up in a tangle of grief, searching for answers, Jack ended up at Temple Shearith Israel. He feels at home at his synagogue, maybe more at home than anywhere else, certainly more than at the cheap apartment he shares with George. Not just a High Holy Days Jew, Jack often stops by the temple to say Kaddish for his father and pass a few words with Rabbi Silverman. That terrible night, Jack had the luck to find a memorial service in progress. He slipped in a back bench and finally cried like a goddamn baby right in front of the rabbi and the whole congregation. It helped, some.

That was Friday, now it's Sunday. Jack throws himself down on the couch. The photo above the fold of the thick Dallas Morning News shows Eisenhower speaking to Lyndon Johnson, the new President. Jack's restless eyes skim right over that piece of shit. Where is the advertisement that sent smoke blowing out of his ears a few days ago? He rummages through the older newspapers littering the coffee table and couch. Here — the front page from November 22 headlining the political controversy swirling around Kennedy's visit — the paper that came out just hours before America lost its champion. Jack quickly flips through to page 14.

Staring up at him is a full page advertisement surrounded by an ominous black border that reminds him of old-time obituary cards. The ad has the nerve to welcome President Kennedy to Dallas in large print before posing a long list of taunting questions about his supposed communist leanings. The worst of it is the name of the person claiming responsibility for this embarrassment. One Bernard Weissman, chairman of a group that calls itself the American Fact-Finding Committee.

Weissman, a Jewish name if there ever was one. Jack feels his back molars grinding.

Jack knows just about all the Jews in Dallas — there aren't that many in this Bible Belt haven — and he's never heard of Weissman or his committee. When he first saw the ad, Jack checked the telephone book right away. *Bet it's made up*, he thought when he found no entry for the name. Just in case, he called his buddy Stanley, the lawyer who helps him with his tax problems. If there's any Jew in Dallas that Jack didn't know, Stanley would. He's in B'nai B'rith — always helping the community — knows everybody. Turned out he'd never heard of Weissman, either.

It doesn't take Jack long to see things clearly. Some outfit is out to attack the President, make him look like some kind of raging commie, and they're too chicken shit to own up to their own words. So what do they do? Invent a Jew to do their talking and take any heat that comes from insulting Kennedy and shaming Dallas.

That's what Jack figured on Friday morning. Now, two days after the unthinkable happened, he wonders if the rant isn't part of a bigger plan. For the umpteenth time, Jack rereads the Weissman ad. His lips curl into a sneer, his hands ball into fists around the thin newsprint paper. Yeah. A five-year-old could see why this ad ran on the day Kennedy was killed. Somebody wanted the President dead and they wanted to make it look like the Jews of Dallas had it in for him.

Shit! Jack smacks his forehead with the heel of hand. He should've talked to Rabbi Silverman about that after the memorial service. Warned him about the trouble that might be barreling down the pike. It's just … he'd been so upset … and he hadn't quite figured things out. Jack shook his head. Still hadn't filled in the details. Yeah, the cops arrested that sniveling punk Oswald. He might well have taken the shot that killed Kennedy and he apparently killed that cop, too. But on whose orders? Who got that ball rolling?

Jack actually saw Oswald on Friday night. In person. After his synagogue visit gave him a small measure of comfort, Jack felt a surge of energy. He wanted to do something for somebody. Do something good. What better than take a bunch of sandwiches and soft drinks to his cop buddies who were working double and triple shifts? So he loaded up some boxes and headed for police headquarters where he had his second lucky stroke of the evening. A press conference was just starting in the basement assembly room.

Well known as an amiable hanger-on at the station, Jack had no trouble threading through the crowd of reporters and climbing up on a table pushed against the back wall of the big room. He had a bird's eye view as a pair of cops in white Stetsons jostled Oswald in. The little creep's defiant smirk, his calm request for legal representation, and his whine of being "just a patsy" told Jack a story he already knew.

A story that tied directly in with Weissman's ad.

That worm Oswald obviously didn't have the balls, or the smarts, to assassinate Kennedy on his own. Somebody else planned the whole thing and put the little weasel up to it. And Oswald thought he was going to get away with it. That's why he was so calm. He thought his bosses would send his fucking legal representation, maybe buy off a few cops and judges, and he'd be out of trouble. Somebody else would be set up to take the fall.

Anger and dread crackle through Jack's veins like summer lightening. A Jew would take the fall. *Blame it on the Jews. Isn't that always the way?*

The apartment door clicks open, and Jack jumps up to see George lugging in a basket of folded laundry. Jack's roommate is a gray-haired man about Jack's age and build, but not nearly so well groomed. He's an old hand at stepping lightly when his roommate is flapped about something. One look at Jack's face tells George the man is seriously flapped.

He raises dark eyebrows in concern. "Ya get any sleep, Jack?"

"A little, yeah." Jack pushes his lower lip up as he carefully positions the lengthwise fold of the newspaper against the coffee table so he can rip the advertisement page free.

"Is that the Bernie Weissman thing?" George asks, knowing full well that it is. After Jack returned home from that midnight press conference, he grabbed George and drove to The Carousel to pick up Larry Crafard, the bum he'd been letting sleep on a cot to guard the club and look after the other dogs he kept there. Then Jack dragged them both to the post office where he harangued the night clerk to find out who had rented the post office box number printed at the bottom of the inflammatory ad. No dice. The guy said it wasn't worth his job to give out classified information. Boy, had Jack been steamed!

"Yeah." Jack nods as he folds the ad into quarters, then eighths. "I'm gonna hang on to it. Might need it."

George looks for an empty spot to park his basket and decides on the end of the couch. "Ya ever figure out who Weissman really is?"

"Don't put that there," Jack snaps. "Whaddya think this is? A Chinese laundry?"

"Er, no. Sorry." George jerks the basket away. Always best to humor Jack. Generous to a fault at times, he could also blow up faster than any man George has ever known.

Jack answers the question, slightly mollified, "No, but I'm not giving up. I know a hell of a lot of people in this town. I'll keep asking around. I'll find out what's really going on."

"You're playing detective," George says with a half-baked grin.

"Yeah, well, a man's got to stand up for his people, doesn't he?" Jack stows the folded ad in his righthand coat pocket, and finishes under his breath, "And stand up for Dallas."

"Well, be careful."

"Whaddya mean?" Jack juts out a pugnacious jaw. "I've always been able to lick any punk who stands in my way."

George shrugs. "It's just … I've been thinking. This Weissman isn't some punk. He — or they — dropped some dough on that ad. A full page doesn't go cheap. Half the rich guys — the oilmen and the bankers — the ones who really run the show around here are Birchers. They've made it plain they have no use for an Irish Catholic president."

Jack nods. *Or for a Jewboy strip club owner with greased-back hair who can't quite lose his Chicago accent.*

George takes a few steps towards the hallway that leads to his room, then turns back. "They're powerful, Jack. Just be careful. That's all I'm saying."

"Okay. Thanks," Jack mumbles. He's checking his watch, set on getting downtown to Western Union. It's close to eleven and Lynn will be waiting for her cash. His dachshund, Sheba, is pawing at his pants leg. She's hungry and probably needs to pee. Where's her leash, dammit?

"Hey!" George stops in his tracks, laundry basket resting on his chest. "Did ya hear they moved Oswald this morning?"

"Shit! When?"

George's voice floats down the hall: "Radio said ten o'clock they'd take him from the city jail over to county. Guess they think he'll be better protected over there."

Jack merely snorts in reply. Protected? *What that sonvabitch needs is a good ass frying that'll make him cough up who hired him.*

Jack grabs Sheba and heads for the Olds parked in front of the outdoor stairs to their second-floor apartment. Before placing the key in the ignition he retrieves his .38 Colt revolver from the glove compartment. *Gotta keep your piece handy when you're carrying money. Never know when some punk will try something on ya.*

On his way downtown, Jack tries to focus on his next move, to clear his aching head of vague suspicions so he can find the answers he needs. A smile actually creeps through Jack's confusion as he makes a mental list of his Dallas pals. Cops, radio DJs, newspapermen, guys who work at the swank hotels and send customers his way. When he makes his rounds up and down Commerce Street, he stops in to shoot the breeze with tons of people. Good people. Sure, he has to listen to Jew jokes with a smile pasted on his face sometimes, but everybody's always glad to see Jack Ruby, and none of his buddies use fighting words like kike or sheeny. Yeah. Birchers and Bible-toting bigots aside, Dallas respects Jack Ruby because he runs a classy club — the only burlesque joint in the city with three runways. No punks allowed. He makes sure the girls stay classy, too. No front bumps or other raunchy moves that could strain Dallas sensibilities and get the Vice Squad crawling up his ass.

Jack finds a parking space in a lot right across from Western Union. Maybe that's a good sign. Maybe he'll get a line on the Weissman thing today, maybe find someone down at the newspaper who has some information on the ad. Information that can protect all the Jews of Dallas. Yeah. He leans toward Sheba and croons, "You stay here, girl. I'll be back soon."

The dachshund knows the drill. With a canine version of an exasperated sigh, she curls her long body into a doggy doughnut in the front passenger seat on top of old newspapers and paper napkins smeared with catsup and mustard. Before he heads across Main Street to save Little Lynn's bacon, Jack runs beringed fingers through Sheba's soft fur. *You're my best friend, girl. About the only thing making sense in this crazy world right now.*

Jack joins the line at the long counter at Western Union. The clerk is copying some guy's information onto a form, then repeating it back to him to make sure. Could he go any slower? While Jack fidgets with the folded ad in his pocket, a couple of old dames take their place in line behind him. They wonder if it's going to rain. Jack tightens his shoulders under his suit jacket, pulls at the knot of his tie. His good mood is rapidly evaporating. *They're talking about the weather, for Chris' sake.* Everybody's going about their business like the world just didn't cave in, like Dallas hasn't become an ugly stain on the country. *Geez, what's wrong with people?*

"It's Jackie I feel the most sorry for," continues the white-haired woman in the yellow pillbox hat. "They'll have to put her on the stand to testify."

"Oh, they wouldn't dare drag her back to Dallas," her friend replies. "Not after what she's been through."

"No." The yellow pillbox gives a decisive shake. "They'll have to put her on the stand — she's an eyewitness — the newspaper said so."

Waves of sorrow for Mrs. Kennedy and little Caroline crash over Jack. All of a sudden he feels as depressed as he had when Lynn called him this morning. Tears stab at the back of his eyes. Fighting for control, he takes a big gulp. Jack Ruby blubbering right there at the telegram office was the last thing he wanted to hear from the gossip mill.

"Next."

Finally. Filling out the money order lets Jack concentrate for a few blessed minutes. But soon, with a definitive stamp of an electronic clocker and a pleasant nod, the clerk sends Jack on his way. His head is really pounding now, and his empty stomach is rumbling. The tears behind his bloodshot eyes have dried up. Anger has again muscled in to take their place.

Jack's thoughts churn like a whirlpool. Every step across the shiny linoleum floor brings a new worry.

He almost hadn't moved down to Dallas when his sister Eva begged him to help her run her supper club, but he had. Even though being a Jew in Texas is a tough proposition, he'd come to love his new home.

Now Dallas is hurting in the worst way. Some of the out-of-town newspapers are calling it the City of Hate. *My Dallas!*

And the Jews of Dallas are gonna hurt in a big way if somebody doesn't do something. Do something about Oswald — that skinny-necked, smirking, little weasel.

For a second, Jack's hand pauses on the door to the street. No — not just Oswald. Like he whined in front of the reporters, Oswald is just the patsy. Who needs to go down, then? The oilmen, the John Birch Society, maybe even the goddamn Communist Party? Jack hadn't gotten too far in finding Weissman, but hey, when you get knocked down, you gotta get your ass off the mat and go again.

Yeah. Jack shoves the door open. *Gotta get my ass in gear. Dallas needs a hero, a guy as gutsy as Kennedy was on that PT boat.*

Out on the sidewalk now, Jack turns his face up to the weak November sunshine, then adjusts the brim of his gray fedora. He's on the move, with lots to do. Where to first? Should he go find Rabbi Silverman? Look into the ad department at the paper? Or get over to his club? He takes a bitter gulp. He really needs to tote up how far he's in the hole after staying closed for two nights.

And? And?

Oh, yeah, the dogs Larry Crafard is supposed to take care of at the club. He can't really count on that boozer. Jack's stomach rumbles again. Maybe he should get some hot food for himself — a plate of eggs over-easy and home fries would go down real good. He could head over to the B & B, a favorite eatery, then go on to The Carousel. Yeah.

Jack steps towards the curb. He looks right, then left down Main Street, and sees a commotion near the entrance ramp to the police department down the block. With senses honed back in his Chicago days, Jack senses a fight — or some excitement — brewing. His muscles tense, he starts toward the station, then stops short. What about Sheba waiting in the Olds? Would the dog be okay? Sure, sure. He'd just hop down the block and see what was up. Probably not much. They took Oswald away over an hour ago.

Jack's feet start moving again. He'd be back for Sheba in ten minutes. He'd skip that breakfast — he's been planning to put himself on a grapefruit diet anyway — and just take Sheba over to the club. He'd feed her, then leave her with Larry and go find Silverman or head down to The Dallas Morning News building. Jack's steps quicken. Maybe he'd decide to open up the club tonight after all. Up to its neck in tension and grief, Dallas could use an outlet, a place to unwind for a couple of hours. That's one small thing he could do for his adopted city.

As Jack nears the building, he sees that the activity is centered on the basement garage. He walks right past a police cruiser and a couple of patrol officers before heading down the ramp. No one pays him the slightest attention. Inside mingled voices bounce off brick and concrete, but Jack can't make out what they're saying. Closer to the foot of the ramp, bright floodlights cause him to blink. *What the hell?*

He shades his eyes. Is Chief Curry giving a press conference? Damn garage is packed like sardines in a tin, but Jack is intent on getting through the crowd. He shoulders his way between reporters, photographers, and TV cameras on tripods. The cameras are all trained on a pair of swinging glass doors to his right. To his left sits a police cruiser. Jack jerks his head around, momentarily dumbfounded. Then it hits him — they must be waiting on the creep. Oswald is still in the building.

In the space of another breath, the doors swing open. Two plainclothesmen flank the small man the world's attention has been focused on for the past two days. Their expressions are grim. His is calm.

Jack's breath starts coming hard. He realizes he could fix this Weissman mess right here, right now.

A Jew killing the man who shot Kennedy — avenging the President with all the world as witness — that would defend the Jews of Dallas from accusations of hating the President. Yeah. Jack feels his chest swell, like his heart just doubled in size. He could make Dallas look good again. He could protect his people. He'd show 'em all that Jewboy Jack Ruby has the balls to be a hero.

His gaze drills right through Oswald's smirk, the same smirk he was wearing Friday night.

"Son of a bitch," Jack bellows.

The .38 in his right hip pocket seems to jump to his hand with a mind of its own.

Two Nights with Suzie Wong
Kirk Landers

April 1970

As soon as Jackson woke up, he knew it was going to be a bad day. His penis felt sore and there wasn't much mystery about why, only what the name of it was and how bad it was going to fuck up his life. He was hoping it was gonorrhea because that could be cured. He wasn't sure about the other stuff.

Wouldn't it be a kick in the head to survive the fucking war and die of some exotic venereal disease he got from a woman he didn't even enjoy?

He got up and went to the bathroom. As soon as he dropped his shorts he knew it was gonorrhea. The tip of his penis was excreting pus and when he peed it stung like hell. He'd read about those exact symptoms in a novel in college. He couldn't remember which one, and yes, it was fiction, but still, he knew this was gonorrhea. Good fucking morning, Vietnam.

The woman in his bed stirred when he came back in the room. Suzie Wong. Her hooker name. She opened her eyes sleepily and stretched, her arms reaching overhead so far her breasts almost disappeared, Jackson watching but not getting turned on, so caught up in his own misery he couldn't have smiled if President Johnson was standing there telling fart jokes.

"Hey, honey, you okay?" Suzie asked. She sat straight up.

"I've got the clap, Suzie," he said.

She bent closer and took his penis in her fingers for a better look.

"No sweat, Jackson," she said with a big, happy smile. "I take you to special place."

"You've probably got it too," he said.

"No sweat," said Suzie Wong. "This Bangkok. Everything no sweat."

"But you'll miss work."

"No sweat. I need vacation anyway. I spend time with you."

"We're going back to Vietnam today," said Jackson.

"I stay with you 'til then," said Suzie. The smile and cheer never left her face, and for some reason, that boosted Jackson's spirits, even though he knew she was playing him for a tip.

Randy and Rose came down to breakfast late, Randy with a somber expression on his face. Jackson and Suzie Wong were sipping beverages at the table on the hotel patio, surrounded by lush green plants and bright red and yellow blossoms.

"I've got good news and bad news, partner," Randy said to Jackson as they sat down.

"All I've got is bad news, so let's get it over with."

"We can't go back today," said Randy. "Our bird couldn't get out."

"Oh, shit," Jackson groaned. "What's the good news?"

Randy's face lit up. "We spend another day in paradise."

Jackson leaned forward on the table, his face cupped in his hands. "I'm broke. I'm going to have to sleep on the street tonight unless you let me cuddle with you and Rose. And I've got a raging dose of clap. And when I do get back to Nam, I'm going to get busted and sent to L-B-fucking-J. This is just fucking perfect."

Randy kept smiling and shook his head in wonder. Suzie put a hand on his arm and gave it a squeeze.

"Damn, partner, that sounds like a trifecta to me," said Randy. "But look at it this way, things can only get better, right?"

"One can hope," muttered Jackson.

Suzie Wong took his hand. "I take you doctor, and you stay Suzie Wong's house."

"I'm broke," said Jackson, like he was confessing to a priest. "I can't pay you."

"No sweat. You stay with me. When you go home, maybe you remember me." She seemed as cheerful as a child on Christmas morning. "Maybe you come Bangkok and marry me, take me to U.S., I work for you, make you rich."

Jackson smiled in spite of his worries. "I can't get married, Suzie."

"I know. Make joke. I take you doctor, you stay with me."

She said it with such finality that Jackson just nodded and said yes. He knew it wouldn't turn out well, but he had no place else to go.

Before they left for the clinic, Jackson settled his bill, moved some of his belongings into Randy's room, and called his mother back in The World. She was on the other side of the planet, in a different time zone and in a different day, and his call would come as a shock to her but there was no way to avoid it.

Her voice was tired and fearful when she answered. He had awakened her from a deep sleep.

"Allan? Are you okay?" she asked, her voice rising with concern. "It's three a.m."

"I'm okay, Mom, I just need a favor. Can you wire me some of my savings?"

"Where are you, Allan? What's going on?"

"I'm in Bangkok. Thailand. On R&R." Jackson tried to sound lighthearted, like it was no big deal. "I ran out of money and I was wondering if you could wire me a thousand dollars at this hotel."

His mother made a series of gasps and exclamations that Jackson could hear, even on a bad transpacific connection. When she recovered, he gave her the name and address of the hotel and the phone number.

"Are you sure you're okay?" she asked, her voice filled with suspicion and concern.

Jackson assured her he was.

"Have you been kidnapped?"

"No, Mom," he laughed.

"You're not running off to Canada?"

"No, Mom," he said. "I just ran out of money on R&R."

Which was pretty much true, except for the R&R part. And the not being in trouble part. And being okay.

*****

Suzie Wong had the driver drop them at a plain-looking, one-story building near the R&R bars. A modest sign identified it as a U.S. military medical facility. The front of the building had two doors.

"That for you," Suzie told Jackson, pointing to one of the doors. "This for me." She flashed him her life-is-fun smile and opened her door.

Jackson watched her disappear, still frozen in place by the knowledge that nothing good ever happened to him when he came in contact with the Army. The door loomed in front of him like the maw of a ravenous animal, waiting to swallow him into the madness of the world's largest corporation, where zealots and morons directed hapless masses to kill and be killed. He tried to convince himself he was just being paranoid again, but he'd danced this dance before, and paranoid or not, he was right about the fucking Army. Still, he had no choice here. He had to see a doctor, even an Army doctor. He opened the door and entered.

It felt like a netherworld inside, not a sound, nothing moving. Like there wasn't another living person in the place, just the dumbass GI with clap. He stepped up to a counter on his left and looked for signs of humanity. Nothing. Then he saw a memo taped to the countertop. It directed him to find his medical problem in a chart on the opposite wall, note the color code it was given, and follow that color of tape on the floor to the stations he needed to visit.

Jackson swore under his breath and looked at the chart. All the possible reasons for visiting the facility were reduced to eight items. Venereal disease was its own category, undisguised by any polite term. It was, Jackson realized, the reason for this facility's being — to treat VD-ridden troops and the girls they infected and maybe the girl they got it from.

Jackson followed the yellow line on the floor to the next station, where he surrendered his fake Temporary Duty Orders to a prune-faced Army nurse. She ignored his greeting, and pointed his attention to a sign that told him to drop his drawers. She inspected his penis, scribbled on a form, gave him the form and his fake TDY orders, and pointed for him to follow the line to his next station. He did, but it kept getting weirder. Not a sound in the place except his footsteps, not another person to be seen except the people who popped up at his various stops to tend to him or his paperwork — always without saying anything.

Three stations later, a stern-looking female nurse, Army to the core, gestured for Jackson to drop trou and bend over, his chest on an exam table, his bare ass hanging in the air. She stabbed him in the butt with a needle, not trying to avoid muscle tissue. It hurt more than it needed to, Jackson taking it as a reprimand, and not caring as long as he got out of there without getting nailed for having fake orders and being AWOL. She gestured for him to get his pants on and follow the yellow line on the floor to the next station.

Jackson's last stop was a Dutch door, the bottom half closed, the top half open. A uniformed enlisted man, a Spec 5, was waiting for him, no expression on his face. He took Jackson's fake TDY orders and the medical form to his desk, and used a typewriter to bang out words and numbers on another form. He came back to Jackson and handed him his orders and an official U.S. Army form listing the details of his medical visit for the treatment of gonorrhea.

"Take this back to your unit and have it added to your 201 File," the clerk commanded. His was the first voice Jackson had heard in this bizarre clinic and his message was insane, even for the Army. Sure, Jackson nodded. Sure, he'd let his company know he was AWOL in Bangkok and got treated for clap, and he'd make sure it was all in his permanent service record so someday, when some company was running a background check on him before giving him the job of a lifetime, they could discover rock-solid proof Jackson served his country as a whoring, deserting son-of-a-bitch who couldn't be trusted.

Not that he'd want a job where they took exception to a soldier doing some whoring.

When Jackson emerged into the fresh air and sunshine, Suzie Wong was waiting for him, beaming.

"You have fun?" she giggled, as Jackson approached. He smiled. She patted him on the butt. "Hurt, yes?"

Jackson shrugged.

"You be fine tomorrow." She laced her arm through Jackson's. "We go Suzie Wong's, see real Bangkok."

Jackson gave her a brave smile, but the truth was he didn't want to see the real Bangkok. He wanted to stay in a nice hotel, eat five-star meals, wallow in air-conditioning, and be treated like a king. What he didn't want was to get beaten and robbed, or hauled off to Long Binh Jail, or even think about having sex. But the only options he had right now were to go with Suzie Wong or to find himself a cardboard box to sleep in until his money arrived.

Jackson figured Suzie Wong for a ghetto tenement, probably with bugs and rats, but Suzie lived in a nice house in a nice neighborhood that Jackson would enjoy living in. The house was small, modest, and immaculate. It had sparkling wood floors and held an unpretentious kitchen and living/dining area with simple bamboo furniture. Stairs led to a main bedroom and a smaller one where a woman was dressing a tiny toddler. Jackson did a double-take as they passed the small bedroom. He had assumed Suzie Wong lived alone, maybe entertaining johns there sometimes.

Suzie smiled at his reaction and led him into the main bedroom. She placed his small bag next to the bed and turned to him cheerily.

"Suzie Wong house okay? Not U.S., but okay?"

"It's beautiful," said Jackson. He looked out a window at the quiet street below, trying to comprehend that Suzie Wong, steamy, dark-eyed sex goddess and professional prostitute, had one foot firmly planted in a lifestyle he could understand.

The woman and toddler from the other bedroom joined them, the toddler smiling and laughing and hugging Jackson's leg, the woman reserved and friendly. She was also quite beautiful, with features similar to Suzie's — long hair falling in sensuous profusion like a Tahitian princess, full lips and flawless skin, and a face and body as radiant and sexy as any of the girls hustling sex in the bars.

"This Malai, my roommate," said Suzie Wong. She said the word "roommate" slowly, making sure she pronounced the syllables perfectly. "And this beautiful baby is Lawana."

At the sound of her name, Lawana lurched to Suzie, who picked her up and hugged her. Malai watched with a motherly smile, and she and Suzie exchanged warm glances.

"Nice to meet you, Mr. Jackson," said Malai in formal English, bowing slightly, enunciating each word carefully. When she straightened, she and Suzie exchanged glances again.

Jackson greeted her and bowed back. The two women seemed surprised at his bow, so Jackson deduced it was a breach of Asian protocol, but he shook it off. He wasn't some damn feudal lord and he had no idea how to act like one.

Suzie and Malai spoke in Thai while Jackson and Lawana rolled a ball back and forth, Jackson glancing up at them occasionally. They spoke casually, Malai nodding several times, Jackson thinking they were well-suited as roommates.

Their conversation stopped and both of them looked at Jackson. He stood.

"You sleep here," said Suzie Wong.

Jackson looked at her questioningly.

"With me," Suzie added, as if that explained everything.

Jackson looked from her to Malai, then back again, finally figuring out that they usually shared the bed. Of course, they just had the two bedrooms and the baby slept in one.

"I can sleep on the floor in the baby's room," he said, not wanting to disturb their order.

Both women objected in unison. It was more than politeness, Jackson realized. No mother in the world would bunk a stranger, a *farang* at that, in her baby's room.

"Or on the floor downstairs."

"No, no," said Suzie Wong. Malai shook her head and waved her hands in front of her. "No, you our guest." The women looked from him to each other, something passing between them.

Jackson thought there was some kind of Asian custom at play here, and to argue any further would be an insult, so he acquiesced. Then he realized, and it hit him like the concussive wave of an exploding rocket, that they weren't just roommates. They were lovers. Roommates didn't look at each other the way they looked at each other.

He hid his shock — he had never known lesbian lovers before — but as he followed them downstairs, his mind was racing. To his surprise, what he mainly felt was understanding. They were probably both hookers before Malai got pregnant, surrendering themselves nightly to GIs who treated them like whores. Of course they'd want the tenderness of a woman after that. He wondered how they made love, or if they made love, or if having sex for money and doing it a lot would turn them off it altogether.

Downstairs, Suzie Wong seated him and brought him water, then went back upstairs and carried a small clothing bag downstairs, Malai following her with Lawana in her arms.

"Malai stay with sister," said Suzie. Malai smiled and bowed slightly.

"We have good time, she help sister," said Suzie.

Jackson figured there was no sister, and he knew there wasn't going to be any boy-girl sex here, not involving him, because his dick felt like a blowtorch every time he peed, and because he wouldn't re-infect Suzie Wong anyway, even if he felt like a million bucks, so really, what was the point of moving Malai? The point was, that's how they wanted to do things.

Suzie embraced Malai tightly, then Lawana, and mother and child disappeared down the street. Jackson watched them go, wondering what it would have been like to share the bed with two women, not for sex, but just sleeping with two soft, beautiful women and feeling their warmth and the soothing strokes of their hands on his skin. It probably wasn't normal, a GI wanting to sleep with two women and not have sex with them, clap or no clap, but fuck normal, Jesus, he was a fucking soldier, how normal could he be?

Suzie led him back upstairs. She seated him on the bed, then sat herself at a makeup table and began un-pinning her elaborate hairdo. Jackson watched, mesmerized, as she unwound a long tress, separated it from her own hair, and carefully placed it on a form. She unpinned the rest of her hair and brushed it out, letting it fall to the middle of her back. She glanced at him in the mirror and laughed. The eyelashes were next, long and dark and elegantly curled. She peeled them off carefully and placed them in plastic holders.

Jackson couldn't take his eyes off her. Suzie's beauty ritual was far sexier than any stag movie or striptease he'd ever seen. She stacked her jewelry on a corner of the table. She used a cream to wipe off the makeup and removed the last vestiges of her lipstick. Then she stood and peeled off her tiny dress, her bra and panties, then turned to Jackson and smiled.

"No more Suzie Wong," she laughed.

Jackson managed to smile, but she was right, and the drama of the transformation left him agape. His sultry, lesbian sex goddess had turned into the girl next door, a pretty young woman with a happy face and a slim figure. If he didn't know she was a hooker, he'd think she was a student or a teacher or maybe a flight attendant.

Suzie Wong wasn't sure how to interpret his silence. "What you think, Jackson?"

"You're beautiful," he said. He wanted to say more, but couldn't think of the words so he just smiled and let the silence cover them like a cocoon. They took a nap then, their bodies intertwined, Jackson's last waking thought being that this was real intimacy. She was a hooker who was probably playing him for a tip, but it was still intimate.

When they woke up, Suzie took him for a walk in the neighborhood, greeting neighbors, waving to shopkeepers, taking his hand now and then, making like they were school kids on a date. She supplied most of the conversation, but she spoke more slowly and less often than when they were hooker and john. Jackson realized that he was seeing the real person, even as he kept most of his person secret.

Suzie purchased dinner from a cart on the street — a plate of rice topped by a fish of some kind, cooked with its head still on. Suzie Wong engaged in repartee in Thai with an older vendor who seemed to like her. They ate their meal sitting on a bench in a small park. The fish was delicious.

They walked on, covering residential streets and commercial strips, Jackson having no idea where they were. Gradually, he realized no one was going to knock him senseless and steal his money, partly because he didn't have any money, but mostly because the people he was meeting were friendly, good-hearted people.

When they were exhausted, they returned to Suzie Wong's house, stripped to their underwear, and slept deeply, Suzie spooning with Jackson, Jackson thinking he'd never felt anything so warm and soft, and wondering what it was like to be Suzie Wong.

*****

Jackson's peace ended with the bright rays of the morning sun. The contentment and harmony of the previous night evaporated and his mind fixed on his urgent priorities. Get his money, get back to Vietnam, and try to slide back into the company compound without anyone realizing he'd been gone. And never, ever go AWOL from a war zone again. Ever.

Suzie got him back to the hotel by nine. Jackson's money wire had arrived. The desk clerk gave him a discreet looking envelope containing U.S. greenbacks, twenties and hundreds. He paid Suzie, including a nice tip, then bought them breakfast while they waited for Randy and Rose.

"You look pretty good for a guy who slept under a bridge last night," Randy greeted Jackson when he and Rose came down.

"Bangkok is a bridge paradise," said Jackson.

"Well," said Randy, "our plane is supposed to come in this afternoon. Call me here around one for a departure time."

Jackson nodded and glanced at Suzie. She was standing so close to him their bodies touched, legs, hips, arms, like they were spooning again, but in a way that other people wouldn't notice. Jackson wondered if this was a hustle Suzie did with all her johns, or just with special ones, or maybe just with him.

They talked about what to do with their half-day of freedom, but Randy and Rose wanted to be alone, and Suzie had to get herself ready for another night in the bar. She invited Jackson to come with her.

"See Suzie Wong beauty secrets," she said.

Jackson said he didn't really have any place else to go, but he was also intrigued. The driver he shared with Randy drove them back to Suzie's neighborhood and promised to return when the flight information was confirmed.

Suzie Wong chatted as they walked along the narrow streets lined with small shops and street vendors. Jackson enjoyed the lilt of her voice and her cheerful spirits, but most of his mind was occupied with a sense of dread he just couldn't shake — dread of going back to the war, of going to jail for desertion, of the aching, soulless, mind-numbing monotony of base camp life in Vietnam. He felt like he was living his last hours and willed himself to enjoy them, thought maybe they should go to Suzie's place and make love since his symptoms were gone, thought it might be nice to have the sex smell on him for the ride back to Vietnam to remind him of his moment of happiness, that flickering candle in the pitch black of the shitstorm he'd been bucking since he enlisted in the Army.

＊＊＊＊＊

Suzie Wong's beauty shop was like an exotic foreign country. Jackson had never been in one, though he'd passed by them often enough, always intrigued by the magical transformations that women underwent in them, always strangely attracted to aromas emanating from such places. He knew it wasn't manly to want go in one, and certainly not manly to enjoy the strange smells of perm solutions, hair-coloring chemicals, baking hair, and the flowery scents of shampoos and sprays. But that had been part of his secret self since he was a child.

Suzie's salon was compact and seductively dim, with most of the light focused on three swiveling chairs, each in front of a mirror and a shelf containing beauty tools. A young woman sat in one of the chairs as a beautician worked on her hair, puffing it up into huge balls as they talked quietly. Another woman, young like Suzie, sat under a high-pitched hairdryer that made her look like a creature from outer space, but sexy somehow, maybe because she looked so feminine and comfortable with herself as she glanced at Jackson and Suzie. A middle-aged hairdresser who had been organizing her tools when they walked in greeted Suzie and bowed slightly to Jackson as Suzie introduced him. The client in the other chair and her hairdresser exchanged secretive remarks in Thai and tittered as they assessed Jackson in the mirror.

"Are you sure—?" Jackson started to ask. He felt wildly out of place, like he was invading the women's bathroom. And yet he couldn't take his eyes off the woman in the chair and what was happening to her hair.

"No sweat, Jackson," interrupted Suzie. She directed him to a chair next to a table holding an array of nail polish bottles. "Men okay here."

"Really?" asked Jackson.

"Some come with girlfriends. Some come to be girls. We call them *kathoey*, lady boys."

Jackson took his eyes off the woman in the chair for a second, long enough to look at Suzie and grimace, like he knew she was having him on.

"No, Jackson. Is true," she said. "They pretty. Some men like them more than lady-ladies."

"Sure."

"I show you *kathoey* later. Maybe you like?"

"Maybe not," said Jackson.

Suzie sat in one of the empty chairs and stared in the mirror as the hairdresser brushed out her long locks, then she followed the woman to a back room. Minutes later, the two emerged, Suzie's wet hair wrapped in a towel. She winked at Jackson, and sat in the chair again, smiling and chatting as the hairdresser wrapped her hair in curlers. Jackson's eyes pivoted between Suzie and the woman in the other chair, whose hair was being fashioned into a towering up-do that made her look like a nymphomaniac to Jackson, who, despite his inner turmoil, still thought like a horny soldier.

The woman working on Suzie wrapped her hair in huge curlers, her tiny hands moving with the speed and dexterity of a pianist's fingers on a keyboard. Jackson was entranced. When Suzie's hair was wrapped, she moved to one of the hooded hair dryers, stopping on her way to pose for Jackson.

"How you like Suzie Wong now, Jackson?" she asked playfully. "Very sexy, yes?"

Jackson smiled, trying to hide his discomfort. He knew he was supposed to find her appearance funny, but what he thought was she was the sexiest woman he'd ever seen, not in spite of the curlers, but because of them. His dick was as hard as iron. Suzie noticed and bent to whisper in his ear.

"You feel better already, no?"

Jackson nodded, and she sat under the dryer and looked at him, smiling once more before turning her attention to a magazine.

Jackson watched the other client rise from her chair and come to the nail station, sitting so close to him he could smell her perfume. She was wearing a mini-skirt and a low-cut top that showed off her cleavage and her slim arms. She smiled at Jackson and said something in Thai to the woman working on her nails. They exchanged smiles and glances at Jackson, then continued to chatter, Jackson trying to watch surreptitiously, while also watching another client go from the hair dryer to the styling chair and get transformed.

By the time Suzie Wong transitioned from the dryer to the styling chair, Jackson was dizzy with images of femininity. It was different than the sexual sizzle in the bars, like the difference between seeing a picture of a naked woman and seeing the actual woman.

"You okay, Jackson?" Suzie called from the chair. She was watching him in the mirror. He couldn't imagine what he looked like, but his pulse was pounding and he was fully aroused and feeling faint.

"Sure," he said. But his voice cracked. He wondered if getting turned on by women in a beauty salon was a sign he was queer.

"You sure?" she asked again.

Jackson nodded.

*****

"I've got good news and bad news," Randy said cheerfully when Jackson called.

"Give me the good news," said Jackson. "I can't remember what good news sounds like."

"The good news is, we can't go back today."

"Jesus Christ!" Jackson swore, thinking now, for sure, they were going to jail. "What's the bad news?"

"Well," said Randy, in his story-telling Southern drawl, "first of all, the company found out we're AWOL, and they sent a lifer to bring us home."

"Motherfucker!" said Jackson, his hands trembling and his head feeling watery.

"Relax," said Randy. "They aren't going to bust us. I told you. They'd have to bust everyone else who ever travelled on these orders, and the officers who signed them would lose their commissions."

"So, why aren't we going home tonight?"

"Turns out Sergeant First Class Bates is giving himself a night on the town. He's already rounded up two girls. We won't see him until sometime tomorrow. We'll go back when he's ready. Probably around lunchtime."

Jackson almost collapsed with relief. Suzie looked at him with concern. He cupped a hand over the phone and briefed her on the conversation.

"You stay one more night?"

Jackson nodded.

"You want Suzie Wong?"

Jackson nodded again and touched her arm with his free hand.

"Should I get you a room?" asked Randy.

Jackson looked at Suzie. "Hotel or your place?"

"My place," she said. "I make you very happy, then you marry me, take me to States."

"Don't bother," he told Randy. "I'll stay at Suzie's and see you in the morning."

He turned to Suzie and stroked her arm again. "You love Malai," he said. "Why would you leave her for me?"

Suzie grinned without embarrassment. "Because I want live in States. I save money and send for Malai and Luwana when I can." Her voice was jovial, like they were sharing a joke, but Jackson could feel the soft drums of a young woman's dream just beyond the jest.

"So I share you with another lover?" He kept it light, not wanting to lead her on, knowing there was no way he'd be marrying anyone, maybe ever, but for sure not until he got his head straight.

"No, Jackson. You have two lovers and a daughter." She laughed gaily and took his hand and they went for a stroll in the soft light of an overcast afternoon in Bangkok.

*****

They sat across from each other on the floor, their food on a low table between them, Jackson handling the chopsticks like an Asian. Suzie Wong chattered all through the meal, a meandering soliloquy on everything from the events of the day to memories of her childhood.

"You like salon today." Suzie said it, she didn't ask it.

Jackson flushed and started to deny it, then silenced himself.

"It okay, Jackson. You love women. I love Malai. Means nothing. Means we love someone. Woman, man, so what?"

Jackson was quiet, but within himself, his thoughts flashed like tracer rounds.

"What's it like to be in your body?" He blurted the words, knowing they were crazy. "How does it feel? Your skin? Your breasts? Looking in the mirror?"

Suzie regarded him curiously, not understanding the question.

"I know what I see when I look at you," said Jackson, "and I know what I feel when I touch you. But what do you feel like to you?"

Suzie looked about and shrugged. "I don't know," she said, pronouncing the words carefully. "I never think like that."

"In the salon today, I kept wondering what it's like to be you," said Jackson. "To be so light and delicate, to have big, sexy eyes and small, perfect hands and feet."

Jackson paused and touched her lightly.

"You looked so... regal. Like a queen. Beautiful. And powerful. Really powerful. Do you feel that?"

Amazement swept over Suzie Wong's face, her mouth slightly agape. "In my village, girl marry or work. I sixteen, old man want marry me. Farmer. Not nice. He want someone cook, clean, fuck. I beg my father, please, no, don't make me do that. He say I must work or marry. Work mean go Bangkok. Sew clothes, one dollar day, all day, twelve hour. Six dollar week. Until your hands and fingers don't work right, or your eyes see blur.

"Or I can work in bars. Whore. Five dollar night. Sometime tips. Ten dollar. Five dollar. Sometimes no tip. Nice clothes. Sexy. Get VD three, four time year. Get hurt sometime. Men fuck me hard. Curse me if dry. Hit me, I talk too much, he can't come, he no like Thai girl."

Suzie didn't cry, but her face was sad, like she was holding back a reservoir of tears. He held her hand softly.

"You see old lady in bar?" she asked.

Jackson looked at her quizzically, then thought about it. "No," he said.

"No old ladies in bars. No old ladies in sewing shops. Only old ladies in families. Grandmas. Suzie Wongs no have families. Suzie Wongs do not get old."

"Jesus," said Jackson, taken aback by the full meaning of what she said. "But you're so happy all the time."

"No help be sad and angry. Still get old."

Jackson looked away from her, cast his eyes around the room, trying to find some sense of equilibrium. He felt like nothing was real. He wasn't a man. A real man wouldn't get turned on by watching women get their hair done. His hooker wasn't a sex object, she was a person with a good heart and a dim future. He could go to jail and not be as fucked as she was.

"How can you..." Jackson stopped. He couldn't think of the right word. "...You know." He shrugged.

"How can I live?" she asked.

He nodded.

"You marry me, take me States." She laughed at the absurdity of it.

"I can't, Suzie Wong." Jackson used her full name for the first time. She noted it with a raised eyebrow. "I'm a mess. I don't know who I am or where I belong. I didn't fit in at home even before I went in the Army, and now it's worse. Nobody likes GIs, nobody wants to hire one. I can't take care of someone else. I'm not sure I can take care of me."

"No sweat, Jackson," she said. "We have fun tonight. You think like beauty salon, we make love. Very sexy." She laughed, and he laughed with her.

✶✶✶✶✶

The driver came for Jackson at eleven o'clock the next morning. He offered to take Suzie Wong along and bring her back if she wanted to see Jackson off at the airport, but she declined. "Too sad," she told Jackson, "but I dream about you." She grinned mischievously and he smiled back.

"I want you to have this," Jackson said, as he handed her a wad of U.S. currency. "It's five hundred dollars. I wanted to give you the rest, too, but I might need to lay bribes to stay out of jail."

Suzie's eyes focused on the money for a second. It was probably more than she'd ever seen at one time, but her eyes shifted back to him and she tried to pass the money back. "I no want you money, Jackson," she said.

She stood on her tip-toes and kissed him softly on the lips and held his hands in hers.

"I wish I could do more," he whispered to her. He put the money back in her palm and gently closed her fingers around it. "Maybe you and Malai can start a business," he said.

She smiled, sadly at first, then impishly. "Maybe you come Bangkok, marry me, make me rich old lady."

He laughed too, squeezed her hands softly, and said, "Maybe." Then he left.

*****

Randy leaned across the aisle of the small airplane and spoke into Jackson's ear above the din of the engines. "You got into it with Suzie Wong, didn't you?"

Jackson nodded soberly.

"Do I hear wedding bells?"

Jackson tried to hide the sadness in his face as he shook his head. "A guy could do worse."

Randy nodded like he knew what Jackson meant, like Jackson had just shared the secret of the universe. He sat back in his seat for a few minutes, deep in thought, then leaned over the aisle again.

"This was one wild ass fling, wasn't it?" Randy grinned.

Jackson smiled a little. "That it was."

"What are you going to tell your kids about it?" Randy asked.

Jackson deadpanned, "Gonorrhea's a bitch."

Randy laughed. "Seriously."

"I'm going to tell them that nothing is real," Jackson said. "Everything you think you see is really something else."

Randy laughed. "Jesus, leave it to you to come away from a week in Bangkok with the most beautiful women in the world with a line like that." He laughed again, then squinted at Jackson. "You okay with that?"

"Yeah, man. Sure. I mean, worrying about it isn't going to change anything, right?" Jackson grinned at Randy, then sat back and closed his eyes. He wished he'd given Suzie Wong all his money. He wished Suzie and Malai could have a business of their own, a café, maybe, or a beauty salon. And he wished he could save Suzie Wong.

Cruel and Unusual
James Lee Proctor

Turns out, Vietnam wasn't the adventure any of us thought it would be. Personally, I'd grown bored with the confines a fenced-in three-hundred-acre farm provided a venturesome seventeen-year-old. Most the rabbits and squirrels had been eradicated, the tank rid of its biggest bass and catfish. The suburbs were closing in and mother was already negotiating with a developer to sell the big parcel on our west side. Since dad got sick, more of the chores were falling in my lap. I knew, everybody knew, my future wasn't in farming and lay somewhere beyond. I knew too much. Problem was, it was all the wrong things. Life choices weren't my strong suit.

Other guys went. Some came home with a hero's funeral; some just came home. Thing is, they'd all been transformed by the experience. Like they had some kind of machine over there that either ground boys up or made them into men. As long as I stayed on the farm, I'd feel like an oak at the acorn stage. I wasn't scared of death. I was more scared of not facing up to it.

But then, there I was, pinned down with the rest of the unit, in a section of jungle that was supposed to have been cleared out, taking heavy fire, our transport shot to hell, in flames, still on the road, its only purpose giving us a little bit of cover, and me, getting all the experience a boy off the farm could ask for, could stand. Three of us were already gone in the ambush including the radio man. There weren't enough of us left to lay down covering fire and gain any kind of position. Behind us, our only way out was a tidal swamp. In the few seconds lull between rifle shots, we could hear Cong flanking us. Our escape route was closing fast. When snipers tried picking us off from trees, holding us up against the embankment for cover, I think we all started thinking about home and family a world away.

There was only me, Marv and Johnny left when the calvary showed up and scattered them. Cap and his band of cowboys made a pass right over the top and wiped out the Cong that managed to get on the other side of us with a wall of machine gun fire. A couple of well-placed rockets across the road scared off the rest. We managed to recover the bodies and got the hell out. Cap said a minute later we would have been overrun. I came to learn the only reason the Hueys showed up was they veered off course from a faulty nav system, saw the burning truck and dove in. I felt the hand of God must had spared us. Cap chalked it up to blind luck. He said better men had died and lesser men survived this idiotic farce. And the longer Marv, Johnny and I lived, the more we came to understand that truth in Cap's words.

*****

Knowing the time, place and method of his own death, a man is likely of a distressed mind. Even if the final hour is years beyond the foreseeable horizon, the manner agreeable to educated, robed justices who deliberate such subjects intently. It's the knowing that squeezes tight across a man's chest. Not the walls, not the bars. I know, because I've seen it on a man's face and smelled desperation ooze from his pores. They've all, well almost all, done plenty of time before, long hard years, each prior stretch with an end date. None were so deluded or stupid to see a release from those stints as freedom, but at least it meant sunshine on your face for a little while, a hamburger and a beer in your belly. Rehabilitation was not an option afforded to these men, the ones on the row. That this day on the row was going to be it, identical to the first one and last one, until their date arrived, made a ten by six cell feel closer in dimension to a pine box.

I did my own time among the general population. Even though I got to go home at the end of my shift, sharing most waking hours breathing the same sour air with humanity's castoffs weighs heavy on a man's self-worth. I could shower it off, at first, but the grime dug itself deep under my fingernails, and stink followed me everywhere like a debt. It reached the point my wife could no longer tolerate it, and she removed herself with the kids to her mother's. By then, I was too invested, all I could say was goodbye. Don't get me wrong. It wasn't that I didn't care. It was the opposite; I cared too much. Probably about the wrong things. I tried stopping her, but I knew better than to make promises I couldn't live with. Besides, when she married me, I was already a prison guard. It didn't work out. I get it. Happens all the time. Guys at work told me to forget her, move on, it was less painful that way, so that's what I did. She was as content as I to pretend 'we' never existed. She married an undertaker, I think. An occupation with its own brand of stink, albeit more respectable.

Cap took me on at the prison after I washed out of school and the sawmill closed up for good. It was my old army buddy, Johnny, gave me the idea. I wasn't even sure Cap would remember me, him being an officer and me an enlisted man. He wasn't a real captain, just a lieutenant. Got the handle Cap from the crew of his flying armada. He took me on straight away, which for me was in the nick of time, and I've been here since. Don't see him much, but says my name, gives me a nod if we come across one another. I never got passed up for promotion. I still call him Cap. Everyone else calls him warden.

These days, when I clock in, the uniform doesn't sport sharp creases anymore, the collar's frayed, there's a mustard stain that's been scrubbed a thousand times but it's not going anywhere. I'm clean shaved, like the rule book says, but I usually miss a spot or two. I've taken to taming my hair with oil. I resemble the old timers on either side of the bars more than I do the recruits. Guarding is no beauty contest. Like I said, I had passed the point of no return a while back. Longevity and suppressing trouble are what's prized and gets you the better shifts. That, and a friend upstairs.

On the row, days pass with a never-ending fluorescent cloud cover. The prisoners aren't just killing time, they murder it, in a slow, tortuous monotony, the guards their accomplices. Routine is what we call it. A creeping cancer is how the inmates say it feels. When the morning lights come up the treadmill starts. There's an illusion of movement without progress, getting past another day with nobody getting hurt. The meal carts come and go. A trustee librarian makes rounds passing along requested law books, Bibles and tattered magazines. I walk them back and forth to the exercise yard, or maybe the visitor's room to see their lawyer. The tedium gets to them, me too, but you miss a beat, show up five minutes late, you see a deeper rage in their eyes. Any day the routine is broken up — someone new checks in, a prisoner makes his date, or someone hastens their own date by cutting a hole in their neck — the tension electrifies your bones.

That's the way things were the day Flannigan came on the row. We hadn't had a new addition in some time and the row was already threatening to spill over into gen pop. A couple of the more reasonable dungeon dwellers with extended stays took up residence in a reconfigured corner of the main prison. Flannigan, an unknown commodity, wouldn't have that luxury until he had some history, which began pretty rough. He was loud, demanding, threatening everyone with everything from death to lawsuits. And it took him weeks to figure out how to sleep through the night. Like infants, new inmates on the row have a way of making everyone around them irritable. Although he'd done plenty of time before coming to the row, he hadn't yet adjusted his mindset for what was to come, and what would never come.

Not long after his arrival though, the big guys up in Washington decided that he and the rest of the fifty-two death row inhabitants, and the ones just like them on every death row throughout the land, didn't deserve what their juries gave them. That separating them from society permanently and forever had been too easy and a prison cell for the rest of their natural lives was probably good enough. And, that if you wanted to condemn someone, it required a new set of procedures. The old system was unfair. Since no prosecutor had the will to reopen and retry any of those cases under the new rules, it wasn't long before everyone went where the lifers did their time, including the guards.

At first, we all thought we caught a break. It may not have been obvious to the casual observer, but an immense weight had been lifted from everyone. Some of the prisoners' whoops echoed through the row for hours, while some with closer execution dates wept. But all were looking at life in the pen for the rest of their days. Even though someone decided they didn't deserve killing anymore, the nature of their crimes was too much for civil society to tolerate. Parole would never be on the table except in the far corners of a criminal's mind where hope and fantasy reside. Their reality was the same; they would still die in prison. The only thing that changed was they just didn't know exactly when.

Turnover within our ranks was pretty rare. When guards came on the row they'd been chosen for their experience, especially for their ability to put out fires without people getting burned. Hours of training were logged, psych evaluations completed. Working in the most secure area of the prison was a perk unto itself. Once on the row, guards didn't want to go back into gen pop. Like the prisoners we watched over, we enjoyed elevated status among our particular animal kingdom. Now, it all meant nothing. The guards got to keep the extra bump in pay they'd been collecting working on the row, and the seniority that came with the position held up too, but we were all tossed in with all the other guards when it came to preferred shifts.

It wasn't too long I was back on nights going in at ten, clocking out after six in the morning. I didn't mind too much. It had its pluses. The parking lot was half full. There was no one at home who cared when I came or went. I could go hours without seeing one of the other guards. Security relied on closed circuit and the strength of the steel bars to do most of the work. I grew accustomed to the quiet and the solitude. I read books between scheduled rounds. It was, I imagined, like watching over a tranquilized tiger, knowing it was dreaming its carnivorous dreams. Everything would be fine as long as the medicine did its job.

One night, this was way past lights-out, I was on my first walk-through and thought I heard something stir down the block coming from Flannigan's direction. You get used to all types of sounds in a penitentiary, anything from the scurry of a rat to the shrieks of terror from men descending into their own special hell. But you keep an ear out for anything mechanical, metallic; that someone is using a tool, or making one. I aimed my light inside his cell.

"That you, Collier?" Flannigan said, a whisper that echoed for anyone wanting to hear it. It had been almost a year Flannigan checked in. His privileges improved with his deportment. He was still on the old row, alone in his cell, but he was starting to be integrated with the general population; meals, even some exercise that was heavily supervised. Now might be the time he was acquiring the means for a shiv.

"I'm not going to gen pop any time soon, am I?"

"Go to sleep, Flannigan," I whispered back to him. "Whatever you got going in there, we'll find it in the morning."

"You got your job, I got mine."

"It's what keeps the doors open," I said. "Or in your case, closed."

Whatever he was doing will forever be a mystery. The report said nothing was found when the morning turtles tossed his cell. He either hid it very well, a first for any con, or I was mistaken. Next time, I would have to be sure.

A week, maybe two, goes by, and I was escorting Flannigan to the infirmary for his quarterly psych eval. The shrink lets him ramble on about his shitty childhood, or some such nonsense, to see if he's normal enough to work in the laundry, trustworthy enough to pick peas. It doesn't take a medical degree to know you keep a man isolated for long stretches and you can't trust him around anyone, including himself.

"You think the shrink's gonna recommend me for a job, Collier?"

"Not my decision, Flannigan. Keep moving."

"But, if he asks you, you tell him I'm not ready, right? A misfit."

I don't answer him. I would probably tell the guy Flannigan was no better or worse than anyone else that had been on the row. But I'm just a guard. My say doesn't mean squat. Flannigan knows that the difference between a good day and a bad day depends on what kind of mood I'm in, so he doesn't press too hard.

Trust. That's an interesting concept in prison. The warden and the shrink can sit around for hours weighing whether Flannigan can be trusted enough to be around other inmates. Me? The only thing I trust Flannigan to do is be a convict the rest of his life. That means making life choices that don't involve the well-being of anyone but Flannigan. Given the situation, that could mean the difference if I go home that morning or not. Put seven or eight Flannigans in a group and the odds don't tip in a guard's favor.

*****

The hard timers, particularly the ones who were on the row, don't get a lot of visitors. They've screwed over most of their family and friends, girlfriends and wives have moved on. Visits tend to be with lawyers or someone associated with their appeal, a game with lower odds than the lottery, but one they all play like winners. If it's the only game in town, you play it.

"There's a contract on me," Flannigan says to me, like a confession, as I double-checked his cuffs and leg irons at the visitors center door. Now, all inmates are paranoid to some degree. Most learn to live with it, swallow it as part of a nutritious dietary regimen. A healthy dose of paranoia keeps guilty men on their toes. Even the guards take a bite once in a while. But Flannigan was not known by me or any one as a worrier. Beads of sweat formed across his brow. His eyes darted around the room, looking in every corner for a sign from Moros.

The problem with Flannigan, like all cons, is they only tell you what they want you to hear. He could be lying, trying to prolong his time out of his cell. Or, he could be telling the truth, some version of it anyway, to serve some other purpose I have no interest in chasing. I can't make those kinds of judgments. I stick to the routine. "C'mon Flannigan, back you go."

He's doing the convict shuffle, his head's on a swivel. "No, really. My new lawyer just told me," he whispers over his shoulder down a stretch of isolated corridor between the blocks. "I need to tell you what he said."

"Shut up, Flannigan, 'less you're wantin' to skip your dinner."

I get him to his cell, the only one he's ever occupied. It's cooler back there but Flannigan's shirt is soaked through under his arms, across his back. I remove the shackles. His breathing is shallow, labored.

"You okay?"

He spits words out like an Uzi does bullets. "I've been trying to tell you, Collier. I'm a dead man. Couldn't tell me who, but he says it's coming Thursday. That's three days. You gotta do something."

"What's coming?"

"The hit. He says it's someone from La Famiglia. Gonna cut their losses. And my throat, I suppose."

"What in the hell are you talking about?"

Flannigan told me his story, the one he used to come clean with the cops, and he did so with all the candor and earnestness of a deathbed confession. I knew parts of his sheet but not the grisly bits. Except that he killed a cop. I never read his confession, had no interest in it. I'm no priest, far from it, but the only times I've ever seen cons make a transition from who they'd been their whole lives to someone you might believe to be sincerely reformed is when we were packing them up for the death chamber. But, when you think about it, Flannigan was right back in the crosshairs of his executioner. He had the time and place. Only question was would it be an uppercut shiv in the gut, or a blade across the jugular?

There hadn't been a gang hit in our prison since a member of the Desperado MC eviscerated a rat who got tied up in immigration detention, but that was gen pop fuck up, a crime of opportunity and five years ago. Should never have happened. Flannigan and the other former death row inmates still got special attention. The chances of something going sideways were slim.

"You gotta help me," he said, pleading harder than he probably ever had in his life.

"I don't 'gotta' do anything."

"Suppose it happens on your watch? You want to get bucked down? What's that going to do to your career?"

He had a point. If it was credible, if he talked to some other guard more sympathetic than me, and said I wouldn't listen, and if he wound up dead, his head crushed in the shower room, it wouldn't look good.

"I'll see what I can do."

"You gonna talk with the warden?"

"I said, I'll see about it."

"You gotta keep the traffic through here to a minimum."

"It already is, Flannigan. Used to be death row, remember?"

"Yeah, I just want to be sure it stays 'used-to-be.' Know what I mean?"

"I'll mention it to the other guards."

"Be discreet, will ya? I mean, don't tell them the whole tale. Just that it'd be good to minimize the number of new faces on the block for a while."

"Sure. Sure, Flannigan. Anything else I can do for you while I'm at it? Wash your car? Pick up your laundry?"

I went to the warden that morning before I clocked out. I told him what Flannigan said about the hit. We'd known each other a long time and he knew I was not one to exaggerate or fall for an inmate's hype.

"Cap," I said, "Flannigan made a complete turnaround from easy-going lifer to scared-as-shit jelly bowl between when I took him to see his lawyer and when I brought him back. He's not prone to fear and he's no actor."

"He's a con, Collier. Part of the résumé includes theater."

"You can't make up the sweat I saw poring off him."

"Nothing to be concerned with," he said, writing entries into a ledger. "I've already been briefed."

"Mind filling me in, Cap?"

He put down his pen, removed his glasses. "You know the man's story, Collier?"

"The high points. Can't say I know the details. Do I need to?"

"Sometimes the devil is in the details. Sit down, son." He called me son when he really wanted me to pay attention. "You're going to have to trust me on this."

✶✶✶✶✶

Flannigan always was a hard case. You have to be for a jury to send you to your death. No one wants to be that person who pulls the string on another human being, least not the kinds of people they pick for jury duty, but no one wants to be the person who lets a killer keep on killing.

At twelve, just after Flannigan's dad split, he began working at a mechanic's garage. Flannigan's journey to the row began with armed robbery at an impressionable fifteen. The minute he got his learner's permit, his older stepbrothers recruited him as a wheelman into their little cottage industry of robbing package stores. Flannigan was big for his age. He looked like he belonged behind the wheel of any car and he was a natural born driver. He liked the power and he liked the speed. The adrenaline was exhilarating. Until it wasn't. One of the brothers took a bullet in the thigh from an old man who'd been held up one too many times. He bled out in the back seat while Flannigan tried to find the emergency room. The judge was lenient. Believed he was duped by the older boys. Believed he'd been shaken by tragedy. At eighteen he got out of juvie with a tenth-grade education and a record that stuck to him like flypaper.

The mechanic wouldn't take him back on. Said business was slow, but Flannigan knew what was what. Wouldn't even look him in the eye, tell him the truth. No one he knew from before would. He was out. He drifted with few prospects for legitimate employment, but a knack for attracting the wrong kinds of people. Sinclair, a guy he knew from juvie, was such a person.

In juvie, Sinclair offered some protection to Flannigan until it became something different, something to be repaid. But Flannigan squared things away with Sinclair, and after the guards broke them apart, broke Flannigan's nose and Sinclair's young lust, they got along fine. Sinclair was seventeen doing his stint for knocking over a dealer's stash house — well sort of. He meant to knock it over but got there just before the narcs, who had been watching the place longer than he had. Turned out they mistook him for the dealer and when they saw him go inside, they finally had their chance to jump. Once it occurred to Sinclair what was going on he ditched the gun and took the possession with intent rap over armed robbery.

Sinclair had a nice little distribution gig going and saw Flannigan as a chance to expand. Flannigan took to dealing the way birds take to flight. They recruited mules, dealers and a small army as a show of strength. He liked the idea that guns weren't the centerpiece of the enterprise. In any illegal activity worth more than ten grand, you need a weapon for protection. It only makes sense. But with drugs, they sold pills mostly, some coke, a lot of weed, a gun wasn't necessary to conduct business. Not like it was in armed robbery. They had their brushes. Some with cops, some with rivals. They got big enough to have a lawyer on retainer. They kept him busy. They hired an accountant to do the laundry. They attracted attention.

It wasn't the cops that kept Sinclair and Flannigan up at night as much as the competition. When you want to expand without growing the whole pie you got to take a bite out of someone else's. At first, when they bumped up against Giancarlo, it was a polite 'excuse me.' Then it wasn't so civil and soldiers marched. In an effort to keep the peace they met to draw up boundaries, but it was clear each side wanted what the other had. It also became clear, once again guns would matter.

Sinclair and Flannigan dreamed up a plan to buy out Giancarlo. They knew the old man had been looking for a way to make his operation legit. He had no living sons, his lieutenants were goons and his daughter wanted nothing to do with it. With enough unencumbered cash, he could melt away on a beach somewhere without looking over his shoulder and turn everything over to the girl. At first Giancarlo balked at the idea, walked away insulted, but by the end of business the next day, after one of his men had been yanked out of the river, he reconsidered. "The idea grows on me," he said. He was old and curious about the value of his legacy. The following day they met, Giancarlo asking for the moon, Flannigan and Sinclair negotiating amounts they didn't have, agreeing to impossible terms and surprising all parties. They had three weeks.

"How we gonna manage this?" Sinclair said to Flannigan, "We ain't got anywhere near that kind of scratch."

"We'll get it."

"How?"

"When it's nailed down, I'll let you know. 'Til then, it's business as usual."

Flannigan went missing for a few weeks leaving Sinclair to cover their entire operation solo on top of wondering if his partner skipped out on him and the deal they'd made. He didn't answer his phone, his apartment was dark, no one had seen him. Five days before the deadline he showed up in the backseat of Sinclair's car, within the frame of his rearview mirror, scaring the shit out of him, almost causing him to swerve off the bay bridge.

"I fixed it," Flannigan said.

"Where the fuck have you been?" he said watching the mirror instead of the road.

"Fixing it. I got it all figured out. Where you headed?"

"I gotta be over to the depot in a couple of hours. See about a delivery. Something you would handle if anyone coulda found you."

"Pull over when you get up to Kelly's. I'll explain it all."

Flannigan told Sinclair he'd been pulling together a crew to knock over one of the richest armored cars that ever traversed the city. Enough money to float the deal with Giancarlo and then some. "It's the run from the port to the casinos downstate," Flannigan said. "Dirty, filthy cash, all of it on its way to the laundromats. Cash no one can trace."

"Yeah, I know. La Famiglia's monthly run. The one no one's supposed to know about, but everybody does. I think they like it like that because it comes with a disclaimer that says don't fuck with us or you will die a painful and slow death. You tired of this old Earth,

Flannigan?"

"Exactly, they'll never see it coming. Even if they do, even if the whole plan blows up and no one walks away with a cent, we win."

Flannigan explained he built his crew with Giancarlo's own men, each recruited one at a time. He'd hid a small tape recorder on himself when they had been negotiating with the old man, and they were not happy to learn they would soon be pounding the pavement looking for work. Experience is prized in any gang but it isn't very portable. Grudges are sticky stuff. Flannigan offered them a chance to join up with him and Sinclair and working this assignment would earn them top spots in the new, expanded organization.

"The beauty of it all is, none of them will be working for us. None of them will make it out of the robbery alive, well except maybe one. All will be identified as Giancarlo's men, the rest unknowns. Giancarlo will be top of La Famiglia's ten most wanted. That beach Giancarlo wants to find will have to be on another planet."

"In another galaxy," Sinclair said. "I suppose you are the one who survives?"

"I better. If I don't there's going to be a lot of unattended cash sitting on an empty road downstate."

"Lemme guess, you're the wheelman. When is this going down?"

"That's a very good question. Could be anytime. Thing is, we won't have much time. The guy I have inside said he could give us maybe a couple hours heads up."

"Who is it?"

"The less you know the better."

"Then we better get set now."

Sinclair was all in. The pieces were falling into place, the plan simple but dangerous by design. Everyone driven by the payoff.

Flannigan hung up the phone telling Sinclair it looked like it was on for tonight. He'd been given the time, the vehicle and the route. For the past thirty-six hours they'd all been prickly with expectancy, especially Giancarlo's men. Beto, the man Flannigan designated to run the crew of seven, five of Giancarlo's best and two recruits, was notified to get his men moving into position. Whatever they were doing, making drops, collecting, it wouldn't matter after tonight.

Flannigan and Sinclair rounded up their girls and hustled to their standing reservation at a well-known, busy steak joint and the perfect venue to stage an alibi. Flannigan tipped the maître d' double, got Jinny to slap his face and accidently spilled a drink on his pants, all within five minutes, just to get people to notice he was there. He excused himself to the restroom, slipped out the back and was gone.

Flannigan pulled behind a clump of switchgrass out on the fen and killed the headlights. He was early. He wired and set the charges like he'd practiced a hundred times the past few days, and strung them across the roadway. Minutes passed like clotting blood. Another pair of lights came into view down the long stretch of road piercing the bruised twilight, a van slowing to a crawl, stopping. It pulled off the road fifty yards up. Flannigan flashed his lights. Beto responded. Dark figures fanned out along the road berm disappearing into the cattails.

The county sheriff said the aftermath reminded him of a firefight his army unit took on, him being the lone survivor. The worst part of this scene, he said, was IDing a man by the tat on his arm, 'Mona,' a tribute to his wife, a woman the man idolized. The bullet entered the back of Sam's head obliterating his face on its way out. The tattoo was the only way. He had coffee with Sam that morning. He'd been a deputy for seven years. Sam drove for the armored car service and did a little security to help make ends meet.

By the time all the jurisdictions trampled the crime scene pointing out each other's inadequacies little usable evidence of the way things went down remained. The armored vehicle was rendered unusable by explosives that ripped a three-foot-wide gash across the road. The doors were open, a body laid partially outside the back. Bodies littered the road and the brush below it, some with multiple wounds, others with head shots that appeared to be executions. The van, the apparent getaway vehicle was still idling when the sheriff arrived on scene. It was clear this was an ambush, but with no surviving witnesses and nobody claiming they'd been robbed, it seemed a lot of very bad people died at each other's hand. Twelve of the thirteen victims had rap sheets a mile long. The last one was clean as a whistle and the only one the sheriff cared about.

The first domino to fall was the inside man at the armored car service who made the fatal mistake of believing he could save his life by admitting his role, and who paid him. Flannigan was long gone by the time the posse was trailing him, but what a posse it was, and it proved relentless. La Famiglia had resources and techniques less sophisticated, less admissible, than the cop's investigative capabilities, but effective nonetheless. Flannigan was as well-hidden as the cash, but knew the only way to stay alive long term was to keep his head down and turn himself over to the law. The money, and where it was stashed, was his only chip on the table. As long as it was out there, somewhere, he might stay alive. That is, until a jury condemned him to death for the murder of a lawman during the commission of a crime.

*****

Cap moved me to days. Made it known to the other guards he wanted me on point around Flannigan 'til this thing was over. I spread word through the ranks that there was credible intel of a hit on Flannigan. That it might be coming in the next couple of days. I said that the warden was making arrangements to move Flannigan to a safe location, soon as he could set it up. "Keep your eyes and ears open," I told them. "If anything looks out of place, you tell me."

The next day, a few minutes after eleven on a colder than normal gray morning, a secure vehicle, a fortified panel van, backed into the prisoner intake area where Cap and I were waiting. Flannigan waited back inside shackled to the prison's plumbing. The only thing he was told was that he was going away for a few days until we could figure who, if anyone, was out for him. Cap said when word of him missing from his cell for extended periods got around, and no one sees him in the exercise yard for a day or two, someone was bound to get curious, ask around the infirmary about him, we'd flush him out.

"You're driving, Collier," Cap said to me, as he motioned to Norris, one of the guards, to bring the prisoner out.

As I replaced the guy in the cab, I watched in the mirror as the warden had Flannigan's feet and hands secured to the eyebolts inside the van. A chest restraint was applied. He was as much a part of the van as the engine block. The warden took a seat on the bench opposite Flannigan near the rear doors.

"Close it up, Norris."

"But warden, we can't let a con out with only a single guard."

"You're not. He's got both Collier and me. Now, close it up."

Norris handed the warden the keys and slammed the doors to the van shut.

"Drive, Collier."

"Where we going, Cap?"

"Just drive. I'll give you directions when you need them."

We made our way through the gauntlet of gates insulating the rulers from the rule breakers, each set of guards expecting us, letting us through with a cursory inspection of the cargo and a nod to the warden, and not happy about a depraved individual like Flannigan reentering the honest world. At the end of the main drive the road in either direction was deserted. "Which way, Cap?"

"Left," the warden called from the back of the van. "Get us to the highway and head south."

I'd been driving about twenty minutes along the interstate, waiting for the next instruction when Cap called out, "When you get to the Rockaway exit, take it. Go west about ten miles 'til you see a diner.'"

"You talking about Marv's, Cap?"

"That's the place."

Marvin Wayne was my unit's sergeant in the army, one of the guys pinned down that day we lost so many men, and Cap helped haul out of the jungle. But days after the rescue, Marv shipped home, his tour complete. I'd never heard Cap even mention his name. But me and

Marv stayed in touch. Marv retired a sheriff's deputy, one of the good guys, and though he never suffered so much as a scrape in Nam he was shot and wounded pulling over a drunk driver. It got him early retirement. His uncle gave him some near worthless property and he opened a roadhouse in the middle of nowhere. His regulars were few, ran tabs and were slow to pay. He tried attracting more people with a barbeque menu on weekends, but it wasn't enough. The last time I was by the place it had been closed for years and I was drinking to Marv's memory.

An empty bourbon bottle, Marv's favorite, was right where I'd left it, underneath a picnic table bench on the front porch of the roadhouse. It was Marv's spot, the place you could always catch him. Johnny and Pete and I killed it after Marv's funeral. Johnny was a survivor, an old army pal. I didn't know Pete, but he told stories about his time in country with Marv, things that reminded Johnny and I about our own times with sarge. Turned out he knew Cap, too. Also turns out, his brother was the deputy Flannigan murdered during the armored car heist, although I didn't know that little tidbit until it mattered.

The roadhouse sign hung at an angle now, across the roofline, having lost its supports when a tree limb fell on it. Weeds grew up through cracks in the asphalt, paint curled up on the siding. A 'for sale' sign that wasn't there the four years prior was now tacked to the front door.

"Park us around back," the warden said, "out of sight."

I do as I'm told. The back of Marv's is cluttered with old beer crates, rusty kegs and debris from the woods staging a slow-motion assault to reclaim the territory it once possessed. The warden tells me to cut the motor and keep a gun on Flannigan while he detaches the prisoner from the van.

"Behave yourself, Flannigan," I tell him as the warden releases the bolt connecting the handcuffs.

The warden steps out the back of the van and tells Flannigan to come on out, carefully. The three of us stand in the gloom, the warden and I facing Flannigan, my gun casually trained on his mid-section, beneath the canopy of oak trees. It's early afternoon, but the atmosphere speaks more to twilight. The only sounds come from the movements in the forest, there's no traffic along the road to disturb nature's business. Some long moments pass. It seems the warden's mulling something important. No one says a word. It's Cap's show.

He checks his watch. "Okay, Flannigan. Take a seat on the bumper," he says.

He complies and I adjust my aim accordingly.

"It's going on one o'clock, Flannigan. Keep that in mind for what I'm about to tell you. And listen carefully. You don't want to waste time with stupid questions or have me repeating myself. At two o'clock a man will arrive here to torture and kill you. I'm telling you this not because I'm trying to scare you, or that I care one way or the other about if you live or die today, but because there is only one way to walk away from this with your life, and if you're smart, a free man."

Flannigan's face was a contorted mixture of fear and excitement. His lips trembled, then started forming words.

"I'm dead serious, Flannigan. Shut the hell up. You speak without permission and I'll have Collier here abuse you like he's always dreamed about."

The warden shot me a stern glance, one that conveyed we were on the same page.

"I know your sheet. I know your raps inside and out. I know exactly why you gave yourself up. You've been sitting on a secret a while now. I want you to tell me that secret."

The warden stepped toward Flannigan, hiked the suit material at his knees and sat next to him. "Put that thing down," he said to me about the gun I now had trained in his general direction.

"Listen to me. As of today, you and I need each other. I've started something in motion now that can't be reversed. You tell me where the money is, convince me why you put it there, how you came up with the plan to stash it there, then take me there, you live. Simple as that. You comply, you walk away with your life and enough cash to disappear. You don't, you die. Got that?"

Flannigan remained rigid, staring into the woods.

"You stall, take too long weighing your options, of which there are few, you might be dead anyway. I have no idea if these La Famiglia guys are punctual or not, or even if they're prone to arrive early. But I assure you I won't be waiting around to find out." He checked his watch.

His gaze still in the distance, Flannigan said, "You coming to the dark side, Cap?"

"Not your concern. You better come up with a better question before Collier puts your jaw out of business."

"So, I show you the money, you show me the door?"

"In a nutshell."

He turns his head to read the warden. "How do I know you don't kill me? Claim I tried to escape?"

"You don't. But which odds do you like better, my word or trying to negotiate with La Famiglia?"

"How do I even know they're coming?" There's a chill to the air, but Flannigan's sweating.

Cap stood to face him. Flannigan's feet are still shackled, his wrists cuffed, hands clasped as if in prayer, looking upward toward his savior. Cap said to him, "Look at it this way, pal. Your prospects are far better today than when you first arrived at my prison. Your death was a certainty. Your appeals went nowhere. Even this morning when you woke up, the best parts of the rest of your life were going to be behind bars. Today I offer you redemption."

"How is it they even know I'm here?"

Cap cut me a glance. Flannigan picked up on it.

"You? Collier?" Flannigan dropped his gaze into the dirt and spit into it. "Fuckin' Judases would sell your own mothers."

I said nothing. I put my gun back on him.

The breeze settled for a moment and I picked up the sound of tires on the pavement rolling toward us from the direction of the interstate.

We all heard it.

"Could be them, could be early," Cap said. "Whatcha gonna do, Flannigan."

He regards Cap with a scowl. "Okay, okay, I'm in." He shakes his head. Beads of sweat shake off and darken the yellow of his prison jumpsuit.

The car rolls past Marv's kicking a cloud of dust from the shoulder, then disappears down the road.

"Spill," the warden says.

Flannigan begins his story too early, takes irrelevant sidetracks, and provides meaningless detail, wasting time and pissing Cap off, no end. He's constantly checking the time.

"You wanted credibility," Flannigan said.

"I want location credibility. I don't want you taking me on a joyride to nowhere. Start with where it is and then why I should believe you."

The location wasn't far, an hour and a half's drive if we hump it, and if it was stowed as he described, would not be hard to get at; no digging, no people around. He was finally giving Cap what he wanted; why he chose that particular spot, how he got it there. That's when I heard a vehicle pull into the parking lot around front.

Then there came a terror in Flannigan's eyes. They darted between me and the warden and the woods, looking for a way out. "Who is it? Is that them?"

Cap looked at me, chuckled, and said, "Not likely."

Footsteps, boots on gravel, emerged from around the corner. A man wearing a ballcap, a denim shirt and work jeans stopped when he saw us. He stiffened to attention, raised his right hand in salute and said in bootcamp cadence, "Ten-hut, recruits. Reporting for duty as ordered, sir." I hadn't seen Johnny in a while, but there was no mistaking him.

The man with him I hadn't seen in years, not since Marv's funeral, but Pete was equally as recognizable. Older, for sure, and dressed down from when we grieved over our buddy, but the blond hair and ruddy face made him singular among many. "Hope you brought along a bottle of bourbon this time, Collier. I sprung for the last one." He nodded a silent greeting to me and Cap, then looked at Flannigan sitting on the van tailgate and said, "Guess we're doing this. Got the location yet?"

"Just now," I said.

"Wait a minute, you're supposed to be my lawyer," Flannigan said to Pete. "You knew about this?"

Pete ignored the question, but not the man. He kept his eyes on Flannigan the way one would an angry, capable animal hobbled by restraints, not out of fear, not for underestimating the cuffs and leg irons, but to grow accustomed to his being there. A good fifteen yards separated the men. Soon they would occupy smaller confines, breathe the same air. Pete was not looking forward to it.

"How far?" Pete asked.

"Hour and a half," I said.

"Maybe I should ride along with Johnny."

"That isn't the plan," Cap said. "Johnny, you got the big truck gassed?"

He nodded he was all set.

"Pete, you're in back with me and Flannigan. Collier, you're still driving, and Johnny follows. Everybody still on board?"

No one said they weren't.

"Good. Load up," Cap said.

I put Flannigan back inside the van and looped the shackles through the restraint rings. For more than an hour, no one in back seemed much in the mood for talking. Cap and Pete sat across from Flannigan who stewed in a broth of shame and rage. Flannigan now knew what was what. He wasn't stupid. Pete posed as one of his lawyers. He had enough information about his case to convince him he was filling in for the guy that he usually saw, information that would have been easy to obtain from someone with access to his records.

"I'm not walking away from this, am I?" he finally said.

Cap looked at him, his face giving nothing away. Pete started to say something, but Cap put an elbow to his ribs and he clammed up fast.

The shadow of the old iron works in front of an orange sky was in sharp contrast to the uneven shapes of the forest when we pulled in at sunset. A gate with a rusty chain kept the honest people and teenagers out. The lack of potential for easily pawned equipment kept the thieves away. The company had moved on years ago and taken everything of any value or sold it for scrap. Anything left behind was either worthless or too heavy to transport.

"This the way you remember it?" Cap said to Flannigan.

Flannigan bent as far over as possible to see what he could through the windshield. The van headlights shot across the darkened empty lot, particles of dust dancing in and out of them the only activity inside the fence line. "It was up and running last time I came in this way."

"Any reason to think the money's not here?" Cap said.

Flannigan shook his head. "I hid it too good."

Johnny rapped a knuckle on my window, holding up a pair of bolt cutters. "Open it up?"

Johnny closed the gate and made it appear untampered with. We drove cautiously across the parking lot past the old administration office, a one level structure separate from the manufacturing outbuildings. There were five identical hangar-sized structures, each with a gaping door, lined up one after the other to the end of the concrete pad.

"Where to?" I said from the cab, staring into the void beyond my headlights.

"Keep going all the way to the end," Flannigan said. "When we get there, I'll tell you what to do."

I heard the click of a cocked hammer and Cap's voice, "We got nothing better to talk about. Tell us now."

I saw he was aiming his gun at Flannigan's forehead. "Hey Cap. Never know when we hit a bump or something out here in the dark." He eased the hammer back and aimed at the floor.

"It's just that it looks like things have changed out here," Flannigan said. "I need to take you there. If I try to tell you how to get there and it's different, you'll think I'm lying."

Cap was thinking it over.

Pete said, "You said it was in a basement. It's gotta be one of these buildings."

"I said a cellar. Just drive to the end of the pavement and stop, Collier."

Fifty yards past the last building the pavement ran out and an expanse of rusted wrecks and worn-out rigging served as trellises for weeds and vines. I pulled to the edge and let the lights settle over the scrapyard. Johnny pulled alongside.

"Okay, where?"

"I tell you, you're never gonna find it. I have to show you."

"There's a cellar out there somewhere?" Pete said.

"Sure is. And I think I'm probably the only living person who knows it even exists. What made it such a perfect place to stash all that cash."

"How do you know about it and no one else does?" said Cap.

"Between juvie and my career that got me sent to the row, I thought I might make an honest living. You know, try it on and see how it felt. I worked here for a while, 'til summer nearly burnt me to a crisp. Boss was a good guy. Didn't mind givin' somebody like me another chance. But, 'cause of my record, he didn't want me working anywhere near the money makin' end of the business. I was pretty good runnin' the forklift and I spent most my time haulin' stuff in and out of here. One day, I come across this pair of doors underneath what's left of an old water tower. Turns out this place used to be a farm before the company bought it and the farmer built himself a storm cellar. I didn't tell nobody about it. Kept it for myself. Spent more than a few hot afternoons down there."

"Some people would still be alive if somebody'd covered you up while you were down there," Pete said.

"Then you wouldn't be looking at a payday, now would ya, lawyer," Flannigan said, and spit.

"How'd you get it in here, I mean if this place was still operating?"

Cap said.

"I had this place picked out from the start. During the day this place is busier than Grand Central, but night time is a reduced shift. The watchman stays in the office. Before the robbery, I come out here and got it all set up. I cut a hole in the back fence, made sure the doors weren't covered up. Comin' in the back way at night I pretty much have the run of the place."

"Where are these doors?"

"Like I said, I gotta show you."

Cap told Pete to put his gun on Flannigan while he unlocked the leg irons. "Here's how it's going to work. You're going to lead us into this field and show us where the cellar is. Simple as that. But you fuck with me in any way and you are an escaped convict. In other words, you're a dead man. Understand?"

Beams from our flashlights bounced around the tombstones of the industrial graveyard. Pete pushed Flannigan along, his gun at his back, a light out in front of him. Cap and I followed with guns at our sides. Johnny was last carrying a pick and shovel, just in case we needed to excavate the money or dig a grave. The only sounds in the night were soft footfalls, the occasional clank of Johnny's tools. Rabbit trails wound their way through the grass and we fell into a single file following one. Flannigan slowed his pace, then stopped and turned back looking at the old plant in the half moonlight.

"It's right around here," he said in a whisper.

"Where?" whispered Pete.

"Is there anyone around that might hear us?" Cap said.

"Lemme see your light a minute," Flannigan said, his voice returning to a normal level, reaching with his cuffed hands toward Pete's flashlight.

Pete flinched at Flannigan's move pulling the light away from him in reflex, keeping the gun leveled at his gut. But Flannigan feigned the move entirely and grabbed hold of Pete's gun hand, twisting it upward while making Pete's finger work the trigger. The shot exploded the night in sound and light, while the bullet traveled from under Pete's chin and shattered his face, blood and bone splinters speckling Flannigan. He fell to the ground and Flannigan stood in front of us holding Pete's gun between Cap and me ready to shoot either of us.

"Drop 'em, boys. First one moves sets the example. You, too, back there. Throw the tools down."

Johnny tossed away the pick and shovel. I heard them tumble into the weeds. I dropped my .38 from my side. I wasn't sure Flannigan saw it so I raised my empty hands, palms out. The warden hadn't moved, hadn't said a word, and Flannigan drew a bead square at his head.

"What's it gonna be, warden?"

I heard the clang of something heavy drop onto a hard, metallic surface.

"Smart. Now, step back." Flannigan picked up the flashlight while keeping his eyes and gun on us. Specks of Pete's blood shone pink through the lens. He told us to kick our guns over his way. Then he spoke his deliberate instructions.

"Now, warden. I want you to listen to me very carefully. Reach into your coat pocket and very slowly remove the key to these cuffs. You will toss them at my feet. Do you understand?"

Cap complied.

"You," he said to Johnny, "come over here and drag your pal off these doors."

Johnny hesitated. Cap and I looked at each other. Johnny was confused.

"Get to it. Or, I'll shoot you and go to the next man."

Johnny moved up around me and Cap and looked down at Pete. A good piece of his head was gone. Gore covered most the upper half of his body. He picked up Pete's ankles like he was testing the weight and gave Flannigan a look that asked where he wanted him.

Flannigan pointed the flashlight into the weeds and said, "Over there, anywhere."

When he pulled Pete away some of the weeds were dragged along under him revealing the rusted surface underneath, the doors covering the storm cellar. Two iron rings lay on either side of the seam separating the cellar doors. Flannigan instructed us to clear off the rest of the debris and vegetation camouflaging them while he stood watch over our work, giving us some light, covering us with the pistol. The doors were constructed of thick oakwood planks and iron straps. There was some struggle to heave open one of them. When the opening stood agape, me, Cap and Johnny lined up near the entrance, Flannigan on the other side shining a beam onto the steps leading inside, I said, "This is the stoutest storm cellar I think I ever seen. Don't women live on farms?"

"You don't hear 'bout too many twisters in these parts," Flannigan said. "Farmer used to run a still, probably down in those woods. This is where he stored his product. Wanna taste? Should still be plenty down there. 'Least there was last time I was down there." He put the light in our faces. I got the feeling he was trying to gauge our intentions — our level of motivation minus any level of fear. My guess is he got a different read from each of us.

"Get down there, boys."

The steps were made from the same heavy oak planks and looked trustworthy in the light disappearing below. I led the way, testing each step before putting my full weight on it, and Cap was two steps after. As we descended into the hole, Flannigan came up around behind us putting light onto the cellar floor. The room was cool like a cave and there was enough ceiling for a tall man to stand upright comfortably. The walls could have been within reach or twenty foot to either side; there was not enough light to know.

"Stop at the end of the steps," he said. "Stay where I can see you."

From where I stood, looking up into the night sky, stars were beginning to come out, stars I hadn't paid attention to in a long time. Flannigan was facing toward us, kneeling, his face illuminated by the edges of the flashlight beam, and although I couldn't see what he was doing I knew he was working the key into the cuffs. I heard the ratchet click and chain rattle, then he tossed them aside. Standing erect, the gun in his right hand, the flashlight in his left, he ordered Johnny to strip and toss his clothes up to him.

Johnny wadded his shirt and pants into a ball and chucked them up the steps to Flannigan's feet.

"The ball cap, too."

Flannigan snagged it by the brim. A lucky catch.

"Thanks," he said. "If you find a way out of there, which I think is unlikely, there'll be a prison jumpsuit waiting for you."

Flannigan walked out of the frame made by the doorway. We all could hear him straining to lift the door, the hinges creaking. Cap, seeing this as perhaps the last best opportunity to save us, himself, started taking the steps in twos. He was halfway outside when the door came crashing on top of him sending him sideways against the wall on the other side. He fell into a heap on the floor. Flannigan's gun was on us, his light showing a bright red streak leaking from the gash across Cap's skull.

Flannigan moved away to the other side, to the other door, and began lifting it.

"Wait!" I cried out to him, "what about the money?"

"Ain't no money down there, you fool." He started to drop the door on top of us, but held it for a second. "I wasn't kidding about the moonshine, though. You get cold enough, thirsty enough, you'll find it."

The heavy door slammed tight against the one that knocked Cap unconscious, the night sky gone from view forever. Up top, I heard him ramming the shovel and pick handles through the iron rings. Then later, I heard him park the prison van over us and shoot out a couple of the tires.

Cap never woke up, but it took him a couple of days to stop breathing altogether. We made all the noise we knew how, but that proved futile. When Johnny about froze, he began pilfering parts of Cap's wardrobe. The homemade whiskey did take the edge off, though.

I counted six days so far. The little bit of light that finds its way down through narrow slits doesn't last long, but with the eyes of a mole I judge my room to be a little bigger than the one Flannigan occupied. Split between me and Johnny, it's about the same.

Knowing the time, place and method of his own death, a man is likely of a distressed mind.

Just Keep Talking
Victor Kreuiter

"These guys bitching all the time … you hear them? Saying they're working their asses off, taking all these risks and the boss don't do nothing and he gets all the money?" Bill Schaefer was eating a gyro, the sauce dripping out, him talking and licking his fingers between bites. He was short and thin, a bag of bones in cheap khakis, always wearing those cut-rate shirts made him look like a refugee. The one time Duane seen Schaefer in a wife-beater he pointed at Schaefer's arm, at the tattoo there, laughing, asking, "What the hell's that about?"

Schaefer went quiet. Inked onto his skinny arm was a sword and some arrows, a crest and the words, *De Oppresso Liber*. He scratched at it, looked away, and finally said: "When you're young you don't know no better. That's what that's about." That was the last time Duane saw Bill Schaefer in a wife-beater.

Schaefer was seventy-three years old and looked like getting to seventy-four was chancy. He had a skinny neck and a sharp little chin, cheeks both shrunken and wrinkled. His eyes were black and they were always blinking, him always looking around like he was expecting something to happen. His thin dark hair was slicked down. Somebody should have told him that look was over a long time ago. How come he was always out of breath? Nobody saw him smoke but he took every breath like it was his last.

Schaefer and Duane were a block down from the gyro truck, standing, waiting for the drop. Duane was eating a gyro, too, wondering if the old man ever stopped talking. It there wasn't food going into his mouth there was words coming out.

"They bitch but don't do shit about it," Schaefer said.

Duane nodded, figuring he had to say something to show he was listening. "What they supposed to do?"

Schaefer humphed and looked up and down the street. He took a drink of his soda, leaned down and put the cup on the ground. When he stood up he frowned at Duane, like Duane would know what that frown meant. Duane pretended he didn't see the frown and asked again, a bit irritated: "What they supposed to do?"

Schaefer shrugged, like Duane wasn't smart enough to follow him. "You got to look out for yourself," he said. If Duane had a dime for every time he heard Schaefer say that. "You got to make your own luck," Schaefer said. His expression was always the same, a weird mixture of fear and anger, a little bit of panic in there, maybe a little desperation.

"Like you're making your luck?" Duane said that, thinking it was a smart comeback.

Duane was not smart. He would never be smart and Schaefer knew that. Everybody that worked for the boss knew that. Duane thought he was muscle, but he wasn't much of that, either. What was in *his* expression? Not much. His face was blank a lot of the times. He had big teeth and a big chin and a big nose and little eyes. He was big in the chest and in the arms and in the shoulders, but he looked like a big grown-up little boy. What was in *his* expression? Mostly he looked like he wanted it to be over. Whatever he was doing, he looked like he wanted it to be over.

Duane and Bill Schaefer had the simple route, the small one. It was the easy one, the one neighborhood ladies watched. Some of the neighborhood men and some of the neighborhood women knew the kids doing the work by name and some of them used. Because they were locals, they could run a tab of sorts, paying up a day late, two days, sometimes three, but they always had to pay. Someone knock on the door, looking for that money? That was very, very bad.

Duane and Schaefer didn't know a thing about those tabs, but the boss did; he was okay with it. It was a community service, that's how he saw it. Them people always owing him money? Made him feel good.

Those neighborhood folks, they might know his name but they would never say it out loud in a courtroom, he knew that. They knew that, too. They might recognize him, but when they did they'd look away.

Duane wasn't smart enough to know he was on the easy route. Schaefer knew it. He knew that him and Duane were the easy grab in case the police needed to grab someone. The police had to do that every so often, otherwise the politicians, the newspapers, the preachers … they'd all get warmed up and that was not good for anybody.

So … Bill Schaefer's eyes were always moving for a damn good reason.

Everybody that worked for the boss thought Bill Schaefer was past his expiration date. He wondered about that, too. He thought about being old and not having much of anything. How did that happen?

"You watch," Schaefer said. Duane heard that and started thinking about what his comeback should be, but he couldn't come up with much except a question. "Watch what?" he said.

"Watch me," Schaefer said. "You'll see." Duane shrugged, didn't say anything, and a kid came up to him and said him and Schaefer should go further down the block and when they see the kid on the bicycle they should follow him to another kid who would have the money; that was how they did it. So Schaefer and Duane go down the block and the kid on the bicycle goes slow and they follow him and a block or so later a kid comes out an alley and hands them a bag of money. That's their last pickup for the day. They walk back to Schaefer's car and drive off, heading away from downtown. They park a block short of their destination, walk the rest of the way and step into a dilapidated brick building. The guy inside the door looks at them but don't say anything and the guy at the top of the stairs does the same. They go through two more doors, deliver the money — the boss doesn't even look in their direction — then walk back down the stairs and when they're back out on the street, when Duane starts walking off, Schaefer stops him, saying, "Duane, that stuff I said. You know, that 'watch me' stuff? It don't mean nothing, okay? You know that, right?" Duane shrugged and Schaefer said "You don't gotta tell nobody, okay? It's just an old man talking too much. That's all it is."

Duane was thinking who would he tell? Nobody listened to him. He knew that. Hell, he was the only one listening most of the time. Him and Schaefer weren't friends or anything like that. They were like all the other teams, stopping by this corner or that corner, driving down one street or another street or circling round like they were watching for something and could do something about something if something happened. Always hoping the boss noticed what they did, always wanting to do things for the boss.

Duane never said anything about anything. Most of the time he didn't know what to say. Most of the time he didn't understand most of what he was hearing. Schaefer talked all the time, mostly about how some gets and some gets others to get it *for* them. "You know how they stay on top?" Schaefer asked Duane. He asked that over and over and over and Duane never answered. "They take advantage," Schaefer said. "They take advantage of a situation, that's all," he said. "They're just looking out for themselves, like we should be doing." Duane thought Schaefer talked too much.

Couple weeks go by and on a Thursday, collections done, Schaefer tells Duane, "Duane, you got to do the pickups tomorrow by yourself" and Duane asks why. Duane's maybe tired of working with the old man, but the old man, he's *somebody* to work with, ain't he? Right off Duane is wondering if he can do it alone.

"I'm not feeling good," Schaefer says. He puts a hand on his forehead, moves it to his stomach. "I got me something, you know? A bug."

So on Friday Duane does it by himself, which he doesn't like one bit but he does it all and he does it right, him feeling better about himself as the day goes along, and it's dark when he parks his car, a block shy of the building where the boss is waiting in the counting room. He's walking into the building when he sees Bill Schaefer's car down the block a bit, past the building. Ain't Schaefer supposed to be sick?

Duane goes in, gets upstairs and sure enough, there's Schaefer, sweating, looking uncomfortable in a chair, head down. Duane gives the money to the guy at the table who sets it next to the pile of money he's counting. The boss, he's sitting on one end of the table, smoking, staring at the ceiling and Duane asks Schaefer "You feel better?" The boss stands up, looks at Duane and says "Why you care?"

Duane knows not to say nothing. The boss says "He your friend? That it? Him letting you go out there alone, doing it all?" Duane doesn't know what to say. Schaefer looks up at the boss and says, "Look, Duane's a good guy and …"

The boss glares, points at him and tells him to shut up. "Shut. Up. Old. Man." he says, and Schaefer shrinks a bit and Duane doesn't know what to say or do and then the boss looks at him and says "Get outta here." When Duane starts to go Schaefer stands up and for some reason Duane stops.

"Did I tell you to stand up?" That's what the boss says to Schaefer. "Who told you to stand up?" He takes a half step toward Bill Schaefer and Duane looks at Schaefer, thinking maybe he should say something to him and he sees Schaefer has his chin up a bit and has some kind of faraway look in his eyes. He's looking right past the boss, like he's concentrating on something far away. The guy at the table has raised his eyes and stopped counting.

Here's what the boss and the guy counting the money and Duane don't know about Bill Schaefer. When he was young, Bill Schaefer found himself alive, standing in a field full of dead people. Soldiers. He was a soldier, too. Standing there in that field of dead soldiers he had to look far away to calm himself. He had to concentrate on his breathing and force himself to stand still and think. He was shaking all over and he kept his eyes closed until he wasn't shaking so much, and then he had to check the dead soldiers, one at a time, until he found the radio and he had to radio it in and before he could do that he had to stay calm and figure out that radio, his hands feeling like bricks. When he figured out the radio he called it in and when they asked him where he was he said it looked like he'd gone down into hell. It took a while before a helicopter came and got him and all that while he was looking for Randolph, that guy from the Midwest he was friends with. Randolph was all the time talking about how they were fools for doing this crazy shit, fighting in a jungle so rich people could get richer. Just that morning, walking on some jungle path, Randolph had said aloud, so everyone could hear: "We gotta get our asses shot so some rich son-of-a-bitch can get two more swimming pools? Who's crazy? Him or us? Who's the crazy ones?"

He found Randolph, blood all over his chest and his neck and his face, dead as hell, and he went blank. Schaefer stood still in a field of dead people and he wasn't shaking anymore and his eyes were wide open and when the helicopter landed they had to scream at him to get him to run.

He couldn't forget any of that. It messed him up. After he was a soldier, back home, he was around people sniffing and smoking and injecting all kinds of shit. For a long time he did that, too. He couldn't remember how or when he stopped doing that, but eventually he got straightened out somehow, thinking maybe there was a chance for him. There's always a chance, right? You got to look out for yourself, right? You got to make your own luck. When he figured that out, when he got straightened out, he was past halfway to being an old man.

He bounced around, did some of this and some of that. That's what his life was like. Truck driving. Gas station cashier. Quick shop cashier. Washing dishes. Kitchen work. Any kind of labor. He didn't live well, but he lived. He got old doing those jobs and then, finding himself old and unemployed, somehow he fell in with Duane. How did that happen? When did that happen? Bill Schaefer couldn't answer either of those questions.

He kept his eyes open and seen the money the boss was making and knew to be cool and just do the job, just do what he was told to do. He kept his mouth shut and put up with being the old man, the butt of jokes, him getting sassed by kids, him smiling it away like he couldn't do anything about it.

"Did I tell you to stand up?" The boss takes another half step toward Schaefer. The boss is pissed. He's always pissed. Why is this old man not listening to him? Why does he put up with this fool?

Schaefer shakes his head like he's weary, like he's old and doesn't understand, and then he reaches behind his back, reaches down into them cheap khakis, pulls out a cheap handgun and shoots the boss right in the face and watches the body slump to the floor. The boss dies wondering how that old man got the balls to shoot him.

The man counting the money is reaching for his gun when he is shot twice and falls backwards off his chair. The money in front of him is undisturbed.

Schaefer knows there's a guy downstairs and another guy at the top of the stairs, two doors away. He holds a finger to his lips, points at Duane then points to a corner of the room, the one behind the door, and watches Duane run there and hunker down.

Right away he can hear those two toughs shouting, knowing they'll be through the door lickety-split. "It's okay," he whispers to Duane. "Stay put."

The toughs enter the room at full speed, guns forward. Bill Schaefer, who once stood in a field of dead soldiers shaking and pondering his luck, shot them both as they entered the room. Two times each. He doesn't even look at them as life leaves their bodies. He doesn't even bother to go looking for their guns.

He turned to look at the safe and the safe was open. Schaefer always wondered why the boss would want that, everyone seeing all that money in that safe. An ego thing? Pride? Every day money coming in, the boss standing around like he's a tycoon, a king, watching his wealth multiply like he'd done it all himself, like he deserved it all. Schaefer knew what kind of car the boss drove around in. He knew where the boss lived. He knew the boss was on top and people on top want to stay on top no matter what it takes. That kind of person, Schaefer knew he got old working for that type of person.

Ten minutes tops, that's all the time it took for Bill Schaefer to gather all the money from the safe and from the table in the counting room and get it to his car. He did it in one trip and before he walked out with all that money he looked at Duane and said "Run."

Fifteen minutes later he was on the interstate.

Twenty-four hours later, when the bodies he left behind were being photographed by law enforcement, he was eating in a roadside diner, seven hundred miles away.

Six months go by and he's seven hundred more miles away. He has a better life. He rents a little bungalow from a young couple. They're nice to him. He calls himself Phillip Hafner now. Phillip tells everybody he meets he's retired. It's true, he is. He's grown a full beard — it's white — and he shaves his head. There's a neighbor lady invites him to lunch sometimes and sometimes he goes.

Another six months go by and he gets talked into a part-time job at the senior center where he's been playing cards in the afternoon, a job in the kitchen. The ladies there love him. He pays attention to the job, mostly washing dishes, and he must know a million jokes — dirty ones, too — and he tells them with a straight face, like he doesn't know he's being naughty, and them women laugh and laugh and ask for more. He talks a lot — tells all kinds of stories — the women eating it up. They egg him on and he just keeps talking, laughing at his own jokes, all relaxed and full of himself.

"Phillip," they say — all of them say it when he's not around — "he's one of those guys done it all and ain't ashamed to admit it." That's what they're all thinking, all of them. Then one of them will say something like "And he's a good man, too. We all see it. Phillip got a good heart."

He brings in donuts some days. And some days he'll take those kitchen ladies for ice creams, them tickled pink and him just keeping on talking and telling those funny stories he's got.

How the Devil Stole Pastor Henry's Soul
K. Arlington Andrews

Traynesha

The night I met *Hen*, the *stroll* was hot and popping like fish grease. All I saw were headlights up and down the avenue, and the johns were almost double parked with the thumping bass coming from their cars. That's when I heard: "What's up beautiful."

He *had* to be talking to me. I was rocking the Gucci clutch I boosted from Macy's and the hot pink outfit matched the streak in my hair.

To keep it totally 100, The coins I make in half a night, beat all those other dusty streetwalking hookers. Who else could he be talking to? He pulled up, I got in, and our conversation just clicked off the bat, ya know? It was like we'd known each other since kindergarten. We talked a little about everything as he drove us to a side street and turned the car off.

"What's a good girl like you doing out here on a night like this?" I couldn't answer. His dimples distracted me. He snapped the straps of my top and my titties spilled into his mouth.

"I know what you want. You looking for a man that knows what to do with all this." Our body heat fogged up the windows when it started to rain, and I knew Hen was different when he insisted on driving me home.

After that first time it didn't take long before he was blowing up my phone, *all* the time. He became one of my regulars, and I didn't know he was a preacher until Dominque and me went to his church on *Save a Soul Sunday*

Every hustler, streetwalker, and gangbanger in the hood, knew about *Save a Soul Sunday*. It was held every first Sunday, at the old House of Transformation on 12th Street.

The streets had been talking about this new preacher that won $2 million in the Lotto. Some said he used to be a low-down-dirty pimp. Said his Momma was a witch from Haiti, and she washed the Mob's dirty money. She cast spells and knew where the bodies were buried. Henry was her only living son, and when she died, she left him the GoGo Strip Joint in Midtown. I heard all kinds of crazy rumors. Some said he believed in voodoo, but I never met that side of him.

All I know is, Hen had a good heart, and did right by his people when He bought the old House of Transformation and turned it into the Dream Center. On *Save a Soul Sunday*, The Dream Center had service, and opened its doors for anyone in need. They gave away food at the pantry, even had day care and job placement help.

*****

He was still Hen to me when Dominique and I went to his church for the first time. I was so nervous; I had no idea what to expect and I paused in the doorway. The choir looked alien in their white robes. A cold shiver went through me as I remembered the last time I'd stepped foot in a church. Momma's funeral when I was little and Momma's lifeless skin against my lips when I kissed her goodbye. I boldly stepped inside the church to see for myself was it really *my* Hen that was the star of this show.

*****

It took a minute for the initial shock to wash over me. I couldn't concentrate on a word he was saying because I was suddenly on fire.

Like flames, Random thoughts flashed through my mind.

Gotta turn in my application at the McDonald's down the street...

These too tight stripper heels is fuckin up my big toes...

The First lady of the church has crazy eyes...

Does she know about me?

I tried to think of anything other than the memory of his delicate touch, exploring every inch of me. His lips, kissing every part of my body, and I couldn't wait to be alone with him again.

*****

Later that evening, tucked under the covers, bolted behind locked doors in the sanctuary of my room at the Grand Hotel, he confessed to me, with an unhinged glint in his eye, that he had made his bed with the Devil, the night he met me.

Surely, he was joking.

But I could tell that he wasn't, as he reached in the nightstand and pulled out a small jewelry box.

"It belonged to my mother. It's very valuable. I want you to have it

No

The sincerity of thought was a wet slap in the face. His Haitian accent was thick and I looked away from his lips. His Eyes were Dead serious when he slid the delicate ring on my finger, and I wondered how he could stir my soul and stimulate my body at the same time.

That night, we read his favorite scriptures from the bible he had give me. I believed him when he said God Loved me despite the whorish life I'd chosen to live.

"Say it, Tray. I deserve to be loved." One morning he snuck up behind me. He knew I hated it when he saw me out of drag but He made me look in the mirror, and he whispered again and again in my ear, "I deserve to be loved," until I believed it myself.

He was always full of surprises. This time with a trip to Indianapolis. I'd be his "assistant" and go with him during the Regional Minister's conference.

I'd never met someone who knew my secret and loved me for it. Maybe it was my spiritual depravity that Hen could relate to. He'd been a liar and a thief, but God had changed his heart and delivered his soul. Every day he was fighting to stay right.

So, how can what we share, be right?

I knew the cracks in his family façade because I had tried to live that DL lie myself, many lifetimes ago. He'd forsaken his wife, who stood faithfully by his side despite his transgressions. Running from his wrongs he'd escape to my room in secret, and I swept open the doors to his madness. Praying and crying, some nights he'd fall asleep in my arms.

I knew that I was surely going to hell, I'd done too much sinning to be saved. But I played along anyway. I loved being myself with Hen. Plus, I needed a vacation.

Dominique

When the dumb bitch called me, it was three o'clock in the morning, and the Caller ID said it was an out of town number. Traynesha lucky I answered. But I already knew the trifling ho needed help. Bitch sounded like a hot mess. Girlfriend was Way Too high and completely hysterical.

I finally got her to calm down when she *said* she was stranded in Indianapolis with Pastor Henry and *begged* me to help get her home.

Bitch, where is Pastor? And she screamed,

Pastor Henry is dead.

My eyes were as wide as shit when she said:

Pastor Henry

Dead

next to me

in bed.

Well, first of all if a married preacher man, worth over $2 million, is laid out naked and dead next to you in bed, being stranded is the least of your worries.

"In fact, you need to change your ENTIRE perspective! This is about you and your freedom. Fuck him and get the fuck out. You Already got money THERE!"

I told the bitch to check his pockets. She found about $2000 and credit cards to choke a horse. She had me on speaker phone as she packed and took pictures of his credit cards. One was a joint account with his wife. I told her to use that one first. until the family finds out he's dead.

But first, and this is the best part, I told the dumb ho to take pictures.

"What Imma do with pi-pi-pictures?" she said between all this fake ass crying.

"Bitch! What you think?" She wasn't *that* stupid. I told her, don't look back and call me when she touched down. That was the last time I heard from her. Claudine, who works housekeeping at the Grand Hotel, was the first one to call me with the T.

Couldn't believe it when she *said* they found Traynesha stabbed to death in her room. Same room the good ole Reverend used to creep to.

You think this street life a game if you want to.

Oh *yes* child, everybody knew Miss Traynesha turned tricks over by Union and Martin Luther King. Made good paper too when she got herself all made up. *Kind-of* reminds you of a broke down Rihanna. I think that's where she met Henry.

Yes sir. Gonna miss that bitch. I used to tell her to sit her crazy ass down. Seems like she was always working some kind of root. But I gotta give it to her. Traynesha knew how to make her coins. They said she was worth it, talking more shit than a little bit.

These younger girls fucked up the game for us real women. All these fake titties and butt implants got these stupid tricks thinking they picked up a *real* woman. Probably that mouth is what killed her. Somebody said it was thirty-seven stab wounds. Fucked that pretty face up.

Now look at the bitch. Dead. Pastor Henry dead *in* bed with his tranny girlfriend. Don't get no better than that shit. Not that I have a problem with it. To each his own.

But I'm thinking to myself, really? Does your wifey know about this shit?

Wifey

Dear Jasmine:

I'm so sorry. I never meant to hurt you. You'll be my baby girl forever and I love you, and my Grandbaby more than life itself. I'm so proud of the woman you've become. Stay strong, because you're the only one who will know the whole truth after you read this letter.

You see I had no choice. Your father's secret indiscretion had gotten out of hand. For years I was silent when he strayed. When he left me for days and indulged his sick tendencies. I tried to remember how much I used to love him. I reminded myself of the man I married and the beautiful soul he had.

At first it was like my prayers had been answered when he won that money. You know how much it was a blessing for our family and the community. We created a ministry together and shelters for the homeless and in some ways your father was a prophet. But Henry was a troubled soul. He had a dark side, like me.

Please don't blame me for snuffing out that little bit of nothing, and that's what she was. A piece of trash, simple as that. That heathen took pictures. Horrible Pictures of your father, my husband, laid-out naked, in the hotel, where they found him. She was gonna tell and sell it all...

I had hired a private detective longtime ago, and I already knew about her scheming ways. So, I wasn't surprised when she called. I went to her room at the Grand with $5000 in cash the heifer told me to bring. I was ready to pay for her silence and be done with it all.

But I wasn't expecting her to be so pretty. She had a confidence that surprised me... so young and comfortable in her own skin. She said Henry loved her and would want her to be taken care of. I laughed in her *face, but she wasn't moved. She informed me that this $5,000 payment would be the first of many more payments to come.*

I KNEW THAT SHE WAS A MAN under all that fake hair and makeup. How could Henry love her, and a fireball of hatred and jealousy consumed me. I couldn't leave her room without making sure we were alone, and I checked her kitchenette for knives of which she had many. With the whisper that this would be our little secret, I slit her fine yellow flesh from ear to ear.

You already know the rest to be sure. They find her slashed to ribbons and I go mysteriously missing. The burden of hiding your father's truth is too much to live with. You will receive this letter and see the postmark from Niagara Falls, New York. I imagine you will call the authorities and alert them to my last confirmed whereabouts as well you should.

I made sure your father's ministry and business affairs were in order before I left. There will be no open casket for me. Please forgive me.

With my Everlasting Love,
Your Mother

Black Mack
Michael Bracken

I rubbed my sweating palms on my faded blue jeans and looked out the living room window at my aging red Peterbilt.

"You can't go out there," my old lady pleaded, her voice on the ragged edge of fear. Her blue eyes were red and puffy; she'd been crying most of the evening.

"I'll be okay," I told her.

"But they killed that guy up north a few weeks ago," she said, pushing herself up from the couch and walking toward me.

"I'll be okay," I repeated. "I can't afford to sit out the strike. I've got a $2,800 payment on the truck next week and the company's willing to double my usual fee for hauling a load to Chicago."

Betty fell into my arms, her long brown hair cascading over my thick forearms.

"I don't want anything to happen to you," she said.

"If I don't drive, I lose the truck. You remember what happened during the last strike." We had been two days away from repossession of my truck, hadn't eaten any real food in a week, and I'd damned near taken Fat Freddie's offer for the Harley I had sitting in the garage. I couldn't go through that again.

"I don't care about the truck," she said between tears. "I care about you."

I stroked her hair with my thick fingers and felt her body shake with silent sobs. "The truck, the bike, and you," I said. "That's all I got."

"John," Betty whispered as she turned her face upward toward mine. "Before you go...?"

I took her chin in my hand and held her face while I pressed my mouth against hers. Betty's full red lips parted, and I slid my tongue into her mouth, tasting the beer we'd shared during the late news.

Finally, I pulled away from her. "It's time to go."

"John?"

"Yes?" I turned from the door and looked back at her. Fear had returned to her face.

"Call me when you get there."

I blew her a kiss, then stepped outside and walked to the Peterbilt. I climbed into the cab, feeling the comfortable bulk of the seat quickly form itself to my shape as I settled into place.

The engine roared to life beneath me and I took one last look at the house, saw Betty standing in the doorway and saw the Harley parked neatly in the center of the garage. Then I drove the truck down the street away from the house and toward the highway. Driving bobtail — without a trailer — made the Peterbilt handle like a two-ton sports car, and I made good time.

Across town, I turned off the highway, downshifted several times, and eased up to a loading dock. I checked with the man in charge, then backed my cab under a load of frozen foods. With help from the guys on the dock — one of them a fellow biker with heavy alimony payments — I quickly hooked up the pneumatic and electrical cables on the truck, double-checked everything myself, then gathered the paperwork and climbed into the cab. I tried my best to ignore the picketers at the far end of the dock entrance. I hated to cross their line, and they hated me for doing it, but this was a question of survival. When I eased the truck toward them, they yelled "Scab!" and worse, but they didn't damage the truck.

My goal was Chicago by dawn and as I eased the Peterbilt and the trailer load of frozen food onto the highway, I realized how easy the trip had been in the days before the truckers' strike, and I realized how many times I'd cruised the same highway with Betty on the back of my bike and the wind whipping through our hair.

I wiped my hands on my jeans, then used the sleeve of my shirt to wipe the steering wheel dry. The highway stretched dark and empty before me and I slowly eased the truck up to the speed limit, and then edged beyond it when I'd passed Smokey's favorite hiding places just outside the city.

Half an hour later my CB crackled, and I heard the first of a series of voices shouting "Scab!" as I passed a usually busy truck stop filled with idled semis.

I saw no other trucks on the six-lane highway, so I knew the insults were meant for me. Even though I sympathized with my brother truckers, I couldn't afford to let my truck sit idle. For me it was a simple matter of drive it or lose it. I lowered the volume on my CB, realizing that important information might cross the airwaves despite the various insults hurled my way.

The insults from the idled truckers at the truck stop had almost ceased when a new voice crackled through the CB. "Hey there, good buddy in the cab-over-pete," the voice said. "I hope you got your ears on 'cause this here's the strike enforcer. 10-4."

I listened, but I didn't respond.

I pressed my foot a little more heavily on the accelerator, watching the speedometer needle creep past 65 M.P.H. and edge its way toward 70.

"Look, motherfucker in the big red one," the voice called. "We got you in our sights. You won't deliver that load, good buddy."

I swore to myself and snapped off the CB. I couldn't tell if the asshole on the other end was making idle threats or if he somehow meant to keep them. Beads of sweat formed on my forehead. I wiped at them with my shirtsleeve and watched the empty highway stretch into the darkness ahead. The rearview mirrors showed me nothing coming from behind. I was alone on the road.

I relaxed, thinking the strike enforcer was nothing but mouth. After all, Illinois had been a pretty safe state to drive through since the start of the strike.

The further I got from the truck stop, the better I felt. I calmed down, my body slowly becoming one with the Peterbilt I'd driven most of my life. I felt the highway beneath me as the truck continued rolling toward the Windy City.

Before long I was safely away from the city and the truck stops that surrounded it, flying through the night on Peterbilt wings. I watched carefully as I passed an occasional car or saw one approaching in one of the southbound lanes. I laughed at a candy-ass with an unmodified Honda when I saw him pull off the road cursing and kicking at the bike.

For almost an hour after I switched off the CB, the trip was incident-free. It stayed that way until a brick crashed through the front passenger window as I drove beneath an overpass. I cursed when the glass flew into my bare arms, cutting me with dozens of tiny sharp edges. Cold wind whistled through the broken window, and I shivered.

I switched the CB back on, then reached behind the seat for my thick wool jacket. While I put it on and zipped up the front, the CB crackled.

"You deaf, good buddy? When the strike enforcer tells you to pull over, you better pull that cab-over-pete off the fucking road. The next time it'll be worse than a brick." The CB crackled quietly for a moment, then from it came, "You got your ears on, motherfucker?"

I didn't respond. I'd finished almost half the trip and I knew I couldn't stop. I couldn't let the striking truckers beat me out of my truck payment. I couldn't let them destroy everything I'd worked for.

A pair of headlights swept down the on-ramp and gained on me. I glanced down at the speedometer, saw I was pushing 75 M.P.H., and realized the car coming up behind me wasn't any late-night joy rider.

I listened to the insults as the car behind me continued gaining, my anger rising. I grabbed the microphone and shouted into it. "The Windy City Express don't stop his truck for no chicken-assed mothers."

"You'll learn, buddy-boy," came the response.

Before long, a late-model brown station wagon with no license plates cut into the center lane in front of me, and the voice crackled through the CB again.

"This is the strike enforcer, good buddy. You pull that Peterbilt off this fucking highway or you're a dead man. You read me?"

The rear window of the wagon opened and a man in a full-face ski mask poked his head out to stare at me. He pointed a gloved finger toward my face, then pulled a rifle from the rear of the station wagon, braced himself carefully, and took aim.

"You had your chance Windy City Express," my CB crackled. "Now you're dead."

I swore. Before I could respond, the man in the ski mask pulled the trigger. A bullet crashed through the remaining glass on the passenger side and struck the roof. I turned the wide steering wheel sharply to get out of the line of fire, but a second bullet punctured the glass in front of me. Then a third bullet ripped into my arm.

I swore again and pulled my foot from the accelerator. The weight of my load helped slow the truck, and the station wagon continued to move on for a moment. Then red brake lights glowed on the wagon's tail and the distance between us closed again.

The CB crackled and I heard a new voice: male and deep-throated.

"This here's the Black Mack," it said, "and I want my good buddy in the cab-over-pete to put the hammer down tight."

I touched my bleeding arm with my good hand — it was sore as hell, but I figured I could get by — then gripped the steering wheel with both hands. My left hand felt wobbly, not closing tightly enough around the hard plastic of the wheel. I told myself it was just the wind and the cold.

When I looked up at the road again, the gunman in the ski mask had repositioned himself, aiming at my cab again. I glanced into the left side mirror and saw a black and chrome Mack truck pulling up along my rear in the fast lane. The gunman barked some order to his driver and the station wagon swerved over into the slow lane ahead of me; now the rifleman had a straight-across shot at me through the broken glass of my windshield. He fired, the bullet spitting over my ducked head and blasting out the window beside me as the Black Mack passed me, its chrome gleaming in the moonlight and the red glow of brake lights. The Mack's air horn roared long and hard as its long silver trailer pushed past the nose of my truck and moved into my lane.

I heard a voice swear into the CB, but the broadcast crackled into silence. I pulled off on the gas, leaving the Mack beside the wagon. The man in the ski mask, hanging half out of the rear of the station wagon, twisted to stare at the silver trailer and the night-black cab. He fired at the Mack, aiming for the massive tires, but missed. Then he spun around toward me and fired two more quick rounds. But I had pulled sharply back into the right-hand lane, and his shots disappeared harmlessly into the night.

I stomped on the accelerator, shifted twice, and rammed into the rear of the station wagon, spilling the masked gunman to the highway and under my Peterbilt. If he screamed, the roar of two huge diesel engines drowned him out.

The Mack started to move over into the right lane and into the station wagon, bumping the little vehicle with its big rear tires. The wagon skidded over the gravel shoulder, then corrected itself, shooting back onto the highway and ahead of the Mack.

I heard the scream of the Mack's engine as the driver shifted, pushing the black and chrome rig ahead of the station wagon again. The driver faked a lane-change ahead of the wagon, twisted the wheel again, and let the chrome trailer slam into the side of the station wagon. Ahead of me, the wagon twisted right, then left, then right again, spun out of control onto the shoulder, then nose-dived into an open culvert. The last I saw of it was in my right rearview. It flipped over and landed on its roof. I'd put a good quarter of a mile between me and the wagon when I saw the red and orange flash of an explosion. The sound came a moment later.

The deep voice returned to the CB with a laugh. "Follow me, good buddy," the voice said. "You've got a load to deliver."

I wrapped my left hand weakly around the CB mike. "Black Mack, you suppose we ought to do something about those friends of ours back there?"

The CB spit static and Black Mack answered, "Those bastards

weren't friends of any trucker, good buddy. You just lay your hammer down as hard as you can now, 'cause you got a load on a reefer gonna get spoilt if you don't. 10-4."

Chilling wind bit my face as it whistled through the broken windshield. As bitter as the night cold was, I felt sleepy. I let my left arm drop to my lap and rest there, feeling thick wetness on the leather seat and on my pants.

"Hey, there, good buddy, you keep awake now," Black Mack called on the CB. "We ain't got but a little ways to go to Chi Town and you owe me 'bout three tall beers."

I laughed, putting my arm back on the wheel, letting the thick fingers wrap around the grip. Black Mack shot ahead on the highway, and I sped up to follow, keeping his yellow and red rear lights right in front of me. Bands of pain tightened across my chest and a fog kept clouding my mind, but I answered Black Mack's call. For the next two and a half hours I followed the black and chrome rig, a two-truck convoy chewing up the highway. The driver's deep voice hammered at me the entire time, joking, singing off-key, talking about roadside women and some damn fine bikes, and forcing me to stay awake when the only thing in the world I wanted to do was sleep.

Just before dawn, almost an hour ahead of schedule, I followed Mack into the truck terminal where I was to deliver my frozen load. Black Mack rolled to a stop near the gate and gave me a long air horn salute as I eased my red Peterbilt to a halt near a loading dock.

Then a wave of nausea swept over me, and I blacked out.

When I woke, I was looking up at the Chicago dispatcher. The first thing I thought of was trouble — for me. I shouldn't have passed out in my truck. But I wasn't in my truck. I was in a hospital bed.

"Did you call my wife?" I asked.

He nodded. "She's on her way. She said somethin' about some guys havin' your hog polished and purrin' by the time you get back."

I tried to smile; Betty knew just what I'd be thinking of. The pain in my arm and the painkillers they'd given me made my thoughts and my mouth work slowly, though.

"You know Black Mack?" I managed to ask.

"Sure, Bud McKay. Big guy with a black and chrome Mack. Helluva guy."

"What kinda beer does he drink?"

The dispatcher patted my good arm. "Why don't you just settle back, huh? Think about drinkin' beer later. You almost bought it last night. When we pulled you from the cab of your Peterbilt, you were soaked in blood. Doctor said you was runnin' on empty, just about."

"What...what kind of beer?" I repeated weakly.

"Oh, Mack? Any kind. Never mattered, sure as hell doesn't matter now. Helluva trucker but not one for unions. Too bull-headed, if you ask me." The dispatcher looked around for nurses, saw none, and pulled a cigarette from his pocket.

"Lousy singing voice, too," I said.

The dispatcher nodded with a grin. "That's the truth. I didn't figure you knew him."

"Yeah," I answered slowly. "He helped me finish the run up here last night. I owe him a beer."

The Chicago dispatcher took a long drag from his cigarette. "Black Mack quit driving years ago," he said. "Would be 65 or 70 by now. His kid was a trucker, too. Down near Bloomington about two weeks ago some goons took potshots at Mack's kid. The kid and his rig went over a guardrail and blew up. Never did find out who did it."

He took another long drag from his cigarette. "The only things Mack had in this world were his kid and his truck. Kept the truck parked in his back yard."

"And Mack? Where's he now?" I asked.

"Downstairs," the dispatcher said. "Everyone was so worried about you... McKay was dead before anyone thought to check his rig. One shot punctured his lung, same caliber as the one they pulled outta you. We found McKay slumped over the wheel, clutching a picture of his boy."

The dispatcher and I sat in silence for a long, long time.

Package of Pain
Kevin R. Tipple

Mike Thornstein sat in his truck in front of his own house as a light drizzle coated the windshield. The package was there again, even though it wasn't supposed to be. He had been promised by everyone that it was all over. The investigation was supposed to have ended months ago. He had been cleared, publicly exonerated, but nothing changed.

It sat there wrapped in plain brown paper on his stoop. When they first started showing up every Friday like clockwork, his colleagues had searched for the sender. Each one had been mailed from a mailbox in Fort Worth. Television had "Walker," but all Mike had were bureaucratic bosses who decided the packages weren't a threat. When the sender wasn't identified after a few weeks, manpower and resources were delegated elsewhere. Mike was still on suspension while awaiting assignment, albeit very unofficially, and the packages were still coming. Something had to be done to end it.

The windshield wipers slapped across clearing the glass. Visible again, the package sat there waiting for him. He turned the engine off and listened to it tick as it cooled. The glass slowly misted over as the drizzle continued. The package dissolved from view into globs of water on the glass. Sitting there, watching the mist fall, wasn't going to solve the problem.

Mike heaved himself out of his old truck and crossed the leaf-strewn yard. Rain and wind had stripped most of the leaves off the trees, leaving just a few to decorate the leaden sky. Everything dripped water and matched his mood perfectly.

The package was small and light, just like all the others. Wrapped in brown paper and twine, it bore the Fort Worth postmark from the downtown office. Beyond that, it was like all the others and would offer up no clues as to the sender. Mike shook it softly as he looked in vain for a return address. Nothing rattled, and it fit in the crook of his arm as he fumbled with the door lock.

Mike got the door open, stepped in and back-kicked the door shut. He wandered into the den and placed the package on the coffee table. His coat went onto the couch as he headed to the kitchen.

The refrigerator beckoned, and he grabbed a beer made from some river out in the Rockies. All beer tasted the same, but this one had been on sale. His only preference was for long-necked bottles. Beer wasn't supposed to come any other way. The top went flying into the sink with a clatter, and Mike chugged the beer down in several large swallows. One soldier down and into the trash. A second one was pulled out and popped open. He took a long swallow and contemplated the job ahead. Fortified, he headed back for the den.

The bottle went onto a small table next to the recliner. Mike switched on the reading lamp and used a car key to slit the package open. Just like the others, there was purple tissue paper inside. He reached inside past the folds, and there was the expected DVD. It was labeled "Continued" in block letters. He popped it into the disk player and, as it began to play, he hit the stop button. The tabs were snapped out so it couldn't be recorded over, and he wasn't ready to watch. The homemade DVDs were a recent addition to the packages and made even less sense than the weird letters.

He sat in the recliner with the package in his lap. He swallowed some more beer while he contemplated the box. The bottle went back to the table, making another wet ring to join its companion. Mike reached deeper into the box and found what he was looking for. Black lace brushed against his fingers as he pushed the tissue paper back. Nestled on the panties was one small bullet with a lipstick mark at the tip. It sounded like some stupid detective novel from the forties, but it was all too real. It was nice to know that this wasn't a threat, according to the bigshots downtown. He wasn't reassured.

Mike twirled the panties on his finger, whipping them through the air. Now he had almost half of a month's worth of panties and they were still coming. This was the sixth bullet, all sealed with a kiss. He knew what he was going to see on the disk; it had been a variation on a theme. He didn't want to watch, but he had too. He tossed the empty box and punched the remote.

The machine whirred to life as he settled back in the recliner. The screen went white with static and then black as the recording began. Words appeared out of focus and slowly sharpened. Some things never change, Mike thought, as the familiar saying appeared. Block letters on white poster board sharpened on screen. Nothing new there at all. The camera pulled back as Mike began to read out loud to the silent room.

"I know what you did. Prepare yourself for the ultimate sacrifice. You are the chosen one."

Whatever. Just like all the others. Originality was a wonderful thing. The screen image faded and then came back with the image of the now familiar woman. The camera focused on a figure on the bed. A woman — at least it appeared to be a woman — was on her back in a black dress and boots. Like before, she lay on her back on the bed with her legs spread open wide in invitation. A small cloth hooded part of her face and all of her hair. She rested quietly as the camera focused in on the pulse beating in her throat. It was obvious that it was beating pretty fast, and as the camera pulled back slightly, Mike could see her chest rise and fall.

He knew what was coming and wanted to fast-forward. At the same time, he was afraid of missing something important as to her identity. It looked like the same room, but the black dress was new. The camera panned down her shapely body and across her long legs. It focused back in tightly against a boot as music began to play in the background. As the beat quickened, the boot began to flex. Mike took another swig of beer and the phone rang.

Hell! It somehow figured just when he was starting to get into it. Part of him dreaded the packages and part of him was turned on. While he thought he knew exactly what he would see beforehand, there was something that made him watch it all. He needed a name to go with that body. He hit the Stop button hard and reached for the phone.

"Hello."

"Hey, Mike, how're they hanging?"

"Tender and unloved, like always," Mike answered.

Leroy guffawed in reply. The ritual greeting had gone back to when they were kids living at home. Leroy was now some hotshot salesman who believed there wasn't a woman he couldn't have. He'd had quite a few over the years and, as a perceived matter of charity, had steered a few Mike's way. Mike had a brooding way about him that most women, while attracted to, couldn't deal with long term. Usually the relationship flamed out in six months and, with a promise to call, the lady was gone.

"Are you still coming over here tonight?"

"Leroy, I'm not. It's been a bad week and I—"

"You got another package, man? Bring it along and we all can watch it and drink a few. Somebody will know her."

Leroy's parties were always the same. He always set Mike up to get laid. It usually ended in failure. The lady was stupid, drunk, easy, or some combination of everything. It just wasn't worth it to get off.

"No, Leroy. I'll pass. Party on without me."

"I'm not taking no for an answer. Shower, shave, and I'll be over to get you. That way you don't have to bring that heap of yours. Don't forget the disk."

He laughed and hung up before Mike could say a word. Mike listened to the dial tone for a few seconds before hanging up. Damn it! He picked the phone back up and punched out Leroy's number. All he got was the squawk of a busy signal. Leroy's newest wrinkle on brother relations, and Mike was tired of it. He kicked his shoes off and sagged back into the recliner. He punched the remote and snapped the reading lamp off as the screen lit the darkened room.

As the video began again, the camera was still focused on the black boot. After a few seconds more, it slowly panned back up the body and focused on the top button of her dress. Manicured fingers came into view as the woman undid the first button. The hands slowly slid down and popped a second button open, then a third. They drifted on down as she kept the dress closed. Soon all the buttons were undone, but her dress was still closed. The woman began to move in the bed and cupped her breasts through the dress.

Mike felt himself begin to respond despite his best intentions. He shifted in the recliner as he watched. It felt like she was performing for just him. He had a voyeuristic streak in him, but this was so much better than watching some woman undress through her blinds as he walked the neighborhood.

The woman cupped herself for another minute or so and then eased one hand lower. Her fingers slipped in between the folds of the dress as she touched herself. Her back arched upward and her dress spilled open to reveal her beautiful body.

Mike shifted again in the seat as he watched. Every week it was a DVD of the same woman, but this was the first time she had actually undressed. Usually it was just her posing in various dresses. Over the weeks, the dresses had become more revealing, as if she were searching for the right dress for him. Sometimes the dress would gape open just right, showing him the full curve of a breast. There was something familiar about her, but since her face was always covered, he wasn't sure who she was. But this was the first time she had deliberately stripped for the camera.

Suddenly she sat up and stared hard right at the camera. Her face was still shadowed by the hood she wore, but the rest of her was very naked. The camera moved in fast until just her lips were in the frame.

"Mike, I hope you enjoyed yourself."

The huge lips twisted in what could have been a smile but could just as easily have been a grimace. It was hard to tell.

"Get cleaned up, and I'll see you at Leroy's. I'll bring another DVD just for you. We'll watch it together."

Another first. Now he knew what her voice sounded like. Husky, but arousing in that whisky sounding voice way. Sure was a weird way to get a date, but maybe that worked for her.

He thought the video was over, but as he reached for the remote, she spoke again. "Trust me, Mike. All your questions will be answered. You will get all this and more, everything you deserve and then some. Later, lover."

The screen slowly blurred and faded to black. The disk stopped and the player displayed the main menu again. He suspected, like the others, the disk had been finalized, so nothing could be added to it.

"Well, that was cryptic," he muttered as he headed for the bathroom.

The shower thundered on, and he soaped himself head to toe as he thought about the mystery woman. She was beautiful, and he wanted her, but he couldn't figure out what her game was. A bullet in a bra didn't make sense. Hell, the whole thing didn't make sense. Who sends packages to people showing themselves naked in a video? The shock of the cold water as the hot water ran out snapped him out of his reverie, and he shivered as he got out.

The doorbell rang as he slid on a fresh pair of pants. He was only half-dressed as he grabbed the towel for another pass at his hair. It didn't matter what he looked like; it was Leroy, after all, and he was late picking him up. Mike ran down the hall and pulled the door open.

"Leroy, where the hell—"

It wasn't Leroy. This was an incredibly beautiful woman who was quite clearly slumming if she was at his door. Lips beneath gorgeous brown eyes parted, and she smiled softly.

"Leroy said you were my type, and for once he was right. Why don't you invite me in while you finish getting dressed?"

She pulled the screen door open. He could feel her chest push through her black strapless dress as she brushed against him. He closed his mouth while she strolled down the hall. No, he thought. She didn't stroll; she floated like an angel. His thoughts of what she could do weren't angelic at all.

"Well, make yourself at home."

He pushed the door closed as Mrs. Peabody across the way looked out her front windows. Mike thought about waving at the old busybody, but the damage was done. The phone lines would heat up as she called all the neighbors. The old guys would wink and nod at him tomorrow from their porches, and the women would shake their heads in disgust. If everyone would stay out of everyone else's life, the world would be such a better place.

"I don't mind if I do," she answered. "I hear you have beer; I'm going to get one. You want one?"

"I'm good. Thanks."

"We'll see about that."

Mike heard the refrigerator open as he went back down the hall. Her voice was husky the way he liked in a woman, and here she was offering him one of his own beers. Unbelievable. Nothing sexier than a woman with attitude and the body to back it up. He turned the corner and stepped into the den.

She stood there, looking at his mail as she lightly ran the wet bottle across the top of her dress. That dress could come off so easily.

He grabbed the mail out of her hands and slid it into an open drawer of his desk. He pushed the drawer closed and looked at her. All he really wanted to do was gaze into those eyes as he made love to her. It must be the aftereffects of the video, he thought. Two women playing games this much in the same evening was too much to handle.

"Are you in the habit of barging into a guy's house and helping yourself to beer? Or reading his mail, for that matter?"

Her eyes twinkled as she smiled. The bottle slowly went up to her parted lips, and she took a long, slow swallow. Her neck stretched back as she tipped and drank the last of the beer. Foam slid down the inside of the bottle and into her mouth. She turned and tossed the empty into the trash.

"I'm sorry, but I really needed that. My name is Lauren, and Leroy sent me over. He thought I should pick you up and convince you to come to the party."

Her hands went behind her back as she stepped forward and looked up at him. She was so very close.

"That is, if I can't convince you to do other things." One fingernail grazed his chest lightly. "Let's party."

The phone rang as Mike was trying to figure out what to say. Talk about being saved by the bell. He went into the kitchen to answer it as Lauren put the TV on.

It was Leroy checking to see if his ride had shown up. He wanted to discuss how hot she looked until Mike convinced him he would never get there unless Leroy let him get dressed. Leroy laughed and suggested a possibility with Lauren and hung up. It probably wasn't legal here.

She waved at him with the remote as he went back into the bedroom.

"Don't get dressed on my account."

He was saved from replying by the blare of the laugh track of some cable show. Mike dressed quickly and ran a comb through his hair. He was done and ready for whatever. Lauren had already switched the TV off and was waiting by the open front door.

"Let's party," she said as he grabbed a light jacket and followed her to the car.

The woman definitely liked black. Her car was a beautiful old black Camaro. He slid into the passenger seat and snapped the seat belt on. The car thundered to life as she put it into gear. She drove with confidence as she sped down the dark residential streets. Leroy always did give good directions, and she drove like she knew the area.

Soon they were out of the neighborhood and headed towards the interstate. Mike glanced over at Lauren and noticed her dress had slid up one leg, exposing a creamy white thigh. It flashed in the streetlights with an almost hypnotic strobe effect. Her muscles bunched and released as she worked the accelerator, moving the car through traffic. He looked up from her legs and straight into her eyes. Lauren smiled and swung her attention back to the road. The dress was left where it was. He smiled to himself. Maybe this evening was going to be fun after all.

She whipped the car around a couple of corners and up the ramp to the interstate. The car roared as they headed north. The radar detector chirped away as they passed a row of restaurants.

"My uncle had this car before he died," Lauren said.

Her voice had changed as well as her attitude. She wasn't playful at all now. She seemed hurt and angry as she whipped the car from lane to lane, avoiding slower traffic. The radar detector kept up a steady squeal as yet more restaurants, with full parking lots, flashed by.

"What happened?"

She didn't answer, but glanced up at the moon roof. The drizzle had stopped, and it looked like the clouds were beginning to part. She snapped the lock and opened the moon roof slightly as she glanced over at him.

"Some bastard shot him and my brother one night."

The car leapt forward as she accelerated around and in front of a semi. The horn blared on the semi. Lauren gave him the finger out the moon roof. She tapped the brakes at the same time, flashing the lights at him, and then punched it, leaving the truck in our dust.

She was way past anything legal, and this was not the time to put a stop to it. Mike understood the need for speed to run from the demons; he had been guilty of this same stupidity. Questions would have to wait.

He settled back in the seat as the car flashed past other drivers, all alone in the night. He was so tired and Lauren seemed to have everything under control. The speed seemed almost peaceful as the tires hummed on the road. Sure, she was going too fast, but there was a certain beauty to it all.

He suddenly became aware that the car had stopped and he was alone. Apparently he had fallen asleep. Mike popped the belt loose and eased the door open. He was nauseous as he stood and felt sweat break out on his forehead. He shivered and leaned over right before he threw up on the gravel. It splashed into the parking lot as the breeze ruffled his hair. Finished, he turned and surveyed the area. Where was Lauren?

It looked like they were just below the dam at the lake. The interstate rumbled as the traffic passed along the top of the dam making the headlights twinkle in the night. The Corps of Engineers had dredged out a deep channel in the old riverbed. Then they had created another smaller lake with its own dam below the large lake and it looked like they were parked near the public dock area for that lake. This was not the way to Leroy's place. He walked forward a little bit and stepped out on the dock.

The boards creaked as he walked out above the black water. Mike walked to the end of the dock, but there wasn't a sign of Lauren anywhere. All he could see was the occasional light from the shore twinkling as it was reflected in the still water. A board creaked behind him, and he turned around. He was starting to get a bad feeling about things, and the puzzle pieces were slowly dropping into place. Talk about stupid.

It was Lauren, and she had the drop on him. It was too dark to tell what kind of gun it was. It really didn't matter; he was defenseless.

"This is it, Mike. You made it so easy for me."

He didn't say anything.

She asked, "Don't you even want to know why?"

"I want whatever you want, Lauren." He slid one foot forward toward her ever so gently. "Why don't you—"

The muzzle flashed and the gun roared as the bullet smashed through the dock inches from his foot.

"I forgot to tell you not to move just yet, Mike. I won't remind you again."

She wasn't making sense and he was worried. Maybe the shot would bring help.

"No one can save you. I promised you'd get what was coming to you, and you will."

"Lauren, I—"

"You killed my uncle and brother, so I started sending the packages.

I wanted to fuck with your mind, not your body." Her voice shook with rage. "I planned for this night. I found out who your friends were, what you liked, every disgusting thing!"

Her voice screeched with her rage. He wasn't sure what to say. Her hands were shaking, and it was clear she was close to the edge.

"They were drug dealers, Lauren. They were the ones that started shooting. I didn't have a choice." He eased a little to the side, closer to the edge of the dock.

"Fucking murderer!" she screamed as the gun fired. His shoulder exploded into pain as he spun off the dock and into the water. He swallowed cold water and choked as he struggled to get to the surface through the inky blackness. He started to panic as he realized he couldn't see a thing.

Suddenly he surfaced and smacked into the underside of the dock, cutting his forehead open. Mike sputtered and spat out water as Lauren stalked across the dock above him. He was freezing as Lauren was screaming something while she kept shooting into the water. It seemed like she never was going to run out of bullets. A shot splintered the dock above and just behind him, burying itself into the wet pillar next to his hand. Then all was quiet.

Mike let the current ease him back out from under the dock. His shoulder felt like it was on fire, and he was sick to his stomach. He was shivering in the water, but he wasn't cold anymore. It was getting very hard to think.

The current pushed and shoved him closer to shore. It pulled him down one final time, before throwing him up and onto the shore. His feet snagged on the shoreline as the taillights of the Camaro came on. Lauren was leaving.

Mike pulled himself up on a rock as the car thundered away. The sound disappeared, but he could see the taillights as it rocketed up the access road along the side of the dam. She was heading back to the interstate.

He waited for the brake lights to flash. But in her rage, she ran the stop sign as she pulled out onto the interstate. The car leapt forward but was no match for the momentum of the tractor-trailer rig that had the speed and the right of way. Metal screeched and sparks flew as the truck pushed the car along the guardrail. Then there was a horrible wail that sounded almost human as the car climbed up and over the guardrail.

The car flipped over and bounced off the front wall of the dam. More sparks trailed behind as it silently fell. The silence was shattered with a thunderclap and then a roar as the falling car ignited into a fireball. Flaming debris plunged down the face of the dam, crashing into the park below. The jackknifed truck was stopped in the middle of the dam grinding everything to a halt. People were out of their cars to join the confusion as they looked down the dam to the smoldering wreckage.

Sirens started in the distance. As Mike turned around, he was lit up by a searchlight from a boat. He waved weakly at it and it suddenly accelerated toward him. White foam curled from the bow, as the blue lights of the police boat began to strobe around him. Help was on the way, but it was a little too late for everyone.

The Brothers Jackson
William Flores

In a news conference late Sunday afternoon, along with his 1st Grade Detective John Barley, NYPD Chief of Homicide Detectives Nicky Calucci gave the following update on the murder of a longtime Queens resident:

"On June 18, 1982, Jimmy Jackson was found dead after being tied up and shot twice in the head. Mr. Jackson's body was discovered by his younger brother Alex Jackson in a back bedroom in their home in Springfield Gardens, Queens, New York. At the time of the discovery, around 7:00PM last evening, it was determined Mr. Jackson had been dead for approximately 24 hours. No signs of forced entry were apparent. It's believed the victim knew his killer and let him into his home willingly. The victim was a 35 year old Black man who lived with his brother over the last three decades.

"No leads have been obtained regarding the identification of the killer thus far. All information from the public leading to a possible suspect would be appreciated and held in the strictest of confidence. We are still in the beginning stages of our investigation, interviewing family and friends, and continue to talk with others who knew the victim. Further updates on this case will be given to the public as they unfold."

Calucci, eager to finish his business with the press, could hardly wait to leave the building. When he did depart, he headed crosstown. He had other pressing matters needing his attention and couldn't wait around to answer more questions from the reporters. He'd told them everything he knew, and didn't have any more to give to anyone. All he wanted was to relax with his mistress. His need to be with her overwhelmed him at this point.

*****

It'd been a week since Calucci had been home or seen his wife and kids. He knew he'd have to first stop by his house to spend some time with them before going to see his side chick Delores Flores. He'd hoped however his family visit would add a bit of peace to their tumultuous relationship. Life at home was at its all-time worst for Calucci. His family hardly saw him, and when they did, it was mostly in passing. He'd be in and out, and used his work as an excuse to be away from their lives.

Unlike his partner Barley, whose wife and family were loving, and spent holidays and weekends together, Calucci couldn't wait to escape to his hidden life. He knew he'd get what he wanted there, and wouldn't be disappointed as he was with his own family. Calucci's love for his wife had died a long time ago. She'd become colder than ever with her husband. In fact, he referred to her as "The Ice Queen" because of her frigidity and refusal to be intimate with him. It'd been years since he last touched her, and she was happy for it.

On the other hand, Calucci and Delores had been in love and business for years. Delores was an old-time street hustler who'd played her hand well. Her and Calucci met ten years ago when she was working the track in Long Island City, and he was investigating a double homicide of two of her friends who'd been murdered by some trick looking for a night of pleasure. They'd struck up a partnership in which their professional skills were used to satisfy, not only themselves, but others in the underbelly of a world they knew best.

Delores fulfilled his most debased needs. She was his business and sexual partner combined. She'd run their trap house and stable of working girls, while he'd provide her cocaine and weed by the weight that he'd steal from precincts' evidence rooms across the city. They both profited and enjoyed their arrangement.

*****

Calucci couldn't fathom how his personal and professional lives were disasters, and like a hurricane, were ruining practically everyone in his path. His drug and alcohol addictions had completely destroyed him emotionally, and left him feeling like he was dying inside on most days. Outwardly though, he wore a mask, a fake front he portrayed to the world of being fearless and courageous, upholding justice. In public, he appeared as a symbol of good and all that was right. He was the top cop. Internally, however, he'd been driven insane by his personal demons called guilt, shame and remorse, from living a sordid double life. He abused drugs and alcohol to blunt his reality, self-medicate, for not being able to meet his personal responsibilities to family and friends.

Professionally, Calucci was a master detective, and held the keys of power and authority amongst men and women on the force. In his professional capacity, he was a high ranking City official with power and control over others. Yet, his sick need to live wildly compelled him toward danger in this world even more. Living on the razor's edge pushed him to no end. Calucci was more than proficient at catching killers, he was brilliant at tracking down the murderers of society and putting them behind bars. He was notorious for his diligence and ability to pay attention to detail. His keen detective skills caused him to be noticed by his superiors early on in his career as he rose up quickly amongst the ranks.

Calucci was very successful at hiding behind his badge and gun. It allowed him to indulge his demons whenever he wanted. It led him astray from his life's work and purpose in the first place. He'd been corrupted for years now, living a life of crime and breaking the very laws he swore to uphold. Deviating from his personal and professional oaths, strict codes of conduct and ethics was driving him to self-destruct. He seemed to be a breakdown waiting to happen.

*****

Calucci stayed at the trap house with Delores for the entire weekend and never made it home. He arrived at his office on Monday afternoon, bleary-eyed and hungover. He was determined to apprehend the murderer of Mr. Jimmy Jackson and bring justice to the Jackson family. Calucci believed the community of Springfield Gardens deserved no less. The question remained however, would he be able to catch the killer in his present mental state of mind?

"Well Barley, what have you got so far in the victimology of this case?"

"It's still too early in the case to tell. My detectives are running down leads on who the victim's friends and associates were, and any lady friends he might have been seeing. We understand, as reported by the dead man's brother, the victim had one main girlfriend. Her name is Caledonia Brown. She's a White woman who lives on Guy Brewer Boulevard near 137th Avenue. I've got men checking out her background and personal data as we speak."

"That's always a good place to start. Okay, let me know where that goes, and get back to me as soon as possible."

"Right, will do."

Days later, Barley huddled with his detectives and afterwards met with Calucci to report his latest update.

"We got preliminary results from the Crime Scene Investigation "CSI" guys. They took photos of bloody shoe prints left at the scene and collected other trace evidence they're still going through. They're checking fingerprints lifted in the house as well. Jimmy Jackson was some character. He's had several minor brushes with the law. According to his rap sheet, he received light slaps on the wrists each time. Mr. Jimmy Jackson had been arrested for misdemeanors, shoplifting, theft of services for sneaking on the subway, and petty theft."

"Has he been convicted on any of these charges?"

"Yes he has. Mr. Jackson was placed on probation for eighteen months for his third shoplifting conviction a year ago. His probation officer gave us a psychosocial history filled with deep insights into his life. I believe this data should reveal a lot about our victim."

"Well, I'm sure you'll give me the details on how Jimmy Jackson's inner springs worked. But first, tell me about his White girlfriend. What's her name, Caledonia Brown?"

"Right, Caledonia Brown. She'd been seen with our victim for the last several months. They were the new couple around town. I understand they lived together on and off in her home. Most folks said they were a young interracial couple in love and would be seen displaying affection in public places. Though others we spoke with said as a couple they appeared weird together, almost like a fat and skinny team; since she's a tiny little, petite blonde woman, and he was a large, really Black complected man. Neighbors informed they'd heard fighting and arguing and saw him get violent with her in the past. He blackened her eyes several times, but she'd always take him back."

"That's interesting. Ms. Brown certainly has a good reason to harm Mr. Jackson, that's for sure. What's your take on her?"

"Well, we're still chasing down some other information on Ms. Brown."

"Like what?"

"We understand Ms. Brown has a long history of mental illness. By her own admission, she'd been hospitalized several times in Creedmore Psychiatric Center. It's a State hospital for the mentally ill here in Queens. And from what we can gather, Ms. Brown suffers from schizophrenia. She has a history of having homicidal and suicidal ideations and has been observed hallucinating in public. This information was reported to our detectives by a few of her close friends.

"Ms. Brown has become violent with her own family members. She stabbed her twin brother during one of her breaks from reality. This attack on her brother, Maceo Brown, occurred when she was just twenty-two years old which led to her first diagnosis of schizophrenia and hospitalization at Creedmoore. She stabbed her brother in his left arm and hand for which he required twenty stitches to close his wounds."

"Wow, sounds like we got a sick one on our hands, a violent little firecracker at that. What else did you uncover?"

"Get ready for this Chief. Ms. Brown, during her last four month hospitalization stay at Creedmoore, met Mr. Jimmy Jackson while he was there as an in-patient. Mr. Jackson also has a history of mental illness. He's been known to have, on several occasions, exposed himself and sexually harassed women in public. His hospital stays at Creedmoore were due to perverted public sexual displays. He's a known stalker of women in and around Queens. Once discharged, Ms. Brown met up with Mr. Jackson and the two of them were together up until his death."

"How tight is her alibi?"

"Funny thing, her alibi checked out. She claimed to have stayed with one of her girlfriends during the last week of Mr. Jackson's life, after kicking him out of her house for the umpteenth time. Her alibi had been verified in several ways. She had receipts and other witnesses supporting it."

"Okay, so now where are we? What about the probation officer's report on Mr. Jimmy Jackson? What does that tell us?"

"It tells us plenty. Mr. Jackson had a pretty rough life, filled with problems from the very start. Actually, it was a tragic life.

*****

"Jimmy Jackson, was a foster child, placed in the care of Ms. Mary Rollins at the young age of six, along with his four year old biological kid brother Alex. When they reached 16 and 14 years old respectively, they moved from Staten Island to Springfield Gardens, Queens; along with 11 year old Mailliw Serolf, another foster child in the Rollins' household at that time. Jimmy and Alex were with Ms. Rollins for ten years. She was all they'd ever known as a steady mother figure."

"Have you interviewed Ms. Mary Rollins yet?"

"That's not possible. She died several years ago of heart failure and left her home to the brothers Jackson.

Jimmy was a big boy. At 16 years old he stood 6'3", and weighed 175 pounds. He was really dark skinned with short cropped hair. He was teased a lot for his color. His temperament was usually jovial, but could fluctuate between anger and rage in an instant. Although registered, Jimmy seldom attended school. When he did go, he'd harass and stalk his female classmates; so much so, he'd been suspended on several occasions for aggressively forcing his unwanted attention on them. He'd make sexual advances toward young girls and was known for acting bizarre around campus. He'd been caught by teachers and classmates touching himself inappropriately in public and, even worse, grabbing their butts."

"Was Jimmy arrested for his predatory behavior?"

"After an attack on a female friend of his, Jimmy was arrested and mandated to Creedmore for observation and treatment. That was the first time he'd come to the attention of medical authorities for his bizarre and psychotic episodes. He'd been in and out of this institution ever since. When he took his medication, he'd be fine for a while; it's when he stopped taking it as prescribed, he'd run into trouble."

"What about his brother who found him, what's the scoop on him? Have you interviewed him yet?"

"Unlike Jimmy, Alex was the opposite of his older brother in most every way fathomable. As kids, they'd get into physical brawls, usually behind Alex's tormenting his brother about dropping out of school or being in trouble again. He seemed to get some sadistic pleasure from demeaning Jimmy. Alex could be cruel to Jimmy at times and Jimmy hated it.

"The more Alex baited his brother, the more violent Jimmy became. He once chased Alex with a butcher knife until Mary got between the two. By this time, Jimmy's temper and violent outbursts were growing intensely; and it took longer each time for Mary to calm him down. Everyone knew, but said nothing, Jimmy couldn't go on like this much longer. Not only was he angry and full of rage most days, his growing paranoia made Jimmy's life a living hell."

"So how do these two end up living together if they were at each other's throats all the time? Has there been any violence between the two since the death of Mary Rollins?"

"Yes, there's been several incidents where Jimmy attacked his brother, and luckily neighbors intervened."

"Were the police ever called in to make an arrest?"

"The police had been called but made no arrests. They'd calm down before police arrived. Alex never pressed charges against his brother even though he'd been bruised in one or two of their scuffles."

"How do we know this if Jimmy never was arrested for assaulting Alex?"

"Police made out written reports. They'd gone to check out domestic calls at the house but that was the extent of it."

"What type of alibi did Alex Jackson provide as to where he was at the time of Jimmy's death?"

"He claimed to have been at home working on an art project all weekend.

According to Alex, the only times he left home were to go to the store for groceries and to a restaurant for dinner. When he returned that evening, he found his brother's dead body."

"Who do you like at this point for the killing Barley?"

"I'm still not convinced of the brother's innocence. They did have a history of violence between the two with Alex coming out on the losing end most times. Also, his alibi hasn't yet been fully verified. I need to do more digging on Alex before I can be convinced otherwise."

"Okay, you do that. Get your men to checkout Alex's friends and local shop keepers where he supposedly went that weekend. Meanwhile, I'm going to find out more about Caledonia. There's something here that's eating at me."

"What's that?"

"Her alibi is just too perfect to be credible. We'll see. Let me know how you and your men make out with Alex."

*****

Two days later inside the station house, Barley met with Chief Calucci to update him on his latest findings regarding Alex Jackson.

"Any news? How did your hunch with Alex work out?"

Before he could give his findings, Calucci's phone rang.

"Calucci here. Yea, I understand. Where is she now? She is conscious, oh, okay. I'll be right over."

"That was a nurse from Jamaica Hospital. Caledonia was taken there after overdosing on her prescribed psychotropic medications late yesterday evening. She's come to and is able to talk now. She'll be transferred to Creedmoore once she's stabilized. I'm going to visit her to see what she has to say and find out why she tried to take his life. I'll catch up with you later."

"Okay Chief, I'll talk with you later."

*****

Calucci entered Caledonia's room and found her sitting up in bed. A nurse's aide stood nearby monitoring her. It was the first time he'd seen Caledonia. She was a pretty young woman, yet looked very troubled. After initial introductions, Calucci began:

"Ms. Brown, we are concerned about your health. How are you doing now?"

"I'm better, thanks."

"Why did you take all of those pills, why did you want to harm yourself?"

"I just felt so stressed. I don't want to go to jail for Jimmy dying."

"Did you kill Jimmy or know who did?

"No, I didn't. I don't know who killed Jimmy."

"Did you harm Jimmy in any way?"

"Well, kind of. I sort of harmed him. I hurt him when I threw him out. He wanted me back but I couldn't take his beatings anymore. I know, I loved him, and he loved me. We just couldn't be together, especially now that he's gone forever. I feel so badly how I treated him the last time I saw him."

Caledonia broke down in tears.

"It's okay Ms. Brown. Don't upset yourself. We're concerned about the death of your boyfriend. What can you tell me about how he died?"

"I really don't know anything about that. I wasn't anywhere around him that weekend, and hadn't seen Jimmy in over a week. I was with friends."

"With friends, huh? So why did your friends deny being with you on those times and days you said they were? Can you tell me why?"

Calucci lied to see how she'd respond.

"I don't know why they're against me. They want to get me in trouble."

"Okay, can you tell me anything else as to your whereabouts at the time in question?"

"I told your detectives all I know, I don't know anything else. If you don't believe me just ask my brother Maceo. He'll tell you, I was with my friend during the entire weekend. Maceo came by to see me and dropped off some money for me, $100. We hung out together for awhile and then he left me at my friend Althea Simmons' home."

"Okay, I'll ask him and Althea both. Meanwhile, get some rest and don't worry about anything. I'll be in touch. Goodbye Ms. Brown, feel better."

*****

Calucci checked with Caledonia's friend, Althea Simmons, at her home. She verified she was with Caledonia the weekend of Jimmy's murder. According to Althea, her and Caledonia spent many weekends together, and even partied with Jimmy and Alex in the past. They were tight for a time until Jimmy started being overprotective, paranoid, and hitting Caledonia. Maceo Brown told Calucci he'd stopped by Althea's and spent time with her and his sister on that weekend. He hadn't seen his sister since Jimmy and her fell out, over Jimmy beating her. He'd simply wanted to check on her, to make sure she was alright. When Calucci asked him if he'd dropped off anything for his sister while she was at Althea's, Maceo told Calucci he did.

"I left Caledonia $100 because she'd called me and said she was broke. This was another reason I went to see my sister."

Maceo Brown also confirmed he'd never visited his sister at the Jackson residence. He'd only been with Althea and Caledonia together in their own homes and in night clubs around Queens.

Back in his vehicle, Calucci felt a drop of blood drip from his nose. He cleaned it with his sleeve. He began sweating profusely. It'd been some time since he'd last had a hit of cocaine or drunk alcohol, and tremors were returning to his hands. These symptoms frustrated him to no end. He could feel the tension building up inside. He needed some cocaine and a couple of doubles of Hennessy to calm down. He had to go see Delores for relief. Calucci was now having physical signs of addiction on the job, and he secretly worried his superiors would get wind of it.

*****

Delores was clad in a tight fitting red bra and G-string when Calucci entered her bedroom.

"Damn, you look good enough to eat Sweet Cakes, and I'm starving."

"Oh Nicky, you sure know how to make a girl feel good. I missed you so Honey. Here's a drink, just how you like it, double Hennessy straight up."

"That's right Sweet Cakes, you know just how to serve me. Get me some cocaine and a joint. I need to relax because my chest feels like it's about to blow up, right out of my body."

Once Calucci snorted four or five lines of the Colombian flakes, he began to feel better. He lit a joint, exhaled through his nostrils, and then looked at Delores through glassy eyes.

"Come here baby. You know what's good."

Calucci began kissing Delores' neck and lips softly.

Delores started with her cat o'nine tails whip, slowly, lightly. She'd hit him harder with each strike. She struck him for at least twenty minutes, leaving his back flaming red. Next, she switched to her heavy wooden paddle and spanked his bottom for another ten minutes. She left him black and blue when she was done. All that time, Calucci could be heard moaning in pain and pleasure through the walls of the trap house. When she tired she dropped onto the bed. Delores knew she'd pleased her man once again, just how he liked it.

"Ah Sweet Cakes, you know me so well. You do me the best. I swear Sweet Cakes, I need you. I love you."

"I know you do Papi. I'm here for you always. You know that right?"

"You damn straight I do."

Calucci and Delores laid there for hours, in and out of sleep, holding each other as if they were afraid to let go of one another.

The next morning Calucci was up bright and early, he felt like a new man. He was ready to tackle the Jackson case. He was reenergized, and excited to go. He lit a spliff, took a few hits of cocaine, and kissed his sleeping mistress goodbye.

*****

When Calucci arrived he noticed he'd beat Barley to the office. He was speeding from the drugs, but more so, from his growing intuition that today would be the day he'd get closer to catching Jimmy Jackson's killer. He finally heard Barley moving around in his office next door.

"Ay Barley, get in here."

"Morning Chief. What's up?"

"When we last spoke you were about to fill me in on your follow up with Alex Jackson. How'd you make out?"

"According to local grocery store clerks and restaurant workers, who Alex claimed served him, none remembered seeing him during the entire weekend, and definitely not on the night his brother was murdered."

"What did Alex say when you told him this?"

"He looked like he was going to faint. He insisted he didn't lie. He couldn't explain why no one remembered him coming into and leaving their place of business. They know him well. He's patronized them many times over the last 30 years."

"Since Alex is determined to stick to his story, I want to carry out another walkthrough of the crime scene to see what turns up. Maybe we missed something. What do you think?"

"It might just work, it just might turn up something. You'll never know if you don't try. By the way, Caledonia's alibi checked out. Nevertheless, I'm still looking into some loose ends in her statement. Let me know what turns up at the Jackson crime scene,"

"Will do."

As a follow up on Caledonia's statement, in a last ditch effort, Calucci ran Maceo Brown and Althea Simmons' fingerprints through the NYPD fingerprint system. Calucci came up with some hits. Maceo Brown had been printed back in 1978 after being arrested on an assault charge. The record showed he did 90 days in Rikers Island and hadn't been arrested since.

Althea Simmons' prints also came back positive. She'd been arrested on a DWI charge in 1979. Calucci immediately cross referenced his findings with those prints identified by the CSI team and got a match to prints found inside the Jackson home. He immediately contacted Barley and had him get a search warrant for the residence of his new suspect. Following his boss's orders, Barley executed the search with his squad of detectives. Meanwhile, Calucci could feel his stomach knotting up. He was closer than ever to closing in on the killer. He met with Barley when he returned from the field and compared notes. They were done finally with this case and Calucci was ecstatic. He'd found the killer. He had Barley set up a press conference for late that afternoon.

In the interim, Delores called Calucci and asked him to come see her. He said he was too busy and couldn't get away. He had too many other issues to resolve and didn't want nor need any distractions. In spite of Delores' pleas, Calucci held fast to his decision not to visit her. He abruptly cut their conversation by slamming the phone down. Calucci felt a pang of relief from not giving into Delores' wants and staying away from the trap house. He knew if he visited his mistress he'd never get home. He felt he wanted to see his wife and kids soon. This was a big deal for Calucci. Making a conscious decision to not set himself up to spend hours on end with Delores. The idea of going home to his family produced a faint smile on his face.

Calucci departed the precinct and headed home. It'd been several days since he'd last seen his family. He took a week off to spend with them and planned to abstain from drugs and alcohol during that time. Although Calucci knew he wouldn't be able to smooth out his family relationships within this short period of time, he was willing to try. For him, this was monumental, especially to do so while abstaining from getting high. But there was still one last thing he had to do to close this case.

*****

On July 20, 1982, the front page of The Springfield Gardens Star Ledger Newspaper read:

HUNT FOR QUEENS MURDERER ENDS IN MONTH LONG POLICE DRAGNET

The article stated that NYPD Chief of Homicide Detectives, Nicky Calucci led a month long investigation into the killing of Jimmy Jackson who was found shot dead in his home on June 18, 1982. The Chief was quoted as follows:

"A list of suspects was developed early on in this case. It was made up of a variety of individuals. It included family and friends of the victim, as well as those close to the case and others living in the community. Hundreds of hours of interviews were held by both City and State institutions. They collected pertinent information, and forensic trace evidence proved to be the capstone to solving this horrible murder. In order to bring justice to Mr. Jackson and his only living brother Alex Jackson, the men and women of the Homicide Squad, coordinated by 1st Grade Detective John Barley, tracked down the criminal who had been terrifying this community over the last 30 days.

"Mr. Maceo Brown was arrested and charged with the 1st degree murder of Mr. Jimmy Jackson just hours ago in the 105th precinct in Queens, New York. Mr. Maceo Brown informed detectives in a written confession the reason for his shooting Mr. Jimmy Jackson. He killed Mr. Jackson to avenge his twin sister, Caledonia Brown. Caledonia Brown had been the victim of several vicious beatings, over the last several months, by her then boyfriend Mr. Jimmy Jackson. We regret Ms. Brown was beaten by the victim, yet no one should take the law into their own hands.

"Mr. Brown was snared by detectives in a search warrant executed in the Brown residence. Fingerprints and bloody shoes confiscated in the search matched evidence found at the original crime scene. The footwear worn by Mr. Brown at the time of the murder left distinct sole marks uncovered by our CSI team and matched their photographed impressions. Also found in the lab were traces of Mr. Jackson's blood on both Mr. Brown's shoes and clothing. Mr. Brown will be arraigned on the charge of 1st degree murder sometime this week in the County of Queens. Finally, I'd like to thank the community of Springfield Gardens for its patience and support of the NYPD and to assure you that we remain in service to you always."

*****

On December 12, 1982, Mr. Macco Brown was given a life sentence with the possibility of parole after twenty five years. He receives weekly visits from his sister Caledonia Brown, and her friend Althea Simmons accompanies her to visits periodically. He is presently being held in the Clinton Correctional Facility at Dannemora, New York.

Martyr
Robert Sumner

Every time Edgar parks in the lot of Fairfax Circle Baptist Church, he can't help remembering forty years ago when he accidentally shut the car door on his son's finger. No bones were broken, but the boy wailed all the way home. It had been inconvenient to have gotten out of bed, fixed breakfast for everyone, shaved and gotten dressed, then driven several miles down Lee Highway only to turn around and go home, but at least it had freed up some time before football started at one.

The boy had been resentful all day, but not as much as when he had come home complaining through tears of being beaten on the floor of a neighbor's basement. Ed walked his boy across the cul-de-sac to talk to Steve Hope about his son's aggression. Steve was a Navy Commander who treated his sons like they were recruits in his boot camp, but even he would have to agree that boys shouldn't beat one another. Edgar had rung the Hope's doorbell and gulped involuntarily when the door opened and an eagle-like head popped through the opening. *Can I help you?* he said in a tone that sounded more like *Is there a reason I need to kick your ass?* Edgar related what his boy had told him. Steve stepped out onto the porch to within a foot of his face and said, *Yer son picked up Robbie's Nerf football, said* This is yer face, *then punctured it with a screwdriver.* His face flashes hot with shame as he remembers that his reaction was to turn to his boy and ask, *Why didn't you tell me that?* and then scurry home with him, his son hanging his head in defeat.

Edgar shuts the door of his burgundy Cadillac and locks it, knowing it is unnecessary. Deacon Unruh waves from across the church parking lot, shouts a "Good morning!" Mrs. Unruh smiles sympathetically. Edgar waves back and replies with a pleasantry. His wife passed away years earlier, but he detects a lingering undercurrent of pity.

On the sidewalk that connects the lot to the church's main building he passes the old yellow farm house re-purposed as an office for Pastor Jennings and an auxiliary space for kids' Sunday school classes. The only real unpleasantness in decades of attendance was when his boy was in fifth grade and a couple of crackpots, new members recently moved from Lynchburg, got themselves assigned to teach his boy's Sunday school class. *I don't like scientists. They always try to prove the Bible is false*, his boy had reported that the woman with the long black hair and aura of sinister, holy resentment had told the class. It had been bad enough when the Sutherlands had shamed the congregation into restricting the annual Halloween party to only biblical costumes. They had said it was on the grounds that ghosts and witches and vampires promoted paganism. So the kids were all reduced to running around in bathrobes with towels strapped on their heads, but this was too far. Sure, it's a Baptist church, but in an affluent suburb where parents generally want their kids to be educated. The parents objected to her telling their children that; the hillbilly woman agreed not to discuss her belief in the satanic origin of science, but soon enough she was back to infecting the kids' minds with other ignorant junk. After a few months, her hillbilly husband was voted down by the congregation when he applied to be a deacon, ostensibly because he had previously been divorced, but really because they just wanted to make the couple feel unwelcome. Edgar eventually felt relieved when they joined a church in Manassas and were never heard from again, and many of his friends expressed the same relief.

He has always been suspicious of holy rollers. Robert Hansen attended church every day and constantly pushed Catholicism on everyone, and yet he had been America's worst traitor since Benedict Arnold. Anyone that fervent must be trying to compensate for some sort of deviancy. Chris Cooper played that creep so creepily in the movie *Breach* it's amazing anyone ever didn't suspect the treachery.

It's the fanatics who ruin everything. There was a fellow at work who was a Muslim and he was fine to work with. Majiz just did his work and made small talk once or twice a day like everyone else. When the office had its annual holiday party, he would smile, eat cake, and chit-chat like everyone else, though the season was meaningless in his religion. If all Muslims were like him, there wouldn't be so many problems in the Middle East. Edgar never talks about his faith to anyone outside church so he appreciates it when that consideration is reciprocated.

He reaches the front doors, greets a few more middle-aged members who are also on their way in, and enters the lobby. An oil painting of their previous pastor faces him from the nearest wall. Pastor Williams was more sincere than his replacement, who shakes your hand and grins so aggressively it feels like he's a politician. Pastor Jennings is on the way out after congregants recently caught him recycling some of his old sermons, like they weren't supposed to notice after hearing them only a year earlier.

Edgar makes his way to a pew about a third of the way back from the pulpit, turns right into it and sits down about half way across. He doesn't like to sit too far forward, which is what the holy rollers do, but he doesn't want to sit too far back because it feels like he is one of the bad students in class, hoping not to be noticed.

He crosses his arms and subtly pats the side panel of his suit jacket to reassure himself that his .357 is still hiding in its holster underneath. He heard from a friend who works in the county clerk's office that everyone who comes in to apply for a concealed weapon permit is a weirdo. His wife warned him that some people might think that of him because he always had a somber demeanor and kept to himself mostly. Their suspicions would be unfounded. He isn't a pervert or some other kind of deviant, he's always been level-headed. Maybe most people really shouldn't have concealed weapons permits; they're too hot-tempered, too aggressive, and some are just lousy shots. But Edgar grew up around guns and fired them plenty of times in basic training, and has always been the kind of upstanding citizen who can be trusted with a firearm. Since he retired he has continued to keep guns at home because he wants to protect himself in case of a burglar, and carries one with him in case of one of those horrible shootings like you keep seeing in the news. He isn't afraid of street crime; Fairfax County is about as safe a suburb as you could hope for, and in recent years even D.C. has become much safer, at least in certain neighborhoods. Not that he goes into the District much anymore.

His civilian job at the Office of Personnel Management gave him plenty more opportunities to defend freedom closer to home with only a twenty minute commute into D.C. The Russian language skills he learned through a six month course at the Defense Language Institute at Monterey during his first year in the Air Force were put to further use after his retirement from the military when he was assigned to keep tabs on a former dissident who had been placed in his neighborhood, conveniently less than a dozen miles from Langley.

Anatoly was provided with a house and a Chevrolet, not the most generous package the U.S. government might provide, but pretty good for someone who was not a KGB colonel or an ex-Nazi rocket scientist. Edgar had volunteered to act as director of the neighborhood block watch, a group of neighbors who took turns patrolling in their station wagons in search of crime, periodically reporting on their CB radios that they still had not found any. He scheduled Anatoly to ride shotgun on the nights when he was on patrol. They would drive around for two hours and discuss what Anatoly had learned from his network of fellow dissidents back home. *Have you ever read Dr. Zhivago?* Anatoly asked once when they were finished talking business for the evening. *No, but I saw the movie,* Edgar replied. *That is fine. Nabokov did not like the book. I thought it was mediocre. The film is wonderful.* Edgar nodded in agreement. *Why do you ask?* Anatoly answered, *You remind me of Yevgraf.* Edgar turned left onto Ranger Road and tried to remember. *Which one was he?* Anatoly answered, *The one played by Alec Guiness.* Edgar nodded in agreement again, then stopped. *I'm not sure I like being compared to a KGB.* Anatoly tilted his head. *Yes, he was KGB, but he was reasonable. He was not a true believer. You see it in the way he tolerates the younger man making sarcasm over the Party prohibiting enjoyment of personal poetry.* Edgar remembered that scene. *Huh. Yeah, I suppose he could have been worse.*

A trip to Clark Bros. to try to teach Anatoly to fire a pistol had been less than satisfactory. It took several minutes for him to work up the nerve to pull the trigger the first time, and several more shots before he would fire with his eyes open and his face not turned away. *I do not understand why I need this. You are supposed to protect me*, Anatoly said. *I'm not always around, and the cops could take several minutes to respond. You're your last line of defense.*

The organist finishes playing her tune. Pastor Jennings leaps up and stands behind the pulpit with a big pleading grin, a gold filling sparkling from a lower right molar. He welcomes the congregation and leads them in prayer. After the "amen," the musical director stands up and directs them in a couple of hymns. Edgar always hopes to hear *The Battle Hymn of the Republic*, the best tune in the hymnal. No such luck so far, just a couple of tunes that don't do much for him. The musical director sits back down and Pastor Jennings grins excessively as he segues into his sermon.

Edgar's mind drifts to when he was young, when the fanatics on the other side wanted to overthrow capitalism and felt justified in murdering millions to do so. He hadn't known much when he graduated from high school and joined the Air Force, but he'd known that America needed to be defended against the communist onslaught. As he saw it, the commies could ruin their own economies if they wanted to. If a few distant countries fell to popular revolutions, then the corrupt governments in those countries probably weren't worth saving anyway. It only became a problem when they tried to impose their hell on other countries.

America's fanatics disagreed. They had wanted a third world war to turn back communism. But war becomes unnecessary when you have a big enough military. With enough of the F-86 Sabres, F-100 Super Sabres, and F-94 Starfires he had seen flying around Misawa, only a suicidal Soviet commander would have launched an attack. A sufficient show of strength keeps the peace. The fanatics thought you had to use those weapons to show the other side that you're willing to use them. In his four years of active duty and twenty-one years of reserve duty afterward though, he never encountered anyone nearly as crazy as that General Jack D. Ripper in *Doctor Strangelove*. What an odd movie. Kind of funny in parts, but odd. One enlisted guy snapped in Wakkanai and shot up a couple of radios and a typewriter with a Tommy gun, but none of the officers Edgar ran into were hardcore nutjobs. It bothered him how some of the guys were too eager to pull the trigger, but reasonable people shouldn't shy away from working with warmongers, it's how they can be restrained.

When he first arrived in Japan he stayed in Tachikawa outside Tokyo for a few days to process in. He had been eager to see some fighter planes or bombers but nothing more interesting than bulky transports flew by. From there he waited for his top secret clearance for about a month at Misawa Air Base, at the northern end of Honshu. That place was a beehive of fighters and bombers criss-crossing the sky, a great backdrop to a month of standby status with no duties other than showing up to roll call twice a day. He went to movies, frequented the base's bowling alley, played Pacheko slot machines at the airmen's club a few times, and napped whenever he wanted to. The only real excitement happened when a five hundred pound bomb detonated on the tarmac. Edgar ended up making Master Sergeant, but Airman Second Class Tomlinson's career ended right then and there.

The three years he spent in Japan after basic training were a great experience, the sort that he felt every young man should experience. Some men would complain about the isolation in Wakkanai, but he enjoyed being away from wearisome society. Being so close to Russia made him nervous at first, but he figured they were fairly safe since the Russians couldn't attack their small listening post without provoking a war. And they got leave every few weeks to party in the big cities on Honshu, so the loneliness never became overwhelming. Tokyo was great, except for one time when he ate a bowl of raw horse meat mixed with a raw egg. It was delicious, but he regretted it when he got the shits for three days. Fortunately, the hotel he stayed in had beer vending machines on every floor, so he didn't have to venture too far. For years he would brag about how he was adventurous enough to try that evil dish. He would also brag about hiking on Mt. Fuji, but the anecdote about the daredevil dinner always got the best reactions.

Kyoto was mellower but had more beautiful temples and even a shogun's fortress with floors that were rigged to creak even if an assassin tried to tip-toe across them. He wished he'd seen that when he was a boy because it would have been an ecstatic dream world. His mom had been sad and worried about him living in such a foreign place. He took a lot of pictures and mailed them to her so she would feel better. Kyoto was great for that, as was Nara. His younger brothers loved the picture he sent back of the adorable little domesticated deer pissing on the stone walkway in front of a giant wooden gateway.

When his security clearance cleared, he took a ferry about ten to twelve miles to Hakodate, where he bought a wood statue of a bear with a fish in its mouth in a gift shop before boarding a train for a slow, noisy ride to the north side of Hokkaido. Small towns punctuated tracts of rice paddies, scrubby trees, and low hills. He was glad when the train arrived near Wakkanai Air Station because he had gotten no practice speaking Russian since leaving Monterey. Sakhalin Island, where the enemy lurked, was visible from the coast.

For ten months at Wakkanai and for another two and half years back at Misawa, he intercepted Soviet military broadcasts, transcribing them in Russian and translating them into English during alternating two hour shifts. Misawa was more fun; the air base was two miles inland from a beach a lot of the airmen would to ride to and from on rented bicycles, though the water was too cold for anything more than brief wading. And he went into town a lot to drink beer and sake and watch a few girlie shows with his buddies, some of whom had been in his Russian class. Some of those Japanese girls were so sexy he had wondered why Japanese men had been so eager to go away to war, but then again, there he was, far from home. He'd even had a cute girlfriend there for a while, until Tomlinson stole her away. *Yer not helpin' her with the bills,* the airman had told him with a smirk. *That's all these Jap whores want.* Edgar had wanted to punch him in the face for that but did not want to experience military discipline. Tomlinson was one of those idiots who thought containment was cowardice. When Edgar had tried to reason with him in the mess hall one afternoon, Tomlinson had called him a "dickless coward." Edgar turned and walked a few paces when Tomlinson almost shouted, *Or maybe yer just not man enough for her.* Edgar kept walking. Later that day the pinging Pacheko balls turned his mind to the safety features of the five hundred pound bombs Tomlinson had to cart around.

*****

It's a shame that so much blood was shed during the twentieth century, but it turned out well for the most part, Edgar thinks as Pastor Jennings droned on. Most of the communist regimes have fallen, and millions more people around the world are enjoying freedom. As horrific as the Cold War was at times, he feels a sense of gratitude that his children are inheriting a much more peaceful world. Sure, there's still conflict, but the wars are getting smaller and terrorism will never destroy America, despite what right-wing fanatics claim. Japan was once dominated by fascist fanatics, but it became as moderate as you could hope for. He had always kept his distance from hippies but he was beginning to believe peace might be possible, and that wouldn't be such a bad thing.

Pastor Jennings wraps up the sermon. A fellow a few pews behind him shouts a perfunctory "Amen!"

Edgar wishes there had been a bomb that could have been tampered with in the Hope residence, but suppresses the thought. Not here, not in a house of worship.

The pastor grins again and steps back as the choir rises and begins the closing hymn, *The Battle Hymn of the Republic.* Edgar's mind breaks off its reconnaissance in the past as the opening martial chords march into his heart. He loves the line about "He hath loosed the fateful lightning of His terrible swift sword." His forearms break out in goosebumps when they get to "As He died to make men holy, let us die to make men free." Whenever he hears that song he imagines his great-grandfather marching into the cornfield at Antietam to brave the rebel fusillade. His blood gets hot as he feels the Lord's fateful lightning coursing through him. He has to concentrate not to let the people around him notice how much it rouses him.

The doors at the back of the room swing open with a high-pitched groan of their hinges. Edgar turns his head at the sound and sees a young man with a thick hippie beard barge in. He steps forward and stops in the back of the center aisle. One of his son's former Sunday school teachers screams. The man raises his factory fresh AK-47 and fires into the congregation. A little boy's head explodes. The man in the aisle fires at the choir. Two of the singers slump over, blood spurting onto their gowns. Pastor Jennings stands up, his grin gone as he knows he is about to ascend to heaven. A 7.62 mm bullet punctures his red tie and topples him back over his velour chair.

Edgar draws his pistol, releases the safety, pulls the hammer back. He forces his stiffened legs to raise him up. He spins and squeezes the trigger. A micro-second of elation. The terrorist grunts and stumbles back, a gratifying blood stain splashing across his shoulder. The congregants around Edgar scream again at the sound of his shot, cover their heads and duck.

His fear dissipates. Time slows. Sounds become spectators to his clarity of action. He once caught a fly in his fist without looking, the buzzing of the insect's wings around the conference room charting a trajectory on his consciousness as his eyes unfocused and God guided the lunge of his hand.

The terrorist looks at him, grins a psychotic grin, and aims his Kalashnikov.

Edgar's trigger finger squeezes.

Glory, glory, hallelujah.

Supply and Demand
Jim Guigli

Stephanie:

Stephanie Burkhardt worried about her husband, Allan. She didn't know why he seemed stressed, but she didn't think he was seeing another woman.

Staring through her kitchen window into the early morning darkness, Stephanie shivered. After a Sacramento Valley summer of long, hot, sunny days spent at the backyard pool, fall's dark shadows chilled her.

She was always up first to start the coffeemaker and bring in the paper. *The Sacramento Bee* lay on the table in front of her, next to a cup of coffee going cold. After picking the paper up and returning it to the table several times, she hadn't read past the date, November 4, 1977. She had always been able to read Allan's moods before. Normally confident, she had to admit she was afraid.

The other woman, history for months now, had been easier to understand. Women knew some men strayed.

Stephanie had easily recognized Allan's deception. He strained to appear normal while he told unconvincing stories about working late on his latest project at Valley Aerospace. He emphasized things that didn't warrant emphasis and skimmed over things that deserved explanation. He'd come home from work and shower again, and then dress in clothes he would wear only to take Stephanie out to dinner. He'd beg off dinner. "No time." He had to go, "Back to work." And when he came home later, he smelled. She didn't need lipstick-soiled shirts or an unsigned note.

Her first impulse was to confront Allan and then throw him out.

Stephanie wouldn't take comfort in denial. But Stephanie wouldn't let vanity and emotion waste everything she'd sacrificed for their marriage. Except for her parents, Allan was all she had. They had no children and few friends. She was forty, mature enough to handle another woman.

Swallowing the pain, she pretended she didn't notice. Like lighting a candle and pulling a woolen throw up to her chin, waiting for a winter storm to end, she waited for the affair to pass. It was over in a few weeks.

But an affair! After all Stephanie had done for him and their marriage. They'd been steadies through high school and married at eighteen, right after graduation. She worked two jobs to support them in a Sacramento studio apartment while he commuted six years to the University of California at nearby Davis for his engineering degrees.

She'd pushed Allan to apply for scholarships, and, after graduation, to find a good job. Then she pushed him to ask for raises and promotions. When his earnings stalled, she pushed him again, to move on to better companies. He would eventually agree, reluctantly. He never shared her ambition or enthusiasm. Tainted victories for Stephanie.

When she showed Allan a new Help Wanted ad from Valley Aerospace, he demurred.

"But Allan, it's the top — you can't do better here than VA."

"You know, Steph, *if* they hired me, I'd still need a security clearance to work there. They'd investigate me. Both of us."

Ignoring his warning, she pushed him to apply anyway and suffered complaints from her parents and neighbors when FBI agents knocked on their doors and asked a lot of personal questions.

But her years of effort had paid off. They now lived in a large house in the suburbs, drove good cars, and put money into savings every month.

And then he fell for another woman.

She didn't want to admit Allan's meeting the other woman could have been her fault. Maybe he'd met her at VA, maybe that Laurie woman in the print room he'd mentioned. She couldn't tell her parents because they always said she'd chosen a weak man. Yes.

True, things had been better after Allan's affair ended. They had more money, cash bonuses that Allan said were for meeting federal project milestones. But now he rarely smiled, even to hide a new facial tic.

She heard Allan up and the shower running. Her cup of cold coffee was still almost full. She poured it into the sink and refilled the cup.

Allan entered the kitchen dressed for work, carrying the same briefcase she'd given him for his first day at Davis. Overloaded with textbooks during his days at Davis, the briefcase had lost its shape, and time had dried and faded the leather. At VA, there was little unclassified work he could bring home, but he still carried the briefcase. She'd offered to replace it many times, but he always refused. He said it reminded him of simpler times.

"Allan, can I make some breakfast for you?"

"No, Stephanie. No time for breakfast this morning. I'll grab a roll at the snack bar. I need to get there early. They're on me to finish something today. Thanks anyway."

"You seem so worried lately, Allan. You know I want to help you. Do you want to talk about it?"

His facial tic appeared again. "No, Steph. Lately there's a lot of pressure at work. But it's nothing you should worry about."

"If you're sure."

"Yes. And I won't be home in time for dinner tonight. I have to finish this work they want today."

"No dinner?"

"No. You go ahead without me. But tomorrow's Friday. If I stay late tonight, I may be able to leave early tomorrow. Get a head start on our weekend."

*****

Allan:

"Hey Allan — you forget?" Jeff Sanderson's arms and tie hung over the partition wall of Allan Burkhardt's cubicle. The afternoon sun through the bullpen windows behind Sanderson turned his blond hair angelic. "Ron wants those drawings for the AM380, *and* your calculations, by the end of the day. Are they finished?"

Allan was lettering notes on the large sheet of vellum taped to his drawing board. He shook his head without looking up. "I didn't forget."

"What do I tell Ron? Yes? No? Better not say no."

"Yes. I'll have it done. End of the day." Allan looked up from the drawing. "*Before* the end of the day, for sure, Jeff."

"You better. Chop, chop. You know, Burkhardt, we don't have time to waste here, like you had at your last job. You've had your clearance for more than a year now. No more months of sitting around counting paperclips while you waited for your clearance to come through. Tell me, Burkhardt, just what *do* you do with all your time?"

Burkhardt looked at Jeff and smiled politely, a smile that used little of his face. "Thanks, Jeff."

Sanderson looked at Burkhardt's old briefcase and smirked. He performed a youthful turn on his heel, toward Ron Waldron's office, and left.

Allan knew Sanderson didn't need a job. Not for money. He had learned Sanderson's parents, like Stephanie's, were wealthy. Sanderson was passing time until he inherited a seven-figure estate and could enjoy all his summer days in his ski boat on Folsom Lake, instead of bugging Allan at VA. No, Sanderson worked only for the joy of dominating others.

Allan finished the last drawing and spent a half-hour checking his numbers, then searching the three-foot by four-foot drawing for things he'd missed. He called one of the engineering assistants to his cubicle and handed her a stack of letter-sized papers to be photocopied.

"Becky, copy and collate these — a set for me, Ron, and the file — all on three-hole in binders. Stamp, number, and record them all as Secret-Rhinestone, Preliminary. Binder cover sheets and spines — log them in, da-dee-da, da-dee-da, et cetera. You know what to do, Becky. Ron's waiting. Okay?"

"Okay, Allan."

When she returned, he took one binder and the drawings and left his cubicle. On the way to the print room, he ducked into the empty office he'd been using and locked the door. When he'd finished, he listened at the door before leaving.

Laurie, the young woman who ran the print room, sat at her desk watching the clock on her wall. She stood and smiled when Allan leaned in over the print room's Dutch-door. Then he held up the drawings.

"Don't tell me, Allan. Five minutes before quitting time, and you want what? Six copies each — right?" She approached him, rotating her hips like his visit was more a pleasure than a problem.

Burkhardt noticed. He was aware some women found him attractive. He didn't know why. Stephanie had singled him out and planned their marriage during high school.

Allan offered a cautious smile as he handed over the drawings. "Just three copies each. Ron wants to see them today. Stamp the copies Secret-Rhinestone, Preliminary. And make and log in a file copy, too. Please?"

"You're blushing, Allan. You'll owe me, again." She smiled and started making the copies. "Folded or rolled?"

"Roll them all together with the originals, please. Ron will sign them later."

"You've got it."

After the machine had spit out the last print, Laurie hit the OFF button and took the originals and copies to a worktable. She carefully lined up the original drawings and copy-prints, and then rolled them all together into a tight cylinder.

"Not too tight, Laurie, or they'll never lie flat."

"Not too *tight*. Yes, *boss*," she said, smiling as she brought the prints and drawings to him. "Anything for *you*."

While she stretched a rubber band over the rolled drawings, her face lost some of its playfulness. She leaned toward Allan and lowered her voice. "Why does Sanderson have it in for you?"

"What do you mean?"

"He asked me what you do in the empty office next door. He snoops around a lot. I think he's creepy — always carrying on like he runs the place — and hitting on me."

"That's just Jeff being Jeff. But don't let him get away with anything."

She handed Allan the roll of drawings and prints. "I won't. But Allan, what *do* you do in the empty office?"

Allan hesitated, trying to control his facial tic. Then he smiled and lowered his voice. "Can you keep a secret?"

"Allan? It's Valley Aerospace, and I work here — don't I?"

"All right, Laurie. Then I'll tell *you*. I sneak into that room and use a miniature camera to copy my work on microfilm... and then I give the film to a Russian spy."

Laurie stood speechless, her eyes searching Burkhardt's face. Then she suddenly laughed so loudly Burkhardt hurried to leave before someone noticed.

*****

Ron:

When Burkhardt entered Ron Waldron's office, he found his boss leaning back in his leather chair, almost horizontal, with his legs crossed and the heels of his cordovan wingtips resting on his desk. Waldron, still young at forty-five, enjoyed his power and status, rewards for years of hard work. Cooing and laughing into the phone tucked between his ear and shoulder, he busied his hands playing with his tie and a crystal *Milestone Achieved* obelisk while he looked out his window toward the foothills. Obviously, he wasn't talking to someone about work, or to his wife.

Burkhardt stood just inside Waldron's office door, patiently waiting with the binder and three-foot-long roll of drawings under one arm. When Waldron noticed Burkhardt, he turned his face away, lowered his voice, and continued his call.

Allan shifted his weight from one foot to the other while he rolled the rubber band back-and-forth over the prints. He hoped the noise from the rubber band was annoying Waldron.

Waldron savored his telephone conversation, mostly listening and smiling. During his wider smiles, he stretched and spread his legs. While Burkhardt waited, Waldron straightened the pleats in his pants, and rearranged other obelisks, a pen set, and a framed picture of his wife and two children on his otherwise empty desk.

Finally, Waldron glared at Burkhardt. He said into the phone, "Hold on a minute, Marla," and wrapped his hand over the mouthpiece. "What's up, Burkhardt? Can't you see I'm busy?"

"Jeff said you were in a hurry to see these drawings and the calculations. Before the end of the day, he said. There are three prints each, too."

"Oh, yeah. Right. Put them on the side table. I'll get to them and talk to you later. You *are* staying tonight?"

"No, Ron. Stephanie has this big dinner planned tonight for her parents. I've missed too many of her dinners. I didn't think I'd have to work late tonight."

Waldron frowned. "You're taking a lot of time off lately, Burkhardt, just when we need you. Be sure to tell Jeff."

"Good night, Ron."

*****

Karl:

On his drive south through mid-town Sacramento, down tree-lined Fifteenth Street, Karl thought about his craft — classic woodwork, and his business — European Custom Cabinets. They were both important to him. His goals were always excellent work, good customer relations, and a small profit to show the IRS.

But his customers, all wealthy, occasionally complained about money, about his fees. Karl would patiently explain the cost of first-class materials and tools, the miscellaneous expenses, and the hours of labor required for the high-quality results they wanted.

"You wouldn't expect me to work for free. I have to buy gas and food, and pay my mortgage, too." He would remind them of all the last-minute extras and changes they always requested. He knew the steps to this dance, and when the music stopped, they hired him again.

Today, again, the complaint was about money. Supply and demand. One of his suppliers wanted more money. Nearing Broadway, Karl reviewed the supplier's position.

The amount of extra money the supplier wanted wasn't significant, but the supplier had coupled the demand with a threat. He'd implied he'd be forced to contact the authorities if Karl wouldn't pay more. He had heard all this before. He hated the shallowness, the pettiness, but he knew how to handle it, how to satisfy a person like this supplier, and make him feel at peace in the end.

To Karl, money was just a tool, like a saw, a chisel, or a plane. Accumulating money was not one of his goals. But signs of an uncertain future and the shallow behavior of so many people he encountered, like this supplier, made him wonder if one day he might have to change his attitude about money just to survive. Perhaps, but today, money remained just a tool.

After a left turn on Broadway in front of the Tower Theatre's complex of white stucco buildings, Karl turned right onto Land Park Drive and then right again onto Burnett Way and into the Tower Theatre parking lot. He brought his white, unmarked box van to rest at the far end of the lot.

Except for Karl himself, the van was the most important asset of European Custom Cabinets. Karl kept the van's engine and other mechanicals maintained, and he'd upgraded the locks and alarm system. Though he had a well-equipped cabinet shop at home, every tool he might need on a job site had a place in his van.

Karl moved from the driver's seat through curtains into the back and stood in front of one of the floor-to-ceiling wooden cabinets he'd attached to the van's interior walls. He opened a drawer and rooted through its contents until he found the right tool. After a brief examination, turning the tool in his calloused hand, he slipped it under his jacket into a chest-pocket in his denim coveralls and stepped down out of the van into the cold.

He glanced at the other people and their cars in the dimly lit parking lot while he locked the van's door and set the alarm, never staring at any one individual, nor letting his eyes dwell on a specific area. Satisfied all was in order, he crossed the lot and approached the ticket booth. He bought a single ticket and entered the theater. The marquee promised 3 DAYS OF THE CONDOR for the weekend. Amusing, he thought.

Modern economics had split the main floor of the old theater down the middle into two theaters, with the balcony converted to a third venue. Karl always used the left main floor theater, next to the parking lot.

Karl's eyes adjusted to the darkness while the coming attractions played and he searched for seating. A Thursday evening show was rarely crowded, but he still carefully chose a section of empty seats in the back row, away from other patrons and close to an exit door leading back to the parking lot. Here he and his supplier could talk, or at least whisper, a safe distance from other Tower customers who might hiss or shush. Karl studied the patrons nearest to him. Not recognizing anyone or finding anyone suspicious, this evening he would again use the Tower Theatre as a meeting place.

Karl stretched his long legs during the opening credits. He appeared to be watching the film but glanced back at the entrance whenever a straggler entered.

The door from the lobby opened, spilling light into the theater. A man cut through the light. The man scanned the back rows until he found Karl, who barely nodded in recognition. The supplier side-stepped down the row, past a few patrons and empty seats, until he took a seat at Karl's right hand.

"Thank you, Karl. I'm glad we can have this meeting," Allan Burkhardt whispered after he sat down.

Flickering light from the screen made Burkhardt's face hard to read, but Karl was sure he could see fear.

"It is no problem," Karl whispered. "We have a business

relationship. We can always talk."

"I'm under tremendous pressure. I don't know if I can do this much longer. That's why I want more money now, before... you know the risk, and I'm... well, I'm afraid." Allan's face twitched. "It's getting harder to find the privacy and time to use the camera. Waldron, I think he's been watching me."

"You're sure?"

"No. But I feel it. And Sanderson, his assistant, too."

"What about the security people?"

"No. Just Waldron and his assistant. The security people are bureaucrats. They wouldn't snoop into anything in our division unless Waldron asked them to."

"And, this Ron Waldron, you said before, he is an important man?"

"Chief Engineer in Division 3000. Advanced motors. He's mostly a manager now, but the man designed some of their best motors. He still lives and breathes rocket motors."

"Okay. Let Karl help you. Here is what I say. When you go back to work tomorrow, just do your job. Do what they ask you to do. Forget about me. Do nothing for me for the next month. See if you still think they are watching you. Then contact me next month in the usual way and we will talk. Simple, yes?"

"Yes, thank you. Good. That's what I'll do."

"Good. You are too valuable to me. You are loyal and productive. I don't want you to do anything risky. I don't want you to worry."

Burkhardt nodded.

"I am going to give you the raise, the extra money you requested. You have made a good argument about your position and the money. And, because I don't want you to bring me anything for at least a month, you will need money until we meet again. Yes? I have the money you requested and more."

"Yes, thank you." Burkhardt slouched forward and wiped his hand over his forehead and through his hair. "I'm sorry, Karl, really sorry. I was wrong to press you. I thought at first I could handle this, but I —

you told me to forget about her, but it's hard. Rachel — is she still around? How is she?"

Karl paused, shook his head, and smiled. "I understand. Romance, of any kind, can be difficult. I had to let her go. She went downriver somewhere. Who knows? You may see her sometime soon."

"Rachel — was that her real name?"

"Your Rachel? It doesn't matter now, but she called herself Lada."

"Karl, you know, I didn't mean what I said… about telling somebody. It's just I've been so worried lately."

"I understand. Don't apologize. It's not necessary."

Burkhardt sat up and looked at Karl. "Maybe I can help *you*. My wife has talked about new kitchen cabinets. You do that kind of work, right?"

Karl smiled. "Many, many times I have made kitchen cabinets. I love to work with wood. My mother, who was German, a professor, wanted me to be a scientist or a doctor. But my Russian father taught me to make cabinets, and to love wood. Talk to your wife and let me know when I can come to see your kitchen. We will talk, and I will make beautiful cabinets for your wife. And because it is you, at a very good price."

"Thank you, Karl. Let me talk to her tonight and we'll make an appointment. You'll come to see our kitchen, maybe stay for dinner?"

"Yes, I would like. Now, I have something for you, something to help you relax. If you want."

"What?"

Karl produced a small plastic bag of powder. He looked around the theater, and then offered the bag to Burkhardt. "Here, do this." He sucked on his finger. "Wet your fingertip, and then dip it into the bag. Coat the fingertip with some powder. Then put the finger in your mouth and rub your gums and tongue. It will not taste good, but you will feel better in a few minutes."

Burkhardt did as he was told.

"Feeling better?"

"I feel a tingle. My mouth is getting numb."

"Numb is good, if you are worried."

"You're right. I am feeling better."

"Good. Keep the bag, but just use a little, only when you need it. And now, your money."

Burkhardt watched while Karl reached into his jacket and removed an envelope filled with twenty-dollar bills.

Karl held the bills in his hand and counted them while he waited for a dark scene on the screen. "I have your money. Do you have something for me?"

"Oh, yes. The AM380 — I almost forgot." As he had done many times before, Burkhardt passed several small cartridges of undeveloped film to Karl.

Karl smiled and put the cartridges into one of his pockets. "And you brought the camera?"

"Yes." Burkhardt handed Karl the tiny Minox.

"When we talk again, I will have a new, better camera for you. You will like it."

"Good."

"Here," said Karl, extending his hand and the bills toward Burkhardt. Burkhardt reached for the bills, but most of them fell to the floor at Karl's feet.

Karl uttered a Russian oath. "Oh. I'm sorry. Let me get them."

"No, no, let me. I've got it." Burkhardt left his seat to kneel on the theater floor.

Karl swung his legs to the left to make room while Burkhardt bent down until his head was low with his forehead pressed against the forward seatback. Allan's hand groped in the dark under the seat, gathering the bills.

The cabinetmaker removed the tool and a thin leather glove from his coveralls and pulled the glove over his right hand. He swung his right leg back over the engineer. The soles of his steel-toed work boots were now flat on the floor, straddling the man searching for cash. Karl bent down.

As soon as his left hand gripped the collarbone at the side of Burkhardt's neck, Karl knew the geography. Even in the darkened theater, Karl could find the spot, the small, shallow hollow every man has at the back of his neck.

Burkhardt, confused, froze at Karl's touch.

The awl, at home in the cabinetmaker's right hand, went in like the times before, with little resistance. The point of the awl followed the engineer's spinal cord through the brain stem, deep into the skull.

Karl had always enjoyed the small noises, the barely audible squish of flesh parting to make way for the awl's long steel shaft and the victim's short, sad moan of pain, sudden understanding, and disappointment. The legs, or sometimes the arms, would twitch for a few seconds, and then go still. Karl's eyes were on the movie patrons closest to him when he gave the awl a final twist and shake. No one had noticed.

Burkhardt had stopped moving. Karl had made Burkhardt feel at peace in the end.

Karl planted his right foot on the back of Burkhardt's head and pushed while he withdrew the awl. He lifted the back of Burkhardt's jacket and wiped the awl's shaft clean in the lining.

Karl waited a few moments for another dark scene on the screen before he picked up some of the cash from the floor, leaving a few bills to go with what was still in Burkhardt's hand. He retrieved and opened the plastic bag, spilled some powder on Burkhardt's hand, and tossed the rest to the floor near the remaining twenty-dollar bills. After returning the empty plastic bag, awl, and glove to his pocket and straightening Burkhardt's jacket, he pushed the dead man's head until it was under the seat as far as it would go. The next person to see Burkhardt might at first think Allan had lost a contact lens.

When the screen darkened again, Karl slipped through the exit door into the parking lot. He was outside before any annoyed film patrons could see who had disrupted their viewing experience.

After scanning the parking lot, Karl checked his watch and hurried to his van. He would just make his appointment at a grand old house in Land Park. The original owners' heir wanted new cabinets.

On his way through Land Park, Karl smiled. He would apply the principles of supply and demand again this weekend. He didn't have to study economics to know the best way to deal with rising prices. You always improve supply.

Karl had already prepared the special rooms at the motel he owned, one for himself and the cameras, and the adjacent room for the new girl.

The man would balk when she showed him the pictures a few days later, at their last date. While he looked, she'd mention the 16mm movie film and sound recording.

"I thought... you — you're saying this was all just a set-up?" he'd say.

She would back away and give him time to consider his few options.

"No, I could live with a divorce." He wouldn't want to meet with this man she knew, the man who could make everything right.

"With no job?" she'd ask.

She'd watch him pace the room, reviewing the photos, as if they could show him a way out. After a short while, he would narrow the options to just one, the only solution.

"All right, Marla. I'll meet with your friend, Karl."

"Good, Ron. He will fix everything." Marla would take the photos from his hand and replace them with a thick envelope of twenty-dollar bills. In time, Waldron would enjoy having more money.

Karl was confident Ron Waldron would be a good supplier.

Author's Note:
Sacramento's Tower Theatre was a *Yavka*, a cold-war meeting place for Russian spies, according to Christopher Andrew, author of *The Sword and the Shield.*

A Prayer for My Daughter
James Roth

Prologue

I picked Yuji up in Kabuki-cho at a video arcade near a sex shop, just where Nobuyuki had told me he'd be. He was playing the video game Divine Fantasy, a sad thing. He was old enough to be my father, but I didn't let him in on how sorry I felt for him. I just went ahead and did what Nobuyuki had paid me to do.

After Yuji had finished the game, he smiled to himself before looking up and seeing me. I forced myself to pucker my shiny red lips and say, "You won a favor!" He stared at me the way an otaku does, so I had to go on and force myself to say what I knew I had to, "Wouldn't you prefer the real thing?"

Poor Yuji, I thought, maybe he's only been with his wife.

I was wearing some heart-shaped fashion eyeglasses with a red frame, what Nobuyuki had told me to do. My lips were a red as shiny as the frames. I was one of those idiot girl video game avatars who'd come to life, and I hated myself for it.

"Maybe we should go to a hotel?" I said.

The love hotel Nobuyuki and I had picked out was the Amour, in that area of Kabuki-cho where the love hotels are lined up side by side to the end of the street. They all have flashy neon signs out front or on the roofs that make couples think they are going to a carnival, and I suppose they are, but one for adults. I'd been in more of these hotels than I cared to remember, here in Tokyo and down in Fukuoka and even a few between the two cities, I'm ashamed to say.

The Amour was a hotel I'd wanted to visit for quite some time, way back to when I was a high school student and first learned about the pleasures of boys, but it was too old-fashioned for them. The boys said it was for middle-aged women whose breasts hung down to their knees. They wanted a room with video games and AI generated spaceships or soccer matches. Boys! I'm past them now. Long past them.

I liked the Amour because the look of it took me out of Japan and back in time. A miniature of the Eiffel Tower is near the entrance, and the facade is made up like a building painters might have lived in long ago. You know, a bit run down but charming. But all that had nothing to do with why Nobuyuki had wanted me to take Yuji there. The reason was that it was across from a Family Mart convenience store, where he wouldn't look out of place standing at the entrance holding a camera.

When Yuji and I passed Nobuyuki, he let the cigarette in the corner of his mouth fall to the street, ground it out with the tip of a shoe, then picked up the butt and put it away in a trash bin in front of the store. He was that kind of man, respectful, even if he liked to pretend he was otherwise. It was only then that he raised the camera and took the photos his client wanted. My job was done. I could've run off then, but on the way to the Amour Yuji and I had talked a bit about life and the distance between us narrowed. He'd got to talking about the sushi company he worked for and the pressures he felt put on him by the president for his section to increase profits. I began to feel closer to him. I had pressures on me too.

Yuji and I slipped past the wall hiding the Amour's entrance and went inside. He booked the expensive Monet room, without me even having to ask for it. It was like he knew who I was, him picking that room. I was thrilled.

He put a ten thousand yen note under the slot in the smoky glass window. An old woman's hand took the bill. We started off toward the room, but the old woman called out, "Sir. Your change."

Yuji returned to the window and took the change.

As we were making our way to the Monet room, a couple came out of another room. The man — or was he still a boy? — was about twenty-five or so, wearing jeans and a white dress shirt. He gave me a good going over as we passed each other. He reminded me a bit of Pirate, scrawny and full of himself, a boy-man girls should steer clear of. His girl elbowed him a good one in the ribs. He deserved it. I'd wanted to, the way he'd looked at me.

We came to the Monet room. Yuji tapped the key card against the door lock, a green light flickered, and we went inside.

What a delight that room was. It was just what I'd wanted, like a room in one of those French painter's ateliers. Against one wall were fake windows. 3D images were in the windows, to make the street scene below them look real. Lining the street were bistros and sidewalk cafes.

I turned around and saw that Yuji's eyes were now totally on me. I had power, and it thrilled me. I'd take him to a private place far away from the stresses he felt, and if he were any good I'd go along on the journey.

I took off my glasses and set them on a counter by the television. I then unbuttoned the first two buttons of my frilly blouse to get Yuji started, but even then he didn't know what to do, and so I took his hands and had him undo the other buttons. Then I slipped the blouse off and tossed it over a painter's easel by a sofa. He stared at my body, as if it were something a person in a museum would admire. I had more to show him, though. I turned around, for him to undo my bra, but I wasn't prepared for his fingers being as cold as icicles. I shivered.

"I'm sorry," he said. "I... I've..."

"Don't think about it," I told him. "Things will come naturally."

I stood on my toes and kissed his neck. It was like kissing marble, he was so nervous. I'd see that he warmed up to me.

"Relax," I told him.

I then put his hands on the waist of my red dress and got him to undo the hasp. It fell to the floor. I stepped out of it. He finally then caught on to how a man should be and put his thumbs under the waistband of my panties and peeled them off. There I was, ready for him. He stared at me in wonder. No, he'd never been with a girl, I thought, only his wife. I was happy to be there with him.

I reached out for his belt and undid it and his pants dropped to the floor. I saw then that he was a man. He wasn't going to be a disappointment.

He searched for the switch to dim the room lights but it took him a while to find it. He was still a bit nervous. I suppose I was too. The first time is always that way. I was about to pull off the ridiculous blue wig I'd been wearing, but he took me by the wrist.

"Please," he said. "No."

"I'm not an Avatar in Final Fantasy now," I said.

"Please."

He looked so pitiful that I couldn't stop myself from giving in to him, but I didn't like it, not one bit, him not wanting to see me for who I was. I'd get him to think differently about me, I decided.

He was good for two rounds. I taught him some new tricks, and he thanked me. After the second round, when we were lying in bed together, he said, "I haven't been that strong since my honeymoon in Hawaii."

"You poor darling," I said. It was the way I talked to customers, and I hated to be that way, playing a role, but I couldn't help myself. It was who I'd become. Then Yuji surprised me in a way that I could never, ever have imagined. He said, "My wife put you up to this. Didn't she?"

"What are you talking about?" I said.

"That man with the camera," he said. "He's my brother-in-law."

That threw me. "What man?" I said.

"You know."

"No, I don't."

"I think you do. If my wife can take a lover, why can't I? A divorce will ruin me, you know?"

"I don't know what you're talking about," I said, lying. His bad marriage was something I didn't want to talk about. My customers told me about their bad marriages, and I was sick of them using me as a counselor, so I said, "We had a good time."

"I love you," he said.

I don't know why some boy-men have to go and ruin sex by saying that, but too many do. I forced a smile.

He said, "I'm sorry."

"Sorry for what? We had a good time."

"Really?"

"Stop feeling sorry for yourself," I said.

We lay there for a minute or two longer before he said, "My company." He paused, having trouble going on with what he wanted to say, but then he came out with it, first saying, "I shouldn't be telling you this."

I was foolish enough to ask, "Why keep whatever it is a secret after the good time we had? You'll feel better if you tell someone."

"It's too dangerous."

"You work for a sushi company, you said. How could fish be dangerous?"

"I don't want to involve you."

"But we had a good time. Go on, tell me."

He started to breathe heavily, he was so stressed. How could I not feel something for him? I calmed him down by running my fingers through his hair. He took my hand and looked me in the eyes and said, "The time I spent here with you was the happiest two hours of my life."

Two hours was how long he'd rented the room for.

I got to thinking about his company, how he was worried about involving me in something dangerous. I knew danger. I felt I was in danger every time I met Pirate, that one day he wouldn't be able to control himself, he was so drugged up with *shabu*. We'd get into a fight that was more than words. But I needed him. He'd gotten me hooked. Junko. I should've known what she was up to.

I thought about telling Yuji about Pirate but held back. I didn't want to burden him with my troubles. He was having a hard enough time telling me what his were, so I thought the best thing to do to get it out of him was to make him think I was leaving. I said, "I should be going."

"Boyfriend?" he asked, what I should've expected him to say.

I told him, "How could you ask such a thing, after the good time we spent together? No. I'm a hostess. It's hard work, you know, dealing with the likes of men who come to me to unload all their problems. I'm sick of it. Just sick of it. I want to go home one day." I saw that he took that personally, so I calmed him down again by saying, "I'm not talking about you. You were great."

"What, you want to go home?"

"I mean, I want a home to go to, one where I feel welcome."

"I know what you mean. I have a home, but it doesn't feel that way. What's the name of the club where you work?"

"The Nankaitou. It's near Tameije-sanno Station," I told him. "Visit me one evening."

"I don't know. I might cause trouble for you."

"Talking with men, pouring their drinks, lighting their cigarettes. It's my job, sucking up to them. You'd be different. I like it, you talking to me."

"Maybe one day. Can we keep on seeing each other this way? That might be better. We could meet at a coffee shop sometimes and maybe even just talk. I need to talk."

I wasn't sure about that, but when his eyes filled with tears I thought of my father and how he might have been like that, longing to see me again. Yuji then mumbled, "You must know a lot of men? You don't have time for me."

"No. They're only customers," I said.

"Do you think we could spend the night together?" he then asked. I didn't think he'd had it in him to ask me that, the way a man would. He'd just burst out with it.

"Tonight?" I asked.

"Please," he said. "Please?"

"To spite your wife? Is that why?"

"No. No! Of course not. I feel so close to you. Really."

"What about your wife?" I asked. "I don't want to get you in trouble with her."

"Why should I care about her? She's going to divorce me anyway. I'll tell her I had to work late and am going to take a room at a hotel. It wouldn't be the first time. She'll be happy to have the house to herself."

He leaned against the headboard. His white, hairless chest looked like a moon.

"I'll spend the night with you," I said, "but I have to call in first, tell my boss I've got plans for tonight."

"Won't I be getting you in trouble?"

"That's sweet. No, my boss doesn't ask questions of her girls. She'll understand."

Yuji put a hand on my thigh and smiled. His touch was now warm and gentle, a nice thing in a man. Pirate's touch was like a robot's, metallic. The way he did it was like one, too.

I'd been sitting on the edge of the bed, preparing to leave, but Yuji pulled me over onto him and we lay there for quite a while, looking up at the fake, twinkling stars in the ceiling. The feeling of the two of us lying there together was so peaceful. I had experienced that with Junichi long back, but only him. Thinking of Junichi, I pulled off that ridiculous bluc wig and flung it onto the floor but no sooner had I done so than I realized I'd made a mistake.

Yuji saw thc scar. He touched my forehead, where the scar was, right at my hairline on the right side of my head. "How did you get that?" he asked.

"It's nothing," I said.

"Tell me."

"A car accident," I said. Thinking of that accident, I had to hold back tears.

"But you're fine now?"

"I broke my right leg. My hip hurts now and then."

"How did it happen?"

I wasn't about to tell him the truth about the accident, so I made up a story.

"Sorry," he said. "Such an unfortunate thing shouldn't happen to a girl as cute as you."

"You didn't have to say that," I told him, "about me being cute."

"I wanted to."

"Okay, then, if it makes you feel better."

He smiled the way a man who's with a girl he cares about is supposed to smile, to my delight and surprise. Seeing that look, I became curious about his worries. I asked, "What is it with your company and those dangerous fish? Go on, tell me. You'll feel better."

He looked at me, his lips trembling, and after he'd gotten himself pulled together managed to mumble, "The yakuza is pressuring me to do something I shouldn't. I've never told anyone about it."

I thought he might break down right there into sobs of fear. I couldn't have that. So I said, "Didn't telling me make you feel better? Come on, now. Cheer up."

He stopped his sniffling and looked at me and got control of himself. The poor man. "It did," he said. "I needed to tell someone."

I knew from my father all about the yakuza and the pressures they put on company men who didn't have it in them to stand up to their threats. But I'd never expected the yakuza to have anything to do with fish.

Yuji mentioning the yakuza kept me thinking about my father and mother. Oh, how I missed them. I knew I could arrange a chance meeting. Yes. I could. But what to say? Could we begin again as if nothing had happened? No. I couldn't admit that I'd been wrong. There will be time. There will be time. For now I had Yuji. I said, "We'll talk some more the next time we meet, but, please, I'm not wearing a silly blue wig."

"Just now and then, if you don't mind? Please?"

"Never again. Never. Accept me for who I am or don't accept me at all."

"Sorry," Yuji said. "I want you to be who you are."

He was a kind man, kinder than I could ever have imagined. But what a mistake it was, continuing to see him. What a terrible mistake.

Chapter One

My name is Kawayama Tomoyuki. I am a homicide detective with the Tokyo Metropolitan Police, and I have a story to tell, but it has less to do with the crime my team and I solved than it has to do with me and the shame I have felt for several years. That shame, the assignment of it, is something that I hadn't come to terms with until I wrote this story. In the West, there are psychologists and counselors who help people in situations that I found myself, even ones in police departments, from what I've heard; but we don't have that kind of culture in Japan. We keep our emotions hidden, and this eats away at us at times. Every culture has its failings, and this, I now know, is one of Japan's. I am, or was, a prisoner of Japanese culture. I faced the shame as stoically as I could, in the spirit of a samurai warrior. I'm proud of that bushido spirit, even if I know how damaging it can be. Many Japanese self-destruct, confronting shame by wearing the proper face to get through the day. No one really knows who they are. Some men resort to alcohol and carousing hostess bars to ease the burden of shame. Women have affairs. Or they drink, too. They're called "kitchen drinkers."

The person I needed to confess to the most to relieve my shame was my wife, Mizuko. We've been married for more than twenty-five years. She needed to know what I learned while my team investigated, and solved, the murder, but I just didn't have it in me to tell her until after the killer was found dead in a flophouse in Osaka. But a brave man who has the bushido spirit took the fall for the murder, admitting to it because of the shame he felt.

I thought before confessing to Mizuko that she might leave me after I told her what I had learned. I don't know how I could have kept on if she had. If that is love, then I love her. Such a thing may sound odd to a Westerner, for a man to realize he loves his wife long after they have married, but such a marriage isn't so rare in my generation. Ours was an arranged marriage, what is called an *omiai*; we were both told by our parents that love would come in time, which it did. So perhaps this is a love story I'm telling you, but certainly not one found in cheap novels or sentimental television dramas involving young people in which the story ends with a marriage. Marriage is really a beginning. Those cheap novels and sentimental dramas are fantasies. A real marriage is not a fantasy. You'll learn about my marriage as you read about the investigation of this murder, which I've done my best to put down as accurately as I know how.

Before I begin the story, I first need to provide you with some background information that will help you to understand Tokyo. Tokyo has twenty-three wards. One is Shinjuku. It is where the murder took place. My desk is in the Shinjuku Police Department building, on the west side of South Shinjuku Station, one of the busiest stations in Japan. It's a station that is used primarily by commuters. I'm one of them. I take the Chuo express line, which has cars that are color-coded orange. The line connects Tokyo Station, where the line terminates, with the suburban towns west of Tokyo. The train makes a stop at South Shinjuku Station, where the cars often empty but fill right back up, before continuing on. The police building is only about a five minute walk from South Shinjuku Station.

My commute begins at Yotsuya Station. Mizuko and I have a traditional Japanese house made of wood and shoji screens not far from the station. We are fortunate in that regard, living in a house and not a massive building of flats, where so many Japanese live. We are fortunate to even have a small garden. In it there are a few pines and maples and one cherry tree, called a *sakura* in Japanese, 桜.

The Shinjuku Police Department building is not far from Tokyo's municipal building, which is where many companies have their headquarters in tall, steel, glass towers. A man involved in the murder, but not the killer, worked in a company headquartered in one of those imposing towers. It's likely that we might have seen each other on occasion on our walks to our respective stations. He took a train out of Seibu Station, a private train line not far from South Shinjuku Station.

On the ground floors of these corporate towers are coffee shops, restaurants, and expensive clothing stores. The office buildings are separated by expanses of green in which there are pines, cherry trees, and maples. This isn't the Tokyo that many foreigners imagine when they think of the city: the shoulder-to-shoulder throngs of people crossing busy intersections, such as the one so often seen on YouTube and on social media sites in front of Shibuya Station, farther south on the Yamanote Line, which circles Tokyo.

The Shinjuku that most foreigners imagine is eastern Shinjuku, where the murder took place. Eastern Shinjuku has pachinko parlors, peep shows, brothels, hostess and gay bars, illegal gambling dens — many popular restaurants — and, conveniently located to all these, love hotels, rows of them on the streets near Seibu Station, the station I mentioned earlier, that the man involved in the murder commuted to and from. Seibu Station serves commuters who live in the western suburb bedroom communities, which is where this man lived with his wife and children in a large, modern Western-style house.

The love hotels near Seibu Station are in an area called Kabuki-cho, Japan's most well-known pleasure district. The love hotels there are kitschy but quaint. Some of them have little ponds out front. Koi swim lazily around in the ponds, which have lily pads and reeds; an electronic recording of frogs and crickets make the hotels seem far, far away from the whish of trains and clatter of pachinko balls, just what lovers are after.

All of the hotels have entrances hidden behind walls, on which there is a lighted display of the rooms that are available. After a couple has decided on a room, they slip around the wall and enter the hotel and pay for their stay, a few hours or the night, by slipping some money under a slot in an opaque pane of glass. It's all very private. The rooms in these love hotels are as clean as the ones in the Keio Plaza Hotel, one of the best hotels in Tokyo. It's in western Shinjuku, not so far from the

Shinjuku Police building. Mizuko plays jazz piano in the hotel's main bar. From time to time I go to the Keio Plaza to have a drink and listen to her play, and when she's finished we take a taxi home after the trains have stopped running, which is around midnight.

One day in October after a typhoon had passed through the city, the weather turned pleasantly cool; the feel of autumn was in the air. My boss, Chief Inspector Saito, called me into his office. I had started out the day as I had most, by leafing through newspapers, the *Mainichi*, *Yomiuri*, and *Asahi*, my favorite, which, I knew from experience, had reporters who were interested in discovering truths, unlike the other two, which I consider to be tabloid scandal sheets, more pictures than copy, but helpful, nonetheless, to a detective who needs to keep up on social trends and what actor or singer is in the news for having an affair or having been arrested for using marijuana, cocaine, or methamphetamine — *shabu* — which is the drug of choice for yakuza thugs, company men, and, regrettably, the young, who often become bored with their corporate jobs or see no future for themselves. A detective never knows when they might need to rely on some information a reporter has dug up to solve a crime, and that was the case with this murder. A reporter from the *Asahi* helped me put together the pieces of this murder, why it happened and who the killer was.

"Good morning, Kawayama," Chief Inspector Saito said.

"Good morning, sir," I said.

"Sit," he said. He liked to order detectives around, to show his authority, but it really meant little, how he acted; it was just the face he wore to get through the day. I'd seen him break down and cry too many times to believe that his gruffness meant anything, even if his appearance, that of a rugby champion with cauliflowered ears and mangled fingers, did promote the image of a tough cop. I have to say, very honestly, that his breakdowns into fits of sobbing, tears flowing down his bulldog cheeks, were not without some justification and understanding, if a person has any humanity in their heart. I remember one case we went on in which a pretty high school girl, about to head off to Tokyo University to study Japanese literature, had been raped and beaten unconscious. The rapist had placed her body on the Odakyu line, a private line that serves the southwest suburbs. The train severed her body. Who wouldn't shed a tear over that? The rapist was convicted and sent to Abashiri Prison up in Hokkaido, Japan's northernmost island, where the winters are long and harsh. When he was hanged, most Japanese rejoiced. We Japanese still carry out death sentences by hanging. The long drop snaps the prisoner's neck. A majority of Japanese support it. Killers who have upset the equilibrium of a civil society deserve the death penalty, I believe.

I think Chief Inspector Saito started off with some small talk about Chinese fighters penetrating Japanese airspace, down in the Okinawa area. Threats from China had become a weekly occurrence. Our F-15s had intercepted the Chinese fighters and escorted them out of our airspace. Like many Japanese, Chief Inspector Saito feared China's growing military and economic power. China had relegated Japan to the number three economic spot in the world. We'd been proud of our rise from the ashes of the Pacific War to become the number two economic power, and for a while some had even thought, foolishly, that we would overtake the United States. It was the same kind of foolish thinking that had preceded our attack on Pearl Harbor and the consequential destruction of most of our cities during the war, turned to heaps of ash by B 29s dropping incendiary bombs.

As Chief Inspector Saito was talking about China, I looked over his head at the park. I saw the tops of maples, and the sight of the trees made me think of the changing of the seasons, when the maples turn blazing reds and oranges. Mizuko and I always take a trip to a *ryokan*, a traditional Japanese inn that has a hot spring, *onsen*, that time of year, to enjoy the sight of the changing colors of the leaves, called *kouyo* in Japanese, and also to soak away our stresses in the sulfur water of the baths. The waters loosen our neck muscles, our shoulders and thighs, and bring us closer together. Husbands and wives, even if the attraction is there, a distance between them can't help but creep in at times, and a trip to a mountain *onsen* helps to bring them back together.

I believe I was thinking of dining on some fresh mountain vegetables, tofu, and charcoal-grilled *ayu*, a sort of freshwater smelt caught in mountain streams, when Chief Inspector Saito growled, "Are you listening to me, Kawayama?"

"Yes, sir," I said, "absolutely."

"The war was long ago. The Chinese and Koreans need to move on the way we did, stop blaming us for their shortcomings."

"We did invade their countries, sir."

"And we've paid billions in repatriations, not to mention that Honda and how many other Japanese companies have set up factories in China and are now employing those peasants who would otherwise be in a rice paddy feeling mud squish up between their toes. They should be thankful for our factories being there, not protesting and demanding apologies. My grandfather died in China in the war, you know."

"You're right, sir, the Chinese should be thankful." I didn't dare mention to him that more than ten million Chinese had died during the war and our occupation of their country, or that some of our doctors had performed vivisections on Chinese, to learn what weapons were most effective. Few Japanese talked about that part of our history. It was too shameful to do so.

"A girl was found dead in a love hotel in Kabuki-cho," he then said. "Terrible. Awful. Go see what happened. Ms. Nodoka and her forensics team are already there. It's the Amour."

I knew of the Amour. It's a quaint hotel that has a model of the Eiffel Tower at the entrance and some fake garret windows on the second floor, all to make it look very French, something out of *The Sun Also Rises* or resembling a bohemian painter's studio. I may be a police detective, but I'm a well-read one, having studied English and American literature at Waseda University.

Chief Inspector Saito had remained sitting in his big chair. He seemed to me to be holding back a tear. Then I thought, Who wouldn't?

I think it was Edgar Allen Poe who said something about the death of a beautiful girl being poetic. I assumed, rightly, that this girl was beautiful, because of the circumstances of her death — in a love hotel — and that she might have been a prostitute. But what did any of this matter, really? What mattered to me was that she had been a couple's daughter. Mizuko and I have a daughter. Her name is Tomomi.

Chapter Two

I left Chief Inspector Saito's office and went back to my desk, which was in a room full of other detectives. Phones were ringing, and the detectives were answering them, saying things such as, "This is a matter for animal control," "You need to contact your nearest *kouban* if you're calling about the theft of a bicycle," and, "Your neighbor's son didn't come home last night? Ask her about him."

This room of detectives wasn't a scene from an American police drama, in which detectives have tattoos and beards and shout obscenities at each other. There were no drunks or suspects in a cage in a corner of the room. The atmosphere was very corporate, indistinguishable from an office in Sumitomo Life Insurance, with the exception of a few uniformed officers, men and women, who had sidearms, revolvers in a holster that were connected to their belts by a lanyard. The plain clothes detectives were dressed in dark suits and white shirts and silk ties. The undercover detectives who dressed in jeans and ragged shirts allowed their beards to grow, their department was on another floor.

I went to the desk of Detective Izuka, whom I had worked many cases with. He is thirty-seven, married with two children, and is beginning to feel the grind of being a very small cog in a giant bureaucratic machine. Like me, he had held aspirations of being someone of importance when entering the police force. He had ranked as a 7th *dan* in the kendo ranking system, one rank below the highest. Police usually take the higher rankings. But the paperwork involved in being a police detective had ground him down. He'd about given up on kendo and was now preferring young, available women to relieve the stresses — and often boredom — of the job. I said to him, "A girl was found dead in a love hotel in Kabuki-cho."

"Again?" he asked.

"Yes," I said. We'd worked a case involving a murdered girl the year before. The married man she'd been meeting had killed her when she'd attempted to blackmail him. She'd hired a private investigator to take some photos of them entering a love hotel. A few days after her murder, the man committed suicide, hanging himself in a business hotel in Omiya, a city north of Tokyo, out of shame. Adultery played a part in this murder, but in a way I couldn't have imagined.

Detective Izuka bowed his head. His daughter was ten, his son eight. He'd come to Tokyo from Toyama prefecture, an agricultural area on the coast of the Sea of Japan, to be another Dirty Harry. I'd had the same aspirations, or fantasizes, to look some criminal in the eye, point my .44 magnum at his forehead, and growl, "Are you feeling lucky, punk?" Unlike me, however, Detective Izuka did have the build of a Japanese Clint Eastwood, albeit a shorter version. I look anonymously corporate. I wear less than fashionable eyeglasses.

Detective Izuka is ruggedly handsome, has broad, square shoulders, a pronounced chin, and his eyes have a playful glint. All these qualities must have helped him out with women, those he was sexually drawn to and those who were either suspects in a crime or witnesses to one. He had a soft touch when it was needed, beguiling out of them honest answers that helped us in our investigations.

Detective Izuka stood, and, as we were walking to the elevator, put on his jacket. "Know anything about her?" he asked.

"Nothing."

"Men," he said. "They don't know how to treat a woman."

This was ironic, coming from him. I said nothing. Maybe she wasn't a prostitute but a scorned lover who'd taken her life, but the possibility that a man had murdered her was more likely. Women don't usually kill themselves in love hotels. They have a reputation they want to protect.

We got into the elevator and took it down to the basement parking garage, where a black and white Toyota squad car was waiting for us. The driver was a police officer in uniform.

He drove out of the basement garage into the daylight and headed in the direction of eastern Shinjuku and came to a railroad trestle that is often used as an establishing shot in news stories foreign journalists file on the peculiarities of Japan and the Japanese, ones about vending machines that sell high school girls' used underwear, gropers on trains, and square melons that go for over ten thousand yen, around a hundred U.S. dollars, and are packaged in handsome cedar boxes.

These loony stories about the fringes of Japanese society aren't accurate representations of the country, because life in Japan, for the most part, is rather boring. Trains run on time. Children wear pressed uniforms to school. Women use bicycles to go shopping. Sales people are welcoming, enthusiastic, and deferential. But none of this would attract an audience. And so those who know Japan only by what they've read of the country or seen on YouTube or the news really have no idea what Japanese life is really like, with the exception of the occasional deadly earthquake or mudslide, when boredom turns to utter panic in a second. That's closer to the reality of life in Japan.

The trains were whizzing past on the trestle, one right after the other, which does make for an eye-catching backdrop for a reporter, and just past the trestle, at night, there is the neon blitz of eastern Shinjuku and Kabuki-cho when night falls.

On this morning the street scene was more commonplace. The sidewalks were filled with commuters rushing off to their companies, carrying bags. Others were stopping off to have a coffee in one of the many coffee shops there. We're a coffee drinking people, make no mistake about that. Tea, yes, plenty of that as well, but coffee is the drink of choice of many, including myself.

In the alleys of Kabuki-cho, crouched under staircases, were those Japanese the country had turned its back on — wizened drunkards rummaging through spent liquor bottles in the bins behind bars and restaurants. They pour out a few drops of liquor into a plastic cup and drink it down. As long as they remain out of sight, we Japanese put up with them. Some social workers now and then try to steer them to shelters, but they're rarely successful. Living among urban outcasts, that's their group, the way being with other police is my group.

The driver guided the Toyota along lanes in Kabuki-cho, passing bars and restaurants and girly arcades, peep shows and brothels, the photos of many of the girls plastered to the walls near the entrances; many of the photos, however, were taken from porn magazines or videos and had nothing to do with the girls inside, who'd come to Tokyo from other prefectures, often from the agricultural north, where there were few good-paying jobs. The touts would come out at around noon to lure in the lunch crowd of weak-willed men who couldn't hold out until returning home or had no girlfriend or were just too stressed from work to put in the effort to find someone. A simple financial transaction between a man and a woman was so much easier for them. Unlike Westerners, mostly Americans, we Japanese tolerate prostitution. Yes, it's morally wrong, but a gray sort of immoral wrong that many of us have engaged in, including myself a few times as a university student before I met Mizuko.

The driver guided the Toyota along a street, passing a Family Mart convenience store and onto a street lined with love hotels — Blue Moon, Liberty, Starlight, and Lemon Tea, which brought back memories. Mizuko and I had been to it a few times before, and even after, our marriage. We'd also been to love hotels in other parts of Tokyo as well to take a break from the city. They're often strategically located near train stations. Do I feel shame for this? Hardly. It's who we are as humans. We have desires, and in Japan there is little private space. The hotels serve a purpose. But now and then there are drug overdoses resulting in deaths and quarrels between lovers. The manager's only recourse then is to call the police, or, sometimes, the yakuza, who often have a hand in the running of these hotels, promising protection, which they do deliver. The yakuza? I wish they didn't exist.

But they do, on occasion, have a place in our culture, by enforcing order in ways that the police can't, and if you continue to read this story of mine you'll learn how I availed myself of their services.

The driver stopped the Toyota in front of the Amour. A police van was there, and members of a forensics team were going to and from it, into the hotel, whose manager was at the entrance, an old man, maybe seventy-five or so, who was smoking a cigarette and looking quite doleful, either because of the bad publicity or his honest contrition. It was impossible to know which.

Detective Izuka and I got out of the car. We were met by Ms. Nodoka, chief of the forensics team. She nodded, issued a professional "good morning," and then added, "Murder."

"How?" I asked.

"Strangled," she said, "with a charging cord for an iPhone." Ms. Nodoka was always very taciturn, didn't waste time with banter, the way some of my male colleagues do. She deserved to be the head of a forensics team one day. "I'm judging she was killed sometime early this morning," she said. "She still has color in her cheeks."

"Any identification?" I asked.

"Jiyumi Harajuku."

"Sounds like an alias," I said.

"My impression as well. The ID looks forged."

Detective Izuka said, "Your new hairstyle is very becoming."

Ms. Nodoka had had long hair, to her shoulders, and now it was short, a bit boyish, brushing the tops of her ears. Her complexion was an elegant, unblemished white.

She glared at Detective Izuka but said nothing, which said plenty. She was too smart to fall for his insipid flattery, unlike the younger women he was successful with.

Harajuku was a station on the Yamanote line, near the Meiji Temple. Young people gather near the station on weekends, the girls in all kinds of elaborate costumes, often in a doll or video avatar motif, and the young men in black leather and bracelets with spikes, how the owner of a pit bull might dress his or her dog. This aspect of Tokyo life, of young Japanese gathering near Harajuku Station, had been the subject of many foreign journalists' stories, to the point that there was no longer a story in the story, and so they had moved on to search for another strange aspect of Tokyo life. Bloggers had already written about love hotels and included videos and maps to Tokyo's more interesting ones, including even reviews of the bed, so stories of love hotels were no longer of interest to foreign reporters.

Ms. Nodoka said, "I have work to do." She went back into the hotel.

"She's getting a divorce," Detective Izuka said.

"I didn't even know she was married."

"I like her new hairstyle."

"She's too intelligent for you."

"I need a change of pace."

"You'll be heading for a divorce if you don't watch yourself."

"My wife would be lost without me."

"Don't flatter yourself," I warned him.

I went over to the manager, who was standing by the window where couples look at the lighted board of rooms that are available. The manager was working his way through another cigarette. He had ground out the first one in a pocket ashtray he carried around in a trouser pocket. He bowed and handed me his *meishi*, business card. Even managers of love hotels have business cards. His name was Tanaka. I showed him my ID and asked, "What do you know about this?"

"I don't know a thing, sir," he said. "Nothing. Nothing at all. I wasn't here at the time, you understand. Nothing like this—"

I said, "You're not a suspect. We just want to know what you know."

He nodded his head, then said, "Mrs. Kikuchi was at the front desk last night and this morning. Shall I call her?"

"Is she inside?"

"She's distraught, the poor woman. She's a widower, you understand, living on her husband's life insurance."

"Not too distraught to talk," Detective Izuka said.

"No, no. She's willing. But she's an old woman who watches TV dramas all night. It's a boring job."

"Take us to her," I said.

Detective Izuka and I, following police procedure to prevent the contamination of evidence, put on white cotton gloves before entering the hotel.

We followed Mr. Tanaka into the small lobby, where there was a kitschy model of the Eiffel Tower beside the opaque pane of glass the receptionist sits behind. Beside the window there was a door. Mr. Tanaka opened it and in a tiny room there was an old woman with hair dyed brown sitting in an office chair. A small television was on a shelf beside her. She was a bit stout and looked to be a drinker. Her cheeks were red and her lipstick a medicinal pink. Many of these front desk clerks drink their way through the night as they watch television dramas. She stood when Detective Izuka and I showed her our badges and bowed. I told Mr. Tanaka that we'd call him if we needed him, and he walked off.

"Please take a seat," I said to Mrs. Kikuchi.

"May I serve you tea or coffee?" she asked. Next to the television there was an electric kettle, tea pitcher, and cups, and tucked away behind the cups a small bottle of *shochu*. It's a Japanese drink made of rice and barley and other grains that is stronger than sake, over twenty-five percent alcohol, that has recently become popular with young women. Why? I have no idea. When I was younger, women thought *shochu* was an old man's drink. None of them would've been seen drinking the stuff.

"No, thank you," I said and remained standing.

"We'll be quick," Detective Izuka said. "We just want to ask you a few questions."

"There were two of them," she said.

That was fairly obvious.

"How old was the man?" I asked. "Could you make a guess from his voice?"

"I'm so sorry," she said. "You're sure you don't want some tea?"

"No, thank you," Detective Izuka said. He added, "Was he young, middle-aged?"

"Customers here, they don't talk."

I could've guessed as much. I hadn't when Mizuko and I had visited a love hotel. Anonymity was why people went to love hotels.

"About what time did they arrive?" I asked.

"I think around six. The news was on. I like Yomiuri. What about you? NHK is too dull."

"So they were planning to spend the night?" I asked.

"The man paid for the night. That true crime story was on TV, about the woman poisoning her husband for his life insurance money. That's why I remember the time."

"What room did they take?" I asked.

"The Monet room," she said. "It's very French, even has an artist's easel as decoration and windows that have views of Paris street life. It's like going to Paris, I'd say. Very romantic."

"Nice touch," Detective Izuka said.

I said, "Did he have a dialect? From Tohoku or Kansai?"

"No. Standard Japanese, very educated and polite, from what I recall. Yes, that's what I'd say. Educated. And a bit shy. I think he and that girl have been here before, but I can't be sure about that."

"You didn't see either of them?"

"Of course not! I'm no snoop. Mr. Tanaka would fire me if I were a snoop. What couples do, that's their business. That's why they come here."

Detective Izuka and I looked at each other. Was their affair a long-term one? Company men do take lovers who are young enough to be their daughters, and these women, well, they take the men for a ride, having them buy them expensive designer clothes and bags, perfumes, and the latest model smartphones.

"Married," Detective Izuka muttered, reading my mind about the man.

"The girl never said anything?" I asked.

"No. Girls are shy."

"You said he was polite?" Detective Izuka said, "but that he hardly spoke. Why do you say he was polite?"

"Well, I got the impression he was. I think he was the man who forgot to take his change a while back. Sometimes drunks show up. They're not so polite. Their breath smells of beer. He wasn't like that. His hand was shaking when he took the change."

I asked her for her ID card and wrote down her address and asked her for her telephone number. "Please don't come to my home," she said. "I live with my daughter, and, well…. She doesn't know I work at a place like this. It would be so embarrassing."

"We'll call first," I said.

"Thank you." She bowed.

Detective Izuka and I went back out into the hallway, where Mr. Tanaka had been waiting, smoking away. I asked him if he had a maid on duty, and he said he did and that she had been at the hotel all night. It turned out that she was the one who discovered the body. Her name was Mrs. Oita.

"We need to talk to her," I said.

"She's in the linen room, waiting. She's an old woman, too, all broken up over this. It's never happened before."

"I wouldn't think it has," I said.

"Mrs. Oita, she's kind of a mother to some of these girls, when the men leave them in the room crying. She's a comfort to them. She enjoys listening to their stories and offering advice."

"Take us to her," Detective Izuka said.

The linen room was at the end of a dimly lit corridor, along which there were doors to the rooms where the action took place. We passed the room where the woman's body had been found. The forensics team was in it, collecting evidence, and a photographer was taking photos. The flash from the camera was like summer lightning.

We came to a door at the end of the corridor. Mr. Tanaka knocked on it.

"*Hai,*" Mrs. Oita answered.

Mr. Tanaka said, "There's a couple of police detectives here who'd like to talk to you."

"Please," she said.

Mr. Tanaka opened the door.

Mrs. Oita was a robust little woman with a wide face and gray hair, very grandmotherly; she was the kind of wholesome woman almost any girl would immediately open up to after a man has dumped her. She was sitting in a wooden chair beside a shelf of towels and bed sheets. There were also boxes of Okamoto condoms on one of the shelves in red little packets decorated with hearts. The better hotels put condoms and Meiji chocolate samplers on the pillows. I think some Meiji executive, after a romp in a hotel, got the idea to furnish the hotels with chocolates to promote the company's sweets.

Detective Izuka and I showed Mrs. Oita our badges and introduced ourselves. She stood and nodded. Another chair was in the room. She offered it, and the one she had been sitting on, to us.

"That won't be necessary," I said.

A canned Boss Black coffee was on a little table beside a small television. She looked at the coffee and said, "You know that old ad with Ei-*chan.* I like him. What about you?" She was referring to Yazawa Eikichi, the so-called Mick Jagger of Japanese rock music, who must have been king when she was young. The suffix *-chan* was usually used to refer to young girls. Using it to refer to him made him seem charming and innocent, which he probably was. I guessed that the younger generation wouldn't have recognized him if he were walking across that crowded intersection in front of Shibuya Station. The young, I suppose, would think he was an old pervert on the prowl if they saw him in

Shibuya, where bored young girls congregate, attracting porn scouts and drug dealers.

"Yazawa Eikichi makes good ads," I said, to loosen her up.

"Doesn't he, though? But he's getting on in years now. I need coffee to get me through the night. Tea doesn't do the trick."

"About what happened in the Monet room," I said.

"It's terrible. A tragedy. The poor girl. No girl should come to her end that way. No. Makes no difference to me who she was. You'll catch the killer, won't you?"

"That's why we need to talk to you," Detective Izuka said.

"But what can I tell you?"

"Maybe you saw the man," I said. "Or the girl? Or saw someone enter the room?" That's the way some of the older, more traditional Japanese are, assuming responsibility for a crime they had nothing to do with. She added, "The couples that come here don't want to be seen, you know?"

"Quite," Detective Izuka said.

"But I can tell you this." She leaned forward. "It's not only men and women who come here. Now and then it's two men."

"You don't say?" Detective Izuka said.

"They like the décor, I believe, those kinds."

I didn't want to point out to her that she had just contradicted herself, that she actually did take a peek at who was coming and going from time to time, and put her on the defensive, and so I said nothing. Detective Izuka knew to do the same.

I said, "Perhaps you could relate to us how you came upon the poor girl, what time it was, what you remember. Just speak freely, please. Don't think we're here to judge you."

"It's only because I need the money that I work here," she said. "I've tried to get work at good hotels. But, I know what those youngsters who do the hiring think — *that old woman, she won't hold out.*" She drank some of the Boss Black coffee. "I've still got it in me, the drive to work."

"I understand," Detective Izuka said.

"And what time was it, about, that you found the girl?"

"A few minutes past seven this morning, I'd say, just as I was about to finish my shift. I knew right away what had happened. I watch Crime TV. I know things. A girl on the floor, naked. What else could it be but..."

"Did you go over to her, to see if she was, well, alive?" Detective Izuka asked.

"I did. But I knew immediately that.... Her eyes were open. She had this lonely stare."

"Do you think she was one of *those* girls?" Detective Izuka asked.

"So what if she was? They have it tough, you know, dealing with all kinds of men. They're sellers of spring."

She seemed to be speaking from experience, which explained why she had ended up as a maid in a love hotel, more than the hiring policies of legitimate hotels. The word for prostitute, when written in traditional Japanese, is 売春婦, *bai-shun-fu*, a woman who sells spring.

Japan has a long history of women working in what we call the water trade. Some of these women are prostitutes, but most are what are now called hostesses who work in clubs. There are plenty of these clubs in Kabuki-cho and other pleasure districts in Tokyo. These pleasure districts are in every Japanese city or town, even small fishing villages, which now have imported hostesses from the Philippines, Japanese girls preferring the status of working in a city. There are soaplands, too, a euphemism for brothels, in these districts. The yakuza run them. Yoshiwara, in the Asakusa district of Tokyo, is one of the oldest pleasure districts. It has a history that dates back centuries. It was a refuge for samurai, merchants, artists, and bureaucrats. They were all equals there, once they set foot in their favorite brothel.

"Who will inform her family?" Mrs. Oita asked.

"A police officer will," I said. I didn't know just how wrong I was about that then. No one told her family. The police never could find her family. Japan's secrecy laws are strict. When a person disappears, we refer to them as the evaporated. There's not much the police can do to help the family track the person down, and so those mothers and fathers who have children who've run away have to rely on private detective agencies, but even they have difficulty finding out who the family is. It's the result of the Pacific War, these strict secrecy laws we have, because before and during the war the government could track down anyone who was opposed to the war and throw them in prison. Or see that they disappeared. Permanently.

"We'll find whoever killed her," I said.

"I hope he ends up hanging from the end of a rope."

"He will," Detective Izuka said.

"So what did you do then, after you realized she was dead?" I asked.

"Screamed," Mrs. Oita said.

"Of course."

"Anyone with a heart would."

She finished off the can of coffee and set it down. "I could do with another," she said.

Detective Izuka said, "I'll get you one."

"There's a machine in the lobby," she said.

He left and Mrs. Oita and I looked at each other. I saw in her eyes a woman whom I could pour out my soul to, all those dark secrets that I hadn't told anyone, those secrets that have brought me to tell this story. "I have many experiences here," she said, "but nothing like this. You can't imagine the stories I've heard. Truth really is stranger than fiction. There were even some men who got left behind and cried like babies. They weren't very experienced with women. Men aren't as strong as they make themselves out to be. I try to get them and the girls back on their feet by lending them an ear. They always thanked me. Sex. It's supposed to be pleasurable, now, isn't it?, not turn one to tears."

"Yes, it is," I said.

"I remember when I was young...."

Detective Izuka then entered the room and handed her a can of Boss Black coffee.

She nodded her head. "Thank you. I need it to get me through the night," she said, repeating herself, the way so many of the elderly do. She went on, "I have terrible backaches. Terrible. A morning bath fixes me up."

"You'll be home soon," I said, "enjoying your bath." I said to Detective Izuka, "We were just discussing the complications of life."

"There are many," he said.

"Making up rooms, that's not all I do, you know. Anyone can do that. I was telling Detective Kawayama that men aren't as tough as they think they are. Women, they're the tough ones."

"I wouldn't know," Detective Izuka said.

She looked at him incredulously.

"My wife is tough," I said.

"Women have to put up with so much more than you men. You wouldn't know what it's like to be groped on a train."

"So what did you do after you screamed?" I asked.

"Why, I ran out of the room and told Mrs. Kikuchi."

"How long were you in the room?" I asked.

"Not more than a minute. How could I stay there?"

"I understand," I said.

"You didn't see anyone all night?" Detective Izuka said, "not even hear anything from the room?"

"Do you think I'd keep this job if I went snooping around? People nowadays have cameras in their phones. I don't want anyone to think I'm that kind of person."

"Maybe they were regulars?" I said.

"Could be," she said. "But I tend to my own affairs. I'm not a snoop."

"You've been very helpful," Detective Izuka said.

"Don't flatter me," she said. "I didn't tell you anything of importance." She drank some of the coffee. "I like my coffee black," she said, "not that syrupy sweet stuff. A woman has to be strong to take on this job."

"Detective Izuka wasn't flattering you," I said. "You've been helpful."

She nodded her head.

We left her there with her can of Boss coffee and went down the hall and came to the Monet room. It was made to resemble a painter's garret room, except for the space over the bed, which had a fake night sky of twinkling fake stars. Two pillows were tossed onto the floor. On a stand beside the bed were two Okamoto condom wrappers.

The bed faced a row of fake garret windows that had holograms of a Paris street, bistros and bakeries and newsstands and sidewalk cafes. People were crossing streets dressed as they had back in the nineteenth century, in overcoats and long dresses and bonnets. In some of the windows there were horse-drawn carriages. What a Japanese sense of detail and ingenuity the room had for the benefit of two people out to indulge in their fantasies.

The girl's body was in a corner, beside the artist's easel, over which hung a pair of her jeans and a boy's white dress shirt. She was naked to the waist, lying on her side. The girl's Louis Vuitton handbag, rather small, no bigger than a bento box — lunch box — had a thin strap with a gold buckle and was on a counter near the bathroom door. The bathroom had, as all of these love hotel rooms do, a tub that was big enough for two people.

Across the room from the girl was a table that had flimsy legs made of wire in a French style. It had a couple of bottles of Kirin beer on it and a dish of peeled edamame shells. An ashtray as well was there, but no cigarette butts were in it. This came as a disappointment. I'd been hoping that there might be a butt there, as an indicator of what brand of cigarette the man smoked, then I saw two balls of tissue — I assumed used condoms — in a trash bin beside the bed. They'd have the DNA evidence we needed. So would the beer bottles and edamame shells. The killer had been sloppy. Maybe he'd killed the girl in a fit of rage. Some men are that way. They think they own the woman who agreed to sleep with them, particularly a woman who is a seller of spring because they paid for her.

Detective Izuka, looking at the condoms wrapped up in tissue, said, "I'll leave it to Ms. Nodoka's team to collect those."

She'd heard him and turned and shot him a cold stare. In return, he smiled. She went back to work.

She and a photographer and a couple of men in her team were still gathering evidence. I knew they'd get to the condoms soon enough. One man was dusting for fingerprints; another was on the bed, holding a magnifying glass and tweezers, gathering strands of hair and placing them in a plastic bag. We'd have plenty of DNA evidence, but none of it mattered, in the end.

Detective Izuka and I went over to the girl's handbag. I asked Ms. Nodoka, "Can we examine the contents?"

"We've dusted it," she said.

I opened the bag and laid what was inside on the table — a bottle of nail polish, red, fake finger nails, those kind with gem stones in them, tampons, a packet of tissues, a cigarette lighter in a silver case but no cigarettes, a bit odd, and a bottle of Gaiac 10 perfume. Detective Izuka said of the bottle, "Expensive stuff. Has a musky, arousing fragrance."

"You'd know," I said.

"Only sold in Daikanyama, I think."

Daikanyama was a very exclusive shop in Shibuya, catering to young, stylish — and wealthy — women.

The girl also had an expensive titanium Zebra fountain pen, a small bar of handmade soap from a shop in Akasaka, tweezers, three tubes of lipstick, all subtle reds, and a cosmetics kit made of bamboo that included a small mirror. Her purse was very supple, elegant goat skin. It had in it more than thirty thousand yen, some change, an ATM card from Sumitomo Bank, and a JTB charge card. The name on the cards was Harajuku Jiyumi 原宿自由美. The Jiyumi was the kanji for beautiful freedom, 自由美. Harkajuku was the same kanji for the train station, 原宿.

I looked at the fake ID card. She was born in the Japanese Heisei year 10 — 1998 — on September 12th; her address was in Bunkyo Ward near

Iidabashi Station. The rent there had to be too high for a young girl like her, unless she was sharing the place with someone, so that stood out as a possible lead, that she had a roommate or lover; or maybe a company man was paying her rent. These girls often did. Then there were forgers I knew that I could lean on to provide me with information about who had forged her ID, to find out, maybe, her real name, but I wasn't holding out for that. A forger probably didn't even know her real name if she had wanted to become one of Japan's evaporated. She was also carrying in that Louis Vuitton bag a pack of Okamoto condoms. Then there were twenty or so of her *meishis*. On them were her name and phone number framed by two Japanese cranes, like those on a JAL airliner. She was a traditionalist. No Hello Kitties or bunnies on her *meishi*.

"She must've had quite the client list," Detective Izuka said.

"Her telephone is missing," I said.

I looked in every pocket of her bag but it wasn't there.

"A girl like her with no phone. Impossible," Detective Izuka said.

"I'll have IT trace it," I said. "We do have her phone number."

Looking at the girl, Detective Izuka said, "Such a pitiful end."

"I've never known you to be sentimental," I said.

I looked over at her body. She was shapely. I could tell that, even if she was lying on her side, her back to us. A towel was draped over her bottom. Strange, I remember thinking, how the killer had had that kind of respect for her, to cover her with a towel. Her youthful breasts were flattened out on the parquet floor. She had a long, elegant neck, the kind French painters would have admired. Sadly, red ligature marks from the charging cord disgraced that neck. Yes, there aren't too many things more poetic than the death of a beautiful girl.

While looking for her phone, I had pulled out a receipt for a restaurant bill at a sushi shop, one for a pair of Prada shoes, one for a taxi fare, and a lottery ticket — Ichiban Kuji. We could easily trace the lottery ticket back to where she had bought it. Most important of all, I found a payslip from the Nankaitou Club. Nankaitou, written 南海島,

means south sea, *tou* means island, *kai* 海 sea, *tou* 島 island. These clubs are where lonely men go to be pampered by young, heavily made-up women who often wear evening gowns. The women pour their drinks and light their cigarettes and do a lot of listening, the way a psychologist does. It's tough work, listening to these arrogant men, who are often wealthy department or section chiefs with clout and managerial responsibilities. They use these hostesses to talk about things they might not risk telling their wives because their marriages are so sour. The Nankaitou Club was in Akasaka, one of the more affluent neighborhoods of Tokyo. This girl had class.

I handed the payslip to Detective Izuka.

"She must've been freelancing," he said. Some hostesses did sleep with customers they got along with. It's a normal thing, when men and women meet and drink. I wouldn't call that selling spring.

Over by the front door was a woman's lavender Montbell windbreaker, and in the shoe rack a pair of high-top Keds, which my daughter Tomomi had worn when she was in high school. Seeing them, a shudder of memory of her in her school uniform rattled up my spine.

"Remember when those long socks were the rage?" Detective Izuka said.

Tomomi had never gone in for them. She said they made a girl look dumb and puffed out her legs to the shape of *daikons*, a Japanese white radish.

"The girls used glue to hold those long socks up," Detective Izuka said.

"How many pairs have you rolled off a girl's legs?"

He said nothing.

"Just remember, you have a daughter," I said.

He groaned.

The photographer said to us, "I've finished," and left the room.

We went over to the girl and knelt. A black charging cord was resting a meter or so away from her head, which was turned to one side. The side of her face was pressed onto the parquet floor. She had a thin, elegant nose, unusual in Asian women, but some are born with them, very straight and Romanesque.

Death hadn't quite set in. Her cheeks were a youthful pink. She had a scar just below her hairline. I thought of her parents, who she was, how she'd come to be in this room, and with whom? Why had he — and I was certain that it was a man — strangled her? What could she have done to provoke him to do such a thing? I doubted that she had done much of anything other than what she'd gone to the room expecting to do. Maybe he had beaten other girls. Maybe he was a psychopath. It was reasonable to think so. I thought that we'd have to go through arrest records and try to narrow down who he was, if the girls he'd beaten had filed a report. But I wasn't optimistic about that. They wouldn't want to be shamed by being in a love hotel with him.

I continued to stare at her. I just couldn't understand why, after this man had gotten what he'd wanted from her, he hadn't just walked out of the room, as other men did when their desire was quenched. She looked like the kind of girl who would satisfy any man. She was indeed cute, even in death. And then a feeling of nausea knotted up in my gut. I feared that I might have to make a dash for the toilet. You see, the girl lying at my feet was my daughter Tomomi.

While the Moon Comes Out of the Sea
Michael Zimecki

City detective Ambrose Pierce was vacationing in Lakeview when the local police chief called to ask him for his help investigating a murder. Out of courtesy, Ambrose agreed to lend a hand. The Lakeview police department was small, consisting of the chief and two officers, both part-time, and didn't have a trained investigator on staff. Although he was on vacation, Ambrose acceded to the chief's request, partly because he was better at acting than relaxing, but also because he hoped the investigation might jumpstart his mental battery.

Ambrose needed to recharge. Lately, he had been having trouble getting started, trouble keeping going, trouble powering through the day. His voltage was low, his battery drained, his tank nearly on empty. That, in fact, was why he was here in Lakeview instead of at a desk hundreds of miles away, whittling away at his paperwork.

It began and ended with his sleep. Ambrose had been sleeping badly of late and the problem had spilled over into every aspect of his life. His doctor thought he might be suffering from a sleep disorder and had recommended a study in a lab, but Ambrose chose to follow his own advice and take some time off instead.

It wasn't helping. Last night, in fact, his sleep had been disturbed by a nightmare. He dreamed that someone or something was chasing him. Ambrose Pierce awoke in a cold sweat; every part of him, his hair, his face, his skin, was wet with perspiration. Sweat soaked his pajamas and even drenched the bed socks on his feet. The dream, he knew, was a symptom of stress in his waking life.

After the chief called, Ambrose took a quick shower and changed into clean clothes and dry socks. The chief had asked to meet at a beachfront bar a half mile or so away from Pierce's rental.

"I can have one of my men come and get you," the Lakeview police chief said.

"No need," Ambrose replied. "It's not a long walk and I could use some air. Cordon off the crime scene and make sure no one moves or touches the body until I get there. I'll see you in ten. "

It took him nearly twenty to walk the sandy beach. The morning air was bracing: the wind was coming in gusts from the lake; it blasted a band of gulls from a sand pit, making them wobble like drunkards before regaining their balance and taking flight. Ambrose pulled the collar of his jacket up. It was late in the season, and the air was cooler than he expected. The chill settled in his bones. About halfway to his destination, his arthritis acted up, exacerbating the joint pain in his knees and the sciatic neuritis in his lower back. He began to regret turning down the chief's offer of a ride as he hobbled along the beach.

He exchanged greetings with the chief when he arrived at Shadrach's Shell Shack, their designated meeting place.

"Call me Billy," the chief, whose give name was William, said, extending a hand.

Ambrose nodded as he shook it.

"So, you're Ambrose."

"Yup."

"Everyone's a Billy, Bob, or Billy Bob out here in the sticks."

"My mother named me Ambrose after her favorite writer, Ambrose Bierce," the city detective said by way of explanation, even though none was necessary.

Billy's face screwed up into a question mark.

"He wrote *The Devil's Dictionary*," Ambrose told him.

"We're all God-fearing people here," Billy said.

"My mother was just riffing on the name, I guess. Ambrose Bierce, Ambrose Pierce...."

The chief gave him a sideways glance. "So your mother called you Ambrose. What about regular folk?" he asked. "They call you Am,

Ambie, Amy, or Amber?"

The city detective suppressed a sudden urge to kill. "None of the above," he scowled. Especially the last two."

"I'm just playin' with you," the police chief said with a grin. "No offense intended."

"None taken," Ambrose lied.

"Why don't I just call you Brody?"

Billy led Brody down to the beach where a Lakeview officer was standing guard over a body in the sand. Two EMTs stood nearby. The coroner, Billy informed him, was en route.

The officer debriefed Ambrose. A local fisherman had found the body earlier that morning and called police. The body belonged to a corpulent man who had been shot in the chest. He was local, too. His name was Luther Geary and he tended bar at the Shell Shack. According to Billy's man, Geary closed the bar around 2 a.m. after announcing last call. Three regulars were in the bar at closing time. After finishing their drinks, two of them drove off in a pickup, the other in a van. As he pulled out of the lot, the van driver saw Geary exit the bar through a back door onto the beach. The bartender, who did not drive, typically used the beach as a shortcut to his apartment in town.

Ambrose bent over the body. Rigor mortis had already progressed to Geary's limbs, putting the time of death at closer to 2 in the morning than when the fisherman found the body at 7.

"Around moonrise," the chief said when Ambrose mentioned the time.

Ambrose stared at him incredulously.

"It rises later and later up here this time of year," Billy said. "That's a fact. But don't take my word for it. You could look it up in the *Old Farmer's Almanac*. Better reading than that dictionary you were tellin' me about, I reckon."

The city detective went back to his work, examining the dead man's hands for soiling or powder burns. There weren't any. There wasn't any powder or other residue on the victim's clothing either. Luther Geary was wearing a scoop neck wife beater, cargo shorts, and a pair of white sneakers with no socks, a little underdressed for the weather, but, hey, he was a big man with a beer gut, a veritable bowl full of jelly that would have made Kris Kringle proud. The scoop neck in his tee exposed a small, oval entrance wound. There wasn't any muzzle impression on the tee, no powder tattooing or scorching around the hole in Geary's chest, and Ambrose inferred that he hadn't incurred a contact wound. He most likely had been shot from a few feet away. The shooter had aimed for center mass, striking his victim next to his breastbone a few centimeters above the internipple line.

Ambrose rose and surveyed the crime scene. There were some shoeprints near the body that most likely had been left there by the fisherman or one of both of the EMTs, but another set of tracks led away from Geary's body, forming a staggered line across the sandy beach. They were footprints, not shoeprints, and they ended by the lake. Unfortunately, the tide had come in, erasing the killer's path along the shoreline.

"So, Brody, what do you think?" Billy asked him.

"I think Shadrach, Meshach and Abednego are going to need a hire a new bartender. And, oh, yeah, the killer got away."

"Brilliant, simply brilliant," Billy said.

Ambrose shaded his eyes from the morning sun while he studied the staggered line of footprints in the sand. "Antalgic gait," he exclaimed.

"Ant what?" the police chief asked.

"The killer walked with a limp. See the length of the stride here, on the left," he said pointing, "and notice how the step length is shorter on the right."

The chief looked down. "Yeah, I see it, now that you're pointing it out." He scrunched up his face at Ambrose. "Spend a lot of time studying footprints in the sand, do ya?"

"Not a lot of sandy beaches in the city," Ambrose laughed. "I've got a bad back and when it acts up I get a little hitch in my step sometimes,"

Ambrose added, "so maybe it's something I'm more inclined to notice."

Ambrose asked the chief to have his man photograph the crime scene. He pulled a foldable ruler from his pocket and gave it to the officer to use to show scale. Ambrose drew a diagram of the crime scene on a pad. When he was finished with his sketch, he asked Billy and his man to help bag Geary's hands to reduce the risk of contamination during transport.

Because the coroner was an elected official, not a medical examiner, the body would have to be taken to an out-of-county forensic pathologist to perform the autopsy.

"Let me know if he extracts a bullet. In the meantime, have your man look for any casings on the beach," Ambrose told the chief. "I know it's a pain in the ass, but I'd like to get some plaster casts of those footprints before we're done here."

Later, the two men watched in silence while the coroner's men wrapped the body in a clean white sheet and placed it in a body bag.

Billy drove Ambrose to the station to interview their witnesses. The fisherman who found the body was a teetotaler who didn't know Luther Geary. The three bar regulars obviously did. They all considered themselves friends of the slain man. None of them bore him any grudges or ill will. Not so for Bob Foley, a patron who had been thrown out of Shadrach's that evening, according to one of the regulars. Foley got into a heated argument with Geary after Geary refused to serve him any more alcohol. The angry man was last seen staggering out of the bar around 1:30 a.m., but no one knew where he went after he left the bar.

Foley, the chief concurred, was a hot head, and had spent some time in the drunk tank.

"We're going to have to pick him up for questioning," Ambrose told the chief.

Ambrose asked the witnesses if Luther Geary had any enemies.

"Other than Foley?" one of them queried.

"Maybe his ex," another announced.

The pair had a long and contentious history, Billy told Ambrose. "She cut him with a knife and once shot out his windows," the chief said. "They've been on the outs for years, but there hasn't been any trouble between them lately."

"We still need to talk to her," Ambrose said

Billy dropped Ambrose off at his rental while he went to gather Foley and Luther Geary's ex, Marena, who had ditched the Geary cognomen and was now going by her maiden name of Marinelli.

Ambrose tried to nap. He took a Resteril his doctor had prescribed him. It had the desired effect, and he fell asleep in a chair by a window overlooking the lake.

He dreamed. His dream shattered the placid surface of the seascape and startled him awake.

In his dream, the moon was rising from the sea. In the pale light of the moon, Ambrose saw someone or something coming for him. He wasn't being chased or followed this time, not like the night before. This time, his nemesis was looming large in front of him. It had claws like a lobster, tentacles like an octopus, and a face like Luther Geary's.

Ambrose felt a sensation of impending threat. He pushed away his covers and sat up in bed. He didn't know how he got there. The sleeping pill was for nighttime use and he really shouldn't have taken it.

Bob Foley had an alcoholic's face with bloodshot eyes, dry, wrinkled skin, and broken capillaries on his nose. He smelled of alcohol, and was unsteady on his feet. Billy helped him to a seat. Ambrose wondered if he suffered from alcoholic polyneuropathy, which can cause numbness in the lower extremities and loss of movement in the feet.

Foley—"call me Bobby"—admitted to being in Shadrach's Shell Shack and getting into a shouting match with Geary.

"I get a little rowdy when I drink sometimes," Foley spat. "That doesn't mean I killed the man if that's what you're asking."

After he left the bar, he went out on the lake bluff that overlooks the water. "I don't like to get my shoes wet or stumble through the sand, especially when I'm buzzed. Just an invitation to fall over. So I kept to the bluff, the weedy, mossy part up there a ways from the beach."

Foley said he went to sleep among a clump of trees, as he often does, when he's had too much to drink. "Home's a hike for me," he said, "when I'm in that condition." He had lost his driver's license a few years back — "that's one thing Geary and I had in common," — so he had to walk wherever he was going. "When I can see where I'm going," Bobby Foley added.

He said he awoke in the middle of the night to the sound of something moving along the shoreline. "The moon was full and I could see someone traipsing around down there. Don't know who it was. Not Geary. It was someone else, but I couldn't tell who it was. I can't even say if it was a man or a woman, not from where I was looking."

"They walked up the beach from where I was and I put it out of mind. Up until, you know, up until what happened."

He said he heard a shot and saw a pistol flash, but it didn't really register with him what was going on. "You know what I mean? I mean, it was just like me seeing little green men, that's what folk might say, that's why I didn't report it."

Ambrose asked him if he owned a gun.

Foley chuckled. "Doesn't everyone?"

Foley reported that he owned a Mossberg shotgun, "a little bitty .22," and a Glock 19. "I also used to own a .357 Ruger LCR," but it was stolen," he said. "Some kids broke into my house and took it. Billy knows all about it. I reported it to the police, but they didn't do nothing."

Marena Marinelli looked like she had just come from the sea. She was sporting a wet-head hairstyle, à la Kim Kardashian or J.Lo, with perhaps a tad too much gel. Ambrose didn't like the look, even though it gave off beachy vibes.

All she needed was a sea foam dress and a pair of fishnet hose.

Instead, Marena was rocking a striped bowling shirt over distressed denim and moto-style boots. In sum, she exhibited a grungy toughness — from her hair down to her feet — and had the personality to match her fashion statement.

She didn't take prisoners. She swore a lot. She wanted a lawyer.

Until she didn't.

"Look, Jack," she told Ambrose, "Luther and I didn't get along. I never should have married the little fucker and I should have divorced him long before I did. There were many nights during our marriage when I thought about setting his bed on fire. I hated his fucking guts, but I didn't kill him."

"The chief said you stabbed him once and shot his windows out. A match, a knife, *a gun*. Maybe you finally hit on the right modality."

Marena Marinelli rolled her eyes, and Ambrose thought she was going to ask for a lawyer again.

"Hey jagoff," she said, after a gulp. "Want to know what I did after I shot up his place? I took the gun I used and tossed it in the lake. That's right, I threw it in the lake. I did it to avoid the temptation of going back and shooting Luther in the face. Pretty piece of metal, too. Smith and Wesson Ladysmith. Six hundred dollars new. Got mine cheap from a bull dyke cop who thought the Ladysmith was too ladylike. Too bad I tossed it in the drink."

"In other words, shithead," she continued. "I don't own a gun no more so there's no fucking way I could have shot him."

Marena Marinelli slammed her fist on the table. And then she walked out.

The chief liked Marinelli for the murder, but he wasn't ready to rule out Bobby Foley.

Ambrose agreed both were in play.

"We've got reasonable suspicion," the chief said. "But we don't have probable cause. We can't get a warrant to search their premises, video their gaits, or take measurements based on what we have. Maybe the autopsy will give us what we need."

Ambrose dreamed he had an appointment with the coroner at the morgue.

He was running late and was having trouble finding the location. Then someone directed him to a building down the street.

The morgue looked liked Shadrach's Shell Shack inside.

Marena Marinelli was dressed as a server. She was waiting on a table in the corner where she took an order from a drunken Bobby Foley, who wobbled on a chair.

Foley was slurring his words as he gave the waitress his order. It sounded like he was saying, "I didn't do it."

"I wouldn't do it with you either," the waitress snipped in reply.

In the center of the room, Luther Geary's body was stretched out atop the bar.

The coroner stood behind it in an apron. He was mixing some chemicals in a flask.

"What can I get you?" the coroner asked Ambrose. "I make a pretty mean Bloody Mary."

It was the city detective's last day in Lakeview, and he was packing up his things when his cell phone rang.

It was Billy.

"Just wanted to let you know we found a bullet," Billy said. "It was lodged under one of Geary's ribs and the pathologist was able to extract it."

"He says it's a semi-jacketed .38 Special caliber bullet," Billy continued. "Which means it could have come from that Ladysmith our girl Marena claims she threw in the lake."

Ambrose nodded thoughtfully, even though Billy could not see him. "Could have," he agreed. "But it also could have come from any gun that fires a .38 Special caliber round. Like Bobby Foley's .357 Magnum.

That soft-pointed present your pathologist found could have been a gift from Foley or the teenager he says took his Ruger. Point of fact, it could have been fired by anyone who uses .38 Special ammo."

"If I wanted cold water, Brody," Billy replied, "I'd throw myself in the lake."

"Look for that Ladysmith if you do."

Billy laughed. "You're a card, Brody. A real cutup."

"Don't you know it," Ambrose said. "Hey," he continued, " I'm sorry I can't see this thing through to the end with you. I really mean that."

"Don't doubt it," the Lakeview police chief said. "I understand. Duty calls at home. I appreciate all the help you gave me, cold water and everything."

After the conversation ended, a light bulb flicked on in Ambrose's head, and he cursed himself for not seeing it sooner.

He called the police chief back.

"I know who did it," Ambrose said, "and I can prove it."

"Okay Einstein, who was it?"

"Mind coming here?" Ambrose asked. "I'd like to talk it over with you in person."

When Billy arrived at Ambrose's rental, the city detective was sitting in a chair, a pair of bed socks at his feet. His service piece, a snub-nose revolver with a blue finish and a rosewood handle, was resting on a window table nearby. Dark clouds gathered in the window, portending a late summer storm.

"Don't see many of those anymore," Billy said, pointing at the revolver. "You old timers are the only ones who still carry them. Those of us in the modern world have all switched to semi-autos."

Outside the window, waves chopped on the beach.

Ambrose reached for the gun. He took it in his hands and depressed the thumb piece, opening the cylinder. He turned the muzzle of the revolver up and pushed on the ejector rod, depositing the contents of the cylinder in his hand.

"Take a look," he said, extending his reach toward Billy.

Resting in his palm were four pristine cylinder cartridges and one shell casing.

The gun had been fired. Once.

Ambrose picked up the spent casing and held it up for Billy to see. There was an indentation on its base where the firing pin had struck it, but Billy had no trouble making out the .38 Special caliber code on the headstamp.

"Keep it," Ambrose told him, handing him the casing. You'll want this, too," he said, extending his service piece handle-first to Billy.

"That's pretty much what you'll need to close the case," the city detective said. "Oh," he added, gesturing at the socks on the floor. "You'll want those, too. They're dry now but there's still some sand clinging to the heels and soles."

Ambrose held out his hands for Billy to cuff them. "You can arrest me now," he said.

The chief looked completely stupefied.

"H-how and why?" he sputtered.

"I can't tell you why, but the how is easy," Ambrose said. "I was sleep-walking on the beach when I shot and killed Luther Geary."

noelle
Sebastian Corbascio

"Am I evil? Yes, I am"
— Diamond Head —

For Diane Hoover

How small their two bodies are in the scheme of things. This high up, you can see everything. Up here, the air is music.

Christina landed on the trampoline on her side, sprung up, then landed on her feet. Noelle landed and hopped off onto the backyard grass. Christina did a backflip off the trampoline, and landed funny on her left foot.

"Oh, damn!" Christina yelled.

She recovered, but fell a few steps forward. Noelle caught her.

Noelle hopped Christina to the edge of the trampoline and sat her down.

"You OK?" Noelle asked.

Christina sucked air through her teeth in rapid breaths.

"I'll be fine, I'll be fine," Christina said.

"Breathe...breathe..." Noelle instructed Christina. "Hold it...breathe..."

Christina lifted her leg, Noelle grabbed the calf, Christina leaned back on both hands. Amy, Christina's mother, all forty-six years of her, threw open the sliding glass door, and bounded towards them.

"What happened?"

"Nothing," Christina said.

"She landed funny on her ankle."

Amy knelt in front of Christina.

"Mom, it's fine, I just need a minute, then I'll walk it off."

Amy slipped Christina's shoe off. Christina winced.

"OK, that's not good," Amy said. "Rotate."

Christina rotated her foot. Christina bit her lower lip, then in and out rapid fire gusts.

"Other way." Christina rotated counterclock wise. She clenched her teeth.

"That OK?"

"Yeah, it's fine."

"Should we get the doctor to look at it?"

"No, it's fine. Just let me, just let me rest it for a little bit." Christina lifted her leg into the air and rotated the ankle again. "Feels better already."

"You sit tight for a little bit," Amy said. "I'll go make us some lemonade."

Amy headed inside. Both Noelle and Christina winced at what was coming.

"How's the ankle, really?" Noelle asked.

"I'll survive."

"You sure?"

"If I don't, tell my mother I love her," Christina said. Noelle blinked rapidly.

"It'll be fine," Christina said.

Amy came out with a tray — lemonade, three glasses, ice.

"Here we are, ladies." Amy set the tray down. Noelle and Christina flashed a look at each other. They cackled.

"What's so funny?"

"Nothing, nothing," Christina said. Noelle looked like she was about to burst. Her face went from red to grape.

"You having a fit?" Amy said to Noelle.

"I'm OK, I'm OK," Noelle said, gasping. Noelle snorted a laugh, the tide broke open.

"Well, I guess I am not going to be let into what's so gosh darned funny," Amy said, balling her fists. Noelle drank the lemonade.

"Wow, this is really good," Noelle said.

"It's really good, Mom," Christina said.

Amy put her glass down.

"OK, I have a lot of stuff to do." Amy stood up. "Stay off the trampoline for the rest of the day." The girls begrudgingly agreed. Amy went inside.

"Hey Amy, you forgot your lemonade," Christina said towards Amy, pointing at the resting glass. They chuckled. Christina hocked a huge lugie and spat a long, tacky phlegm string that would not detach from her lips. Noelle drew and hocked a lugie. The whale fell from her lips. Christina got up and limped towards the garden hose.

"Are you sure you're OK?" Noelle asked. Christina nodded and turned on the garden hose. She drank, gargled, and spit. She offered the hose to Noelle. Noelle drank and gargled. She spat and took more.

"Whoever invented Splenda isn't going to hell," Christina said, "because I don't think they're bad people, but…"

"…but they'll have some penance to do," Noelle said. Christina snorted a laugh through her water.

"A lot of penance," Christina said. They laughed. They coughed water. They slapped each other's backs.

*****

Cheer practice. The Umbria Wildcats. Christina made it through her routines, but was wincing at the pain in her ankle and sweating buckets. Noelle watched Christina airborne in a toe touch jump. Her face was contorted, like she was swallowing glue. A bead of sweat off her forehead landed on Noelle, right between the eyes. She caught Christina in a cradle, and let her down. Christina limped.

"Hey, you still…?"

"No, I'm fine," Christina said. She corrected her limp as she approached the camera and interviewer from *High School Sports*. Noelle watched Christina shake hands with the interviewer. The camera sun gun came on. Even from the back, she could see Christina turning It on.

"Last year was the first year Umbria didn't bring home the pennant in the last five—"

"Yeah, the last five years—" Christina said.

"—last year, when there was a sort of a vacuum after Sylvia Swann led the team—"

"—two years in a row—"

"—two years in a row, and before that Justine Piccard—"

"Justine, right—" Christina said.

"—and the list just keeps going on and on all the way back to before anyone can remember."

"Yeah—"

"What do you think it is about Umbria that makes so many spirit champs?"

Noelle muttered: something in the water?

"I dunno, could it be something in the water?"

The host and Christina both chuckled.

"No, I think, I just think that Umbria is a cheering town, like some towns are football towns, and other towns are soccer towns, and others are big baseball towns. Umbria has always been about cheer. And whatever's in the water."

Real laugh.

"Thank you Christina. We wish you the very best of luck in the upcoming finals."

"Thank you, and thanks for talking to me today."

"Thank you." The host turned to the camera man. "I think we got it."

Chris Weaver came up behind Christina and swept her off her feet. Christina squealed loud. Chris laughed like a Hun. They chitchatted. Christina bounded in Noelle's direction, Chris in hand.

"Hey," Christina said in Noelle's direction. "His dumb ass is making me sit through the new *Transformers*. Wanna come?"

"No, no, I'm OK," Noelle said.

"C'mon, it'll be fun," Christina said.

"Not really into it."

"*Please...*"

"Not my kind of movie," Noelle said.

"Not me either. I need someone to talk to," Christina said.

"No, sorry."

Christina pouted.

"I know I'm a bad person, but I just can't stand what's his name," Noelle said.

"You are not listening to music while we're watching the movie," Chris told Christina.

"I don't do that." Chris shook his head.

Christina embraced Noelle.

"I'll call you later."

"K."

"'late." Chris said to Noelle, chucking deuces. As they walked away, Chris turned his head and nodded at Noelle.

✶✶✶✶✶

She lay in bed. Noelle's home bordered the freeway just beyond the unplowed fields. A peach painted cinder block wall muffed the freeway howl. Her blankets were scratchy; she had kicked them into a mound at the foot of her bed. The bottoms of her feet itched; she wake-dreamed about hosing Christina's blood off wooden floor; she, Noelle in an all-white hazmat suit, goggles, and particle mask. It was creeping close to 2:30 am. Her mouth tasted like lead.

She got up, went to the bathroom, and brushed her teeth until her gums bled. She flossed. Blood. Mouth rinse. Streaks in the sink. She looked at herself in the mirror. Blood on her lips. She smiled. Blood between her teeth. She darted her tongue in and out, it strangely white.

The stuffed animals on her shelf watched her in bed with their black eyes. She stared at her window. Condensation. She texted Christina. She texted Chris. She propped her phone up with her pillow and watched and waited.

Noelle came out of the sliding glass door, dressed in her nightie and carrying a flashlight. She approached the wall and climbed over. She walked on the plowed unplanted fields. Big rig trucks passed every few seconds. In the darkness, they were like comets. She found herself at the side of the road. The trucks passed full speed, the wind coming off them like a giant hand shoving her backwards and lifting her upwards.

*****

Teacher droned on. Noelle had her head in her hands, trying not to nod off. Her phone lit up in her hoodie pocket. She checked it. Chris.

CHRISBALLZ: Last night wasnt as good as the 1st one.

She looked over her shoulder to Chris, two rows back and catty corner. He was taking notes. Listening to Teacher. Focused and straight-A-ed.

RARANOELLE: 1st...?

CHRISBALLZ: transfs

RARANOELLE: I herd that

CHRISBALLZ: C issoooooo into that shit but she wont admit it

RARANOELLE: u sure?

CHRISBALLZ: TOTLY

Noelle snorted a laugh. Some noticed. Teacher didn't.

RARANOELLE: Ya she is

CHRISBALLZ: its like playin legos except on a movie screen

CHRISBALLZ: And all the noise makes me sleepy

RARANOELLE: Sleepy?

CHRISBALLZ: I know weird, huh?

CHRISBALLZ: rather b w/some1 I can chill with and talk to instead of going to the movies

RARANOELLE: u can't talk to C?

CHRISBALLZ: i can & i cant.

Noelle looked over her shoulder. Chris didn't meet her eyes, but lifted his index finger off the desk and gave her a tiny wave.

RARANOELLE: What do you mean?

CHRISBALLZ: hard to talk about

RARANOELLE: ???

CHRISBALLZ: Talk ltr Teach is onto us

Noelle faced forward and clasped her hands together on top of her desk. Teacher went on.

*****

Asleep. A tap came on her window. She woke. Another tap. A shadow, male. Chris tapped his cell and shone it on his face. Noelle got out of bed and slid the window open.

"Hey wha—"

Noelle silenced him.

"What are you doing here?" Noelle hissed.

Chris held up four beers in a sixer ring.

*****

Noelle and Chris walked on the unplowed fields. The beer was as sweet and cold as ice cream. The bubbles went up her nose.

"Where'd you get these?" Noelle asked.

"My brother's home from college," Chris said.

"Cool."

"He won't drink with me, but once in a while, he'll throw me a sixer. He feels sorry for me that I still have to live in Umbria."

"How's Christina's ankle?"

"You'd know better than me," he said. Noelle shrugged.

"Wait, she doesn't tell you anything, either?" Chris said.

"Depends."

"What she told you about her ankle?"

"Nothing," Noelle said.

"It's probably broken in four places." Chris belched. Noelle shoved Chris. He fell.

"Oh, shit!"

Noelle helped him up.

"You OK?"

He laughed.

"Yeah, I'm OK. I planned that."

"I could tell. You OK?"

"Yeah, I'll be fne. Why am I wet?"

"Oh, shit the beer…" Noelle guffawed.

"Great. Laugh it up."

Noelle's laughing was more liked undulating. Even in the half light of the trucks she could see Chris' pants were a big wet diaper.

"You are fucking evil, Noelle."

*****

Noelle climbed back inside.

"You gonna be OK going home?" Noelle whispered. Chris checked his watch.

"I'm pretty much a dead man."

Noelle smiled.

"You deserve it."

Chris nodded. His aw shucks face. His wet cat demeanor. They hesitated. They kissed. He put his arms around her. She pushed them away.

"One more," he said. Chris pantomimed "a teeny one."

They kissed. Tongue.

"Let me in."

Noelle looked over her shoulder.

"I can't."

"Sure you can."

She looked at him gravely.

"Going once…going twice…"

He saw the no in her eyes and in her shoulders. Chris slid off the window sill. He jumped the concrete wall. He trotted across the plowed field. He didn't turn around.

*****

In the locker room, the Umbria Wildcats, dressed for practice, Coach Linder, pacing.

"…this regional final will lead us to the Nationals. The Nationals are broadcast on ESPN. We can win this."

Her eyes at Christina.

"We can win this. We can also lose this."

Her eyes sweeping everyone. Faces were grave. Gretchen Stiller, who prayed constantly, prayed.

"The time to keep our focus is now," Linder continued. "Umbria isn't what it used to be, we know that. This cheer team wasn't what it used to be—"

Noelle looked over at Christina, who listened to the speech with downcast eyes, nodding solemnly at the bullet points. Noelle listened, but only heard something akin to a mule braying.

Linder led the team in a chant:

"Take it back! Take it back! Take it back!"

The Wildcats did a relentless workout without music. It was as if they had waited to sweat for years, and could let it spray now. The junior cheer teams were also practicing. Young eyes watched the Wildcats. Most of the young eyes watched Christina. They rehearsed the full down. It was a perfect Christina Reed 360, perfect enough for her to brand it. Camera phones caught it, little fingers posted it, little fingers captioned in capitals, went wild with the exclamation points.

Noelle caught Christina.

"Thanks, pardner," Christina said.

Christina hopped from the cat's cradle to her feet. She threw her arms in the air in a V-shape, and turned and V-ed to four corners of the bowl. Other athletes stopped and applauded. Noelle applauded. Christina signaled that they go again.

Up Christina went into the air. Noelle took a half step backwards. Christina came down. Noelle took a full step forward. Christina fell into Noelle's arms.

"That was the last one," Noelle said. Christina nodded. Noelle set her down. Christina winced. The auditorium cheered. The duo took a bow. Noelle showcased Christina. The applause increased. They embraced and scampered away. Only Noelle was close enough to see that Christina's jaw was clenched tighter than a sprung bear trap.

✶✶✶✶✶

Noelle strapped a backpack with two 15lb sandbags and a 10lb sandbag inside and ran against traffic on to the oncoming lights. Her legs burned, but she tightened the backpack strap, hugging the pack even closer to her body, then picked up the pace. A truck lit her up with its high beams. Across the field, Noelle saw a figure lingering in front of the peach concrete wall. The figure waved. Chris. A sixer.

"What's up?"

"What are you doing here?" Noelle asked, unwrapping her backpack from around her. Cool air attacked her back.

"Thought you might want to hang out. What are you doing?"

"Big meet's coming up, thought I'd get a workout in," Noelle said.

"Now?"

"Couldn't sleep."

Chris smiled.

"A lot on your mind?"

"Couple things."

"Oh. Like what?"

"This n' that."

He moved closer to her.

"Kinda not in the mood right now."

She picked up her backpack and moved towards the wall. "You should go."

"Why?"

"Christina's my best friend."

Chris shrugged.

"Don't you care about her?"

"Yeah…"

"Then what…"

"I think I'm gonna be moving on," he said. "I think I might already have."

"You're going to break up with her?"

Chris shrugged.

"So what am I to you?" she asked.

"A friend. Definitely a good friend."

"What was that the other night?"

"That was...that was me after a few beers." He chuckled.

"Uh-huh."

"Yeah, I just…"

"Why are you here now?"

"Uh…" He cast his eyes downward, chuckled, and fondled the beer can top.

"Can I have a beer?" Noelle asked.

"Yeah..." He pulled a beer out of the plastic holder and handed it to her.

"Thanks."

She stepped back, and threw it at him full force. It hit him square on the forehead. He stumbled backwards. He held his forehead, sucked in air, then wailed in pain. She covered her mouth, time stopped. Chris attacked her, failing. Noelle dodged his swings and jabs, ducking, sidestepping. Noelle stepped and crushed a dirt clod, which momentarily threw her off balance. Chris landed half a hammer punch to her ear. He came back to earth. They stared at each other both panting, Noelle held the side of her head.

"Fucking cunt…"

He marched away.

*****

Practice. Noelle watched Christina warm up. She turned and saw Chris in the stands, joking with his friends. His Backpack Which Held Eternity fastened to his back. He pointed at the goose egg on his forehead like it was a badge of honor. He was pantomiming something.

Noelle turned back to look over at Christina, expecting her to be across the room. Christina was standing less than a foot away from her. Noelle jumped out of her skin.

"Oh my God, I'm so sorry."

"You scared me."

"Do you want to work on the aerial?"

"You sure it's OK?" Noelle asked.

"Yeah, it'll be fine."

"I dunno…"

Christina got into position.

"C'mon, while I am still warm."

"Um, let's get some of the others," Noelle said, and dashed towards a cluster of Wildcats. "Hurry up!"

Noelle stopped halfway and put two fingers in her mouth and whistled. Teammates came.

"OK, ready?" Christina said, collecting nods from the others. Noelle heard Chris' definitive laugh, she looked over. He and the other boys brayed like asses at something. Christina performed backflips into Noelle and the base's arms. They threw Christina up high. Noelle watched Christina's back in the air. Noelle's back leg steadied, heel down. Christina came downward. Noelle loosened her back leg. Christina drinking from the back yard hose the other day. She straightened her back leg. She and the base caught Christina; she dismounted. Wild applause. Christina's canned nod to the fans. Christina jumped into Noelle's arms and gave her a kiss on the cheek. Cameraphone flashes. She jumped out of Noelle's arms and rallied her team mates.

"Go again! Go again!" Christina whopped and hand clapped. Christina, airborne. Noelle already had had her sixth birthday party and they were now at Christina's sixth. They were in the living room, and all the lights went out. Amy came out of the kitchen with a birthday cake with six lit candles. The candles cast weird shadows. The kids sang Happy Birthday. Christina blew the candles out. Black. So black that Noelle thought this is what nothing feels like. Noelle loosened her leg. Christina fell through Noelle's arms, and hit the floor on her tailbone. She bounced. She landed, fell over onto her shoulder, half on her collar bone. Pause. No movement. She let out a huge breath, inhaled a lungful and howled like a gut shot wolf. Did the phones capture Noelle looking excited and smiling? She covered her mouth. The whole auditorium realized at once that Christina wasn't getting up. Noelle rushed to her.

"Are you OK?"

Christina's eyes darted everywhere. She groaned. People, like a great wave came up behind Noelle, hands pulled Noelle away and pushed her to the side. Noelle watched the auditorium feed like lions on the fallen Christina.

*****

In the ambulance, Christina was stretched out on the gurney. Her legs couldn't move. Her head was in a brace, she could feel herself drooling out of the sides of her mouth. Her eyes darted around looking at all the ambulance bric-a-brac. Amy was yelling in tongues. The follow cars were stacked high. Other cars joined. It became a procession that stretched a block and a half. They were crying and praying, praying and crying.

Inside the ER, the doctors worked on her. The waiting room was packed to capacity. Flowers arrived as if by magic. Noelle sat in one of the plush, dark purple chairs. A few well-wishers approached Noelle and tapped her on the hand, asking her if she was OK. Noelle blathered something unheard by the well-wishers. A few conciliatory words, more hand pats, and then the retreat, as if they were fleeing a burst sewer pipe.

Pastor Bill knelt and led a prayer with other kneelers; others who could not kneel prayed in their seats. Noelle wasn't invited to join in. Martin, Christina's dad, sat shell shocked, while Amy prayed on her knees, a mandala of support around her. They finished one prayer and began another. A doctor came in and took Amy and Martin inside an adjoining room, and closed the door. Noelle could see the conference through the long meshed door window. Amy covered her mouth, Martin covered his mouth. The doctor excused himself, opened the door and a flood of pleading and whimpering rolled out for the seconds the door was open, until the door closer closed it, and Martin and Amy continued to be a silent movie through the mesh window. Amy burst into tears. Martin held Amy.

Chris came in with his father. He nodded at Noelle, and sat with Christina's parents. He got the news, and he hung his head. His head came up, tears in his eyes, and he covered his mouth. Noelle texted him.

RARANOELLE: What up??

Chris took out his phone, saw who it was from, and put it back in his pocket.

*****

Noelle was in bed. Her cell pinged

CHRISBALLZ: She mit nvr walk again...

CHRISBALLZ: ...i don't knw wht 2 do....

CHRISBALLZ: ...she broke 3 vertebrae...

Noelle turned to the wall, her face a frozen scream.

CHRISBALLZ: ...cryin in the dark...

*****

In the interrogation room, Noelle watched the surveillance camera watching her. The door opened and a plainclothes female police officer, late twenties, stern, no-bullshit demeanor. Hair pulled back in a ponytail, a steel grey pants suit with sharp, dagger-like lapels.

"Hi Noelle, I am Offcer Timmins. I want to remind you that you are still Mirandized and anything you say or do can and will be held against you in a court of law, I want to remind you also that you can stop the questioning at any time and request an attorney be present."

Noelle nodded.

"I need to hear you say it."

"Yes."

She sat down opposite Noelle and opened the file. She took a hospital report out and read, spinal x-rays in full view.

"OK...why'd you drop Christina?"

"What?"

"Why'd you drop Christina?"

"I guess my left leg support wasn't strong enough."

"Tell me more about that."

"Ok, um...what do you want to know? "

"The move where you dropped her. What's it called?"

"Backflip aerial."

"Tell me about that."

Noelle explained the routine in great detail. Officer Timmins listened stone faced.

"Tell me about you guys."

"Um, what about us?"

"You're best friends."

"Since about the age of eleven," Noelle said.

"But you knew her longer than that?"

"Yeah, sort of."

"How so?"

"Um, I guess everyone kind of knows each other in Umbria. It's small."

Timmins nodded.

"We were in kindergarten together. Then I guess we were in different classes and then we sort of ran into each other again in the fifth grade, and like, started having lunch together, and kinda went from there."

"Why'd you drop her?"

Noelle swallowed.

"Like I said, my back leg wasn't braced enough."

"Were you jealous of her?"

"Huh?"

"Jealous. She's the most popular girl in school, she has that hot little boyfriend, Chris. Is that his name?"

"Yeah."

"He's cute."

Noelle shrugged.

"I don't like him."

"No?"

"Not really."

"He voluntarily handed over his cell phone and there are a lot of texts in there between you and him."

"Yeah, so?"

"From where I'm standing, you guys were pretty friendly."

Noelle thought.

"Maybe I was being friendly, I mean, he's my best friend's boyfriend."

Timmins picked up one of the x-rays, looked at the corner notes and held it up close to Noelle's face.

"OK. You know that Christina has a broken vertebrae and another fused. Did you drop her on purpose?"

"What?"

"Did you drop her on purpose?"

"Why would I ever do something like that?"

"I dunno, you tell me."

"I didn't."

"Didn't what?"

"Drop her on purpose."

"They'll go easier on you if you fess up."

"But I didn't do anything."

"You'll be primary or lead or whatever it's called, now with Christina out of the way."

"Probably," Noelle said.

"Definitely."

Stillness.

"Chris came and visited you a few nights ago. Said you two kissed."

Noelle looked at her lap.

"Did he tell you he was breaking up with Christina?"

"Yeah…"

"Something here I don't get. Chris is going to break up with Christina to start dating you, and you drop her, breaking her back. You already have the guy, why do you drop Christina?"

"I didn't."

"Didn't what?"

"Drop her on purpose."

"So what happened?"

"I miscalculated or something, and she came down too strong, I think and just…my muscles didn't…we'd worked out all day and I guess I was tired, but thought I could keep going or something. Christina always pushed and pushed, you know. I mean, she sprained her ankle playing on the trampoline in her backyard a couple days before and almost broke it, but she didn't sit out practice."

Timmins stared at Noelle for a long time. She reached into her wallet and pulled out a business card.

"This is my card."

Noelle took it.

"Anytime you need to talk, call me."

"OK…"

"If there's anything you want to get off your chest."

Noelle read the card. Officer Noel Timmins.

"You're free to go."

"You and I practically have the same first name."

"What a coincidence."

Noelle walked out of the interview room and down the carpeted halls which smelled like brand new everything. A shiver went up her back. She turned, and there was Timmins, badge gleaming on her belt, staring Noelle down as she approached the elevator.

*****

Spirit Regionals. The crowd noise was deafening. Music pounded. Noelle came into the arena in the lead of the Wildcats. Umbria's support section stood and cheered. Huge banners, waving Wildcats flags, noise makers, a girl blowing a trumpet. Several Umbrians had signs with a silhouette of a black swan inside a circle and slash. Placards of roast goose, with all the fixin's. On the other side of the arena, the Swans waved large poster size pictures of silhouettes of dead cats with x's through their eyes and tongues hanging out.

"…It has been the Swans' year thus far, and last years win at the nationals, the experts are saying that they are going to take it again," the announcer said.

"Yeah, they did have some stiff competition from the Wildcats, but with that unfortunate accident that put the Wildcats best aerialist into a wheelchair—" the second announcer continued. The first announcer whistled. "—that put Christina Reed in a wheelchair has put the Swans on most favored to take the pendant again."

Music changed.

"And the Swans are just about ready to start their set."

The Swans performed. Their 4 whip was top shelf, and the dance was a bass thumping track where there were four centers of aerial stunts that stopped on a dime in unison, then started after applause erupted. But there was a lack of emotional commitment. Noelle couldn't explain it. Maybe the team was infighting, maybe they all had colds, maybe someone broke up with their boyfriend and they were all sad about it, whatever, but they were phoning it in. The Swans' sell sold nothing. Noelle looked over at the judges. Expressionless. The Swans took their finale. Their section stood and applauded and cheered to the point of tears and bloodletting.

"Another great performance by the Swans," the first announcer said.

"Let's see what the judges have to say."

The judges held up their signs. The Swans led. Their section went crazy. Noelle scoffed. The Swans were fourth to go out of eleven.

"And the Wildcats are up," the first announcer said.

"Where is Christina Reed right now?"

"Last I heard, and I can't back this up, she is at home recovering."

Christina watched the match from her hospital bed. Chris sat beside her.

"Don't know, but I've heard that the family is keeping it very private right now, something we can all respect I think."

"And here is Noelle Duchamp, the Wildcats' spotter, now aerialist. She has been a strong performer—"

"She sure has—"

"—and now it's up to her to rue the day, as they say."

Chris watched Noelle. Christina glanced over, and saw Chris watching Noelle. His lips parted, he made fists, knuckles white.

Noelle.

First position. She went into sort of a trance where she could hear nothing, see only a small tunnel in front of her, and her muscles took over.

The routine began. She was up high in the air. She could have flown away if she wanted to. The floor raced up at her. Noelle did a 360, and turned into her landing at the last possible moment. She grabbed the kinetic energy and did front flips and came down on one knee and threw both arms into the air in a victory V. The auditorium exploded.

The Wildcats continued. Noelle was weightless. She was outside herself. She carved her name into the wood of the trophy case. The Hall of Fame trophy case in the auditorium that held awards back to the 1940s. Something in the water. The whole team tumbled and ended with a handless backflip that was so precise, Christina was taken aback.

Forward tumble, splits, the end. But wait. The vinyl scratched effect on the soundtrack stopped everything. Noelle put one finger in the air. The crowd quieted. A flamenco rose through the speakers as the Wildcats lined up in two lines facing each other. Basket tosses. Perfect sync. Christina watched as four of her teammates being tossed in opposite directions, met the apex at the exact same moment. If she had stopped the video, looking straight on, the three airborne girls would be hidden behind Melinda Carrigan.

The basket toss went into a toe touch. Then a single kick double full. Single kick double fulls long enough for the crowd to fill their lungs and gasp. Everyone landed, arms shot out. The Wildcats were one big flower, every girl's nostrils wide, every girl's eyes burning.

The auditorium exploded. The Wildcats dog piled Noelle, then threw her on top of their shoulders. The crowd stomped the floor in time. Noelle ascended the stage. They handed Noelle the silver cup. The Swans got first place by a hair, but the Wildcats were the crowd favorite. Noelle smiled, waved, and hugged official looking people. She took the silver cup and turned to leave the podium. Linder stopped her.

"Hey aren't you going to say a few words?"

Noelle turned back to the podium. "Um…"

Cheers.

"I want to dedicate this to my best friend and um mentor, I love you Christina!" Noelle shot the trophy into the air. The crowd erupted. Christina sat frozen. Noelle was thrown backwards two steps by the crowd's roar. Linder caught her. Noelle cried hard into Linder's shoulder. The crowd chanted her name. She wiped her eyes. This was really real.

*****

The celebration went well into the night. Noelle wanted to evaporate. Chris was on top. Noelle was somewhere else. The trophy glimmered on her dresser in the dim light from outside. Mom knocked on the door. They stopped.

"Honey?"

"Oh fuck!" Chris hissed.

Chris flew out of the bed and scrambled on his clothes.

"Noelle?"

"Yeah?"

"Is there someone in there with you?"

Pants on, Chris threw open the sliding glass window and jumped out, and ran barefoot.

"Noelle, open this door right now."

Noelle opened up.

"What the hell is going on?"

Noelle shrugged. Mother scanned. She saw the open window. She saw the messed up sheets, again the open window, and the look on her daughter's face. She came inside the room and looked out the window, then looked under the ledge. She turned and faced her daughter.

"Who was in here with you?"

"Chris."

"Chris who?"

"Chris Chris."

Mother swallowed.

"What was he doing here?"

Noelle shrugged.

Slow burn.

"Don't ever do that again," Mother said.

"Do what?"

"Go back to bed."

Mother left.

*****

The doctors ran tests on Christina. Prognosis: she hadn't gotten worse, but she hasn't improved, either.

"We should tell the parents what the child's options are at this point," an intern said.

The lead physician looked at the x-rays in the lightbox.

"Let's hold off on that," the lead physician said.

"Why?" one of the interns asked.

"We make room for miracles in this business, Dr. Chu."

*****

Noelle arrived dressed to the nines and carting a huge mixed bouquet. Noelle appeared at the threshold. They both screamed with abandon. Noelle ran to Christina to hug her, but stopped inches away.

"Can I give you a hug?"

"Fuck, yeah."

They embraced. They squealed.

"You look amazing," Christina said. Noelle stepped back, gave a spin.

"This all for me?" Christina said towards the bouquet. Christina took the bouquet. "They're beautiful."

Noelle hovered to sit on the bed.

"This OK?"

"M-hm."

They took hands.

"How are you doing?"

Christina shrugged.

"OK, I guess," she said. "They aren't sure what's going to happen to me."

"What do you mean?"

"The vertebra is broken and fused with the one on top of it. It's pinching the spinal cord, so I only have partial feeling below the waist."

Noelle swallowed.

"Wow, that sucks."

"Wanna hear something else?"

Noelle nodded. A keep-from-crying smile spread over Christina's face.

"Chris broke up with me."

"What?"

Christina nodded solemnly.

"Why?"

"He said that he was, he had been, been in love with me, but now, now he only loved me. Or loves me or whatever. He said that we had run our course."

"He's worthless," Noelle said.

Christina shook her head. She looked out through the ajar room door towards the hallway.

"We never had sex," Christina said, voice low.

"No?"

Christina shook her head.

"But you said…"

"…I know. We didn't go all the way. I didn't want to. I couldn't."

Noelle nodded.

"I really want to think that he broke up with me because I'm paralyzed, but, but I can't think that he's that mean, and always was that mean, like I didn't know him or something."

She sobbed.

"You think that if I had done it with him, we'd still be together?"

"I don't know."

They drew in closer together.

"I don't have any feeling down there anymore," Christina half-whispered.

Noelle froze.

"I'll never have those…experiences again."

Christina sobbed quietly, laboriously, her entire body doing a slow whiplash. Noelle held her. Christina heaved, and screamed like a jet engine into Noelle's belly.

*****

Noelle found herself in the peach hospital hallway in front of the peach elevator, and pressing the button. There was an incessant hum, a fusion of florescent lights, AC, and air pressure which pressed on Noelle's ears. The elevator arrived. She rode down. It was one of those long elevators which took in gurneys. Her knees gave way and she collapsed.

*****

In class.

RARANOELLE: Two words: FUCK YOU

CHRISBALLZ: ???

Noelle didn't text back. She dropped her phone from a foot and a half up onto the top of the desk. Teacher turned, everyone turned. A few seconds of silence, and Teacher turned back and everyone else turned back.

*****

Closed rehearsal, empty stands. Noelle was trying to do the new routine. Linder was barking at her.

"OK, OK, I'll try it again."

She did a bad landing and stumbled.

"Duchamp." Noelle scampered over. "Your head's not in the game. What's going on?"

"I dunno, Coach, I might have the flu. Threw up this morning."

"This morning?"

"I'll be fine before finals, don't worry."

*****

Christina was trying to walk holding herself up on bars. She poured sweat.

"One foot in front of the other…one foot in front of the other…"

Christina exhaled all her air. She fell onto her elbows.

"Up…get up, Christina," the therapist egged. Christina looked over at Amy, bloated in tears. Christina pushed herself back up. She dragged her left big toe, and planted her left foot. She lifted her hands two inches off the bars. She stood on the foot for a breath, then steadied herself. Right foot, right toe drag, plant right foot. Left big toe…

*****

The Vanagon pulled into the driveway. Martin got out and took out Christina's wheelchair and unfolded it. He helped her into the chair. He drove her up the new wooden ramp they had had built.

"I can do it," she insisted.

"OK," Martin said, letting go.

*****

Dinner time, no carbs, gluten free bread, filtered water. Bonnie, Martin's second wife, a tanning bed victim. Blake was six, and his father's twin. Christina forked a purple heirloom tomato wedge.

"Hey Christina," Blake said.

"What?"

"How come you can drink a drink, but you can't food a food?"

Chuckles.

"Good question."

"And um, how come it's called a drive thru, if you stop? Wait…"

"I get it," Christina said.

"People buy me to eat, but never eat me, what am I?"

"Okra?" Martin suggested. Guffaws.

"Nooo…"

"What then?" Christina asked. Blake picked up his plate.

"A plate. Get it?"

She mussed his hair.

*****

Evening; Christina shot baskets in the driveway. Everything a shade of orange. She made one. The ball bounced to the grass. She wheeled over. The garden hose was dripping. She rolled towards it. She turned the handle counterclockwise. She thought of that perfect day in the backyard, drinking from the hose to get rid of the Splenda aftertaste. One last counterclockwise millimeter and the water stopped. She pulled the hose and coiled it. She rolled back onto the concrete. She shot baskets. Her mind traveled to Noelle's support leg. Christina shot a basket. Missed. Christina chased the ball and retrieved it. Noelle's leg was slightly bent at the knee. The floor came rushing at Christina, and she saw Noelle tuck her arms three inches inward. Christina set the ball on her lap. Her head hurt bad.

*****

"It's the big day for the State, if you're a spirit squad fan, they're out in force tonight."

"Looks that way Jim, I know that there are some empty streets in some California towns tonight."

"We can count on Scarsdale, Charlotte, Hemdale, Meade, all being a little less populated."

"Them and a few others no doubt. And what about Umbria?"

"Umbria, as a few of our viewers know, is the dark horse in this competition."

"What a story—"

"What a story, indeed."

"How are the Wildcats looking?"

"They're clearly a favorite, everybody loves a good comeback story, and if the Wildcats pull it out, they will have theirs for sure."

Noelle texted.

RARANOELLE: Where are u?

Christina watched the competition with Martin, Bonnie, and Blake. Her phone buzzed. She looked at the message.

Noelle stared at her phone. Nothing. She approached the Wildcats' bench and sat. The lights in the stadium went down and a roar climbed out of the crowd. The Falcons took the floor. They began. Noelle rechecked her phone. Nothing. She swallowed.

The Wildcats were up. Noelle texted Christina.

RARANOELLE: Are you watching?

Christina watched Noelle take her position on the floor. The Wildcats began. Noelle airborne, turns and faces downward, and takes a header into the floor. The entire stadium stands in disbelief. The music stops and the coach, team members, paramedics dog pile Noelle. She can't breathe, her chest is heaving up and down, her legs are akimbo to the rest of her. "I can't move, I can't move—"

Noelle saw the floor come at her, and in the last moment, recovered for a good, but not perfect landing. Noelle stood, her arms a V.

Teams waited for the final outcome.

"Third place for the Bronze, Aridale." The Aridale Sooners team exploded along with their fans. "And for the Silver, Umbria, the Umbria Wildcats," Noelle and co. stood and cheered.

"—and for the Gold, The Falcons." The Falcons roared. Threw signs at the Wildcats. Sore winners.

Noelle took the trophy, held it above her head to the love of the crowd. She stepped off the podium and approached the beaming Linder. Noelle embraced her hard, they danced. Noelle whispered in Coach's ear.

"I quit."

Coach looked at Noelle and didn't unpaint her smile. She planted her cheek on Noelle's.

*****

The party was in full swing. Teens everywhere like ants on cut fruit. In the living room, four drunk girls were booty dancing on the coffee table. Noelle was sitting on the stairs, drunk, and yelling into her phone.

"Hit me back, K?"

She put the phone in her lap and stared at it. A girl came down the stairs and put her hand on Noelle's head to steady herself. Noelle threw it off. The girl slid down the stairs and landed flat on her rear end at the bottom. She laughed hard.

Noelle's phone rang. Christina. Noelle answered.

"Hey."

"Hey."

Noelle squeezed past the logjam of teens at the front door.

"How are you?"

"Congratulations."

"Yeah, I coulda, I coulda done better. Were you watching?"

"Of course I was watching."

Noelle made her way off the porch, across the grass and into the surrounding woods.

"How come you didn't come?" Noelle asked.

"I dunno, too much excitement. My doctor says I have to rest."

"Oh, OK. Hey."

"What?"

Noelle swallowed.

"I have to tell you something."

Noelle double checked if she was out of ear shot.

"What?"

"Wait, not over the phone."

"What is it?"

"I…," she took a deep breath.

"No, not over the phone."

"You can tell me over the phone."

"No."

"Tell me."

Noelle exhaled a breath so staccato it was like a drum roll.

"I have to make it right, I have to make it right," Noelle blubbered.

"I know."

"I am so sorry," Noelle said. "I am so fucking sorry…"

Christina said nothing. Noelle sucked in a lungful of air. She put the phone back to her ear. Nothing. She threw her phone into the woods. Christina listened to Noelle in the distance, braying like a wounded donkey.

*****

Noelle woke up on a child's bed in a child's bedroom, an avalanche of pink. Noelle came in to the bathroom, saw two boys sleeping in the bathtub. She approached the toilet, pulled her pants down and peed. She flushed, approached the mirror, looked at herself, and saw the black felt pen markings all over her face, some words some drunk asshole or assholes tried to spell. "SLU(indecipherable", "F(indecipherable)", "KU(indecipherable)" etc. There was a fully rendered upside down cross between her eyes. She sighed. She found soap and washed.

*****

Christina's back x-ray came back and the doctor put it onto the light board. His eyes widened. He put another x-ray onto the light board, another surprise.

Christina lifted herself on the rings. She performed a tumble, her legs strapped together. The therapist was as surprised as Christina. Christina took a deep breath and did it again. She laughed. She inhaled a lung full of air. When she exhaled, tears formed.

"I think that's enough for today," the therapist said.

"Yeah, I think you're right."

They chuckled.

*****

Christina woke up. It was still night. The time was now. She grabbed her phone, and selected a video: *Mom*.

*****

Noelle lay in bed, half asleep. Her phone lit up. Link from Christina.

Play.

You are a stupid piece of garbage, you know that? You know that your father didn't leave me, he left us. To run off with that shitty skank and have kids, just to prove to the world the he can stiiiilllll get it up. And he left me with you— Jump cuts. Montage. Camera hidden behind a vase:—*you're still underage, and I can have you emancipated, I've looked into it, believe me and I know aaalll the laws and procedures and stuff, and guess what missy? You're still eligible for foster care, not that anyone'd want you, I sure don't—* The videos taken over a two year period. Bizarre angles. *You've gained weight, heifer. Heifer, heifer, heifer—* Camera hidden discreetly in what looked like a bookshelf; Amy a whirling dervish of insults at Christina; not an instant of Christina fighting back; camera on the floor stashed behind the gum tree planter; peeking through a kitchen cupboard through the slightly ajar door; uncut of Amy skillfully checking the perimeter before unleashing; *(distorted) all you do? Fail? I mean, at everything? Do you do it on purpose? Is that how—* her head swivels 150 degrees around, her face cracks a smile at something outside the car. Seconds pass. Only the sound of exterior cacophony at a shopping mall parking lot? Amy's head follows something that appears in frame, a man walks past the car. Amy's eyes follow. Man out of earshot, Amy:— *is that how you get back at me? For all thethethe time and effort and goddamn money I put in? For what? For what?* In the car Amy driving, static shot of the grey seat cloth, Amy's bile a raging river, she bangs the steering wheel until it warps; Christina turning up the radio so the cars next to them can't hear. *Stupid, insolent, looks like a whore half the time, thinks she is somebody but doesn't want to put in the work to be somebody*

Noelle looked at the list of recipients. Coach Linder. Principal Bengstrom. Sheriff Haggarty. All of the Wildcats. Top shelf family matrons. Wildcat sponsors. The list was at least a hundred names. Noelle watched the number of views climb and climb. She toggled back and restarted six times. 235 views. 187 shares.

*****

Christina was sitting up in the middle of the bed, legs folded, and watched the sunrise. She rocked in place, singing a wordless, repeating motif. Something a monk would sing in an empty cathedral. Another message arrived to her exploding inbox. Then another. She kept singing.

Your Ticket to Freedom
Martin Zeigler

Dear Mr. Rickets,

I bet you're counting the days now. All your tricks and schemes to delay what's coming to you have run out, leaving you no choice but to face the dead certain.

No more time-consuming and pointless appeals. No more finagling interviews with the local networks in the hopes of swaying public opinion. No more penning open letters to our governor, begging him not just to commute your sentence but to pardon you altogether.

Sure, you're probably still raising your fists to the heavens and crying out how the cards have been stacked against you. But this time no one's listening. No one's listening, because they can no longer hear you. Not the courts. Not the networks. Not the governor.

The only ones who can hear you are the cons in your cellblock, but they're yelling right back at you to shut up. Or however they word it behind bars.

Which leaves you with the counting. With your staring at the calendar taped to the cinderblock wall and adding up all the Xs until the final X.

And when the Big Day arrives, you'll quit with the days because there won't be any more to count, and you'll start with the hours, the only hours you have left, and you'll pray they'll pass slowly.

But they won't. They'll fly by in a heartbeat, assuming you know what a heartbeat is.

I, too, have been counting the days. To the same Big Day. The third of next month at eight AM. The date handed down at the sentencing.

You'll be there because you have no choice.

I'll be there because I've been invited.

And on that day and at that hour, justice will be dispensed. I will witness it. You will experience it.

And that will be that.

My daughter. She also counted the days. Different kinds of days entirely. The number of days until her first college class. Until her first piano lesson. Her first rewarding evening of volunteer work. Days having everything to do with beginnings and nothing to do with endings.

At nineteen, brimming with the optimism of youth, she assumed that since life was so wonderful, it would naturally last a very, very long time. No way could her world come to an end.

That's what she said to me one morning, in a moment of exuberance. That she was going to live forever.

I had to smile. "Really?" I said. "Forever?"

"All right," she conceded with a smile of her own. "Maybe a million years."

The day she said this was the day her world did come to an end.

That was four years ago. Remember that night, Mr. Rickets? Four years ago?

Of course you don't. You were too far gone.

But surely you remember your trial, don't you? How each and every one of your drinking buddies took the stand and testified against you, made statements about that night which you, to this day, call a pack of lies, even though you still don't remember a single thing that happened?

You were all at a place called Tiny's Tavern, sitting at the bar. You, Mr. Rickets, were filling your belly with beer and launching into a tirade against all the injustices of the world. Injustices which included women who turned down the drinks you bought them. Women who only dated guys that worked out in gyms. Women who refused to see what a nice guy you are.

When you finally needed to take a break but found the restroom line too long, you did what you usually did. You staggered out of Tiny's to relieve yourself in the park across the street.

Fifteen minutes later, when you came stumbling back inside, your buddies reared back in horror. One of them said you reminded him of those old photos of coal miners, where all you could see through their blackened faces were the whites of their eyes. In your case, the blood was so thick, it might as well have been coal.

And before the tavern door had time to swing shut, there you were, tottering on the barroom floor, thrusting something high into the air like a victory cup, and slurring at the top of your voice, "I don' know wha' this is! I don'!"

The *this* in your fist was an eight-inch chef's knife, still dripping blood, as if it had just recently served its purpose.

Your friends were the first ones out the door, rushing across the street to Heldon Park to see what happened, if anything.

Well, something had happened. And they called 911.

That's where you were that night, Mr. Rickets, no matter what you recall.

As for me, I was home watching TV. I clearly remember the special report, the anchor warning us that what was about to follow might be disturbing.

"The body," he said. "Of a young woman," he said. "Was found in Heldon Park earlier tonight," he said. "Her face slashed beyond recognition."

The words "young woman" triggered within me an immediate alarm, a protective reflex, which quickly subsided into relief when I remembered that my daughter was upstairs in her room, studying for a college exam.

Except I suddenly realized it was a Tuesday. Tuesday nights were when she donated her time to one of the local soup kitchens.

But which soup kitchen? There were several in the area. She had mentioned the name once, but it slipped my mind. The only ones I could think of at that moment were the soup kitchen downtown and the one at Heldon Park.

It had to be the downtown one, I told myself.

That's it. It was the soup kitchen downtown.

Because it couldn't possibly be the one at Heldon Park.

A flickering on the TV caught my eye, and I looked up at the screen, at a photograph of a necklace with a silver and emerald pendant.

The anchor was saying that if anyone could identify this pendant to please call the number at the bottom of the screen.

The photo lingered so people could jot down the number, and then it was back to regular programming.

I didn't need to jot down anything, because, although my daughter's pendant was silver and emerald, it was different. It was special. It was a gift to her from her grandmother, and she treasured it.

She wore it wherever she went, and I was always sick with worry that someday someone would snatch it from her. I didn't want her to come home heartbroken.

And then the photo that was just up there on the screen came to mind, and I breathed a sigh of relief. No, nobody had stolen the pendant. If someone had stolen it, there wouldn't be a photograph of it.

A thought struck me just then. Something my daughter had said weeks ago. That she would be switching from the downtown soup kitchen to the "nicer" one for a while.

"Nicer one?" I asked.

"The one near Heldon Park."

And that's when the pieces fell into place, exposing my blind stupidity. There was only one pendant. And only one reason there was a photograph of it.

In a heart-dropping panic I bounded up the stairs, screaming her name, and threw open her door. The light from the hallway rushed in ahead of me, illuminating her bed, freshly made; her dresser, its lotions arranged just so; her desk, plain and pristine, awaiting her next assignment. At a glance, her room was as she always left it whenever she went out, a sanctuary to return home to.

Do you know what loss is, Mr. Rickets?

Since I doubt that you do, I'll tell you what it is. It's picturing that room with nothing out of place ever again.

That's all I have to say.

You can continue counting now.

See you next month.

*****

Postscript

Hey, Rickets, did my letter have you going there, at least for a little while? Did I come across as one of the enraged, bereaved, broken parents of the dearly departed, getting in one last word before you make your own departure?

Come on, my friend, do you really believe the actual parents would make the slightest effort to write you and express their displeasure over your shredding their daughter? They couldn't give two shits about you. And even if they did, they wouldn't follow up on it. As all those doddering seniors out there on Medicare are fond of lamenting, the world has changed. No one takes the time to write letters anymore.

Except that I took the time. Poured a lot of loving sweat into it, too, if I say so myself. And what you just finished reading up above, between the *Dear Mr. Rickets* and the *See you next month*, is the culmination of my hard work.

Look, Rickets, I realize you have a lot on your plate, what with that pesky lethal injection looming on the horizon, but I would really love to share with you some of my favorite passages from my letter. The highlights, if you will. And, yes, even some of the lowlights — which, I confess, were as much a kick to put down on paper as the good stuff.

This shouldn't take long. And I'm pretty sure you won't be disappointed. In fact, there might even be a pleasant surprise waiting for you at the end, although I can't guarantee it.

So what say we get started!

First of all, I loved playing the part. I've never been a parent myself, let alone a parent of someone who gets sliced up into bloody strips of flesh, and so I hope I filled the role convincingly. But I have to wonder, Rickets, if, at any time during your reading, you had to touch your finger to your chin and ask yourself: My God, which parent is this? The daddy of the dearly departed or the mommy?

I never say, do I?

I suppose I should have inserted somewhere a helpful "as her mother, I taught my daughter how to bake cookies" or an "as her father, I once bought my daughter a pair of needle-nose pliers," but I didn't.

And do you know why?

Because it never occurred to me. Once I started typing as a generic parent, I kept on hammering away full-speed ahead, letting the creative juices flow, making things up as I went along. Not as a mommy or a daddy but as a sort of best-of-two-worlds *mommydaddy*.

It is a nice touch, though, don't you think? Not dealing with the momminess or daddiness of it all? The omission was purely by accident, but since it is a nice touch, I'm inclined to think of it as something I intended all along.

Speaking of nice touch, how did you like my repeated use of the phrase "counting the days?" You, Rickets, counting the days. Me, the mommydaddy, counting the days. How the dearly departed daughter once counted the days before she stopped counting things altogether. The repetition sounds almost literary doesn't it?

On the other hand, mommydaddy continually referring to the daughter as "my daughter" is probably a repetition I could have avoided. Why didn't I just have mommydaddy use her name?

Well, because yours truly, who wrote as mommydaddy but didn't know the real mommy or real daddy, didn't know the real daughter either. Or her name. Or any of their names for that matter. And still doesn't.

Hence, the liberal sprinkling of the words "my daughter" throughout the piece.

So maybe it's time to fix that. To make things easier and less cumbersome down the road, let's decide on a name and stick to it. I vote for the plain and simple Dee Dee. As in "mommydaddy's daughter Dee Dee" or as in "Dee Dee, the dearly departed."

Which brings us to Dee Dee's firsts. Did you like how I handled those passages in my letter? Dee Dee's first college lecture? Dee Dee's first tickling the ivories? Dee Dee's first dishing out hot soup to the cold and starving?

I paint her out to be real saint, don't I?

Was she really like that?

Beats the hell out of me.

If Dee Dee's life story had come out at the trial, I wouldn't have known. I wasn't there, and I wasn't particularly interested. The thing is, you were there because it was your trial, and yet you wouldn't have known either. You were too busy wishing the whole courtroom drama would get over with so you could go back to chugging brewskies.

So I could've said just the opposite and got away with it. That Dee Dee, or whoever, was an unrepentant slut who one day shoved a grand piano out of a third story college lecture hall window, sending it crashing onto a couple of cold, starving bums huddled around a burn barrel.

You wouldn't have known.

But in the end I chose to portray her as a pure-as-the-driven-snow virgin with one of those yellow cardboard haloes attached to the back of her head, the way they are in those age-old art museum paintings.

Why?

To make her demise all the more tragic. And to make you, Rickets, feel really, really god awful. Maybe, with luck, even a tiny bit guilty.

Even though I know you aren't.

Do you see where I'm going with this?

Back to Tiny's Tavern is where I'm going. And so are you.

Now that *tiny* portion of my letter, so to speak, was pretty much taken word for word from what your drinking buddies testified to at your trial. All except for the bit about your looking like a coal miner. That was my contribution all the way. As well as the business about you hoisting that knife into the air like a victory cup. Yes, you did raise the knife. Your buddies testified to that. But I deserve full credit for the victory cup reference.

You like?

Anyway, you were there at Tiny's that fateful night, bitching about the world and filling up your bladder, when, at some point, you left the bar to empty said bladder in the park across the street. Fifteen minutes later you came back.

So what happened during that quarter hour?

Well, just so happens I was on my haunches, quietly finishing up, when you came stumbling through the bushes. I pretty near jumped out of my skin. I thought at first you were some creature that roamed Heldon Park, but one whiff of stale beer told me you were just some drunk roaming the bars across the street.

Still, that didn't ease my mind any. Here I was deep into my work, and there you were looking in my direction. What to do? What to do?

Nothing, as it turned out. First of all, it was dark out. Second, I had a ski mask on. And most of all, you were blind-as-a-bat blotto. Your eyes were on me, but your cerebrum was out for the night, and your primitive brain was trying its best to keep you from landing flat on your face. It was obvious you had no idea anyone else was there, living or dead, even though they were both just a couple feet in front of you.

So I kept at it.

Until I heard your zipper and the splash of piss. That's when I figured it was high time I quit slashing and got going. And I would've taken off like a bat out of hell, except I had a better idea. A sudden inspiration, as it were.

I got to my feet and waited. And waited and waited. And when you finally finished watering the bushes and zipping back up, likely by pure instinct, I took my gloved hands and smeared your face with blood, applying a double coat to your forehead, and thickening it up around your cheeks. I then opened up your hand, placed my well used chef's knife in your palm, and curled your fingers around the handle, giving them an extra squeeze to solidify your grip. After all, I didn't want you to let go of the evidence prematurely.

After a gentle shove on my part, off you staggered, back through the bushes and onward to your primo watering hole.

And off I sprinted in the opposite direction, leaving my completed project behind for the police to uncover and for the real mommy and daddy to sob over whenever they learned the news.

Mommydaddy, on the other hand, didn't have to learn the news. Mommydaddy, meaning me, already knew the news. And would go on to weave a fanciful but touching and often suspenseful tale about special reports and nonexistent pendants and loss having to do with the bed never needing to get made.

But all worded in a sensitive way.

For a sensitive guy like you, Rickets, who is probably asking right now, "So where's my surprise?"

This is it. This postscript.

Look, Rickets, I might not have paid much attention to Dee Dee in the news, but I couldn't get enough of you. The more that came out, the worse it got for you and the better it got for me. One look at your character traits, and any suggestion that something else might have happened that night other than you having yourself a party with an eight-inch chef's knife would have been met with ridicule.

Face it. You're a drunk. A mean, loud, obnoxious drunk. You're no great shakes when you're sober either. You hate women. You have few male friends. And those male friends you do have are more than happy to testify against you in court.

What's more, you're a nuisance. Your daily open letters to the governor, pleading for every kind of release imaginable, including roaming totally free in the countryside, are still the stuff of late night comedy shows, some of which have been hosted by the honorable governor himself.

And on top of all that, you're ugly and have a last name that's a disease.

And, in the end, what has been your sole defense? That even though you didn't remember a single thing about that night, you couldn't have possibly done any of the things you're accused of because — well, because you're such a nice guy.

And what's so funny is that, even though you're nowhere near being a nice guy and are in fact a total asshole, you're guilty of absolutely nothing whatsoever. Up to now you've never been accused or even suspected of a single crime. And now you're facing a personal version of end times for something you didn't do.

But cheer up. Because what this postscript amounts to is a confession, pure and simple. All you have to do is hand it over to your jailers, and they'll pass it on to the authorities, who will know how to proceed, given that my fingerprints, which are on file, are all over every page.

Look at this letter, along with all its additions, as your ticket, Rickets. Your ticket to freedom.

✳✳✳✳✳

Post-Postscript

Except for one thing.

My letter to Rickets, the postscript with my confession, and this post-postscript I'm typing up this very second aren't going anywhere. None of it will be mailed off to anyone.

Least of all to Rickets.

There will be a blizzard in hell before that poor bastard ever hears from me.

Unless he manages to push another one of his open letters onto social media. In which case I might just decide to dash off a reply, with words along the lines of, "Rickets, I know for a fact you're innocent, but I don't care. You post one more open letter, and I'll head out there to death row and give you the shot myself."

But of course I won't do that. How would that look?

Besides, as annoying as he can be with his open letters, Rickets still deserves the right to be put to sleep by professionals.

I just wish that, over his remaining few days, he comes to accept, for his personal well-being if nothing else, a cold, hard fact about life: that some people enter this world, get framed for murder, and then get executed.

I, myself, have come to accept not just one but two cold, hard facts about life. The first one being that, for all the time and effort I've spent composing this letter, no one will ever read it.

Nevertheless, that time and effort have provided me with plenty of practice.

Practice at what?

Faking empathy.

Throughout the main body of my letter, touching and heartfelt examples abound.

Take the part where I have Dee Dee confidently claiming she'll live to be a million years old...on what just happens to be the very same day her life gets snuffed out!

To be able to put such maudlin, sentimental pap like that down on paper without collapsing into fits of hysterics is a talent, pure and simple.

What's more, this ability to step into other people's shoes — or, more precisely, to *pretend* to step into their shoes — may very well prove indispensable should something like a school shooting rear its irritating head. After all, who's going to put their trust in our leaders if they can't even shed a phony tear over a handful of dead students?

Which leads to the second cold, hard fact I must accept. Namely, that killing one human being at random simply won't be enough.

For let's be honest. I need something — some meaningful activity — to distract me from the endless political turmoil of public life. And I'll be damned if I'll spend whatever free time I have building homes for charity.

But perhaps this is a matter best left for another time, another place, another park.

For now, I've whiled away enough hours here in my gubernatorial chambers. It's high time I hit the delete button and resume the duties as befit my office.

The Last Gunfighter
John Bertram Fawet III

From: jbfawet@yourmail.com
Sent: April 5, 2022 09:30
To: pmmm@charltonmagazines.com
Subject: The Last Gunfighter
Dear Ms. Hathaway:
Attached you will find my short story "The Last Gunfighter."

Having been forced into involuntary early retirement, although I feel fine, I was casting about for what to do with my life. My therapist suggested I combine my love of literature with my desire to have a positive impact on the world, so I have decided to write on topics that are of vital importance in today's society. My story addresses the issues of mass murders, mental illness, and gun control, versus our second amendment right to own weapons. My initial thoughts for titles were "I'm AK — You're AK," and "Guns and Neuroses," but I felt those were too frivolous for such an important subject, when there are over 39,000 deaths from guns here in the US every year, and so many mass shootings (around one per day) that most are deemed not important enough to qualify as front-page news.

I've put a lot of thought and effort into crafting what I feel is an excellent story, one that I believe will both entertain and enlighten, and I hope you will find it worthy of publication in your fine magazine.

Thank you for taking the time to read it.

Yours sincerely,

John Bertram Fawet III

*****

From: pmmm@charltonmagazines.com
Sent: April 5, 2022 09:55
To: jbfawet@yourmail.com
Subject: RE: The Last Gunfighter
Thank you for submitting your story for consideration at Perry Mason's Mystery Magazine.
You can check on its status here:
http//pmmm.magazinesubmissions.com/view/651322
Sincerely,
Julia Hathaway
Editor, Perry Mason's Mystery Magazine

*****

From: pmmm@charltonmagazines.com
Sent: May 12, 2022 11:03
To: jbfawet@yourmail.com
Subject: RE: The Last Gunfighter
Dear John:
Thanks for letting us read your story "The Last Gunfighter." We gave it careful consideration, but did not think it best suited to any of the spaces we currently have open. We hope you will soon find the right publication for the story, and that you will continue to think of PMMM when you have new work.
With best wishes,
Julia Hathaway, Editor
Perry Mason's Mystery Magazine

*****

From: jbfawet@yourmail.com
Sent: May 12, 2022 11:30
To: untamedpress@yourmail.com
Subject: The Last Gunfighter
Mr. Brennan:
I have attached my story "The Last Gunfighter" for consideration in Edgar Allan Poe Mystery Magazine.

When I was first let go from work, on account of a supposed disability, I was, quite frankly, at a loss for what to do. I was angry. Angry at my bosses for depriving me of my job and main reason to live, angry at my country for not giving me the support I needed, and angry at the world in general.

However, rather than cursing the darkness, I decided instead to light a candle and try to make this world a better place, hence my maiden effort at fiction writing. I trust you will find it not only entertaining, but also enlightening, in the glow it casts on such important topics as mass murder, mental illness, and guns in our modern American society.

Thank you for looking at my creation.

Sincerely,

John Bertram Fawet

*****

From: untamedpress@yourmail.com

Sent: May 12, 2022 11:45

To: jbfawet@yourmail.com

Subject: The Last Gunfighter

Submission received.

Maxwell Brennan

Editor, Edgar Allan Poe Mystery Magazine

*****

From: untamedpress@yourmail.com

Sent: May 28, 2022 09:35

To: jbfawet@yourmail.com

Subject: RE: The Last Gunfighter

John:

Thanks for letting me read "The Last Gunfighter." It doesn't feel like a fit for EAPMM, so I'm going to pass and wish you luck placing this elsewhere.

Maxwell Brennan

Editor, Edgar Allan Poe Mystery Magazine

*****

To: submissions@crimesaplenty.com
Sent: May 28, 2022 09:58
From: jbfawet@yourmail.com
Subject: The Last Gunfighter
Dear Sirs:

I have written what I feel to be a powerful story for modern times, "The Last Gunfighter," which you will find attached.

Guns. They are everywhere in modern American society. Someone disrespects you? Blow him away. Don't like your neighbor? Blow her away. Bullied at school? Blow them away.

The politicians have been helpless to do anything about this, but you know who can effect changes here? Us, me and you, together. It is said that the pen is mightier than the sword, and I believe it can also be mightier than the gun; all it requires is the courage to take a stand. Editors have godlike powers over the stories submitted to them, which is why I am praying you will do the right thing and publish my creation, "The Last Gunfighter."

I hope you enjoy it and will use it, to help make this a better world.

Thanks for your consideration.

Yours,

John B. Fawet

*****

To: jbfawet@yourmail.com
Sent: May 28, 2022 10:05
From: submissions@crimesaplenty.com
Subject: RE: The Last Gunfighter

Thank you for submitting "The Last Gunfighter" to Crimesaplenty. Your submission was successful.

You may check the status of your submission at any time by visiting this link:

https://hardstone.moksha.io/submission/status?id=427&uid=5fac46 70.

Your submission id is 5fac4670. You can use that number to check the status of your submission through the online tracking feature of the Moksha submission system, though of course you will also be contacted directly once a decision has been made about your story one way or another.

*****

To: jbfawet@yourmail.com
Sent: August 19, 2022 09:13
From: submissions@crimesaplenty.com
Subject: RE: The Last Gunfighter
Dear John,
Many thanks for the submission of The Last Gunfighter.
Sadly, on this occasion, we are going to decline to take this forward.
Best wishes and kind regards,
Jack Conlan

*****

To: submissions@mysteryforum.com
Sent: August 19, 2022 10:00
From: jbfawet@yourmail.com
Subject: The Last Gunfighter
Sirs:

Attached you will find my submission "The Last Gunfighter."

"Submission" — that's a pretty strange word in this context, when you think about it. I submitted when they told me I couldn't work anymore because I was "disabled" (sorry, I should say "had a disability." "They," whoever "they" are, tell me I'm supposed to use *people-first* language if I want to be politically correct). I submitted when they put me in the hospital. And I submitted until I could prove to them I was healthy enough, and safe enough, and reliable enough at taking my medicines, to be let out.

Well, I'm done submitting. As fictional anchorman Howard Beale said in the film *Network*, "I'm as mad as hell, and I'm not going to take this anymore!" One of my ways out is through my writing, and my first step in this direction is the short story I'm sharing with you for consideration by your magazine.

Thank you.

John Fawet

*****

To: jbfawet@yourmail.com

Sent: August 19, 2022 10:23

From: submissions@mysteryforum.com

Subject: RE: The Last Gunfighter

Hi John,

Thank you for your interest in Mystery Forum. We have received your submission and look forward to reviewing it.

Thanks!

Mystery Forum

*****

To: jbfawet@yourmail.com

Sent: November 28, 2022 14:19

From: submissions@mysteryforum.com

Subject: RE: The Last Gunfighter

Dear John Fawet,

Thank you for sending us "The Last Gunfighter". We appreciate the chance to read it.

Unfortunately, the piece is not for us as we publish a different style of fiction in our print edition.

If you wish to submit another piece, you can get a sense of the type of fiction we publish by picking up a copy of Mystery Forum and browsing through the Fiction section.

Thanks again.

Sincerely,

Mystery Forum

*****

To: nmm@charltonmagazines.com

Sent: December 12, 2022 09:17

From: jbfawet@yourmail.com

Subject: The Last Gunfighter

To the editor:

After I was released from a psychiatric hospital, for some mental issues, now thankfully resolved — not from a prison, since in the immortal words of President Nixon, "I am not a crook" — I cast about for changes in the world while I was detained, and it was immediately obvious that gun violence, gun control, and mental illness constituted an epidemic in our society, and that something needed to be done about it, hence my short story "The Last Gunfighter," which I have included with this email.

I will admit this story has been rejected by other magazines, which is why I took the step of hiring a so-called professional editor to look it over and offer some suggestions. Her main point was that I needed to "tighten it up." She said I tend to ramble, going off on tangents and veering from the theme, weakening the focus of the story, making it harder to appreciate the points I am trying to make, and annoying the reader who is not interested in my sidelights. I don't see this at all; my comments are uniformly cogent and pertinent.

She said I should follow the advice of Stephen King in his book "On Writing." King apparently writes a first draft of his novels and then edits them down ten percent. However, if he's such a great writer, how come you never published a story of his? One point for me. I wonder if she was just a scam artist.

One other thing she did say was for me to know my audience. You said the same thing on your website, that it would be helpful to read some back issues to get a feel for the magazine, so I purchased four years' worth (no Stephen King!), and did revise my story accordingly. It is now a perfect fit for your magazine, and I look forward to seeing my first paycheck as a published author any day now.

Or was your comment about reading back issues just another con job?

John F

*****

From: nmm@charltonmagazines.com
Sent: December 12, 2022 09:30
To: jbfawet@yourmail.com
Subject: RE: The Last Gunfighter
Dear John:
Thank you for submitting your story to Notorious Mystery Magazine for our consideration. We look forward to reading every story. Because of the volume of submissions, our response time is currently at an average of six to eight months. We appreciate your patience with us as we catch up.

You can check on your submission status here: http//nmm.magazinesubmissions.com/view/816635

*****

From: nmm@charltonmagazines.com
Sent: June 19, 2023 09:58
To: jbfawet@yourmail.com
Subject: RE: The Last Gunfighter
Dear John:
Thanks for letting us see "The Last Gunfighter." It's well written, but ultimately, it doesn't quite come off for me. I am going to pass on this one, but I hope you'll keep us in mind for future submissions.

Sincerely,

Laura Lattimore

Editor, Notorious Mystery Magazine

*****

From: jbfawet@yourmail.com
Sent: June 19, 2023 10:12
To: info@mysterymonthly.com
Subject: The Last Gunfighter
Karen Carson, if that's your real name, the world is going down the toilet more and more every day, and nobody's listening. First it's the bosses controlling ordinary people like me and hiring doctors to force you out of work by saying you have a disability while they ride about in

their limos and yachts and private jets.

And then there's the politicians sitting on their fat asses while they look the other way. Of course whenever anything happens they make a big show of claiming they'll do something this time and offering hypocritical thoughts and prayers while all the while they're raking in the money from Big Oil and Big Pharma and all those other "corporations are people too."

And let's not forget the foreigners doing their part to destroy our great nation. I'm not talking about just the ones you hear about streaming across our borders daily I'm talking about the ones the media covers up that you never hear about the ones the bosses smuggle in on those yachts and jets I spoke about earlier so they can stock their private armies all while preparing for the coming war when they will take away everything that is rightfully ours.

It's all of them together the bosses the doctors the foreigners the politicians all those sons of bitches one vast conspiracy to keep themselves on top while screwing the rest of us.

Our world as we know it is falling apart and me along with it and I'm feeling powerless to do anything unless you print my story "The Last Gunfighter" to wake everybody up to the crisis if only you have the guts to print it or are you like the other publishers I've contacted in their pocket too? I'm begging for you to do the right thing and rescue us before it's too late.

John

*****

From: info@mysterymonthly.com

Sent: June 19, 2023 15:30

To: jbfawet@yourmail.com

Subject: RE: The Last Gunfighter

Thank you for submitting your story to Mystery Monthly! Our response time ranges from 3 to 6 weeks. You can use the link below to check the status of your submission:

Check Submission Status

*****

From: info@mysterymonthly.com

Sent: August 13, 2023 11:02

To: jbfawet@yourmail.com

Subject: RE: The Last Gunfighter

Dear John:

Thank you for submitting your story "The Last Gunfighter" to Mystery Monthly.

I enjoyed reading your story, but unfortunately, I will not be accepting it.

I wish you the best of luck in finding a home for it.

I would be happy to read more of your work and sincerely hope that you will continue to send your mysteries our way.

All the best

Karen Carson, Editor

*****

From: jbfawet@yourmail.com

Sent: August 13, 2023 16:02

To: Talesofcrimeandmystery@yourmail.com

Subject: The Last Gunfighter

heres my story The Last Gunfighter. ive been fighting the good fight but im getting exhausted and running out of energy. can you publish it and save me? youre my last chance.

J

*****

From: Talesofcrimeandmystery@yourmail.com

Sent: August 13, 2023 16:28

To: jbfawet@yourmail.com

Subject: The Last Gunfighter

Hi J,

Thank you for your interest in Tales of Crime and Mystery. We have received your submission and look forward to reviewing it.

Thanks!

Tales of Crime and Mystery

*****

From: Talesofcrimeandmystery@yourmail.com
Sent: August 20, 2023 09:45
To: jbfawet@yourmail.com
Subject: RE: The Last Gunfighter

We regret that we are returning your story "The Last Gunfighter" unread. We have made the difficult decision to suspend the magazine for now. We trust you understand why we have chosen this course of action, made in light of the shocking and senseless tragedy that took place in our offices earlier this week.

The Usual Unusual Suspects

Vinnie Hansen fled the winds of the South Dakota prairie and headed for the California coast the day after high school graduation.

A two-time Claymore Award finalist, she is the author of the Carol Sabala mystery series, the novels *Lostart Street* and *One Gun*, as well as over fifty published short works. Still sane(ish) after 27 years of teaching high school English, Vinnie has retired and plays keyboards with ukulele groups in Santa Cruz, California, where she lives with her husband and the requisite cat. For news and updates, visit

https://vinniehansen.com/ for news and updates.

Vinnie first appeared in *Crimeucopia – One More Thing To Worry About* with *Killer on the Loose*.

V. S. Kemanis has written short fiction for magazines and anthologies including *Ellery Queen's Mystery Magazine*, *Mystery Magazine*, *Mystery Tribune* online, *Autumn Noir*, *The Crooked Road Vol. 3*, *The Best Laid Plans*, and *Me Too Short Stories*. Other publishing credits include six Dana Hargrove Legal Mysteries and five award-winning or nominated collections of short fiction. She has recently retired from her career as a lawyer in New York's criminal justice and court systems and is also a former board member of Mystery Writers of America, New York Chapter.

David Krugler writes historical mystery and suspense fiction. His novels, *The Dead Don't Bleed* and *Rip the Angels from Heaven*, follow a naval intelligence officer trying to capture Soviet spies inside the top-secret atomic bomb project during World War II. His short stories have been published in *Mystery Magazine*, *Ellery Queen Mystery Magazine*, and *The Mysterious Bookshop Presents the Best Mystery Stories of the Year 2023*, edited by Amor Towles. Writing historicals comes naturally to David, who works as a professor of history. When not in the archives, classroom, or at his desk, he enjoys world travel. Learn more about David and his writing at www.davidkrugler.com

Robert Jeschonek is a *USA TODAY* bestselling author whose fiction has appeared in *Black Cat Mystery Magazine, Punk Noir, Yellow Mama, Pulphouse Fiction Magazine,* and other markets around the world. His young adult fantasy novel, *My Favorite Band Does Not Exist,* won the Forward National Literature Award and was named one of *Booklist*'s Top Ten First Novels for Youth. Visit him online at www.bobscribe.com, find him on Facebook, also on X as @TheFictioneer.

Beverle Graves Myers is a storyteller based in an old Victorian neighborhood of Louisville, Kentucky. Her studies in history help her make earlier eras come alive, and her first career as a clinical psychiatrist gave her insights that contribute to unforgettable characters. Bev's published work includes the Tito Amato Mystery Series set in baroque Venice and numerous short stories. Visit her website at www.readbeverlemyers.com for more on Bev.

Kirk Landers launched his professional writing career in the US Army, writing profiles of his fellow Basic Trainees for the post newspaper to get out of KP and guard duty. After military service, he became a staff writer and editor for special interest consumer magazines, a staff writer for *Time-Life Books,* co-author of the biography of self-help writer Napoleon Hill, and chief editor for several trade magazines. He writes crime fiction under a pen name. His first Kirk Landers novel, *Alone on the Shield,* told the story of Vietnam era lovers who broke up over the war meeting on a wilderness island forty years later.
He first appeared in *Crimeucopia – Through The Past Darkly,* with *The Parking Lot.*

James Lee Proctor is a writer of short stories and novels and treats every character with as much brutal honesty as they deserve. His motto: If you're not laughing or crying, I'm not doing my job. He is the author of

Borderline, a Texas crime novel, and *The Rules of Chance*, a collection of 11 stories about how automobiles bring people to destinations they could never have imagined. He lives in the Piney Woods of East Texas with his wife, author M.E. Proctor. Author Page: https://www.amazon.com/stores/James-Lee-Proctor/author/B0CM2HDD4D

Victor Kreuiter lives, reads and writes in the Midwest USA. His stories have appeared in *Ellery Queen Mystery Magazine, Halfway Down The Stairs, Bewildering Stories, Tough, Frontier Tales, Del Sol SFF Review, Literally Stories*, and other online and print publications. His story, *Miller and Bell* — originally published in the August, 2022, issue of *Mystery Magazine* — was selected to appear in *The Mysterious Bookshop Presents the Best Mystery Stories of 2023*.

K. Arlington Andrews is currently a High School teacher at KIPP HS in St. Louis, after moving from Chicago 10 years ago – though he's not a fan of the city ("I long to go home to Chicago.")

Michael Bracken's short fiction has appeared in *Alfred Hitchcock's Mystery Magazine, Ellery Queen's Mystery Magazine, The Best American Mystery Stories*, and in many other anthologies and periodicals. He first appeared in *Crimeucopia – We're All Animals Under The Skin* with *Soiled Dove*.

Kevin R. Tipple is a multiple term past President of the Short Mystery Fiction Society. He reviews books and short stories, watches way too much television, and offers unsolicited opinions on anything. His short fiction has appeared in magazines such as *Lynx Eye, Starblade, Show and Tell*, and *The Writer's Post Journal*, among others. *Mystery Weekly Magazine* published his story, The Damn Rodents Are Everywhere, in May of 2021 and soon had to change their name to *Mystery Magazine*. His short story, The Beetle's Last Fifty Grand, appears in the 2022 anthology, *Back Road Bobby and His Friends*, and everyone involved

seems to have survived the experience unscathed. His short story, Visions of Reality, appears in *Crimeucopia—Say It Again*. Earlier this year, the *Notorious in North Texas: Metroplex Mysteries Volume III* anthology was released and includes his short story, Whatever Happened To...? Also released earlier this year is the anthology, *Larceny & Last Chances: 22 Stories of Mystery & Suspense*, which includes his crime fiction short story, The Hospital Boomerang.
Fully trained before marriage, Kevin can work all major appliances and, despite a love of nearly all sports, is able to clean up after himself.

William Flores is a retired Licensed Social Work Consultant, who lives with his wife and grandson in New York City. He's published three short fiction stories listed on the Reedsy Blog, and one autobiographical story with *Story House*. At 71 years old, he runs two miles a day, and works out regularly. He enjoys writing short stories involving detective mysteries, and poetry about inner city street life.

Robert Sumner is an attorney living in California with his two unbelievably adorable dogs. His fiction has appeared in *Mystery Tribune, The Emerson Review, Riprap, Jokes Review, Corvus Review, The Penmen Review*, and *The Quotable*.

Jim Guigli is a student of many interests: SCUBA diver, auto-mechanic, and gunsmith, served as an Army Security Agency Russian Voice Intercept Operator in Japan, studied Judo, played basketball, was a career mechanical designer for National Labs LBNL, SLAC, & LANL, trained at Gunsite with pistol & shotgun, designed and supervised firearms competitions, toured Quantico as an FBI Citizens Academy graduate, designed a 400 sq ft kitchen addition to his house, and earned BFA and MA degrees in Art/Photography. Jim is an active member of SMFS, PSWA, & Sacramento CWC.
Publishing History: Won 2006 Bulwer-Lytton Fiction Contest Grand Prize. The Grand Prize sentence and one other were published in *It Was a*

Dark and Stormy Night, by Scott Rice, Friday Books, London, 2007. Self-published 2013 Kindle Bart Lasiter novelette, *Bad News for a Ghost.* Other Bart Lasiter appearances include *Looking for Mishka, (Rock and a Hard Place Magazine, Issue 7, Winter 2022),* and *Cane Mutiny (May 2022 Pulp Modern Flash). Listen to the Gunsmith* appeared in the *July 2022 Guilty Crime Magazine.* Two new non-Bart pieces — *Ben Hurt* and *Not Funny* – appeared in *Guilty Crimes Magazine* during 2023. His *Blood on the Stairs* appears in *Crimeucopia – We'll Be Right Back – After This!* He has also written various articles for the *PSWA newsletter* and NorCal Chapter newsletters of MWA and SinC. Website: www.jimguigli.com

James Roth is a writer of fiction and nonfiction. His work has appeared in several magazines and journals. His first novel, *The Opium Addict*, is forthcoming from Hear Our Voice, LLC. A second novel, *A Prayer for My Daughter*, set in modern Japan, is a noir/literary mystery that should be out in 2024. He has taught in Japan, China, and Zimbabwe and likes to say he was "Made in Japan." His parents lived there during the American occupation but he was, to his and his mother's lasting regret, born in a military hospital in the U.S. He is presently a fellow in the U.S. State Department's ELF Program at the Jordan Media Institute in Amman, Jordan. www.jamesroth.org.

Michael Zimecki is an attorney by day and a writer at night, and the author of *Death Sentences*, a novel published by Crime Wave Press. He is also the winner of a *Golden Fedora Award* for Poetry from *Noir Nation.* His novella, *The History of My Final Illness*, about the last five days in the life of Joseph Stalin, was previously published in *Eclectica Magazine,* while other work has appeared in *Close to the Bone Magazine, The Dark City Crime and Mystery Magazine, Guilty Crime Story Magazine, Harper's Magazine* and *Hoosier Noir,* among other publications. He lives in Pittsburgh, Pennsylvania, with his wife, Susan, and a black cat named Mr White.

Sebastian Corbascio was born and raised in Oakland Ca, and showed a very early affinity towards writing fiction — plays, short stories, novellas — and was thus a horrific student.

Later he became involved with making films "because, as an art form, there is none more expensive or frustrating." Of his output, he states "Those I like, and those that were popular are an inverse equation. *The Devil and Alexa Jones* is my favourite. No one who dwelt outside the criminal underground understood the ending. Cops, bangers, dealers, gangsters' molls, and attorneys got it immediately. The rest had to ask me to explain."

His novel, *Sarah Lugar* is available here:

https://www.amazon.co.uk/Sarah-Luger-Sebastian-Corbascio-ebook/dp/B07K61DBVL

The Devil and Alexa Jones — https://www.imdb.com/title/tt3072078/

Martin Zeigler writes short fiction, primarily mystery, science fiction, and horror. His stories have been published in a number of anthologies and journals, both in print and online.

Every so often (okay, twice), he has gathered these stories into a self-published collection. In 2015 he released *A Functional Man And Other Stories*. More recently, in 2020, a year we will all remember with fondness, he released *Hypochondria And Other Stories*.

Besides writing, Marty enjoys the things most people do. And besides those, he likes reading, taking long walks, and playing the piano.

Marty makes his home in the Pacific Northwest.

Jon Matthew Farber, when not writing under the nom de plume of ***John Bertram Fawet III***, is a pediatrician in northern Virginia. He is a member of the Mystery Writers of America, with previous publications in *Ellery Queen* and *Black Cat Mystery Magazine*, among others.

Investigators and investigations are the mainstay of most Crime fiction sub-genres. Everything from the original *Golden Age* of country houses and the amateur sleuth, through to the high tech ultra-modern 21st Century – a place where the cyber investigators sometimes appear to be baffled by old-fashioned motivations of power and greed, and human foibles such as love and revenge.

So is there any real difference between the Private and the Public Sector investigators? Not much, if writers are to be believed, and the two can often be found straddling both sides of the 'what's legal procedure?' fence.

Of the twelve authors contained within, eleven are voices new to the world of Crimeucopia - and although the theme is *Investigators*, the material ranges from Cosy, through to not too Hardboiled - and most are touched with a vein of humour, be it light or dark. Rather like a box of chocolates…

Paperback ISBN: 9781909498327 eBook ISBN: 9781909498334

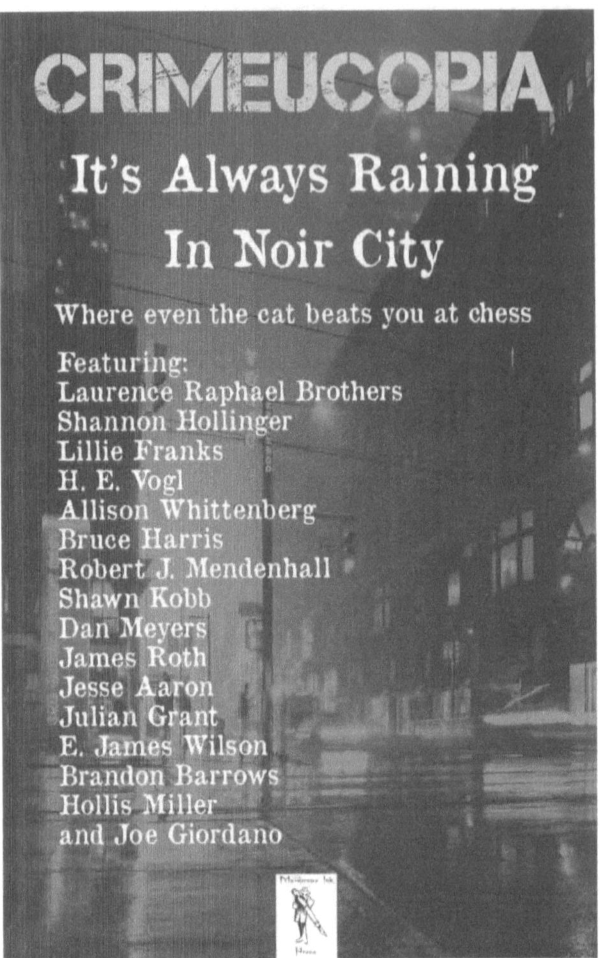

Is the Noir Crime sub-genre always dark and downbeat? Is there a time when Bad has a change of conscience, flips sides and takes on the Good role?

Noir is almost always a dish served up raw and bloody - Fiction bleu if you will. So maybe this is a chance to see if Noir can be served sunny side up - with the aid of these fifteen short order authors.

All fifteen give us dark tales from the stormy side of life - which is probably why it's *always* raining in Noir City....

Paperback Edition ISBN: 9781909498341
eBook Edition ISBN: 9781909498358

It Was In The Year Of….

Historical/Period Crime short fiction ranging from Cosy. Noir, PIs, Narrative Crime, and a whole spectrum of Crime sub-genres in between

21 authors — Gary Thomson, Edward St. Boniface, Terry Wijesuriya, Frances Stratford, Dennis E. Delaney, Joan Leotta, Hope Hodgkins, Karen Odden, J. F. Benedetto, S. B. Watson, Hal Dygert, Merrilee Robson, John G. Bluck, David Hagerty, Avi Sirlin, Karl El-Koura, Penny Hurrell, Kai Lovelace, Maddi Davidson, J. Aquino and Kirk Landers — take you from 420 BC through to AD 1969, and give you a criminal history, laid out in a case by case Crimeline.

Paperback 9781909498587 eBook 9781909498594

Alright My Son, Say No More, Leave It 'art!

As I best recall, it was one afternoon here at MIP Towers – must have been a touch after the start of tiffin, so around 4.35pm – when some smart young cove decided to politely call attention to himself by saying he had a proposal: 'Why can't we do an all-British Crimeucopia?'

And, bless my soul, after several pots of tea — Darjeeling (mid-season second flush, naturally) the general consensus was a resounding: 'Why not indeed?'

From there was born this anthology, containing, we hope, stories that, were you to cut them in half with a knife, they would flash you their Union Jacks without a moment's hesitation.

Rule Britannia - Britannia Waves The Rules features fiction from
Daniel Marshall Wood, Gerald Elias, S. E. Bailey, Alexander Frew,
Kelly Lewis, Carew S. Bartley, Madeleine McDonald, Edward Lodi,
Michaele Jordan, J. Aquino, David Rich, Kelly Zimmer, Sharon Richards,
T. K. Howell, Maroula Blades, David William Johnson and Harris Coverley

The fiction ranges from general British cosy, through Harry Palmer and George Smiley territory, before going deep into very British Modern Noir. And as with all of these anthologies, we hope you'll find something that you immediately like, as well as something that takes you out of your comfort zone – and puts you into a completely new one. In other words, in the spirit of the Murderous Ink Press motto:

You never know what you like until you read it.

Paperback: 9781909498501 eBook: 9781909498518

This is the first of several 'Free 4 All' collections that was supposed to be themeless. However, with the number of submissions that came in, it seems that this could be called an *Angels & Devils* collection, mixing PI & Police alongside tales from the Devil's dining table. Mind you, that's not to say that all the PIs & Police are on the side of the Angels....

Also this time around has not only seen a move to a larger paperback format size, but also in regard to the length of the fiction as well. Followers of the somewhat bent and twisted Crimeucopia path will know that although we don't deal with Flash fiction as a rule, it is a rule that we have sometimes broken. And let's face it, if you cannot break your own rules now and again, whose rules can you break?

Oh, wait, isn't breaking the rules the foundation of the crime fiction genre?

Oh dear....

New Crimeucopians *Aran Myracle, Alexei J. Slater, Gerald Elias, Terry Wijesuriya, Issy Jinarmo, Larry Lefkowitz,* and *Vinnie Hansen* smoothly rub literary shoulders with a fine collection of familiar Crimeucopia old hands: *Bob Ritchie, Michele Bazan Reed, Nikki Knight, N. M. Cedeño, Wendy Harrison, Andrew Darlington, Madeleine McDonald, Joan Leotta, H. E. Vogl* and *Jesse Aaron.*

All 17 tell tales that will make you realise there's always going to be One More Thing To Worry About….

With 16 vibrant authors, a wraparound paperback cover, and pages full of crime fiction in some of its many guises, what's not to like?
So if you enjoy tales spun by
Anthony Diesso, Brandon Barrows, E. James Wilson, James Roth,
Jesse Aaron, Jim Guigli, John M. Floyd, Kevin R. Tipple, Maddi Davidson,
Michael Grimala, Robert Petyo, Shannon Hollinger, Tom Sheehan,
Wil A. Emerson, Peter Trelay, and Philip Pak
then you'd better get
CRIMEUCOPIA - Strictly Off The record
by the sound of it!

Boomshakalaking is a variant of the expression Boomshakalaka, currently recognised as a boastful, teasingly hostile exclamation that follows a noteworthy achievement or an impressive stunt — the meaning similar to *in your face!*

Which is why this anthology is subtitled *Modern Crimes for Modern Times*, because most, if not all, are not your 'regular' crime fiction pieces — in fact some quite happily dance along the edges of multiple genres and styles, while others skew it like it is.

Of the 14 who appear in this anthology, 8 are new Crimeucopians, and even we have to admit that this is one of the most diverse Crimeucopia anthologies so far, and still sits under the umbrella of Crime Fiction.

As with all of these anthologies, we hope you'll find something that you immediately like, as well as something that takes you out of your comfort zone – and puts you into a completely new one.

In other words, in the spirit of the Murderous Ink Press motto:

You never know what you like until you read it.